CW00980759

Renewal and Resistance

Paul Collins (ed.)

Renewal and Resistance

Catholic Church Music
from the 1850s to Vatican II

PETER LANG

Oxford • Bern • Berlin • Bruxelles • Frankfurt am Main • New York • Wien

Bibliographic information published by Die Deutsche Nationalbibliothek.
Die Deutsche Nationalbibliothek lists this publication in the Deutsche National-
bibliografie; detailed bibliographic data is available on the Internet
at http://dnb.d-nb.de.

A catalogue record for this book is available from the British Library.

Library of Congress Cataloguing-in-Publication Data:

Collins, Paul, 1965-
 Renewal and resistance : Catholic church music from the 1850s to
Vatican II / Paul Collins.
    p. cm.
 Includes bibliographical references and index.
 ISBN 978-3-03911-381-1 (alk. paper)
 1. Church music--Catholic Church--History--19th century. 2. Church
music--Catholic Church--History--20th century. 3. Catholic
Church--Liturgy--History--19th century. 4. Catholic
Church--Liturgy--History--20th century. I. Title.
 ML3002.C65 2010
 264'.020209034--dc22

                            2010022643

ISBN 978-3-03911-381-1

© Peter Lang AG, International Academic Publishers, Bern 2010
Hochfeldstrasse 32, CH-3012 Bern, Switzerland
info@peterlang.com, www.peterlang.com, www.peterlang.net

All rights reserved.
All parts of this publication are protected by copyright.
Any utilisation outside the strict limits of the copyright law, without the permissi-
on of the publisher, is forbidden and liable to prosecution.
This applies in particular to reproductions, translations, microfilming, and storage
and processing in electronic retrieval systems.

Printed in Germany

Contents

Acknowledgements   vii

THOMAS DAY
Foreword   1

ECKHARD JASCHINSKI
The Renewal of Catholic Church Music in Germany/Austria,
France and Italy in the Nineteenth Century   13

PAUL COLLINS
Emissaries to 'a believing and a singing land':
Belgian and German Organists in Ireland, 1859–1916   29

KIERAN ANTHONY DALY
The Dublin Eucharistic Congress:
Tra le sollecitudini in the Phoenix Park   53

HELEN PHELAN
Ireland, Music and the Modern Liturgical Movement   73

BENNETT ZON
Victorian Anti-Semitism and the Origin of Gregorian Chant   99

THOMAS E. MUIR
Catholic Church Music in England: The 1950s   121

KEITH F. PECKLERS, S.J.

The Evolution of Liturgical Music in the
United States of America, 1850–1962   151

ANN L. SILVERBERG

Cecilian Reform in Baltimore, 1868–1903   171

ROBERT A. SKERIS

Musica sacra in the Archdiocese of Milwaukee, 1858–1958   189

SUSAN TREACY

A Chronicle of Attitudes towards Gregorian Chant in
Orate Fratres/Worship, 1926–1962   211

JOHN DE LUCA

Disputatur inter Doctores: A Disagreement between
Two Australian Bishops on the Binding Nature
of a Papal *Motu Proprio*   237

JOHN HENRY BYRNE

Archbishop Daniel Mannix and Church Music in
Melbourne, 1913–1963   251

Notes on Contributors   271

Index   277

Acknowledgements

My thanks go, first, to all of the contributors to the volume, and to Thomas Day for gracing the book with a foreword and for his valuable suggestions. Sincere thanks also to Graham Speake, Shirley Walker Werrett, Laurel Plapp and Gemma Lewis of Peter Lang for their help in preparing the manuscript for publication, and to Dr Gareth Cox and Cyprian Love, OSB, for reading through and commenting on portions of the book. I acknowledge, too, the help of Norma O'Neill and Elizabeth Brosnahan of the library of Mary Immaculate College, University of Limerick, both of whom were kept busy acquiring inter-library loans on my behalf. Grateful thanks also go to Leo Collins, whose untiring commitment as a research assistant I greatly valued. I am indebted, furthermore, to the Research Directorate of Mary Immaculate College, University of Limerick, for seed funding in support of this project. Finally, and most importantly, I thank my wife, Martina, for her encouragement and support, particularly when the project was nearing completion.

THOMAS DAY

Foreword

All of the information on the following pages could be read as a collection of facts – various ideas, ecclesiastical decrees, people, attitudes, controversies, and events – pertaining to the Roman Catholic Church's efforts, during the nineteenth century and the first half of the twentieth, to cultivate a more appropriate liturgical music for its Latin Rite. Looking at those facts from the distance of time, however, there is also a temptation – a very alluring one – to see in that information a pattern that keeps repeating across the centuries, and the pattern is this: a continuing cycle of *action* followed by *reaction*. To put it another way: (1) a type of liturgical music becomes widely accepted; (2) there is a reaction to the perceived inadequacies in this music, which is then altered or replaced by an improvement. (Sometimes the improvement is supposed to be a return to an original purity that once existed.) The improvement, after first encountering resistance, becomes widely accepted, and eventually there is a reaction to its perceived inadequacies – and on the cycle goes.

It is true that sometimes human beings can easily deceive themselves by imagining all kinds of patterns and grand historical frameworks where there is only one event after another. But this book is about music, an art, and in the history of the arts in the West there is, indeed, a recurring pattern that has continued for more than a thousand years: 'the new' in Western art and music pushes aside 'the old', usually in the name of improvement. When 'the new' becomes old, the pattern is repeated. Compared to the arts in some other cultures, these shifts from old to new have been rather rapid. The art historian looking at ancient Egyptian and Chinese art over the centuries perhaps sees stylistic changes, but they are assimilated within a slow-moving continuity. The art historian looking at Western arts since the Middle Ages perhaps sees continuity and assimilation, but also a series of distinctive stylistic shifts. Romanesque, Gothic (in various varieties), Renaissance, Mannerist, Baroque, Rococo, Neo-Classical, Romantic, Gothic Revival, Victorian, a large assortment of styles labelled 'Modern', and so forth, all started as improvements that contradicted an existing style and which were later eclipsed by improvements. It is an oddity of history that over the centuries, the Catholic Church in the West – which has always emphasized its unchanging character – went along with fashion and changed the art and architecture of its churches to fit into this pattern of improved styles replacing old styles, at least until the Modern style first arrived.

The history of Notre Dame Cathedral in Paris provides a good visual example of the Catholic Church adapting to new styles. The original building, a Romanesque structure, was torn down to make way for architecture in the modern and daring Gothic style. Even before this building was finished, the architects modernized it further by adding features from newer versions of the Gothic style that were coming into fashion. Then Gothic went out of fashion and, as far as knowledgeable people were concerned, the cathedral was an embarrassment, a monstrosity put up by medieval barbarians (the Goths) who were ignorant of ancient Greek and Roman art. Tearing down the building and constructing something new was too expensive, so over the years, the old building was improved here and there. Stained glass windows were smashed and replaced by plain glass that let in more light. Decorations and furnishing in a Gothic style were also thrown out. Very large paintings were hung in the nave in order to edify the faithful but also to hide the barbaric-looking Gothic arches. For Napoleon's coronation in 1804 (as we know from Jacques-Louis David's painting of it) a kind of Neo-Classical theatre set was constructed inside the building; this interior facade in the modern style hid the building's Gothic features. Then, in the following decades, people once again began to see great beauty in the old Gothic cathedrals, and the architect Eugène Viollet-le-Duc (1814–79) did his best to improve Notre Dame by restoring it to something close to its original glory.

Chant, like Notre Dame, had its own history of being battered by successive attempts to improve it. We can trace this pattern of improvements back to the eighth century when Pepin the Short and his son Charlemagne tried to abolish local liturgical rites and replace them with the rituals and chants used in Rome. The complications of this story do not have to be recounted here. We should just note that these rulers justified their efforts as improvements: a replacement of the local chant with music that seemed to have the prestige of history behind it and the authority of the papacy. (The symbolism of an entire kingdom and, later, an empire united by the same liturgical music was another incentive for enforcing the change to the Roman chant.) The result of this encounter between Frankish and Roman traditions of liturgical music was Gregorian chant, and during the rest of the Middle Ages the reaction to this music (and perhaps its perceived inadequacies) was a series of improvements that could only be described as exuberant:

- Tropes (new words) were added to the chants. A liturgical drama could even be inserted into a liturgy for special occasions
- The old-fashioned melismatic Alleluia could be replaced with new sequences
- Music notation for chant began to replace an oral tradition
- Polyphony took the old chant melodies and simultaneously blended them with new melodies

All of these innovations first developed in the lands that were originally part of Charlemagne's empire (where the Gregorian tradition of chant first developed) and all of them are signs of a restless energy for improvement that continued across the centuries and still continues today. It could be argued that these well-meaning improvements contributed to the decline and disfigurement of Gregorian chant. When we listen to the slow pounding of the *Dies Irae* quoted in the last movement of the *Symphonie Fantastique* by Berlioz (the way he heard that music sung in his lifetime), we get some idea of how centuries of trying to improve chant nearly destroyed it.

Action and reaction: the chapters in this book, either directly or indirectly, pick up this recurring pattern at the point in history where Roman Catholicism reacted to the Enlightenment – and if that phenomenon in European history was about anything, it was improvement.

The typical college or university lecturer who has to provide a quick description of the Enlightenment usually begins with the reaction in Europe to years of unrest and hideous warfare in the name of religion. The lecturer then explains that many Europeans, turning away from the authority of religion and received traditions, looked instead to the power of reason as their guide. At some point in this lecture, students will hastily scribble something like the following oversimplification in their notebooks (or type it into their laptops): 'The writings of enlightened thinkers like Diderot, Rousseau, Voltaire, Hume, and Kant will lead directly to freedom, democracy, religious tolerance, progress, technology, science, and everything good in the modern world.'

To enliven the class the lecturer might show a well-known visual representation of what the Enlightenment was trying to achieve: the frontispiece of the great French *Encyclopédie* (published mainly between 1751 and 1780). In this engraving, Truth, depicted as a beautiful woman, is radiant with light; next to her, Reason and Philosophy remove the veil from Truth's face; below them – in gloom and darkness – are faces of people looking upward at this luminous apparition. The allegory's message is clear: the intellect and reason will free the human race from ignorance and lead the way to greatness. There was also an implied message that many people at the time must have seen in this picture: down there in the deepest gloom of perpetual ignorance was the Catholic Church; for the sake of improvement and progress, it had to be either forced into subservience to the state or eradicated.

An entire lecture – perhaps an entire course – could be devoted just to the determined efforts of enlightened rulers in Catholic countries to weaken the Catholic Church. For the purposes of this book, what concerns us here is one aspect of this campaign against Roman Catholicism: the utter disdain for the contemplative life. The thinking behind the scorn went something like this: people in monasteries and cloistered convents did not do anything useful for society; they just wasted nearly all of their time every day on prayers and liturgy, which were sung, such behaviour being both preposterous and an impediment to progress.

Here is a small sample of how governments dealt with the perceived uselessness of the contemplative life. Between 1700 and 1768, the French monarchy closed 122 Benedictine houses. By 1792 the new revolutionary government had abolished all of the remaining Benedictine monasteries in France, and when its troops conquered other countries, the government abolished monasteries there as well. In the name of enlightenment, the enormous monastery at Cluny was not only confiscated; most of it was also demolished and the rubble put up for sale. The Holy Roman Emperor Joseph II (1741–90) had no patience with the kind of holy life practiced by the contemplative orders; as part of his efforts to make the Catholic Church an efficient state agency under Hapsburg rule, he closed down 876 monasteries and convents.

Thomas Jefferson gives us a helpful insight about what was going on here. In a letter to Roger C. Weightman dated 24 June 1826, Jefferson described his hopes for the ideals expressed in the Declaration of Independence. Fifty years earlier, he had written the first draft of that statement about freedom and in this letter he predicted that the Declaration would eventually be 'the Signal of arousing men to burst the chains, under which monkish ignorance and superstition had persuaded them to bind themselves [...]' Note the way the word 'monkish' connects with 'ignorance and superstition' to form a coherent unit. Note the association with 'chains'. Anything 'monkish' was abhorrent to Jefferson, and that certainly must have included music or ritual that was reminiscent of a monastery.

Long before Jefferson was even born, the Catholic Church was dealing with critics who were attacking it for monkish backwardness. One way of responding was a tactic from the Counter-Reformation: the use of modern art to show that the church was a vibrant, forward-looking institution in the modern world. A famous example is the interior decoration of St Peter's Basilica in Rome. Using the language of contemporary art, this riot of baroque ornamentation energetically announced that the church had not just emerged from the challenge of Protestantism, it had triumphed. In the eighteenth century, Austrian and German Catholics (including monks) showed they were not afraid of modernity by building churches in the fashionable Rococo style.[1] The music of Mozart's Masses for Salzburg's cathedral, Haydn's Masses, and even Beethoven's *Mass in C*, communicated

---

[1]   I recall visiting one church whose interior was a delightful Rococo confection. Then I looked more closely and noticed traces of Gothic arches. It was really a medieval

in the language of a modern musical style that seems to proclaim faith in a
God who is cheerful, benevolent, and un-monkish – the Enlightenment's
idea of a perfectly acceptable sort of deity. (The aristocrats who commissioned such music wanted that.)

A general reaction to the cold certainties of the Enlightenment was
well under way towards the end of the eighteenth century. We can see this
in the *Sturm und Drang* movement in German literature during the late
1760s and into the early 1780s and then later, with a much more international scope and lasting impact, in Romanticism. The Romantics surren-
dered themselves to powerful emotions, feelings, and spiritual yearnings;
to solitude; to the pagan power of nature; to the local folk culture. They
wanted music that would help them to immerse themselves in that sur-
render. They also found much to admire in the Middle Ages – sometimes
idealized as an era of chivalry and noble deeds from the pages of Sir Walter
Scott's *Ivanhoe* (1819), sometimes dramatized as the source of the 'Gothic',
where mystery lurks in the darkness beneath every pointed arch.

The Catholic Church, consistent with its behaviour over the centuries,
took what it found useful in modern art influenced by Romanticism. An
example of this was the building of new churches in the old Romanesque
and Gothic styles. This new-old architecture appealed to modern tastes and
at the same time showed the world that, contrary to what was said during
the Enlightenment, the church's cultural accomplishments in the Middle
Ages were impressive. Architecture was easy enough, but adapting the music
of Romanticism to the liturgical needs of the church was another matter.
The musical language of Romanticism frequently demanded the attention of the listener with its overstretched emotions. That grand theatrical
gesturing in so much Romantic music (even instrumental music) can be
thrilling in the opera house and the concert hall, but could that musical
style fit into the liturgical objectivity of the Roman Rite?

A large portion of *Renewal and Resistance* is about the answer to that
question, or to put it another way, about the Catholic Church's reaction to
liturgical music in a style influenced by Romanticism. For many Catholics

---

building that had been modernized during the eighteenth century by covering the
interior with thick layers of, as it were, whipped-cream and cake-icing decorations.

of the Latin Rite, that reaction was favourable, even enthusiastic; they saw nothing wrong with beautiful modern music that was also uplifting. Songs by Rossini and Mercadante, and elaborate Masses by Gounod, Franck, Cherubini and others sounded 'normal' – contemporary music that people could 'understand'. It was also art that met the highest standards of excellence and for that reason, was appropriate as liturgical music. At the same time, however, such music was too difficult for the great majority of choirs, so an assortment of minor composers (extremely minor) produced abundant quantities of easier liturgical compositions that approximated Romantic grandeur. It did not matter if this music mangled the Latin text or reminded the faithful of opera and operetta. According to a way of thinking that had prevailed perhaps since the seventeenth century, liturgical music only provided a background enhancement; the priest, by reciting the required words, took care of the complete liturgical text by himself.

By the middle of the nineteenth century a reaction against Romantic music in church emerged in the Cecilian movement. The Cecilians, mostly Catholics who spoke German, thought of themselves as reformers who were going to lead the faithful away from error (liturgical music that merely entertained during Mass) and back to truth (liturgical music that was an integral part of worship and prayer). They found their source of pure liturgical music, untouched by worldly associations, in the late sixteenth-century music of Palestrina and other composers of the Roman school.[2] They also extolled the virtues of Gregorian chant.

The efforts of these Cecilian reformers have been criticized: for disfiguring Renaissance music and chant with interpretative nuances that were more appropriate for nineteenth-century Romantic music; for using a faulty edition of chant published in Regensburg; and for devoting so much of their energies to mediocre neo-Renaissance music by contemporary composers. With all that said, the Cecilians were nevertheless right about so many things, including two somewhat radical propositions for the nineteenth century: (1) a wonderful unity between liturgical music

---

2   More information about this glorification of Palestrina can be found in James Garratt's excellent *Palestrina and the German Romantic Imagination: Interpreting Historicism in Nineteenth-Century Music* (Cambridge: Cambridge University Press, 2002).

and liturgy had existed in the past and it needed to be brought back to the modern world; (2) modern congregations were quite capable of liking liturgical music from the past, and even intensely identified with it as an extension of their own inner prayer.

Restoration – bringing back music of the past – had a central place in the Cecilian movement's agenda. Restoration – returning to correct and wholesome practices after years of disorder and confusion – is a constantly recurring theme in *Renewal and Resistance*. Replacing the bad (or at least the misguided) with the good from the past might look like a simple proposition, but it is not so simple. Sometimes it can set off another reaction, an especially destructive one if the restoring process is handled badly. An explanation of that statement requires a lengthy digression.

After Napoleon was exiled to St Helena, the Catholic Church in Europe began what could be called a restoration campaign. There was much to be restored. Monks and nuns moved back into empty monasteries and convents that had been taken from them and they restored the contemplative communities that had once existed in those places. The Jesuits were restored as a religious order. The First Vatican Council restored, reaffirmed, and strengthened the primacy of the pope. Leo XIII promoted a restoration of scholastic philosophy, with an emphasis on St Thomas Aquinas. The papacy recovered territory it had lost to the French.[3] These territories were lost again, this time to the new Kingdom of Italy. The popes never did regain control of the Papal States, but in 1929 a financial settlement and sovereignty over the Vatican and some other properties amounted to a reasonable form of restoration.

Very soon after becoming pope in 1903, Pius X proclaimed the following in the fourth paragraph of his first encyclical, *E Supremi*, promulgated on 4 October: 'We have no other programme in the Supreme Pontificate but that "of restoring all things in Christ" (Ephesians 1:10), so that "Christ may be all and in all" (Colossians 3:2).'[4] He followed that statement with

---

3   In 1809 the Vatican's archives, on the Emperor Napoleon's orders, were confiscated and sent to Paris. The archives were returned after Napoleon's exile, but some items disappeared in transit.

4   See <http://www.vatican.va/holy_father/pius_x/encyclicals/documents/hf_p-x_enc_04101903_e-supremi_en.html>, accessed 26 June 2009. 'On the Restoration of

his *motu proprio* on liturgical music, *Tra le sollecitudini* (22 November 1903), which is essentially about restorations: bringing back the traditional wisdom that liturgical music functioned as a part of a liturgy rather than as a decorative parallel to it; bringing back a restored version of Gregorian chant; and encouraging the use of old polyphony.[5] This would be followed by what amounted to the pope's official recognition of the scholarly work done at Solesmes Abbey on the restoration of Gregorian chant to something closer to its original sound. Later, Pius X would launch a project to publish an improved edition of the Vulgate (Latin) Bible, the church's official Bible – an immense scholarly undertaking that was really about restoring this text of this Bible to its original Latin form. A reorganization of canon law, the Vatican bureaucracy, and the Vatican's official journal for publishing its decrees (*Acta Apostolicae Sedis*) – projects he initiated – could all be described as efforts to restore order where there had once been insufficient order.

The campaign of Pius X to restore was not motivated just by a determination to tidy up disorder or to improve liturgical music; rather, as *E Supremi* makes clear, the new pope was reacting to a modern world that horrified him: 'We were terrified beyond all else by the disastrous state of human society today. For who can fail to see that society is at the present time, more than in any past age, suffering from a terrible and deep[-]rooted malady which, developing every day and eating into its inmost being, is dragging it to destruction?' This disease was the 'apostasy from God' that leads to ruin. 'We must hasten to find a remedy for this great evil, considering as

All Things in Christ' is in the title of this encyclical, and some version of the word 'restore' ('restored', 'restoration' or 'restoring') occurs ten times in the document, including the title.

5   At the conclave that elected him pope in 1903, Giuseppe Sarto, the future Pius X, wept when it looked certain that the cardinals were going to choose him. He begged them to find someone else. Perhaps one reason he wept was because he knew that, like two of his predecessors (and two of his successors), he would be the Prisoner of the Vatican – trapped inside the walls of the Vatican because of feuding with the Italian Government. Perhaps he also wept because he knew that once inside the Vatican, he would have to endure appallingly bad liturgical singing. (For an example of the Sistine Chapel's singing in 1902 and 1904 and also a castrato voice, consult *Alessandro Moreschi: The Complete Recordings* (Opal CD 9823, 1987)).

addressed to Us that Divine command: "Lo, I have set thee this day over the nations and over kingdoms, to root up, and to pull down, and to waste, and to destroy, and to build, and to plant" (Jeremiah 1:10)'.[6]

What could be called the pope's agenda for liturgical music – *Tra le sollecitudini* and the publication of a restored Gregorian chant – produced reactions that went in two main directions. One direction was a series of restorations that produced good results. Monks, nuns, and seminarians majestically sang Gregorian chant in the restored Solesmes version, while visitors who heard them were deeply impressed not just by the art and beauty of this old music but also by the deep piety that this music could express. The sound of chant and a few items of Renaissance polyphony inspired Catholics at congresses and conferences and in some parishes and cathedrals. Catholics who spoke German, Polish, and various other European languages maintained their vigorous tradition of singing vernacular songs during the Low Mass and took that same vigour into their choral singing for the High Mass in Latin. Above all, the sung liturgical texts were once again restored to their place as essential parts of a liturgy rather than background decorations.

Then there were the countless churches and chapels that went in another direction – but what word could describe it? Perhaps 'anger'. There was good reason for the anger, considering what was going on in many choir lofts, mostly in Italy and English-speaking countries: the singing of operatic favourites, like the sextet from Donizetti's *Lucia di Lammermoor* and the quartet from Verdi's *Rigoletto*, refitted with Latin words; the neglect of chant; the sacred music in a flimsy contemporary style that imitated opera and operetta, and so forth.[7] The result of all this anger was timid choral

---

6   As n.4, paragraph 3.

7   In 1922 the Society of St Gregory of America published *The Black List: Disapproved Music*, a list of works that were 'not in accordance with the MOTU PROPRIO' and 'clearly antagonistic to the principles enunciated in the document issued by Pope Pius X' (see <http://www.musicasacra.com/pdf/blacklist.pdf>, accessed 26 June 2009). The publication lists some masterpieces by Mozart, Rossini, Schubert, and other famous composers, but mostly contains forgettable atrocities by contemporary composers. The St Gregory Society, which made valiant efforts to improve

music that suggested fear and trembling. All 'unliturgical' music may have been expelled from the church, but so had anything that symbolized the devotion and best efforts of a community. To be fair, many choirs were just too intimidated by the challenge of singing the music of the Latin High Mass according to the uncompromising liturgical standards.

In the nineteenth century there were all kinds of efforts to restore sacred music to a golden age that had once existed. In the middle of the twentieth century, especially after the Second Vatican Council, there was a reaction to this restoration: a yearning to restore liturgical music to an even older golden age, when congregations (not choirs) filled the churches with their singing of psalms, antiphons, responses, litanies, and so forth. Once again, this was a reaction that went in two directions: (1) congregations welcomed the opportunities to participate and liturgical rigidities were relaxed; (2) not just anger but fury. That righteous indignation of some liturgists! Those denunciations of old sacred music! Those demands of contemporary composers that all previous liturgical music be swept away (and replaced with theirs)! In the name of participation, everything in church music would have to change. The old regimentation of the past (for example, priests, seminarians, nuns, and novices chanting their way through Vespers and Compline, with the precision of soldiers in a marching drill) would now be replaced with the new regimentation – congregations force-marched through four hymns at every Mass.

The next reaction has already begun. Pray that it will not be angry.

Renewal and Resistance contains selected scenes and episodes from this unending story of imperfect human beings trying to express in their music the perfection of God. The task is impossible and endless, but must be done.

---

the liturgical music of Catholics in the United States, also published a *White List*, containing 'approved and recommended' music (see <http://www.musicasacra.com/pdf/whitelist1947.pdf>, accessed 26 June 2009). While chant and polyphony of the late Renaissance feature in the *White List*, the St Gregory Society, like the Cecilians of the nineteenth century, mostly endorsed easier sacred music that was by approved contemporary composers.

ECKHARD JASCHINSKI

The Renewal of Catholic Church Music in Germany/Austria, France and Italy in the Nineteenth Century

The 1903 *motu proprio* of Pope Pius X, *Tra le sollecitudini*, was the high point of many decades of development in the history of Catholic sacred music, the effect of these developments lasting until the Second Vatican Council. The three main roots to which the developments can be traced lie in politics, intellectual history, and liturgy.

Germany/Austria

The term *secularization* sums up the economic, political, and intellectual consequences of the 1803 *Reichsdeputationshauptschluss*, particularly for the Catholic Church in Germany. The act of secularization that began at that time was considered primarily as compensation: the occupation of territories to the left of the Rhine by France was accepted by Prussia and Austria, but only at the price of allowing both states to take advantage of the ecclesiastical domains to the right of the Rhine. Those domains, including their territories, began to be distributed to the secular rulers.

The Catholic dioceses were partly under the supervision of Protestant authorities. This was the case particularly for the Prussian provinces, Rhineland and Westphalia. As a result of this, a constant theme was the frequently uttered demand for freedom from the bonds of the state church system (*Staatskirchentum*). With regard to Prussia especially, this difficult relationship can be delineated. The Cologne ecclesiastical controversy (*Kölner Kirchenstreit*) of the 1830s was followed by the joint initiative of completing Cologne Cathedral and the establishment of a Catholic department within the Prussian Ministry of Education and the Arts to which only Catholic officials could be appointed.

In German Catholicism during the second half of the nineteenth century, the way out of the state church system was increasingly regarded as ultramontanism. This growing leaning towards Rome caused fierce Protestant polemics, so much so that there was little distinction between 'Catholic' and 'anti-national'.

Devotional practice saw a rediscovery of baroque forms. Once again prayers and pilgrimages attracted large crowds and were perceived as a demonstration of an awareness of Catholic identity. In clerical circles that favoured restoration, tendencies arose that challenged the achievements of the Enlightenment. The liturgical expression of these tendencies could be seen in the clearly marked space of the chancel reserved only for the priest, as well as by the restriction of the laity to the nave. An architectural expression of the same leanings was the structure of the ideal neo-Gothic nave of the church building.

The growing power of the laity became apparent in the flourishing of associations (Katholischer Verein Deutschlands, 1848), as well as the emergence of large events (Deutscher Katholikentag, 1848).

The influence of the Age of Romanticism

At the turn of the nineteenth century, a new intellectual trend emerged among literary figures, namely Romanticism. This trend did not see the genuine fulfilment of life in ordinariness, but rather looked for it beyond everyday life, in the spectacular, mysterious, and unusual. This ideal alternative world could be best embodied in music. Music, especially of the Renaissance and Early Baroque, was rediscovered and presented as the ideal. To imitate this 'pure musical art' ('reine Tonkunst') even more purely (without dissonance) became a goal for the Cecilian movement in the restoration of church music.

Two literary figures, Heinrich Wackenroder (1773–98) and Ludwig Tieck (1773–1853), are regarded as founding fathers of Romantic musical aesthetics. According to them music has the advantage of escaping linguistic and thus rational capture, because it touches the 'heart' immediately – 'heart' being understood as a metaphor for the human emotional experience.

According to the Romantics, music embraces human beings in their wholeness and opens up new areas of awareness to them. It is even a language pointing to a divine origin. Music becomes the experience of religion, and by opening up religious dimensions, it becomes sacred devotion. The art of music, metaphysically infused in this way, becomes music religion: the audience becomes a community, and the concert hall, the room in which compositions are ritually celebrated. Musical art is an alternative plan to reality, not its image. The opportunity, opened up by sound, to accompany the human being into a different world is eventually interpreted as eschatological. Understood as redemption, music assumes the genuine purposes of religion.

Reflecting on the music of his time, the jurist, writer and musician Ernst Theodor Amadeus (E.T.A.) Hoffmann (1776–1822), in particular, emphasized the essentiality of instrumental music to the idea of Romanticism. In his review of Beethoven's fifth symphony (1810), Hoffmann states that music is 'the most romantic of all arts – one might almost say the only one that is *purely* romantic',[1] for music opens up to the human being an unknown realm, one that has nothing in common with the surrounding, outer, material world, one in which every feeling defined by concepts is left behind in order to dedicate oneself to the inexpressible.

This ideal world, emerging in instrumental music, is said to appear in sacred music as well, admittedly only in the sacred works of earlier times, but including even those which are not limited to liturgical events. Hoffmann called Renaissance polyphony itself a cult, and in his essay 'Alte und neue Kirchenmusik' (1814), he describes the ideal of music as a 'sacred musical art' ('heilige Tonkunst'):

1   David Charlton (ed.; trans. Martyn Clarke), *E.T.A. Hoffmann's Musical Writings: 'Kreisleriana', 'The Poet and the Composer', Music Criticism* (Cambridge: Cambridge University Press, 1989), 236.

The music that is purest, holiest, and most suitable for the church must therefore be that which arises from the heart purely as an expression of that love, ignoring and despising all earthly things. Palestrina's simple, dignified works are conceived in the highest spirit of piety and love and proclaim godliness with power and splendour.[2]

The literary figures' ideal of *musica sacra* was at first interdenominational and found its way through the educated middle class gradually into the music of the church. Choir singing evolved within the middle class, and an appropriate *a cappella* repertoire was compiled for them.

The jurist Anton Friedrich Justus Thibaut (1772–1840) taught at Heidelberg, where, from 1811, he also directed an amateur choral group that performed oratorios by Handel as well as *a cappella* music of the Renaissance. Both as jurist and musician he stood for a firm historicity, calling for a return 'to the roots'. He was entirely filled with a devotion to art, through which musical tradition evolved into classicism. In his widely-read book, *Über Reinheit der Tonkunst* (1825), he sternly rejected instrumental music inside the church.

Attempts to reform liturgy and music in the Age of Restoration

By the early nineteenth century, Catholic sacred music faced two threats: secularism and impoverishment. The operatic style was so popular in liturgical music that melodies from operas were used during the Mass, while radical directives of the Enlightenment restricted sacred music in such a way that artistically and spiritually everything became sober and down-to-earth. These threats were countered by the ideal of ancient music. Contemporary music, moreover, was regarded as theatrically shallow, secular, and lascivious. Behind the search for a pure style of sacred music, a drama was brewing, the consequences of which continue to have an effect to this day:

---

2   Ibid., 358. For more on Hoffmann's 1814 essay and the Romantic idealization of Palestrina, see James Garratt, *Palestrina and the German Romantic Imagination: Interpreting Historicism in Nineteenth-Century Music* (Cambridge: Cambridge University Press, 2002), 36–47.

the total separation of the profane and the sacred. The religious attitude of the Romantics towards moralism and asceticism implied that music could not develop freely within the liturgy.

In the middle-class concert halls, on the other hand, a new style of sacred concerts developed, beginning in 1829, when Mendelssohn reintroduced Bach's *St Matthew Passion*. Compositions like Brahms's *Ein Deutsches Requiem* (1867–9) were written specifically for the concert hall, and no longer had roots in the liturgy. So, a true renewal of sacred music could not come from that direction. What was required was a hearkening back to the foundations of Christian faith.

Developments in the German-speaking areas

One of the most important mentors in this respect was Johann Michael Sailer (1751–1832). For the design of the sacred service, he took a well-balanced view. Since the liturgy is the action of the entire church, singing by the congregation has liturgical relevance. On festive occasions, however, the choir has its place as well. Although Sailer preferred the use of the vernacular in the liturgy, he did not make it absolute. He kept aloof from the rationalists' overstated demands for simplicity. Simplicity should not sink into banality.

With Sailer's appointment to membership of Regensburg Cathedral Chapter in 1821, a centre for liturgical renewal was established. The personage connected with the fulfilment of Sailer's ideas was Carl Proske (1794–1861), a Silesian physician and music-lover whom Sailer appointed as director of music at the cathedral in 1830. In order to gather genuine liturgical music, Proske made three visits during the 1830s to Italy, where such music was said to be found still intact. He also promoted Thibaut's thoughts, primarily in his collection *Musica divina*, the first volume of which appeared in 1853.[3]

3 Carl Proske (ed.), *Musica divina* 1 (Regensburg, 1853); see also Garratt, *Palestrina and the German Romantic Imagination*, 141–4.

The programme of musical reform, however, met with the disapproval of the cathedral chapter. At the time, work on the construction of Regensburg Cathedral, begun in the Middle Ages, was brought to completion, and it was hoped that the new building would be ennobled by music equally pure. This music, however, was falsely equated with the Gothic style of the cathedral, the view being held that simple chant, accompanied by organ, was most appropriate for the Gothic cathedral.

Further development was influenced by one of Sailer's pupils, the liturgist Franz Xaver Schmid (1819–83), who published a two-volume manual on the liturgy in 1832 that was keenly studied by the Regensburg circle and embraced as a basis for the reforms.[4] Schmid distinguishes between ceremonies in a narrow sense, performed by the celebrant in accordance with the instructions of the church, and liturgical actions of the faithful which need only the approval of the church. These new conceptions were developed later on in the direction of centralistic and clericalist ideas. Initially, Schmid effectively propagated valid insights on the nature of liturgy and sacred music that reflected the old Roman tradition. Accordingly, sacred music upholds not only a supportive function, but rather forms an integral part of the entire liturgy.

A common combat against the attacks of liberals opposed to the church around the middle of the nineteenth century engendered an increasingly militant Catholic consciousness that promoted the renewal of the church by looking to the past. Not to be overlooked is the juridical thinking that was applied to the liturgy: liturgy consists mainly of ceremonies, established and prescribed by rubrical norms.

On this breeding ground of intellectual history (Romanticism) and liturgical history (Enlightenment versus Restoration) the Cecilian movement of sacred music reform began to thrive. The concrete establishment of a relevant organization had forerunners in Cecilian associations in Vienna and Munich. Regarding the content of this reform movement, the basis was laid first by papal statements on the function and form of sacred music. Of central importance was the reference to the Council of Trent (1545–63), as well as the encyclical letter *Annus qui* of Pope Benedict XIV (1749). These general papal instructions, however, did not provide concrete criteria

---

4   Franz Xaver Schmid, *Liturgik der christkatholischen Religion* (Passau, 1832–1833).

regarding the design of contemporary pastoral music in the middle of the nineteenth century. As early as 1563, the council fathers had decided that further regulations concerning the practice of sacred music should be delegated to the provincial synods. For the Cecilian movement this was primarily the diocesan synod held in Cologne in 1860, which had a far-reaching effect on the development of sacred music in Cologne, and at which detailed instructions for liturgically appropriate sacred music were set down.

Under the leadership of the archbishop of Cologne, Cardinal Johannes von Geissel (1796–1864), it was decreed that the traditional and popular symphonic sacred music for choir and orchestra was to be substituted by Gregorian chant and Renaissance polyphony. The use of instruments in divine worship, furthermore, was to be reduced to a minimum, and women were to be excluded from the liturgically defined ministry of the choir, their voices being replaced by those of boys, for whom special choir schools were to be established. The reform aimed at a solemn sacred music suitable to the sublime dignity of the liturgical action. Everything regarded as 'noisy', 'distracting', 'unholy', and 'weak' was henceforth to be banished from liturgical music.

Eight years later, during the assembly of German Catholics in Bamberg in 1868, the Allgemeine Deutsche Cäcilien-Verein (ACV) was founded through the initiative of the Regensburg diocesan priest and musician Franz Xaver Witt (1834–88).[5] During the First Vatican Council Pope Pius IX approved this society with the papal brief *Multum ad movendos animos* (1870), and the society thus became an organization under papal regulation. The association was to report on the status of sacred music directly to Rome on a regular basis. Other countries, including France, the Netherlands, the United States, Poland, Austria, Ireland, and Italy, followed with the founding of similar associations. Thus, the sacred music of various countries became a concern of the Vatican congregations, and the appropriate regulations were to be integrated into a corpus of laws relating to sacred music.

5   From 1876, the ACV was known as the Allgemeine Cäcilien-Verein für die Länder deutscher Zunge, and from 1956 as the Allgemeine Cäcilien-Verband für die Länder der deutschen Sprache.

Like Proske, Witt too had liturgical renewal on his mind, advocating that sacred music ought to be reintegrated into divine worship. He made a sharp distinction between the outer form and the inner nature of celebration, the priestly ministry forming the bridge between the inner nature and the outer performance. Thus, liturgy is priestly ministry, understood only in connection with priesthood, which alone is authorized to carry out the celebration. Consequently, Witt wanted only men and boys to sing in sacred services. From this point of view, the faithful have no influence at all on the liturgical celebration. They are onlookers, whereas the choir is a participant. The choir does not stand in for the people, because the people cannot play any role in the liturgy. This led to the distinction between 'liturgical' and 'non-liturgical' services. Only in Masses not subjected to the regulations for singing, that is, the 'private Masses' of a priest, was the assembly's singing in the vernacular permitted. According to a manual by Paul Krutschek, *Die Kirchenmusik nach dem Willen der Kirche*, congregational singing in the liturgy was not only to be frowned upon, but also to be rooted out: the true praise of the Lord consists in obeying the rules.[6]

This implied a revocation of all those processes of enculturation that had ever occurred since the Roman liturgy was adopted in other countries. Gregorian chant, for example, is seen as liturgical song in a strict sense. While Gregorian chant was conceded this high rank only formally, in reality the works of classical Roman polyphony were regarded as artistically superior; a few questionable creations of Cecilian composers were included as superior works.

With the establishment of sacred music centres and the widespread introduction of the ACV, liturgical and musical training was fostered as well, and church choirs were founded everywhere. Thus, the standard of sacred music, including singing by the congregation, was raised.

The Cecilian representatives were concerned with bringing sacred music from its independence and secularization back into the liturgical domain. However, they did not view the liturgy as an activity that could be changed at will, but rather as a rite set down by law. Sacred music had

---

6   Paul Krutschek, *Die Kirchenmusik nach dem Willen der Kirche* (Regensburg: Pustet, 1897).

to obey stringent legislation, including the exclusion from the liturgy of both secular music for sensual pleasure (theatrical style) and folk songs. For these types of music artistic quality was secondary.

The Cecilian representatives tried not only to recommend suitable works from the past for adoption, but also to influence the development of sacred music in a restorative sense. Numerous less gifted composers were supported, if they followed the ideal of Palestrina's classical vocal style. Because of this, Catholic sacred music almost completely lost contact with the style of the period. Prominent musicians of the time no longer had much interest in liturgical music, and some of them even tried to beat the Cecilian representatives with their own weapons: the motets of Anton Bruckner, and above all the composer's Mass in E minor (for eight-part choir and wind players) and Liszt's *Missa choralis*, are among the few successful attempts at composing in a Cecilian style and yet with authenticity.

France

During the eigtheenth century, a group of reformers centred in Paris made significant strides in achieving lay participation in Catholic worship. Known as Jansenists, these reformers shaped what could be considered a French Catholic rite, a rite in the language of the people that would consciously engage them in the heart of worship. Although the Jansenists eventually were condemned by Rome for various teachings, their liturgical reforms continued to influence official worship and popular devotion in France.

In 1833 Prosper (Louis-Pascal) Guéranger (1805–75), a priest of the French diocese of Le Mans, revived Benedictine life in the old priory of Solesmes. His rule of the order, based on that of the Order of Saint Benedict, was approved by the pope in 1837, and in the same year Guéranger became the lifelong abbot of the monastery. The revival of Solesmes was based upon two main principals: scientific studies and the celebration of the liturgy.

One result of Guéranger's studies of liturgical history and theology was the three-volume manual *Institutions liturgiques*, which covered all areas of liturgical studies.[7] The second volume (1841), in particular, presents a critical treatment of the unique French liturgies that led to conflict with some French bishops. Guéranger's principal work is considered to be the multi-volume *L'année liturgique*, which began to appear in 1841.[8] For the period of the liturgical year after Pentecost, the work was continued by Guéranger's confrère Lucien Fromage. This work offers a complete commentary on the liturgical year, as well as translations of the texts in the Roman breviary and missal into the vernacular. For its commentary Guéranger employed many texts from other Western and Eastern liturgies, as well as from authors of religious writings. To a great extent this work promoted interest in the celebration of the liturgical year and had a lasting influence on piety that was based on the liturgy. Guéranger was, nevertheless, devoted to a clerical view of liturgy, for he rejected not only any incursion of the vernacular into the liturgy, but also kept the wording of the Canon of the Mass, though spoken by the priest in an inclusive plural, hidden from the assembly.

For a dignified celebration of the liturgy that would redound to the glory of God, an uplifting type of song was essential. The available editions of liturgical Gregorian chant, however, were totally insufficient. Thus, to begin with, there was a practical necessity to prepare the books required in the abbey, and Guéranger entrusted responsibilty for that enterprise to his confrères Dom Paul Jausions and Dom Joseph Pothier. Around 1870 their work seemed to be finished, but publication was delayed, and only in 1883 did the Gradual appear, the Antiphonary following in 1891.[9]

The systematic research of the old manuscripts of Gregorian chant resulted in a series of editions, *Paléographie musicale*, the first volume of which (facsimile Hs 339 of St Gall) appeared in 1889. This is regarded as

7   Prosper Guéranger, *Institutions liturgiques* 1–3 (Le Mans: Fleuriot/Paris: Débécourt, 1840–1851).

8   Guéranger, *L'année liturgique* (Paris: Oudin, 1841).

9   *Liber Gradualis* (Tournai: Desclée, 1883; 2nd edn Solesmes: Imprimerie de Saint-Pierre, 1895); *Liber Antiphonarius* (Solesmes: E Typographeo Sancti Petri, 1891).

the birth of Gregorian palaeography, because with the support of a precise reproduction of the original sources, made possible by photography, the manuscripts' old handwritten neumes could be explored and analysed. Twenty-one volumes in two series have been published to date, reproducing some of the most important manuscripts with their original notation.[10]

This first stage of restoration was marked by the pioneers' dedicated hard work. It was, however, also a period of research using exploratory, uncritical, and not yet perfected methods, with which it was hoped to attain practical solutions at any cost.

Despite the research of the French Benedictines and their editions of manuscripts of Gregorian chant, there was, in 1868, a move to update the *Editio Medicaea* (1614–15) by the Regensburg Cecilian Franz Xaver Haberl (1840–1910). This version of Gregorian chant, mutilated beyond recognition, was recommended as obligatory by Pope Pius IX in 1873, with printing rights for thirty years. Thus, an edition of authentic Gregorian chant for the universal church was blocked for decades.

Dom Guéranger managed to hold up classic Roman liturgy as the model for public and private prayer. His liturgically centred reform generated great enthusiasm for the Roman liturgy, especially in certain French and German monasteries.

In Germany, two brothers, Maurus and Placidus Wolter, opened the former convent of Augustinian canons at Beuron as a Benedictine priory in 1863. Five years later Maurus Wolter became the monastery's first abbot, and in 1872 he founded Mardesous in Belgium, which was initially led by Placidus Wolter. From Beuron the monasteries of Erdington in Birmingham, Emaus in Prague, and Seckau in Styria were founded in 1876, 1880, and 1883 respectively, while Maria Laach was resettled by monks from Beuron in 1892.

Dom Guéranger was a great admirer of the thirteenth-century Saint Gertrude of Helfta, who aligned her *Exercitia spiritualia* with the liturgical

---

10   *Paléographie musicale* 1–21 (Solesmes: Imprimerie de Saint-Pierre/Tournai: Société Saint-Jean l'Evangéliste, 1889–1958 (first series); Tournai: Desclée, 1900–1924 (second series)).

year and the service celebrated daily. In 1863 Guéranger edited her writing in French, while the following year Maurus Wolter published his own *Gertrudenbuch*, which closely follows Guéranger's work. Also, in his *Praecipua Ordinis monastici Elementa* (Bruges, 1880), Wolter, like Guéranger, explained the great importance of the Benedictine rule and the liturgical celebration in monasteries, particularly those of the Beuron congregation.

The most frequently mentioned Benedictine monk in Germany during the nineteenth century was Pater Anselm Schott (1843–96) from Beuron Abbey (and later of Maria Laach Abbey). During his stay at Maredsous (1876–81) he saw that his confrère Dom Gérard van Caloen was working on the two-volume, bilingual *Missel des fidèles*, published in 1882. Although a number of German translations of the missal were already available, Schott decided to publish yet another, which was to be a single-volume handbook for regular Mass-goers. It did not include a Latin version of all the texts, but instead gave brief explanations of the most important liturgical texts. Schott understood it as 'a sort of compendium of Dom Guéranger from whose *Année liturgique* most of the explanations are derived [...] a book for devotional use, to put it in one's pocket and take it away.'[11] In 1884 it appeared as *Das Meßbuch der hl. Kirche (Missale Romanum) lateinisch und deutsch mit liturgischen Erklärungen. Für Laien bearbeitet von P. Anselm Schott OSB aus der Beuroner Benediktiner-Kongregation.*

Schott wanted to make the church's treasury of prayer more 'available and familiar' to the faithful. This intention would have been met, according to Guéranger's example, if Schott's missal had included the *Vesperale* as well. The practicality of the book would otherwise have been lost. Yet, to the editor, it was so important that nine years later (1893), as 'a sort of addition' to the missal, he edited his *Vesperbuch (Vesperale Romanum) lateinisch und deutsch, enthaltend die Vespern des Kirchenjahres.*

The Benedictines, therefore, had made a genuine effort to revive the liturgy, to celebrate it impressively, and to publicize its content through widespread translations of the liturgical texts and their commentary. But the number of those who possessed these publications and attended liturgies with deeper understanding remained relatively small. While aesthetically ambitious services were celebrated in Benedictine monasteries, their classical

---

11   Letter dated 28 June 1883 to the Herder publishing house.

beauty filling many of those attending from outside with enthusiasm, the liturgical celebrations in the parishes themselves had not changed very much. Moreover, although the Schott missal went through many editions and was widely available, it was used by only a few people attending the services.

To Prosper Guéranger, only the Roman liturgy was of importance. The numerous diocesan liturgies in France were suppressed; the oriental liturgies were overlooked. 'Catholic' meant 'Roman', and that meant 'Latin'. The centralization of the church before and after Vatican I fostered these endeavours and was in part supported by them.

The new theological approaches, in so far as they were opposed to religious individualism and emphasized the liturgy above all as a celebration of the community, were in accordance with the dominating Benedictine conception of liturgy. Guéranger would not have had any sympathy for Valentin Thalhofer's *Rituale Romano-Eystettense*. There was obviously a confidential agreement, however, between Thalhofer and Schott. The Eichstätt theologian had encouraged the Beuron Benedictine to publish the German *Vesperbuch*. Yet despite his knowledge of the historical development, Thalhofer, like Guéranger, held the view that the Roman liturgy must essentially adhere to the Latin language, and that to introduce the vernacular into worship meant to give up the Roman liturgy, no matter how well and how exactly it might be translated. The possibility of changing the predominance of Latin as the exclusively valid language of the liturgy was not taken into consideration.

Closely bound to the Roman liturgy, Gregorian chant demanded too much of congregations due to its use of Latin and its complex melodic line. Since, however, the vernacular in the liturgy was strongly rejected, Latin choir song had to be employed for the solemn form of the sacred liturgy.

The musical arrangement of the liturgy clarified the way things really stood regarding celebrations: one had the abbeys with their High Mass and Gregorian chant in the Middle Ages; the parishes with their choral music in the style of Palestrina during the Counter-Reformation; and those parishes that preferred Viennese music during the Baroque. The people certainly sang during some of the sacred services. Yet worship song in the vernacular was not regarded as genuine liturgical song any more than the praying of devotions during the Mass could be regarded as liturgical prayer.

What attracted people more were devotional practices outside of the liturgy: Blessed Sacrament and Sacred Heart prayers, the rosary and May devotions, Corpus Christi and rogation processions. The celebration of the Mass in front of the Blessed Sacrament was uniquely appreciated. On the other hand, people were satisfied with receiving Holy Communion just once a year, and this often occurred outside of Mass. The number of those who took the church law of 'reverently hearing Mass' each Sunday seriously was still quite high, yet the number of those who stayed away from Sunday service, especially among the workers in the cities and industrial areas, gradually increased. For a long time the church did not know how to counteract the trend.

Italy

The 1749 encyclical letter of Pope Benedict XIV, *Annus qui*, had already responded to abuses in Italian sacred music. Although harmonized singing accompanied by organ and orchestra was still allowed, it was not to include anything profane, secular, or theatrical. The instruments permitted were organ, strings and oboe, in so far as they supported the singing. Prohibited instruments included timpani, brass, flutes, psalteries and lutes, because of their association with theatrical music.

During the first half of the nineteenth century several relevant reforms were decreed for the city and diocese of Rome, the first appearing in 1824. The condition of sacred music in Italy throughout the nineteenth century, however, continued to leave something to be desired. It could happen, for example, that during a baptism celebration on the anniversary of the freedom fighter Giuseppe Garibaldi (*d*1882), his hymn would be played. Popular operas by Verdi and Puccini, as well as other secular influences, had a strong effect on sacred music. Verdi himself, however, made a sharp distinction between sacred and profane music.

During the pontificate of Leo XIII the Congregation of Sacred Rites issued two decrees on sacred music (*Regolamenti per la Musica Sacra*), in 1884 and 1894 respectively.[12] The first *Regolamento*, drawn up in the spirit of Cecilianism and in cooperation with the Società di Cecilia, wanted, according to the covering letter, to put a stop to abuses that had crept into Italian churches. The second *Regolamento* was shorter than its predecessor. For the first time Gregorian chant and sixteenth-century polyphony were emphasized. Nonetheless, other guidelines, primarily those concerning the supervision of sacred music, were less rigid. The reason for this was probably that the new prefect of the Congregation of Sacred Rites, Cardinal Gaetano Aloisi-Masella, thought little of a strict Cecilianism.

Giuseppe Sarto (1835–1914), who became Pope Pius X in 1903, was an experienced pastor. As a student, and later at the diocesan seminary in Padua, he received a thorough training in sacred music, becoming choir-master of the seminarians during his last year of theological studies. As a priest he oversaw the singing in his parishes, founded both small and large choirs, and taught Gregorian chant to his congregation. While bishop of Mantua (1884–93), he founded the *schola cantorum* at the seminary, where he also taught courses in sacred music and chant. He convened a diocesan synod in 1888, and in certain passages of the synod's conclusions, statements regarding the reform of sacred music can be found which go beyond the *Regolamento* of 1884 in their strictness: the seminarians were to receive genuine liturgical and musical training; bands were not to perform in processions; Gregorian chant was to be promoted; musical instruments other than the organ were to be excluded from churches; and women were not to be allowed perform in choirs or orchestras.[13] Responding to a questionnaire issued by the Congregation of Sacred Rites in 1893, Sarto submitted a *votum* (report) on the state of sacred music, while, in 1895, as cardinal-patriarch of Venice (since November 1894), he published a

---

12　See Robert F. Hayburn, *Papal Legislation on Sacred Music, 95 A.D. to 1977 A.D.* (Collegeville, MN: The Liturgical Press, 1979), 137–43.

13　See Hayburn, *Papal Legislation on Sacred Music*, 198–200; also Anthony Ruff, *Sacred Music and Liturgical Reform: Treasures and Transformations* (Chicago/Mundelein: Hillenbrand, 2007), 274.

pastoral letter on sacred music, the regulations therein being based on the 1894 *Regolamento*, to which the letter indeed refers.

In view of the slow pace of reform within the church, it was obvious that Pope Pius X, newly elected in 1903, would take the initiative. His *motu proprio* promulgated on 22 November 1903, *Tra le sollecitudini*, focused on the renewal of the liturgy, and more particularly, the renewal of sacred music. The document did not, however, set off a revolution. Instead, it incorporated broad continuity, including initiatives that had lasting effects due to their energizing quality. Thus, on the one hand it embraced previous positions, such as a juridical view of the liturgy, an exclusive emphasis on priesthood, and a clericalist attitude towards the choir, while on the other hand, the *motu proprio* mentioned the phrase 'active participation in the sacred mysteries', thereby giving impetus indirectly to the 'awakening of the Church in souls'.[14] Compared with the sacred music regulations, the motto 'active participation' proved to have more far-reaching implications in the course of time, given that it was to become the leitmotif of the liturgical movement after the First World War.

---

14   See Romano Guardini (trans. Ada Lane), *The Church and the Catholic; The Spirit of the Liturgy* (New York: Sheed & Ward, 1935), 11–31.

PAUL COLLINS

Emissaries to 'a believing and a singing land': Belgian and German Organists in Ireland, 1859–1916

Land of Belgian and German organists

On the 2nd of January 1879 classes began at the church music school established by Jaak Nikolaas Lemmens (1823–81) at Malines (Mechelen) in Belgium. Formerly known as the École de Musique Religieuse, which was founded by the acclaimed Belgian organist, teacher and composer the previous year, the new Lemmens Institute offered courses in religion, liturgy and church Latin, plainchant, organ, piano, harmony, counterpoint and fugue, and sacred music composition. In March 1879 *Lyra Ecclesiastica*, the monthly bulletin of the newly formed Irish Society of St Cecilia, brought news of the opening of the Belgian 'church music training school' to its readers.[1] An English version of the school's prospectus, published '*in extenso*' by the bulletin, noted that the new academy of sacred music, 'under the august protection of His Eminence the Cardinal Archbishop of Malines; of their Lordships the Bishops of Belgium; and under the direction of M.J. Lemmens', had been founded 'for the purpose of training and advancing to the highest degree of proficiency, organists, choirmasters, and vocalists, for the service of the Holy Catholic Church.'[2]

At a time when church music in Belgium was perceived to be entering a new era,[3] Lemmens hoped that his academy would form each of its

---

1   See *Lyra Ecclesiastica: Monthly Bulletin of the Irish Society of St Cecilia*, March 1879, 51.

2   Ibid.

3   See *Lyra Ecclesiastica*, July 1879, 86.

pupils into 'the ideal which is required: an eminent professional in a true Christian.'[4] The prospectus requested, therefore, that each diocese send a small group of carefully selected musicians – only those 'with evident signs of vocation' – for training.[5] Among the first pupils to enrol at the academy was a 'Mr Hanrahan' from Limerick, who travelled to Malines because of the paucity of opportunities in Ireland for those who wished to receive comprehensive training as an organist-choirmaster.[6] Indeed, the absence of a training infrastructure in Ireland for aspiring church musicians, a situation that endured until the late twentieth century, led to a reliance on the part of many Irish dioceses on the services of foreign organist-choirmasters, mainly from Malines, the Kirchenmusikschule at Ratisbon (Regensburg), and the school of music at Aix-la-Chapelle (Aachen).[7] The extent of this dependence on musical expertise from mainland Europe was to become clear by 1930, when the Brussels correspondent of the *Irish Independent*, dubbing Ireland the 'Land of Belgian organists', commented:

> Some of the best Belgian organists, trained at the Inter-Diocesan School at Malines, have left their country to go to Ireland, there to act as professors of music and as organists [...] In Belgium it is believed that the best musicians migrate to Ireland on account of the wonderfully melodious old organs and because Irish audiences are very appreciative of their efforts.[8]

While the article cites the names of ten Belgian organists employed at Irish churches, cathedrals, and colleges, this number did not 'exhaust the list.'[9]

---

4   *Lyra Ecclesiastica*, March 1879, 52.
5   Ibid., 51.
6   Ibid., 53.
7   See Aloys Fleischmann, 'The Organization of the Profession', in Aloys Fleischmann (ed.), *Music in Ireland: A Symposium* (Cork: Cork University Press, 1952), 83; also Joseph J. Ryan, 'Nationalism and Music in Ireland', PhD thesis, National University of Ireland, Maynooth, 1991, 220.
8   'Ireland, Land of Belgian Organists – Remarkable Facts', *Irish Independent*, 22 August 1930, 8.
9   See letter from 'Marcato' to the editor, *Limerick Leader*, 6 September 1930, 10. The writer asserts that there were 'at least four more' Belgian church musicians at work in Ireland at the time, 'in Carlow, Waterford, and at Mellary and Roscrea colleges'.

One of the Lemmens Institute's most distinguished laureates, Belfast-based Arthur de Meulemeester (1876–1942), himself acknowledged in 1936 that the 'great and famous' church music school at Malines was represented in Ireland by 'so many of its erudite disciples.'[10] The fact that these musicians secured key organist posts in what was 'essentially a believing and a singing land' did not, however, meet with wholesale approval.[11] While the Irish hierarchy, eager to engender leadership in church music by the easiest and most economical means, favoured the appointment of Belgians and Germans to important organist-choirmaster positions, others viewed the employment of foreign musicians in these roles as a deliberate snubbing of native musical talent. One letter writer to the *Limerick Leader*, J.A. Smyth, argued that Irish musicians were often superior in ability, and should have been encouraged by the same unpatriotic pastors who rebuffed their talent:

> There is no logical excuse which the clergy can allege towards veiling their impatriotic [*sic*] attitude by employing foreign organists, while the services of men of equal, if not of superior, ability can be secured at home. We have yet to procure the information as to the number of Irish organists that are employed in Belgium, or in any other European country. I doubt if one could be found. The Belgians are too patriotic to spurn native talent by employing Irishmen, even though they were Gounods or Mozarts [...] Had those [Irish] talents been protected and developed,

---

The organists already mentioned in the *Independent* article were Karel Seeldrayers (Westport, Co. Mayo), Arthur de Meulemeester (Redemptorist Church, Clonard, Belfast), Michel Van Dessel (Dundalk Cathedral), Ernest de Regge (Ennis Cathedral), Antoine Toulemonde (Clongowes Wood College, Sallins, Co. Kildare), René Segers (Longford Cathedral), Jozef Delafaille (Newry Cathedral), Albert de Meester (Sligo Cathedral), Louis Evers (Galway Cathedral), and Jozef Cuypers (Newbridge, Co. Kildare). Brief biographies of these ten organist-choirmasters appeared in the Belgian journal *Musica Sacra* in June and September of 1930 (see Albert de Schutter, 'De Laureaten van het Lemmensgesticht in Ierland', *Musica Sacra*, June 1930, 81–94, and September 1930, 192–5).

10   Arthur de Meulemeester, *The Reform of Church Music* (Dublin: Catholic Truth Society of Ireland, 1936), 110.

11   See Arthur de Meulemeester (ed.), *St Cecilia's Hymn Book* (Dublin: Cahill & Co., 1911), preface.

as they should have been by the clergy and hierarchy, they would have far surpassed everything in contemporary Europe [...] The men of talent are flung away, and the people and clergy, in the depth of their folly, have, with an unnatural aptitude, clasped everything foreign and inferior to their bosoms, and have lavished public money in so doing.[12]

Interestingly, Smyth invokes *A History of Irish Music* by Irish music historian, organist, and composer William Henry Grattan Flood (1859–1928) in support of his claim that 'in every period [...] Ireland possessed musical talents often superior to those of any other European country.'[13] It was Grattan Flood who, in October 1914, addressed a communication to the Chief Secretary's Office in Dublin claiming that German organists in Ireland were spies.[14] Earlier, in 1902, concluding a lecture on 'The Original Melodies of Thomas Davis's Songs', Grattan Flood had advocated an institution 'which was one of the dreams of Thomas Davis – an Irish School of Music.'[15] He remarked that if such a school was established, Irish organists could be trained there and eventually fill positions in the 'thirty-five important Catholic churches in Ireland occupied by German organists.'[16]

Competent native organists were certainly to be found, as were opportunities for such musicians to cultivate their ability. It was possible to study with a foreign musician already domiciled in Ireland, and there were also the chances afforded by the organ competitions in music festivals such as the Feis Ceoil and Munster Feis.[17] What became of these native organists, however, and why were more of them not appointed to important posts

12   Letter from J.A. Smyth to the editor, *Limerick Leader*, 6 September 1930, 10.
13   W.H. Grattan Flood, *A History of Irish Music* (Dublin: Browne and Nolan, 1905).
14   See Registered Papers of Chief Secretary's Office, National Archives of Ireland, 1914/18218.
15   'The Original Melodies of Thomas Davis's Songs – Interesting Lecture by Mr. Wm. H. Grattan Flood', *Freeman's Journal*, 7 November 1902, 6.
16   Ibid.
17   The Feis Ceoil Association was founded in Dublin in 1894–6 to promote the general cultivation of music in Ireland, and more particularly Irish music. The first of the association's annual music festivals, which featured thirty-two competitions (vocal, instrumental, and composition sections) as part of its programme, took place over one week in Dublin in May 1897.

as they became vacant? These very questions were posed in late 1907 in David Patrick Moran's Dublin weekly newspaper *The Leader*. Reporting on music and painting at the Munster Feis, the columnist 'Lee' queried in passing why Ireland was failing to produce native organists, given that every Irish-based foreign organist he ever knew had 'one or more organ pupils year after year.'[18] Lee's piece drew an immediate and 'considerably astonished' response from the organist of St Patrick's Church in Cork, Eugene O'Mahony, 'one of the singularly fortunate "Irish" organists' to have secured a position in his native land.[19] O'Mahony, who claimed to have been offered the post of organist at a US cathedral in 1906, confidently asserted that the problem in Ireland lay in the failure to employ native organists, not produce them:

> The talent and ability are here in abundance, the means of cultivation are here also, but when a vacancy does occur, which would give an Irish organist an opportunity of displaying the aforesaid talent and ability, he must respectfully stand aside to make room for outsiders, and, as a result of this 'No Irish need apply (at least at home) policy', nearly all the great churches in America have Irishmen as organists. This is more curious from the fact that, there, they are in open competition with a great number of continental organists [...][20]

While the appointment of foreign organists was undoubtedly a cause of concern in Ireland because of the limited number of organist posts and the amount of unemployment in the music profession, the contribution of these musicians to church music in their country of adoption was considerable. Fr Michael Tracy, a one-time professor of ecclesiastical music at St Patrick's College, Maynooth, reflecting on the excellence achieved by the many foreign organists who had worked and were still working in Irish churches, endorsed the policy of employing such musicians, noting that the results 'justified the procedure.'[21] He continued:

---

18 'Lee', 'Music and Painting at the Munster Feis', *The Leader*, 28 September 1907, 87.
19 Eugene S. O'Mahony, 'Irish Organists', *The Leader*, 5 October 1907, 100.
20 Ibid.
21 Fr Michael Tracy, 'The Training of the Organist and Choirmaster', in Aloys Fleischmann (ed.), *Music in Ireland* (as n.7), 143.

These men are usually highly efficient organists and in most cases excellent choirmasters. Any opposition felt towards them was due to the fact that they tried to introduce
approved liturgical music to a country where the prevailing standard of taste in this
matter was rather poor; and also, perhaps, to the pardonable jealousy of native musicians who realized that, given similar opportunity for training in a recognized centre
of sacred music, they might have produced equally good results.[22]

Though not the focus of this chapter, the role that such musicians played
in musical life outside of the organ gallery deserves passing mention: they
were active in founding music schools and directing bands and choirs,
while those among them who were composers produced arrangements of
Irish folk songs.

Early Belgian arrivals

The first of the Belgian organists to arrive in Ireland was almost certainly
Charles Louis Nono (1834–95).[23] A graduate of the Academie van Schone
Kunsten in Roeselare, he arrived in Ennis, Co. Clare, in 1859 to take up
the dual appointment of organist-choirmaster at the Pro-Cathedral of St
Peter and St Paul and music teacher at St Flannan's College.[24] The following year the *Clare Almanack* informed its readers that at the unfinished
'Parish Roman Catholic Chapel' in Ennis there had just been installed 'a
magnificent organ, built by Mr. White of Dublin, which cost the large sum
of £600', noting further that 'Monsieur Nono, the organist', had 'formed

22   Ibid., 144.
23   See Herman Kerstens, *Vlaamse Organisten sinds 1900 in het Buitenland*
     (Norbertijnenabdij van Tongerlo: Kempense Cultuurkring, 2002), 7.
24   See John Chartres Molony, *The Riddle of the Irish* (London: Methuen, 1927), 33.
     Nono became a member of the nascent Irish Society of St Cecilia, being listed in
     the supplement to the April 1879 issue of *Lyra Ecclesiastica*.

a choir for sacred music.'[25] Monsieur ('Mons') Nono evidently possessed a fine bass voice too, as he took part in a performance of the motet *Splendente te, Deus* (KV Anh. 121) by Mozart at a concert in St John's Cathedral in Limerick in May 1864, during which the celebrated English virtuoso W.T. Best (1826–97) inaugurated the cathedral's new three-manual Hill organ.[26] Interestingly, the two other key participants in the concert were also from mainland Europe, both having arrived in Ireland only two years before, in 1862: Francis Prosper De Prins (1829–84), from Louvain, the 'popular' organist of Limerick's Redemptorist church (Mount St Alphonsus), who sang the solo bass part in the opening movement from Rossini's *Stabat Mater* and in Sir John Stevenson's duet 'O Lord, our Governer', and Mainz-born Caspar Anton Wötzel (1828–73), 'the untiring and skilful' organist of St John's Cathedral, who acted as conductor on the occasion.

As the focal point of Catholic church music reform during the late nineteenth century was Germany, it was to the Kirchenmusikschule at Ratisbon (Regensburg), founded by Franz Xaver Haberl (1840–1910) in 1874, that Irish ecclesiastics had looked in order to supply the Irish church with badly needed musical expertise. Six years before the founding of the Ratisbon school, German efforts at reform had peaked with the establishment by Franz Xaver Witt (1834–88) of the Allgemeiner Deutscher Cäcilien-Verein and the journal *Musica Sacra*, the latter propagating the new society's reformist principles. Francis De Prins and his brother, Léopold, who became organist at St Mary's Cathedral in Cork, were, like other Belgian and German organists of the period, devoted advocates of Cecilian reform.[27] Francis, 'possessing great musical taste, with the power to impart it successfully to others', had previously 'occupied the eminent position

---

25 *Clare Almanack*, 1860, 46. One of Nono's sons, Donatus, also taught at St Flannan's College and succeeded Charles Louis as organist at the cathedral.

26 'Opening of the Great Organ, Saint John's Cathedral. – The Oratorio', *Munster News*, 18 May 1864, 3.

27 There were, of course, notable indigenous musicians who were staunch Cecilians, like Joseph Seymour (organist at St Andrew's Church, Westland Row, Dublin), Brendan Rogers (organist at Dublin's Pro-Cathedral), and John Murray (organist at the Cathedral of the Assumption in Thurles, Co. Tipperary).

of organist to the Dominican Church of his native place, Louvain,'[28] and was probably recruited for the Limerick appointment by Belgian-province Redemptorists, who had established their order's first community in Ireland at Limerick in 1853.[29] Reporting on the formal dedication of Mount St Alphonsus, which took place on 7 December 1862, the *Munster News* noted that the 'musical portion of the proceedings', under the direction of De Prins, was rendered by 'the first exclusively male choir formed in Limerick, in a Catholic Church', the choir numbering 'close on seventy.'[30] It was further remarked that when the Belgian organist first assembled his 'choral corps of one sex', its members

> were with few exceptions ignorant of music. They began no further back than two months ago, and yet on Sunday last, they rendered the service in a manner that reflected infinite credit on their talented instructor, and the judgment of the Fathers in having secured his valuable services.[31]

Even before the appearance of the first issue of *Lyra Ecclesiastica* in 1878, Francis and Léopold De Prins had edited a quarterly journal, *St Cecilia* (from 1876),[32] and the brothers were enthusiastic members of the Irish Society of St Cecilia and committed supporters of its bulletin.[33] Of *St Cecilia* and its editors, *Lyra* gave the following assessment:

28   See 'The Redemptorist Fathers. – Dedication of Mount St. Alphonsus Church – Sermon by the Most Rev. Dr. Moriarty', *Munster News*, 10 December 1862, 3.

29   Other Redemptorist foundations were to follow at Dundalk (St Joseph's, 1876) and Belfast (Clonard, 1896), both of these communities employing Belgian organists. Redemptorists in Baltimore, the first episcopal see of the Roman Catholic Church in the United States, were also supportive of liturgical music reform during this period (see Ann Louise Silverberg, 'Cecilian Reform in Baltimore, 1868–1903', PhD thesis, University of Illinois at Urbana-Champaign, 1992, 287–9).

30   *Munster News*, 10 December 1862, 3.

31   Ibid.

32   'St. Cecilia. Quarterly Journal of Catholic Church Music by the best ancient and modern composers. Edited by MM. De Prins. London: Burns & Oates. Dublin: M.H. Gill & Son.'

33   Francis and Léopold were listed as members of the Irish Society of St Cecilia in the supplements to the March and April 1879 issues of *Lyra Ecclesiastica*. The June 1879

This ably-conducted and beautifully edited publication has now been before the public for two years, and was the first practical effort made in this country to bring Cecilian music within the reach of our choirs and choristers. The Messrs. De Prins have been favourably known for many years past (one in Limerick and one in Cork), as almost the only organists who persistently applied themselves to upholding and practically applying the principles of the Cecilian Society in their respective choirs, and the selections they have already published in their quarterly journal prove the soundness of their judgement in Church musical matters, as well as their artistic discernment.[34]

In the autumn of 1878, shortly before the establishment of the 'St. Cecilia society' in Dublin, Léopold had cause to defend Cecilian ideals in responding to a series of letters written by the then twenty-two-year-old organist of Limerick's cathedral, Joseph Smith, to the editor of the *Munster News* on the topic of church music reform.[35] In the first of his letters, Smith took issue with those who held that Gregorian chant was '*par excellence* the music of the Church' and 'the one musical language alone capable of expressing the emotions of the mind acted upon by feelings of love and reverence for God.'[36] How could a 'style of music' which fulfilled its intended aim centuries ago be expected to do so with equal effectiveness 'in an age which requires far more powerful stimulus to emotion of any kind, and when even the involuntary critical faculties have reached so high a development'?[37] The affective power of Gregorian chant could never match that of 'modern music' in awakening awe and reverence, contrition and joy – 'those deep

---

issue requested subscribers in the Limerick region to forward their annual subscriptions to Francis De Prins, while earlier in the same year, Francis and Léopold were among the first to report to *Lyra* on liturgical music outside of Dublin (see Kieran Anthony Daly, *Catholic Church Music in Ireland, 1878–1903: The Cecilian Reform Movement* (Dublin: Four Courts Press, 1995), 51).

34   *Lyra Ecclesiastica*, January 1879, 40.

35   See editorial comment entitled 'Church Music', *Munster News*, 24 August 1878, 3. Letters by Smith appeared in the *Munster News* on 24 August, 31 August, 7 September, and 28 September 1878, while De Prins's responses featured on 31 August 1878 ('The Question of Reform in Church Music') and 14 September 1878 ('Reformation of Church Music').

36   'The Reformation of Church Music', *Munster News*, 24 August 1878, 4.

37   Ibid.

feelings [...] which it is the province of all sacred music to excite.'[38] In his second letter Smith concluded that the value of plainchant ultimately resided in a 'negative' rather than a 'positive excellence':

> In other words, its adoption is generally advocated, rather by reason of its comparative freedom from the abuses that are sometimes connected with figurate music, than on account of any worth or beauty of its own. Such a recommendation, however, is hardly sufficient to convince us of the desirability of its general revival.[39]

In his letter of 14 September, Léopold remarked:

> If Mr Smith had had the good fortune to listen to some of the Cecilian choirs in Germany (as I had a few weeks ago), he might, *perhaps*, change his opinion as to Gregorian music [...] Adoration, devotion, and heavenly thoughts are the results of such angelic music [...] I trust that some day Mr Smith will have his eyes opened, and be converted, and that then he will use his *humble quill* in praise of the Angelic Song he now has the bad taste and *simplicity* to deride.[40]

Further evidence of the De Prins brothers' commitment to Cecilian ideals may be gleaned from the accounts they forwarded to *Lyra* in 1879 of their St Patrick's Day and Holy Week liturgies. In May, for example, Francis reported on the Holy Week ceremonies at Mount St Alphonsus:

> The music sung on Palm Sunday at the blessing of the palms and the procession which followed, was that prescribed in the *Processionale Romanum*. The Ordinary of the mass sung on that day was Haller's *Missa Quarta*; the Proper of the Mass was sung in Gregorian [...] The Mass on Easter day was Haller's celebrated *Missa Assumpta est*, for four equal voices; this Mass is, perhaps, one of that grand composer's finest specimens of Church Music we know of.[41]

After the establishment of the church music institute at Malines in the same year, the brothers, it would seem, took an added interest in developments in sacred music in their native country. On Christmas Day 1882 Francis

---

38   'The Reformation of Church Music (Continued)', *Munster News*, 31 August 1878, 4.

39   Ibid.

40   'Reformation of Church Music', *Munster News*, 14 September 1878, 4.

41   *Lyra Ecclesiastica*, May 1879, 72.

introduced a *Messe en re* by Lemmens to Mount St Alphonsus,[42] while *Lyra's* music supplements of 1883 included 'two little motets for three voices' by Palestrina, which had been forwarded to the bulletin by the Limerick-based Belgian. The motets, the bulletin noted, 'were first published [...] by direction of the Cardinal Archbishop of Malines, a great lover of real Church Music.'[43] Following the death of Francis in the summer of 1884, the July/August issue of *Lyra* lauded the influential Cecilian's efforts at promoting 'the standard of true liturgical music':

> The Irish Society of St Cecilia can badly afford the loss which it has sustained in the death of one of its most sincere and zealous working members, Mons F.P. de Prins of Limerick [...] Years before our Society was established, the standard of true liturgical music, in opposition to the frivolous style which then prevailed, was raised in the Redemptorist Fathers' Church in Limerick by the Messrs de Prins, with the joyful approbation of the Fathers and there, under the cross of the mission the true music of the Church has flourished and waxed strong in a congenial atmosphere [...] Setting himself steadily against the 'solo' system and thus depriving himself at first of the countenance and help of most of the educated musicians, who were strongly devoted to this system, Mons de Prins, out of untrained material, educated, trained and brought to efficiency, a choir of forty men and boys, now for the most part readers of music and capable of singing, in a style which leaves nothing to be desired, the most difficult works of the ancient and modern church writers.[44]

Three days before De Prins's death, it was reported that Limerick man P.J. Murray had been appointed to the 'important position' of organist at Mount St Alphonsus. After Murray's departure from Mount St Alphonsus a mere two and a half years later, the Redemptorists advertised the vacant position, and endeavouring to appoint a musician who would maintain the high standard set by De Prins, requested that 'none but a thoroughly competent person need apply', adding – not surprisingly – that such a person 'must be a Cecilian and well versed in plain chant.'[45]

42   See *Lyra Ecclesiastica*, February 1883, 15.
43   *Lyra Ecclesiastica*, September/October 1883, 64.
44   *Lyra Ecclesiastica*, July/August 1884, 54.
45   See *Munster News*, 19 January 1887, 2.

The ensuing eleven-year period from 1887 to 1898 saw the engagement of at least two local organists at the church before 'the Fathers' once again opted to appoint a Belgian, this time Lemmens laureate Jozef Bellens (1876–1939). A composer of sacred music and works for organ, Bellens's output included a motet, *Salva nos, Domine*, for SATB and organ, and a *Missa prima* and *Ave Maria*, both for two equal voices and organ.[46] Like his fellow countryman and organist Joseph Sireaux, who was based in Dundalk, Bellens became involved in the relief of Belgian refugees at the start of the Great War, being a member of the reception committee that welcomed forty such refugees to Limerick in December 1914.[47] He remained in Limerick until 1919, when he returned to Belgium to teach music at a seminary in Hoogstraten.[48] On behalf of Bishop Robert Browne of Cloyne, who had enlisted his help in sourcing a qualified organist-choirmaster for St Colman's Cathedral in Cobh, Bellens contacted the institute at Mechelen and secured German-born Alphonsus Graff, who remained at St Colman's from 1902 to 1908. In a letter to Browne dated 19 October 1901, Bellens assured the bishop of Graff's suitability for the position:

> It gives me very much pleasure to let you know, I have succeeded in getting a really good musician for your cathedral, Mr Alphonsus Graff, a German by birth, but now a naturalised Belgian. He studied at the School for Churchmusic, the well known Lemmens Institute, established in Mechlin by the bishops of Belgium, over which the great catholic composer Edgar Tinel is director, and where I studied myself. His diploma from this school qualifies him to hold the position of organist and choirmaster in any church or cathedral [...] I must say, that your Lordship will be fortunate in securing him.[49]

At St Joseph's Church in Dundalk, the Redemptorists engaged Belgian musicians from 1903. In that year Jan Juliaan Stuyck (1880–1957), who graduated from the Lemmens Institute in 1901, succeeded Thomas Vincent Parks

---

46 These three works appeared in supplements to the Belgian journal *Musica Sacra* in 1897/98 (17/12), 1911/1912 (31/3–7), and 1912/1913 (32/5) respectively.

47 See 'Belgian Refugees', *Limerick Leader*, 23 December 1914, 3.

48 See 'Departure of Mr J P Bellens', *Munster News*, 26 April 1919.

49 From the Bishop Robert Browne Papers held at Cloyne Diocesan Centre, Cobh.

as organist.[50] Like his own successor, Joseph Sireaux, who was employed from 1905 to 1910, and who subsequently became organist at St Patrick's Church, Dundalk (1910–19), Stuyck returned to Belgium after the Great War.[51] Following Sireaux's move to St Patrick's, Firmin Van de Velde (1888–?) was appointed organist at St Joseph's (1910–12), being succeeded by Jan Baptist Van Craen (1864–?) in 1916.[52]

The most significant of the early Belgian appointments was undoubtedly that of Arthur de Meulemeester by the Redemptorists in Belfast in October 1898. Lauded as 'the ideal church organist – a man who combined brilliant musical genius with deep and fervent piety',[53] de Meulemeester was a prolific composer of sacred music and 'a tireless campaigner and leading voice in the area of church music reform, not only in the north of Ireland, but throughout the country.'[54] The touchstone for all such reform, according to the Belgian, was Pius X's *motu proprio* on the renewal and regulation of sacred music. Commenting that 'the Law on Church Music' had been 'completely and clearly laid down' in the 1903 papal document, the Clonard organist echoes R.R. Terry's earlier observation that

50   Stuyck was also a composer, his works including an *Ave Maria* for SATB and organ, op.10, and a Toccata for organ, op.21.

51   With the opening of a Belgian Relief Fund in Dundalk in 1914 and the arrival of Belgian refugees, Sireaux ('J. Siraux'), in a letter to the *Democrat and People's Journal* (14 November 1914, 5), expressed his thanks to the people of Dundalk for their support of a fund-raising concert (see also *Democrat and People's Journal*, 7 November 1914, 5).

52   Kerstens claims that Van Craen, who graduated from the Lemmens Institute in 1890, spent a period as organist of Carlow's Cathedral of the Assumption (see Kerstens, *Vlaamsa Organisten*, 24). The register in Fleischmann (ed.) concurs with this, noting that Van Craen was at Carlow in 1892 (*Music in Ireland*, 161). A year later, in 1893, Van Craen was appointed organist to St Peter's in Phibsborough, Dublin (see *Lyra Ecclesiastica*, November 1893; also Daly, *Catholic Church Music*, 147).

53   E.H. Jones, CSsR, 'Chevalier de Meulemeester, K.O.L., K.O.C.B.', *The Redemptorist Record* 6 (September/October 1942), 151.

54   Mary Regina Deacy, 'Continental Organists and Catholic Church Music in Ireland, 1860–1960', MLitt thesis, National University of Ireland, Maynooth, 2005, 86.

> The Holy Father has spoken, and matters which were regarded as subjects for discussion have been removed from the region of controversy to the region of obedience [...] The day for individual comment and for individual expression of opinion has happily gone for ever [...][55]

De Meulemeester, who entered the Lemmens Institute in 1894, was a student of Edgar Tinel, and graduated at Mechelen in 1898. At Clonard, he established himself as an energetic 'apostle of the liturgy and champion of good church music', and the Clonard Domestic Archives remark upon the accomplishment of the Belfast church choir under his direction.[56] Clonard's Domestic Chronicle records, for example, that at the laying of the foundation stone of the Redemptorist church by Bishop John Tohill on 4 October 1908, the music

> was rendered in a faultless style by the meticulously trained choir of Clonard under the conductorship of Monsieur de Meulemeester, the well known organist and composer. All pieces were sung with rare beauty and taste, the solemnity and impressiveness of the sacred music being fully expressed.[57]

De Meulemeester's sacred music was regularly sung by Clonard choir, his motets, in particular, being included on all major feasts.[58] One notable occasion that featured a work by the Belgian was the 'opening' of the new organ on 26 May 1912:

> At the twelve o'clock Mass the following, among other pieces, were beautifully sung by an augmented choir:– 'Singenberger', 'Jesu Dulcis Memoria', 'Ave Maria Arcadelt', Lemman's [sic] 'Easter Sonata', and Meulemeester's 'Hymn to St. Cecilia.' M. Meulemeester presided at the organ, and the effect produced by the superb instrument, played by a master hand, was indeed memorable.[59]

---

55   R.R. Terry, *Catholic Church Music* (London: Greening, 1907), 39–40.
56   See James Delaney, 'Church Music Reform', *Irish Ecclesiastical Record* 68 (July–December, 1946), 242. For a fascinating insight into de Meulemeester's interaction with Redemptorists at Clonard, see James Grant, *One Hundred Years with the Clonard Redemptorists* (Dublin: Columba Press, 2003), 189–94.
57   Clonard Domestic Chronicle 1, 124.
58   See Jones, 'Chevalier de Meulemeester', 151.
59   *Irish News and Belfast Morning News*, 27 May 1912, 6.

For de Meulemeester, writing in 1935, the presence of so many Belgian organists in Ireland was something of 'a grateful reversal of history': if the 'Irish Apostles of early Christendom' had shaped the faith and culture of Belgium, it was now the turn of Belgians in the early part of the twentieth century to 'come and help to restore to Ireland the glories of ecclesiastical art [...]'[60] Keenly aware of the competent, loyal service given by Lemmens graduates to the Irish church, de Meulemeester stressed the need for 'more judicious' organist appointments. Failure to make appointments 'with the necessary discrimination' had led to a situation where good organs were 'in the hands of "executioners" instead of "executants," – in the hands of so-called organists.'[61] Substandard organists and choirmasters were directly responsible for the poor condition of sacred music in Ireland, the shortage of 'efficient' organists being 'at the root of most existing defects in the art of Sacred Music.'[62] In 1905, thirty years before he wrote his handbook on church music reform for 'all who are concerned in the progress of ecclesiastical art', de Meulemeester had attempted to fulfil the 'crying necessity' for training for Irish organists when he 'submitted a scheme for an interdiocesan School of Church music' to Bishop Henry Henry of Down and Connor.[63] Due to the bishop's sudden death, however, the proposal progressed no further.

Heinrich Bewerunge and other German musicians

The Westphalian-born priest, musician, and scholar, Heinrich Bewerunge (1862–1923), like de Meulemeester, knew that the training of organists and choirmasters would have to become 'the pivot of reform.'[64] In an article published in the *New Ireland Review* in 1900, Bewerunge, who had been

60 De Meulemeester, *The Reform of Church Music*, 110.
61 Ibid., 77.
62 Ibid.
63 Ibid., 74.
64 Ibid., 68.

appointed to a new chair of 'Church Chant and Organ' at St Patrick's College, Maynooth, in 1888, outlined the qualities required of one who would 'judge on the suitability of any music for Church services.' His description accurately profiles the musicians from mainland Europe that secured positions at Catholic cathedrals and churches in Ireland at the end of the nineteenth century:

> First of all he should be a pious Catholic, and, more particularly, be thoroughly familiar and sympathetic with the Liturgy of the Catholic Church. Secondly, he should be a good musician with a good historical training. He should have a fair knowledge of all the principal classes of music, and be particularly familiar with Gregorian Chant and the Palestrina style, the two classes of music that admittedly form the culminating points in the history of Church music. Of these two kinds of music he should thoroughly understand both the technical construction and the spirit that pervades them, and he should be able to perform them in a satisfactory manner.[65]

The reason for the dearth of such 'men' among Ireland's church musicians was as clear to Bewerunge as it would be to de Meulemeester over thirty years later:

> [...] we are severely handicapped by the almost complete impossibility for our young musicians to get a proper training in Church music. One of the results of this impossibility is that a considerable number of the more important positions of organists have to be filled with musicians imported from England or the Continent. This is not as it ought to be. But even apart from this, the general condition of Church music in this country is sadly affected by the want of opportunities for the training of organists and choirmasters.[66]

Bewerunge's appointment to the influential academic position at Maynooth confirmed the 'foreign' organist as a commanding figure in Irish Catholic church music, and Bewerunge, no doubt, was highly influential in the appointment of German organists to churches in Ireland and elsewhere,

---

65   Heinrich Bewerunge, 'Cecilian Music', *New Ireland Review* 13 (1900), 82. In his prospectus for the institute at Malines, Lemmens had already remarked that 'in order to direct Church Music, or to play in the house of God the noble instrument that alone becomes it, the fervent Christian and the skilful professional must be united in the same person' (see *Lyra Ecclesiastica*, March 1879, 51).

66   Bewerunge, 'Cecilian Music', 84.

as the career of Rudolf Niermann attests. On 7 February 1908, the parish priest of St Oswald's in Ashton-in-Makerfield (Liverpool archdiocese), Ardfinnan-born former Maynooth student Fr James O'Meara, wrote to Bishop Browne of Cloyne, recommending Niermann as a successor to Alphonsus Graff:

> Herr Niermann has asked me to write you a testimonial letter on his behalf. Through Father Bewerunge I secured his services to help my organist and teach my choir while he is disengaged. I have no hesitation in recommending him. He is a thoroughly trained musician and understands Church music and choir training perfectly. He has done excellent work here even in a few weeks and I feel sure he will prove a valuable acquisition to any church that secures his services permanently.[67]

Despite the bleak picture painted by Bewerunge in 1900 regarding the training of Irish Catholic organists, some efforts had been made to ameliorate the situation. In addition to Irish-based continental organists taking on students, some Irish organists, like C.J. Hanrahan from Limerick – mentioned at the outset of this chapter – had travelled to Mechelen and elsewhere to undertake further study. The 'Cecilian Intelligence' section of the January 1880 issue of *Lyra* proudly announced that

> at a *concours* given by the organ class in the recently established church music school of Malines, under the direction of M. Lemmens, an Irishman and a member of our society (Mr. Hanrahan of Limerick) distinguished himself, and was warmly commended by the critical jury present.[68]

Alois Volkmer, a stalwart Cecilian first mentioned in *Lyra Ecclesiastica* in 1879, was Joseph Seymour's predecessor at St Andrew's Church in Westland Row, Dublin, and taught organ at St Patrick's College, Maynooth (prior to Bewerunge's arrival there) and at the Royal Irish Academy of Music.[69] In 1880, *Lyra* included a notice advertising organ lessons at the RIAM,

---

67   From the Bishop Robert Browne Papers held at Cloyne Diocesan Centre, Cobh.
68   *Lyra Ecclesiastica*, January 1880, 8.
69   Volkmer is listed as a member of the central council of the Irish Society of St Cecilia in *Lyra Ecclesiastica*, January 1879 (p.33; see also Daly, *Catholic Church Music*, 47, 116).

Catholics being urged to consider the particular merit of studying under Volkmer:

> Catholic pupils will have a special advantage in studying under Herr Volkmer, as besides his acknowledged ability as an organist and contrapuntist his acquaintance with the Catholic Liturgy, acquired during his residence in the church music school at Ratisbon, will enable him to prepare them in all that they should know to fit them for the position of organists in our churches.[70]

The previous year, pleased to announce that 'a fair beginning' had been made regarding the introduction of Cecilian works to some of Dublin's major churches, *Lyra* noted that

> In St. Andrew's, Westland-row, it [Cecilian music] is no longer a novelty, as for some time past under Mr. Scott, as choir-director, assisted by Herr Volkmer as organist, and a select choir, some of the most beautiful *morceaux* of the Cecilian catalogue and many of its masses have been rendered with true devotional effect.[71]

Hans Conrad Swertz (1858–1927), born in Geldern in Rhine-Prussia, also studied at the Ratisbon Kirchenmusikschule, and was appointed assistant organist to Herr Thinnes at St Vincent's Church in Sunday's Well, Cork, in 1879. Influenced by continental sacred music practice, Vincentian Fr Edward Gaynor (1850–1936) had formed St Vincent's Palestrina Choir at the Cork church in the 1870s, and may well have been responsible for recruiting Swertz and his predecessor. Thinnes, who returned to Germany after Swertz's arrival in Cork, had introduced works by German Cecilian composers to St Vincent's, and was described as 'a *real church Musician*, a man who knows as if by instinct what is suitable and what is not for the House of God, and who will admit of nothing else.'[72] In 1890 Swertz was appointed organist and choirmaster at the Cathedral of St Mary and St Anne in Cork, and he also taught organ, singing, composition and advanced

70 *Lyra Ecclesiastica*, January 1880, 8.
71 *Lyra Ecclesiastica*, January 1879, 36. The same report on Cecilian music in Dublin further remarked that at High Mass on St Andrew's Day in 1878, 'the organ accompaniments, preludes, and interludes were all of a character with the vocal portions of the Mass and played with Herr Volkmer's accustomed ability' (ibid.).
72 Letter from Fr J. Hanley (St Vincent's) to *Lyra Ecclesiastica* dated 2 January 1879 (published in *Lyra Ecclesiastica*, February 1879, 46).

harmony at the city's newly established school of music. When he immigrated to Philadelphia in 1906, his son-in-law, Aloys Fleischmann senior (1880–1964), succeeded him at the cathedral.

Fleischmann was the most significant German church musician to arrive in Ireland after Bewerunge. He studied at the Royal Academy of Music (Königliche Akademie der Tonkünste) in Munich and had been a student of Joseph Gabriel Rheinberger (1839–1901). After taking up the post of organist-choirmaster at the cathedral (where he remained until the end of 1960), he endeavoured to implement the principles of the 1903 *motu proprio*, which had famously called for the exclusion of women from choirs.[73] In addition to substituting boys' voices for those of women, Fleischmann abandoned the Masses of Haydn, Mozart, and Gounod, and in obedience to the decrees of the *motu proprio*, privileged plainchant and sixteenth-century polyphony. This transition, involving both personnel and repertory, proved a difficult one for the cathedral's congregation, and provoked much opposition at first.[74] Fleischmann's reconstituted choir consisted of approximately fifty boys and forty men, and as well as singing plainchant and works by a variety of sixteenth-century composers, they also performed works by Rheinberger and music by Fleischmann himself and his contemporaries, including Vinzenz Goller (1873–1953). Within five years of arriving at the cathedral, Fleischmann had won the plaudits of clergy and laity alike. In 1908 the cathedral administrator hailed the German as a

73   De Meulemeester, zealously supportive of Pius X's desire for the reform of church choirs, would later remark that 'female voices are naturally sentimental [...] rather than inspiringly devotional: they please the ear, – but disturb the heart and mind; they are unsuited for truly religious music, however impeccable and artistic their renderings may be' (*The Reform of Church Music*, 23).

74   The exclusion of women from choirs in the wake of the *motu proprio* undoubtedly caused considerable disenchantment among singers, organist-choirmasters, and clergy. After establishing fine mixed choirs at St Vincent's and at the cathedral in Cork city respectively, Fr Gaynor and Hans Conrad Swertz were among those completely disillusioned by the ban on women imposed by Pius X. Such disappointment must have been further sustained by what one writer described as the 'more or less general view [...] that the Holy Father sent his message to the whole world when he really desired merely to correct some musical abuses in Italy' (H.T. Henry, 'Music Reform in the Catholic Church', *Music Quarterly* 1 (1915), 102).

'master' in the training of boys' voices,[75] while a later administrator affirmed that the organist had earned the 'golden opinions' of people throughout Cork city.[76] In 1916, however, Fleischmann was sent to Oldcastle in Co. Meath with about 450 other German civilian internees, and was transferred to the Isle of Man two years later. During his absence from Cork, which lasted until September 1920, Fleischmann's wife, Tilly, fulfilled his duties at the cathedral.

Brothers Alphonse and Gustav Haan also held posts at Irish cathedrals during the late nineteenth century, Alphonse at St Mel's Cathedral in Longford, and Gustav at the Cathedral of the Assumption in Carlow. In 1888 Alphonse, a faithful Cecilian, responded to *Lyra's* request for reports on church choirs:

> Dear Sir, – As invited by *Lyra Ecclesiastica*, I beg to communicate a brief statement about St. Mel's Cathedral Choir, Longford, which is conducted by the organist, Mr. Alph. Haan, and *is entirely voluntary*. It consists of thirteen singers at present, who meet twice a week for practices, each practice lasting three quarters of an hour. As this country, and this town particularly, is very damp, colds are frequent, and consequently attendance at practices at certain seasons rather irregular.[77]

The extant correspondence between Alphonse and his former teacher at Regensburg, Haberl, reveals how difficult it was for Haan to come to terms with the dismal state of church music in Ireland, and more particularly, the poor condition of the cathedral organ at St Mel's. In a letter dated 30 December 1895, he remarked that he could detain his mentor 'for hours with lamentations, headaches, litanies, etc. about Irish church music.'[78]

---

75 Testimonial letter (10 February 1908) written by Canon Richard McCarthy for Fleischmann's application for a post in Germany (Fleischmann Papers, University College, Cork, archives).

76 Testimonial letter (29 May 1911) written by Canon Martin Murphy for Fleischmann's application for a post in Augsburg (Fleischmann Papers, UCC archives).

77 *Lyra Ecclesiastica*, August 1888, 84. See also Daly, *Catholic Church Music*, 100.

78 See Ian Curran, 'Late Nineteenth- and Early Twentieth-Century Catholic Church Music Reform and Its Impact on Ireland', MA thesis, Mary Immaculate College, University of Limerick, 2007, 73–4.

Depite the 'difficult circumstances' at Longford, where the choir received 'no encouragement whatsoever, either moral or material',[79] Haan's commitment was unflagging, as evidenced by the following account of the Holy Week ceremonies of 1889:

> The very extensive programme of Holy Week music, as contained in the 'Officium Hebdomadæ Sanctæ', Ratisbon edition, was rendered, as usual, with elevating solemnity, appropriate to the sacred functions, by the rev. clergy, as well as by the [cathedral] choir, and with strict observance of the liturgical laws, from the 'Hosana Filio David', at the blessing of the Palms, to the 'Deo Gratias Alleluja' on Easter. His Lordship Most Rev. Dr. Woodlock, who was celebrant at all functions, was highly pleased with the performances, especially of the 'Tenebræ' Good Friday morning, and High Mass on Easter Sunday. The music was taken mostly from the 'Officium Hebdomadæ Sanctæ', from four Masses, by Witt; two by Schweitzer, and one by Singenberger. The motets were by Palestrina, Lotti, Witt, Zange, and Haan.[80]

Gustav Haan (*d*1922), who succeeded Jan Baptist Van Craen as organist of Carlow Cathedral in 1894, also taught music to the seminarians at St Patrick's College, Carlow. Given this latter duty, which involved the establishment of a college choir, his appointment was almost certainly inspired by Bewerunge's arrival at Maynooth six years earlier. Haan's dedication is best captured, yet again, in press reports of the important cathedral ceremonies of the liturgical year, in which the cathedral and college choirs participated. Such reports also complement *Lyra* in offering a window on the repertories (largely Cecilian) of church choirs during the late nineteenth century, the works of Witt, Haller, Mitterer, Kaim, Singenberger and other Cecilians constituting the staple diet of many choirs during this period.

> On Easter Sunday [...] The music was exquisitely rendered by the combined Cathedral and College choirs, Mr Haan presiding at the organ, and the music was as follows: – Proper of Mass and Credo (Gregorian), Kyrie, Gloria, Sanctus, and Benedictus from Mass in honour of St. Ignatius, by Jos. Gruber; Agnus Dei from Mass in honore Spiritus Sancti, by Singenberger; Offertory piece, 'Regina coeli jubila.'[81]

79 Bewerunge, reporting on music at St Mel's Cathedral in *Lyra Ecclesiastica*, June 1893 (p. 43).
80 *Irish Catholic*, 4 May 1889, 6.
81 'Conclusion of Holy Week at Carlow Cathedral', *The Nationalist and Leinster Times*, 2 April 1910, 4.

The celebration of the great feast of Pentecost commenced on Saturday morning [...] The music was excellently rendered by the College choir. Mr G. Hann presided at organ [...] On Whit Sunday was Solemn High Mass at 11 o'clock [...] The music was beautifully rendered by the combined Cathedral and College choirs and was as follows: – Proper of Mass and Credo were Gregorian, Kyrie (new) was by Hohnerlein, Gloria, Sanctus (new) and Benedictus were by Gruber; Agnus Dei by Singenberger. Offerory piece was the Offertory of the day, 'Confirma hoc Deus,' by Canon Haller. Mr G. Haan conducted.[82]

Hans Merx, who moved from Youghal in early 1904 to become organist at Tuam Cathedral, was also responsible for establishing a college choir, that at St Jarlath's College, where he had been appointed professor of music.[83] The choir first sang at Mass in the cathedral in February 1905, the *Tuam Herald* noting that 'they had three beautiful Masses in unison, by German composers.'[84] In May 1905 Merx returned to Youghal and subsequently held posts at the cathedral in Cobh and in Canada.

82 'Whit Sunday at Carlow Cathedral', *The Nationalist and Leinster Times*, 21 May 1910, 4.

83 Merx studied in Aix-la-Chapelle (Aachen), with 'Professor Steinhaur' in Düsseldorf, and at the conservatoire in Cologne (see 'A New Organist for Tuam', *Tuam Herald*, 6 February 1904, 2). At the age of seventeen in Aix-la-Chapelle, Merx 'had already passed [...] all those difficult examinations which are required in Germany for the conferring of those Diplomas as Organist and Choir-master which are at least equal in academic value to the degree of a B. Mus. in the United Kingdom. The examinations, which lasted eleven hours a day for three days, included the following subjects: – Organ and piano-playing, choir-conducting, Gregorian Chant and Liturgy, Harmony and Counterpoint, and a thorough knowledge of the old masters of Church Music, especially of the sixteenth century composers, such as Palestrina and Orlando di Lasso' (ibid.).

84 'Some Memories of the Tuam Cathedral Organists', *Tuam Herald*, 19 March 1949, 6. The choir sang publicly under Merx's direction, however, as early as April 1904, when 'the service of "Vespers" was inaugurated in the Cathedral' (see 'The Catholic Church', *Tuam Herald*, 23 April 1904).

Conclusion

The many Belgian and German organists employed at Catholic cathedrals and churches in Ireland during the latter half of the nineteenth century and early years of the twentieth provided stalwart musical leadership in a church that had repeatedly failed to afford its native musicians the opportunity to avail of proper training in sacred music in Ireland. Despite the efforts of de Meulemeester and the Ennis-based Belgian organist Ernest de Regge (1904–58) to address the issue of training, it was not until 1970, with the establishment of the *Schola Cantorum* at St Finian's College in Mullingar, Co. Westmeath, that an Irish episcopacy began to remedy the situation. Until then, successive generations of continental organists would continue to render their services to the Irish church.

KIERAN ANTHONY DALY

The Dublin Eucharistic Congress:
Tra le sollecitudini in the Phoenix Park

On the 1903 feast day of the patron saint of music, St Cecilia, Pope Pius X made an historic attempt at the restoration and reorganization of liturgical music in Roman Catholic churches with the publication of his *motu proprio, Tra le sollecitudini*. The new pope had already made known that the primary aim of his pontificate was to 're-establish all things in Christ', and slightly more than three months after his election he chose a subject close to his heart with which to begin the revitalization of his church's worship.

The main part of the *motu proprio*, the 'Instructions on Sacred Music', was the capstone of many years' work by Cardinal Sarto (later Pius X) on liturgical music, and the vigour of its text is unique in sacred music legislation. Its sections review the general principles of ritual music, outline the various kinds of sacred music to be regarded as liturgical, specify liturgical text and external form, and attend to the topics of singers, instruments, training, and even the length of service music. The impact of the document was immediate, although it was received worldwide with less than unanimous approval. To many, the unpleasant reality of the document was the banishment from church services of 'religious' music – music of a general religious character – and its substitution by a liturgically correct music specific to a particular celebration. This, and the consequence of a heightened value afforded to congregational participation, suggested the imposition of a more inelegant type of music than was customary. In addition, misinterpretation of the pope's letter and of subsequent documents from Rome promoted a fashionably adverse reaction to the reform.

Due in part to the propaganda of the Irish Society of St Cecilia (established in 1878), the flames of dispute had already been fanned in

Ireland prior to 1903.[1] Articles in periodicals and letters in newspapers had appeared spasmodically over the years and embroiled personages such as the educationist W.F.P. Stokeley, the Galway landlord and littérateur Edward Martyn, and Fr Heinrich Bewerunge, the founding professor of sacred music at the national seminary in Maynooth. The controversy continued with the publication of the *motu proprio* and was sufficiently topical for it to be chronicled in James Joyce's short story *The Dead*. While an ordinary parish priest or curate occasionally offered a printed opinion, the Irish hierarchy tended to avoid the public conflict. After 1903 Archbishop William J. Walsh took a cautionary approach to the legislation and made concessions to diocesan parishes. His *schola cantorum* at Dublin's Pro-Cathedral struggled through its early years in acquainting congregations with the 'new' plainsong of Solesmes, but by the decade's close, his cathedral choir had aquired a favourable reputation. The main protagonist in Irish church music reform from the previous century, Bishop Nicholas Donnelly, instituted his own *schola* in 1908 at St Mary's Church, Haddington Road, and by the close of the Edwardian period a small number of those Dublin parishes unaffected by the earlier Cecilian reform movement had modestly adapted to the demands of the pope's *motu proprio*.

During the following fifteen years, the political and social climate in Ireland redirected the public's attention from matters of church ceremonial.

---

1   Where sacred music existed in nineteenth-century Irish Catholic churches and cathedrals, it was extravagantly secular in style – a celebration of music and musician rather than of the sacred text – and accordingly only approximately liturgical. The establishment of the Irish Society of St Cecilia (and the regular publication of its bulletin, *Lyra Ecclesiastica*) during the final quarter of the century introduced a reform movement to Ireland which challenged the prevailing concept of *musica sacra*. Reaction to the reformers from professional musicians, much of the clergy, and from congregations was habitually adverse. There was an appreciable shift in bias when the newly elected archbishop of Dublin, William J. Walsh, declared for reform, and again when Fr Heinrich Bewerunge took up the cudgel on behalf of German interests. Controversy, however, remained on the agenda during the life of the society and indeed, thereafter. For a documented review of the Cecilian reform effort, see Kieran A. Daly, *Catholic Church Music in Ireland, 1878–1903: The Cecilian Reform Movement* (Dublin: Four Courts Press, 1995).

The country lurched from civil agitation to world war to a war for independence and finally into the divided country's civil war, the rancorous aftermath of which extended towards the close of the 1920s. If one effect of this enduring hostility was a certain curtailment of religious practice despite the considerable prevailing commitment to Catholicism, it was perceived by the Irish church as an indication of a divided people that had lost much reverence for religion and the church. The hierarchy decided to make a determined effort to unite Irish Catholics in Christ, and the centenary of the passing into law of the Roman Catholic Relief Act proved to be its first large-scale effort at so doing.

Walsh's successor, Archbishop Edward J. Byrne, needed an expert organizer, and accepted the enthusiastic and highly motivated Francis O'Reilly. O'Reilly, executive secretary of the Catholic Truth Society of Ireland since 1918, a member of the Order of Knights of Saint Columbanus and intimately concerned with Catholic Action, was a shrewd and autonomous administrator. Placing O'Reilly as his effective yet inconspicuous manager suited Byrne's disposition and the state of his increasingly poor health. Under O'Reilly's meticulous supervision, the 1929 celebrations proved a spectacular and thoroughly Roman Catholic success.[2] In the area of music, as in other areas, the emancipation centenary celebration was as much a rehearsal as an event, and when Archbishop Byrne's 1930 pastoral letter announced that Dublin would host the Thirty-first Eucharistic Congress, a basically unchanged organizing committee was already at work planning a rally with an international flavour:

> We are not undertaking this Congress in a spirit of emulation or in competition with any Congress held before [...] Our whole object is to bring our people [...] to a closer and more intimate knowledge of Jesus Christ.
>
> Even at this distance from the Congress I would call on all the faithful to prepare for it spiritually by prayers for the success of the Congress, accompanied by earnest effort on the part of each one to come nearer to Our Eucharistic Lord.[3]

---

2   The minutes of the Catholic Truth Society of Ireland subcommittee meetings indicate that preparations for the coming event were under way as early as December 1926.

3   *Irish Catholic Directory* (Dublin: James Duffy, 1931), 584–5.

The preparations

Archbishop Byrne called the first official meeting of his standing committee
for January 1930.[4] By springtime, O'Reilly had organized the constitution
of the main committees and called the first official meeting of the General
Committee of the National Council of the Eucharistic League for September. In the meantime, various subcommittees were being assembled and
set to work. Monsignor Michael Cronin, vicar general and parish priest at
the Church of the Three Patrons, Rathgar, was an early appointment to the
chairmanship of the music subcommittee, and he called the first meeting
for Thursday, 9 October 1930.[5] The committee consisted of four Dublin
priests actively involved in liturgical music – Michael Dempsey, DD; John
Fennelly, CC; George W. Turley, CC; and John Kearney, CSSp – together
with *ex officio* members Fr Daniel Molony and Francis O'Reilly.

The initial work of the music subcommittee was concerned with the
selection of material and the production of the official publication which
would provide an official text of the music and words for all congregational
hymns and chants to be performed during the congress. During the first
meeting, Cronin outlined the provisional central programme for June
1932, detailing the services during which congregations were expected to
participate actively in the sacred music.[6]

Choosing the congregational music proved to be a simple enough task.
The list produced at the second meeting, just five days later, on 14 October,
differed very little – even in its order – from the list that appeared on the
contents page of the hymn book published early the following year by the
organizing committee:

4   The committee was composed of his three vicars general (Bishop of Thasos Francis
     Wall, J. Dean Dunne, and Monsignor William Walsh), Sir Joseph Glynn, Charles
     O'Conor, the architect J.J. Robinson, Senator Thomas Farren, the director of organi-
     zation Francis O'Reilly, and the curate Daniel Molony as secretary.
5   See Music Subcommittee Minute Book (9 October 1930), Dublin Diocesan
     Archives.
6   Services were planned for each day from Sunday 19 June to Sunday 26 June.

Mass	Latin Hymns	Programme for Procession
Missa de Angelis (in modern notation, incl. the response and episcopal blessing)	*Veni Creator* *O Salutaris* *Tantum ergo* *Te Deum*	*Adoro te* *Lauda Jerusalem* *Pange lingua* *Lauda Sion* *Magnificat VIII*

Hymns in English and Irish
Come, O Creator, Spirit blest (7 verses)   *Jesus my Lord, my God, my all* (3 verses, Irish and English)   *Holy God, we praise thy name* (3 verses)   *Soul of my Saviour* (3 verses)   *To Jesus' Heart, all burning* (2 verses, Irish and English)   *Sweet Heart of Jesus* (2 verses)   *Hail, Queen of Heaven* (3 verses, Irish and English)   *Faith of our fathers* (3 verses, Irish and English)   *Hail, Glorious St Patrick* (3 verses, Irish and English)   *God bless our Pope* (3 verses)

Congregational music chosen for the Thirty-first Eucharistic Congress.

The remaining meetings of the music subcommittee during 1930 were devoted to matters of music copyright, the translation of various hymn texts into Irish, and the choice of melody – or in some cases melodic variant – for each hymn. The preferred rule of thumb dictated that melodic choice was determined by familiarity and by the common usage in Dublin parishes. At the final meeting of 1930, on Monday, 15 December, the attention of the subcommittee was directed to new issues: the musical preparation of the congregations, the constitution of the liturgical choirs, the disposition of the chosen music, and the coordination of the musical forces. The musical director for the congress, Vincent O'Brien, was invited to an early January meeting of the subcommittee to discuss the priority issue for 1931, namely the final congress Mass in the Phoenix Park.[7]

---

7   Vincent O'Brien (1871–1948) came to wide public notice after Archbishop Walsh appointed him director of the newly established cathedral choir in 1902.

The meeting focused on individual preferences for the Common of the Mass and the difficulties presented by the siting of the service in the open air:

> A discussion took place about the music for the Mass in the Park. It was decided that the music should be the Missa Brevis (Palestrina) for four voices. It is decided that the Choir should consist of 400 or more Men and Boys' voices and in order to get this number of singers the Choir Masters of the various City and Suburban Churches should be asked to co-operate [...] It was agreed that the Responses during the Mass should be harmonised. The *Credo*, however, to be in plain Chant.[8]

There is no recorded reference to the Proper of the Mass. It was possibly presumed that the 'Choir in the Park', as it was dubbed in the minutes (later the 'Palestrina Choir'), would have little difficulty in chanting the Mass of the Blessed Sacrament, as most of the Proper was identical to that sung during the annual diocesan Mass for the feast of Corpus Christi. On receipt of Archbishop Byrne's notice of approval, dated 19 January, a letter was drafted and sent to a number of the more important Dublin churches requesting assistance with the formation of the proposed choir. By the middle of March, the music subcommittee had estimated that a 460-strong choir was available and called its Palestrina Choir to practices on 15 (boys) and 16 (men) April in the Pro-Cathedral under the direction of Vincent O'Brien. The *Irish Independent* reported on the rehearsals and itemized the constituent parts of the boys' choral group.[9] Three hundred copies of the *Missa Brevis* ordered in March were distributed the following month.

Soon after the committee had sent out the first letters to church choirs, the secretary invited Dublin schools to prepare the music for the Common and Proper of the children's Mass scheduled for the penultimate day of congress week. Concerned that the preparation of so much plainsong

---

8 Music Subcommittee Minute Book, 12 January 1931.
9 'The choirs in attendance were: The Pro-Cathedral, St Andrew's, Donore Ave., Francis St, Aughrim St, Glasthule, the Presentation College Dun Laoghaire, Whitefriars St., Corpus Christi, Fairview, Haddington Rd., St. Mary's C.B.S [Christian Brothers' School], Richmond St. C.B.S., Brunswick St. C.B.S., Westland Row C.B.S. and Francis St. C.B.S.' *Irish Independent*, 16 April 1931, 10.

might prove probematic, the committee decided to have a very large choral group (originally fixed at 2,000 voices) placed near the altar to lead the congregation of children. In order to assist the assimilation of the Mass in schools, it also proposed that the plainchant *Missa de Angelis* replace the *Missa Orbis Factor* as the set piece for the diocesan liturgical music examinations due to be held in the spring of 1932.

In September 1931 the venue for the weekly rehearsals of the congress Palestrina Choir was changed to University College Dublin's city centre Aula Maxima, and the October examinations of the boys of the Palestrina Choir were held in the Bishop's Room there. The groups were tested on their knowledge of the motet *Ecce Sacerdos* by Max Filke (1855–1911) and on the Sanctus and Agnus Dei of the *Missa Brevis*, with 508 boys proving able for the tasks set. This number was larger than had been expected, and the committee took fright. On 19 October a decision was made to impose restrictions on the larger choirs but not on the Pro-Cathedral Choir. The choir of St Mary's Church, Haddington Road, was one of those affected. Seán Forde was a boy chorister at the time and recalled years later that while he had been chosen for and sang at the congress Mass, his friend, Gus Kearns, missed the event:

> The present centenary of John McCormack's birth brings me back to the time when I was a boy in the Phoenix Park that Sunday and the way we were placed. I had a good view of him [McCormack] and it was certainly a marvellous experience [...] The boys had to go through a test here before they were sent forward to the Eucharistic Congress choir, and when we went over and became part of it we still had to go through a test – well the boys did anyway.[10]

> I can remember taking part in some rehearsals for the 1932 congress. Myself, Michael King and all of the lads had to go into the Model Schools building opposite the Pro-Cathedral for a couple of try-outs. I remember hearing that Vincent O'Brien was happy with our singing, but I can't recall now why only part of the Guild made it to the Phoenix Park for the Sunday congress Mass. All the bigger boys went though, and the men. Some time before the congress, the master [choirmaster] told us that

10 'Death of a Choir' ('Talkback' series), prod. Donal Flanagan (1st broadcast RTÉ, 17 July 1984).

we all couldn't go. I remember he came over to my desk and said, 'Augustus, you'd
be walked on. You'd never make it to the Gloria.' And that was it. I was out. I was
only a little disappointed with that because I'd been a year then in the Guild, but I
do remember that a few of the small lads shed a tear or two, especially when such a
fuss had been made of the thing.[11]

Finally, in the year of the congress, the subcommittee turned its attention to
the other services: the Thursday and Friday pontifical Masses, the evening
massed meetings and the short services on Monday and Wednesday. It was
quickly agreed that the Pro-Cathedral Choir would lead the congregation
at both the Monday and Wednesday services (some simple Benediction
hymns) in addition to the liturgical music at the pontifical Mass on Thursday. The Dublin Priests' Choir, conducted by Fr Fennelly, was appointed
to sing Friday's pontifical Mass in the Pro-Cathedral and take a central
position in the Sunday procession, while volunteers were requested to lead
the congregations at the Thursday and Friday mass meetings.

A choir of men was easily recruited from the Palestrina/congress Mass
Choir early in the year to sing at the Thursday meeting, and some convent
secondary schools were asked to provide a choir to sing at the women's
meeting on the Friday night. It soon become apparent that the uptake from
convent schools was larger than required, and during April, an attempt was
made to restrict the numbers. Eventually it was decided to ask only three
convent schools to produce singers for the Friday meeting and for radio
broadcast on the Dublin station 2RN.[12]

Singing at the Mass Meeting of Women
It is suggested that there should be three Groups of singers and that the following
Convents should be asked to send each a group consisting of not more than 20 of
their best past pupils, who could sing the hymns in Irish and English: – Dominican
Convent, Eccles Street; Loreto Convent, St. Stephen's Green; and Holy Faith Con-
vent, Haddington Road.

11   Interview (18 February 2002) with Augustus Kearns, who joined the Guild of
       Choristers of St Cecilia, Haddington Road, in 1930. Author's private collection.
12   The call sign 2RN refers here to the national radio service. The station 'Radio Athlone'
       was temporarily opened for the Eucharistic Congress. See Maurice Gorham, *Forty
       Years of Irish Broadcasting* (Dublin: Talbot, 1967), 81.

Broadcasting of hymns in advance
Father Turley is to arrange with Mr. Clandillon in this matter. The hymns are to be sung by ladies selected from the three groups that are to sing at the Mass Meeting of Women.[13]

During these last few months, longstanding topics of debate regarding the Sunday ceremonies such as accompaniment, amplification, and broadcasting were finalized. O'Brien nominated his two brothers and a friend, Andrew Keane, as assistant organists for Sunday's ceremonials. This resulted in the absence from the defining congress ceremonies of the prominent musician Brendan Rogers, who in 1932 was celebrating his fiftieth year as Pro-Cathedral organist.[14]

What is apparent from the record of the music subcommittee meetings is the conscious attempt to reflect the specific demands of Pope Pius X's *motu proprio*. The members succeeded in maximizing congregational integration into the liturgical and devotional ceremonies while nurturing an appreciation of plainchant melodies.[15] The quality of chant chosen for the children's Mass Common partially reflected the low level of plainsong appreciation in Ireland, but the final liturgical performances were in marked contrast with the situation generally in Catholic churches at this time, where chant was considered to belong essentially to the clerical domain. Active congregational participation in a *Missa Cantata* was practically non-existent, while the music, delivered by an adult gallery choir, was rarely perceived as integral and more often than not, was regarded as elitist.

The theme of inclusion was one which permeated the various subcommittees in their preparation for the congress and heightened the perception

13   Music Subcommittee Minute Book, 11 April 1932.
14   Rogers, who died towards the end of 1932, had been similarly omitted from the final emancipation celebration.
15   The effort to realize the concept of *participatio actuoso* within a large community celebration resulted in a bewildering variety of 'special' choirs. It is worth noting that, although not specifically recommended, a congress in the pattern of the early twentieth-century assembly for spreading propaganda was absolutely in keeping with the spirit of the *motu proprio*, especially Section VIII ('Principal Means') and the concluding paragraph 29 (Section IX).

of the Dublin faithful as one large congregation. This integration of cleric and secular, professional and tradesman, rich and poor, inspired a specific 'congress' attitude in all aspects of the celebration. G.K. Chesterton noted how little was on display of fashion, faction or opinion, of how the city spoke with a single, simple voice. The population worked together to provide facilities, accommodation, sustenance, and transport. It built altars and prayer corners, and decorated the streets and buildings with flags, banners, and symbols. No area of the various villages that made up Dublin wanted to be left out. Chesterton found it extraordinary that there was so much display of a congress atmosphere in those hidden places where there was no expectation of it being noticed, except by its own inhabitants:

> The extraordinary thing was this. I have driven through many such arcades and triumphal arches in many festive cities. And of nearly all of them it was true to say that any man who strayed from those festive highways would find the festivity fading away. He would find more or fewer flags in this or that sidestreet; he would not even expect to find so many as there were in the main street. In this one festivity all that common sense was reversed. It was truly like that celestial topsy-turvydom in which the first shall be last. Instead of the main stream of colour flowing down the main streets of commerce, and overflowing into the crooked and neglected slums, it was exactly the other way; It was the slums that were the springs. *There* were the furnaces of colour; *there* were the fountains of light; it was as if whatever hidden thing shone here and there in those passionate transparencies was shining in the darkest place; as if the dark heart of the town pumped forth that purple blood, ending in a mere trickle along the highway. I know no other way of describing it; for I have never seen anything like it in my life.[16]

Division, in a city and country eviscerated by strife, was conspicuously absent, even within areas where conflict was conditioned reflex behaviour.

---

16   Gilbert Keith Chesterton, *Christendom in Dublin* (London: Sheed & Ward, 1932), 14–15. Chesterton had journeyed to the Irish capital not just to record the event but also to take part in it, thereby celebrating the tenth anniversary of his conversion to Roman Catholicism.

The music of the ceremonies

On Monday 20 June, the papal legate, Cardinal Lorenzo Lauri, arrived at Dún Laoghaire (then Kingstown) and processed to the newly widened Pro-Cathedral, where he was welcomed by what Archbishop Byrne had earlier, in a pastoral letter, termed, the 'chaste beauty of the sacred psalmody'. The plainchant antiphon *Ecce Sacerdos*, which opened the short reception service, was chanted by the clerical congregation, led by the Pro-Cathedral Choir and accompanied by Brendan Rogers. The organ played out the recessional procession, and the legate continued on to the archbishop's residence in Drumcondra.

Tuesday was the social day in preparation for the official opening of the congress. A state reception in Dublin Castle was preceded by the Irish hierarchy's garden party at Blackrock College, where the legate was received on a bright sunny afternoon by the president of Blackrock College and future archbishop of Dublin, John Charles McQuaid. About 20,000 people attended the event in the specially prepared grounds of the college. An extended round of vigorous applause welcomed the legate as he appeared on the balcony overlooking the vast crowd of dignitaries, and the instinctive response to his blessing encapsulated the mood of the Dublin congress:

> When the Blessing was over three cheers went up from the multitude. There was a moment's pause, then somebody started to sing and in a minute the whole crowd was singing in perfect unison: '*Faith of Our Fathers, Holy Faith*,' etc.[17]

The churches of Dublin were filled that evening for the final services of welcome. As the Sacred Triduum came to an end, the spiritual preparation reached a climax on the shortest night of the year. One Dublin priest ordained in 1932 recalled the crowd around St Mary's Church, Haddington Road, at 3 a.m., and the words of a bus conductor on his way to work, bewildered by the scene: 'It's like the last day!'[18]

---

17   *Irish Catholic Directory* (Dublin: James Duffy, 1933), 605.
18   Letter from Revd John Meagher. Author's private collection.

The legate arrived for the opening ceremony in the Pro-Cathedral shortly after 3 p.m. on Wednesday to the strains of Filke's *Ecce Sacerdos*. The Pro-Cathedral Choir led the congregation in the plainchant hymn *Veni Creator Spiritus* before addresses were read from Pope Pius XI, Archbishop Byrne, and the Eucharistic Committee. After Solemn Benediction (*O Salutaris*, *Tantum ergo*, and *Adoremus*), the congregation and choir sang *Faith of our fathers*.

The second official day of the congress, Thursday 23 June, was proclaimed with midnight Mass in all archdiocesan churches and with a city – streets, commercial buildings, and private houses – illuminated until dawn.[19] Searchlights scrawled words like 'adoremus' across the Dublin sky, and the numinous nocturnal display prefaced the fundamental activity of the congress, namely three days of sectional religious services, sectional meetings, and general meetings. The daily pontifical Masses characteristic of such congresses tended to be rather more representative in nature, as indeed they became the physiognomy of the Thirty-first International Eucharistic Congress.

At the mid-morning Mass in the Pro-Cathedral, Vincent O'Brien conducted the Pro-Cathedral Choir in Palestrina's four-part *Lauda Sion*. The plainsong Proper for the votive Mass of the Blessed Sacrament was sung from the *Liber Usualis*. Most of this Proper is taken from the Mass celebrating the feast of Corpus Christi, and parts are similar to the Mass for Whit Sunday. Heinrich Bewerunge's successor at Maynooth, Michael Tracy, explained the practice of such duplication in his congress article 'The Music of the Mass', parenthetically revealing the clear familiarity a choir such as O'Brien's had with this votive Mass chant:

---

19   Recalled by Dubliners as the 'Wednesday of the midnight Masses', the evening began with Exposition of the Blessed Sacrament in all Dublin churches (city and suburbs) from 9 p.m. The churches, however, were already filled (hundreds of thousands had flowed into Dublin by then) before people began to arrive for midnight Mass. The result was that congregations heard Mass kneeling in the streets outside. The situation was most acute in city churches, with missal pages reportedly being carefully turned up to half a mile from church gates.

When a new feast was introduced a Mass already in use was applied with its text and music to the new feast. Sometimes the melodies of one Mass were adapted to the words of a new Mass. Examples of these two processes may be seen in the Mass of the Blessed Sacrament. Here the Introit (*Cibavit eos*) is the same as that of the older Mass for the Monday following Pentecost. The Gradual is that of the twentieth Sunday after Pentecost. The Offertory and Communion are adaptations of the Offertory and Communion of Pentecost, where by slight changes of the music the melody is fitted to a different set of words.[20]

The majority of the Proper was undoubtedly chanted in pure Gregorian for the Thursday pontifical Mass, but there is reason to believe that the Gradual (*Oculi omnium*), Alleluia (*Caro Mea*) and Offertory (*Sacerdotes Domini*) were chanted in harmony rather than in the plainsong of the *Liber's* melismatic melodies. Archbishop Byrne's directive was that the music of the congress should follow Dublin norms, and according to the testimony of choir members, the usual Dublin practice (in the growing number of churches where the Proper of the day was sung) was to sing these long and complicated sections in simple fauxbourdon style.

The choir additionally sang Palestrina's *Sicut Cervus* on the conclusion of the chanted Offertory *Sacerdotes Domini*, and Gregor Aichinger's *Jubilate Deo* after the Communio of the day, *Quotiescumque manducabitis*. The Palestrina piece, rubrically set for the vigil Mass on Easter Saturday, was one of the choir's speciality items, while the Aichinger piece may have been suggested by the recent appearance of the Chester edition of the work.

On Thursday evening, a mass meeting of men held in the Phoenix Park consisted of prayers and addresses. The male voice choir, conducted by O'Brien, led the congregation in hymns which were sung in Irish and English throughout the course of the service, the order of the hymns and verses being detailed in the congress handbook. Benediction followed the addresses (all of the sung music was taken from the hymn book) and closed a day of impressive sacramental and devotional music that matched the splendour of classical polyphony with the immediacy of popular hymnody.

---

20 Michael Tracy, 'The Music of the Mass', *Irish Ecclesiastical Record* 39 (1932), 620.

The clerical choir at Friday's Mass (24 June) chanted the Proper for the day – the feast of the Navivity of St John the Baptist. Plainchant from *in festo Nativit. Joannis Baptistae* was much less familiar to choirs and congregations in Dublin, and the diocesan priests' choir, no doubt, paid extra special attention to its preparation.[21] The euphonic Introit antiphon *De ventre matris meae* might have been rather demanding, but both the Communion antiphon, *Tu, puer*, and the Offertory, *Justus ut palma*, are more compact pieces. In the circumstances, it is entirely possible that the Gradual, *Priusquam te formarem*, the Alleluia (also *Tu, puer*), and the Offertory were chanted in pure Gregorian rather than in the recitative style of the previous day's pieces. For the Common of the Mass Fr Fennelly chose from the modern polyphonic repertoire with Ignatius Mitterer's *Missa in honorem S.S. Sindonis*, op. 76, a TTBB Common that had also been sung by the Clonliffe choir at the 1929 centenary. The more immediate appeal of the modern polyphonic style may be deduced from this typical newspaper report:

> The music of the Mass was rendered by a special choir of priests of the Archdiocese of Dublin, under the direction of Rev. John Fennelly, C.C. Donnybrook. Their singing was magnificent, both in the severe strains of the Plainchant and in the rich harmonies of Mitterer's Mass, every word of the music being expressed with unfailing accuracy. Even the least musical in the congregation must have felt the quiet appeal of the Kyrie, the robust joy of the Gloria, the solemn dignity and brilliance of the Sanctus, the simple beauty of the Benedictus, the tranquil devotion of the Agnus Dei.
>
> The choir showed itself to best advantage in the majestic Motet, 'Cantata [sic] Domino' (Hasler) which was sung at the Offertory, giving a rendering that will live long in the memory of those present.[22]

The Friday evening mass meeting of women, like the previous night's meeting, was held in the Phoenix Park. The 'special choir of ladies' accompanied the legate's entrance with a performance of Filke's *Ecce Sacerdos* and thereafter led the congregation through the hymns.

---

21   Fennelly had plenty of time to prepare the Proper, which was apportioned for his choir early in the preparatory period. The music subcommittee minute book records how more problematic was the preparation for the Common of the Friday Mass.

22   *Irish Independent*, 25 June 1932, 5.

The spectacle of the children's solemn pontifical High Mass, which began at noon in the Phoenix Park on Saturday 25 June, caught most reporters' imaginations, with more than a thousand children – girls in wreaths, veils and communion dresses, boys in white trousers and jerseys – marshalled on the green plain of turf. Six of the nine cardinals attending the congress processed in the splendour of their robes to their individual thrones for this first Mass at the newly constructed altar. Loudspeakers carried the voices to every part of the parkland, while homes all over the country and abroad tuned into the Mass on their radio sets.

The choir of secondary school children led the young congregation in the hymn *Naomhuigh-se mhAnam* (*Soul of my Saviour*) before introducing the clerical hierarchy into the open-air cathedral that was the Phoenix Park's 'Fifteen Acres' with the familiar *Ecce Sacerdos* by Max Filke.[23] The Gregorian Introit *Cibavit eos* was chanted, and then the almost 3,000-voice choir of students began the Kyrie of the *Missa de Angelis*. The overwhelming aural effect of the massed children's disciplined singing was testified to in the voluminous reports of the Mass, which included references to the 'angel voices' of the children. The secondary school choir's (some 700 voices) chanted Proper of the Mass of the Blessed Sacrament alternated perfectly with the primary school group's singing of the *Missa de Angelis*.[24] The Offertory motet was a three-part arrangement of Griesbacher's *Adoro te*, and the service concluded with congress hymns while Cardinal Lauri spent some time walking among and meeting the waiting congregation.

For a reported one million Roman Catholics in Dublin on Sunday 26 June, their waking hours were fully given over to the final elaborate function, which lasted for more than six hours. The tripartite service began with pontifical High Mass, continued with a solemn procession from the Phoenix Park to O'Connell Bridge, and concluded with Benediction. Each discrete section had been programmed to include at least one innovation, such as the broadcast voice of the Holy Father at Mass and the city-wide

23   The hymns at Saturday's service were practically all sung in Irish.
24   Some voices had been raised in protest at the use of this musically inferior Common. As early as 1930, a plea arrived from a Paris-based priest for a Common other than the *Missa de Angelis*. See EC20, Dublin Diocesan Archives.

loudspeaker system for the procession. Even at a distance of over seventy-five years, the concept of staging such a spectacular event is breathtaking. Unfortunately, the sheer size of the undertaking (and its success) can be a self-defeating distraction when assessing elements of a service essentially concerned with adoration of and devotion to the Eucharistic Body. No contemporary account indicates that the occasion itself distracted from the worship. On the contrary, the reports of the day contain many references to reverential silence, ceremonial convention, prayerful participation, and the idea of Dublin being, for that day, a city-cathedral.

The 'Palestrina Choir' at the pontifical Mass, composed of men and boys drawn from the city choirs of the archdiocese, sang the Kyrie, Gloria, Sanctus, Benedictus, and Agnus Dei from Palestrina's four-part *Missa Brevis*. Motets included in the Mass were Palestrina's *Exultate Deo* (at the conclusion of Mass) and Franck's *Panis Angelicus* (with John McCormack as soloist) after the Offertory.[25] The choir of student priests chanted the complete Proper of the Mass of the Blessed Sacrament. Finally, the huge congregation chanted the plainchant Credo III, alternating verses with the choir according to directions in the congress hymnal. St Patrick's bell rang at the consecration, symbolically linking the faith of the Irish people of 1932 with that of 432, the year in which the national saint was believed to have arrived in Ireland. Vincent O'Brien directed the choirs and congregation, and Louis O'Brien accompanied on a harmonium which, for the occasion, had been amplified up to the level of a church organ by a specially constructed audio system installed at the foot of the altar steps. Vincent's other brother, Joseph, was in charge of the amplification details and the transmission of the mixed sound to the distribution point of the public address system.

It was expected that the voice of the pontiff would be broadcast at the beginning of Mass, and while the celebrant and sacred ministers stood waiting, the choir sang the Clemens non Papa motet *Tu es Petrus*. After a short delay the Mass proceeded, and it was not until just before the final

---

25   McCormack had originally been asked to sing at the conclusion of the Mass. This is confirmed in one of the letters sent by him to the organizing committee, in which he rejected the notion of a second piece. See EC15, Dublin Diocesan Archives.

blessing that, for the first time in history, the voice of the Holy Father was heard to address his Irish flock. Speaking in Latin, he greeted the congregation and delivered his apostolic blessing. This was the first time that an international eucharistic congress had been directly addressed by a pope, and according to Boylan, 'over the whole great multitude surged a tide of pride and gratitude and exultation.'[26] Appropriately, the choir followed the final blessing with the motet *Exultate Deo*.

A thirty-minute break after the conclusion of Mass allowed time for refreshments before the solemn procession bearing the Blessed Sacrament began to leave the Phoenix Park. The *Irish Catholic* reported that the procession began at three o'clock and took more than three hours to complete the short distance between the park altar and the altar erected at the west pavement in the middle of O'Connell Street Bridge. Leaving the Park in one great column of twenty-four abreast, the procession soon split into four columns following three different routes to the city centre. Loudspeakers were hung at regular intervals along each of the routes – the northern and southern quays, the North Circular Road, and the Thomas St/Dame St route.

> All the streets along which the processionists pass will be covered by the local broad-casting system. All the processionists, separate though they be, will be at the same time singing the same hymns and reciting the same prayers [...] the pace of the procession should be about two miles per hour and will be set by the stewards.[27]

The mainly clerical procession accompanying the Blessed Sacrament took the quays route and included a choir of diocesan priests and the Irish Army's principal military band. The clergy walking in procession were provided with a leaflet specifying the verses of the five Latin hymns and chants which they were required to sing from the congress hymn book, initially in the order *Pange Lingua*, *Lauda Jerusalem*, *Adoro Te*, *Lauda Sion*, and the *Magnificat*.[28] They were instructed to sing every alternate verse only

---

26   Patrick Boylan (ed.), *The Book of the Congress* (Wexford: J. English, 1934), 190.
27   Ibid., 40.
28   See 'Instructions for Clergy walking in Procession', EC2, Dublin Diocesan Archives.

of the *Pange Lingua* and *Magnificat*, and to be silent while the other verses were sung in harmony by the choir of priests. This diocesan priests' choir, augmented for the procession to 200 voices, sang all the verses of *Lauda Jerusalem* and *Lauda Sion*, while the remaining clergy sang the refrains. The *Adoro te* was sung in unison by all. The leaflet also drew attention to the use of a short instrumental interlude between verses. The diocesan choir also performed the motets *Verbum Supernum, O Esca Viatorum*, and *Sacris Solemniis*.

All other processionists, as well as those lining the routes, were required to sing only the congregational hymns specified in the hymnal (mainly those in Irish and English), but were recommended to join in the unison singing at will. Each sung piece concluded with the recitation of some decades of the rosary and the short *Adoremus in Aeternum*. During the three-hour procession, a detachment from the choir in the Phoenix Park led the singing of the congregational hymns over the public address system. Accompaniments on the harmonium were provided alternately by the two O'Brien brothers, Louis and Joseph, and by Andrew Keane, organist at Whitefriar St Church.

A great deal of the success of the procession – and of the congress in general – depended upon the effective operation of a modern public address system. Weeks of planning and co-operative preparation between T.J. Monaghan's staff in the Irish Post Office and the London firm of Standard Telephones and Cables Ltd preceded an installation period of twenty-five days, during which some 500 loadspeakers were installed. The effect of the public address system was to create the atmosphere of a huge open-air church. While the majority of the people could have seen little of the Park Mass, everyone could hear the celebrants, the music, and the blessings, and could follow the ceremony with ease. Similarly, the procession was essentially an aural experience for many who attended the occasion. This atmosphere might be said to have survived as the keynote of the congress, which was broadcast worldwide.

Microphone pick-up points in the Pro-Cathedral, at the altars in the Phoenix Park and on O'Connell Bridge distributed sound over the Fifteen Acres (thirty-four loudspeakers) and along the fifteen miles of processional routes (400 loudspeakers). The speakers were so carefully positioned (in the Park, each pair, pointing in opposite directions, were placed atop lines of wooden poles) that the huge areas were amply provided with sound, yet without interference between near and distant speakers. The layout also successfully minimized the time-lag between microphoned choirs and congregation. The apparant result was continuous audibility (not the shortest breakdown of the system was recorded) without any echo even across the River Liffey, from one side of the quays to the other. Without the system, it would have been impossible to synchronize the singing of a congregation so vast in the Phoenix Park (where those at the back of the throng were fully half a mile away from the altar) and so diffuse along the processional routes.

> The broadcasting facilities were so arranged that singing in the Procession was synchronized, with the voices of those taking part wherever their location and the effect was marvelous. Each Procession moving at the same time toward their place of assembly, sang in unison with the other Procession by this electrical system which enabled them to hear whether they were in time or not. The music was led by a Main Choir which remained in the Park. When the Procession reached the Altar on O'Connell Bridge, the Main Choir stopped and the Processional Choir was substituted, as a basis of synchronization. It took four hours to move the 80,000 people in Procession for Benediction, at O'Connell Bridge.[29]

Shortly after seven o'clock, the papal legate prepared to complete the final service of the congress. People were packed along the thoroughfares radiating from O'Connell Bridge – on O'Connell St, D'Olier St, and on the quays north, south, east and west of the altar. Even the Liffey itself sustained a floating congregation. Out of sight of the altar they congregated around loudspesakers, in Marlborough St, along the routes of the procession, and in the Phoenix Park. In places where the sound from the nearest loudspeaker might fail to carry on that warm summer's evening air, private radio sets were called into service in personal attempts to remain linked to an event which had captured the country's complete attention.

---

29 'Music Features International Eucharistic Congress in Dublin', *The Caecilia* 59 (1932), 235.

At the beginning of congress week, the momentum generated by the long preparations had conspired to deflect superficial attention to the spectacle of the event: the dramatic arrival of the papal legate on the *SS Cambria*, the ceremonial splendour of the Lord Mayor's coach, the temporary structures (like the round tower at College Green, the city gates at the urban boundary with Merrion, and the altars on O'Connell Bridge and in the Phoenix Park), the dramatic illuminations, the cavalry escorts and military salutes. By the week's end, the sacred fuctions had re-focused attention on the essential nature of the event. Music was integral to these functions, in absolute obedience to diocesan regulations and fully in accordance with the letter and spirit of Rome's reforming instructions published at the beginning of the century. The avoidance of utilizing music as a dramaturgy and its retention as a liturgical element in the services helped assemble a lesson in the power of unanimity. As a result, the 'Congress was not a great religious spectacle [...] performed before a cityful of spectators. It was a great religious function in which everyone took the fullest possible part.'[30]

The final Benediction on O'Connell Bridge reprised the music of previous days and was led by the choir of diocesan priests arranged conventionally 'in the choir' at the front of the altar. The mighty congregation had little need now of a hymnal, with whole streets chanting the *Adoremus* and *Laudate* from memory to provide the inspiring spectacle of an entire city at prayer.

30   Alice Curtayne, 'The Story of the Eucharistic Congress', *Capuchin Annual* 3 (1933), 74.

HELEN PHELAN

Ireland, Music and the Modern Liturgical Movement

Introduction

In 1984 Seán Lavery, an Irish Columban priest and chant scholar, estab-lished a church music quarterly called *Jubilus Review*, with a mission to 'provide a Forum for an examination of matters musical and liturgical [...] in the Church in Ireland.'[1] The publication concluded four years later when Lavery accepted a new missionary assignment in Jamaica. In his final address as editor, he noted that post-conciliar musicians and liturgists must recognize that 'there need be no conflict between Latin and the vernacular, between the singing of the choir and the role of the congregation, between art music and congregational song.'[2]

In his work on the study of early Christian worship, Paul Bradshaw reminds us that ideological statements may tell us more about what is not happening than what is; that 'authoritative-sounding statements [...] need to be taken with a pinch of salt.'[3] This tenet could be usefully applied to Lavery's statement, which might indeed reveal a great deal of conflict between Latin and the vernacular, choral and congregational song, and high art and popular aesthetics in the years following the Second Vatican Council. The post-Vatican II tensions between the 'altar and the choir-loft' and the later 'worship wars' of the 1990s point to a history of division and polarity, wherein music became a powerful metaphor for sectional

---

1   Seán Lavery, 'From the Editor: An Introduction', *Jubilus Review* 1 (1984), 3.
2   Lavery, 'From the Editor', *Jubilus Review* 4 (1987), 523.
3   Paul F. Bradshaw, *The Search for the Origins of Christian Worship: Sources and Methods for the Study of Early Liturgy* (New York: Oxford University Press, 1992), 68.

ideologies.[4] Gregorian chant emerged as a dominant metaphor for Tridentine nostalgia, conservative morality, and revisionist interpretations of the remit and consequences of Vatican II.

Lavery's statement is all the more interesting in this context because, not only does it suggest a future ideal which transcends these divisions, but, consciously or not, it speaks to a past, historical ideal: a pre-Vatican II reality rooted in the very values of the so-called 'modern liturgical movement'. The unfolding of this 'modern' renewal of Christian liturgy was to involve both a restoration of Gregorian chant and the introduction of the vernacular – a great embrace including the glories of the liturgical past as well as the pastoral voice of the corporate body at worship. Lavery's words reach back to a part of the creation narrative of this movement, where chant and liturgical rehabilitation went hand in glove.

In the aftermath of the council, it is a sad irony that, if pastoral, liturgical reform and Gregorian chant started the journey as partners, they ended it as representatives of opposing forces and camps. Peter Jeffery notes that one of the victims of this split was Gregorian chant itself: 'One unfortunate result of this polarisation has been to postpone what should have been an immediate response to the Council's directives, namely the objective reassessment of the chant in the new light of liturgical renewal.'[5] One step towards this re-assessment of the place of Gregorian chant in contemporary liturgy lies in a re-evaluation of its role and function in the modern liturgical movement. The emergence of this role is developed through three 'lenses': one focused on the early development of the liturgical movement as a monastic phenomenon, rooted in the Solesmes revival; the second, on the emergence of a pastoral imperative and the championing of liturgy as a site of justice; and the third, exploring the uniquely Irish story of the relationship between liturgical renewal and chant in the years leading up to the council.

---

4   See Gerard Kock, 'Between the Altar and the Choir-loft: Church Music – Liturgy or Art?', in David Power, Mary Collins, and Mellonee Burnim (eds), *Music and the Experience of God* (Concilium Series 202; Edinburgh: T. & T. Clark, 1989), 11–19.

5   Peter Jeffery, 'Chant East and West: Towards a Renewal of the Tradition', in *Music and the Experience of God* (as n.4), 22.

A modern and medieval enchantment

In his review of Katherine Bergeron's 1998 publication on the revival of Gregorian chant at Solesmes,[6] Jeffery notes that 'the story that Solesmes tells about itself and the story that is told about it by the apostles of "folksy guitar masses" both cry out for deconstruction.'[7] Depending on who is telling the story, Solesmes may be evaluated as the site of, for example, the restoration of the Benedictines in France, the emergence of the new science of musicology, or the fabrication of a wholly invented form of rhythmic interpretation for chant performance. The origin-narrative of Solesmes has been much rehearsed.[8] The renewal of the monastery, and indeed of monasticism in France, emerged from a history of monastic suppression and destruction across Europe and particularly in France, so that, 'by the end of 1790 revolutionary legislation had effectively emptied the monasteries, convents and cathedrals of France', to the extent that the word *vandalisme* was coined by the former bishop of Blois to describe such wanton destruction.[9] By the 1830s, intellectuals and artists such as Victor Hugo began to alert the wider public to the loss of France's cultural heritage through the destruction of these national treasures. This aesthetic argument resulted in a renewed appreciation of the architectural inheritance of France's monasteries and cathedrals, but it would take a young priest called Prosper

---

6   Katherine Bergeron, *Decadent Enchantments: The Revival of Gregorian Chant at Solesmes* (Berkeley and Los Angeles: University of California Press, 1998).

7   Peter Jeffery, 'Solesmes High Mass – or Low ?', review of Katherine Bergeron, *Decadent Enchantments*, in *Early Music* 27 (1999), 483–5 (at p.485).

8   Lavery devotes the entire final issue of *Jubilus Review* (4, 1987) to the story of Solesmes. J.D. Crichton's *Lights in the Darkness: Fore-runners of the Liturgical Movement* (Dublin: Columba Press, 1996) is an interesting Irish publication which concludes with a concise sketch of the movement, identifying Solesmes as the inaugural energy. A comprehensive account of Dom Prosper Guéranger's role in the story of Solesmes is given in Dom Louis Soltner (trans. Joseph O'Connor), *Solesmes and Dom Guéranger, 1805–1875* (Brewster, MA: Paraclete Press, 1995).

9   Bergeron, *Decadent Enchantments*, 1–2.

Guéranger to make the connection between the restoration of the physical space and the activity for which that space was designed:

> [...] is it not time to remember not only that your churches have suffered damage to their walls, their vaults, their age-old furnishings, but that, more importantly, they are also bereft of the ancient and venerable canticles they once held so dear?[10]

In 1833 he organized the purchase of the abandoned priory at Solesmes and commenced a grand re-imagining of Benedictine life in France, rooted in the revival of its liturgical life of chanted prayer.

Guéranger's imagined community was both romantic and modern in its scope and vision. It was romantic in its backward gaze towards an idealized, medieval golden age of ecclesial stability, liturgical and musical splendour, and unquestioned papal authority. Robert Winthrop makes the point that neither Guéranger nor any of his original volunteers had any prior monastic experience, and were leading a project which required the recreation of a way of life and a form of prayer which, in all likelihood, they had no opportunity to experience ever at first hand.[11] But their sense of mission was not as provincial as the restoration of the immediate history of Solesmes priory (which seems to have been a modest affair), or of the revival of the most recent liturgical chant books (the 'corruption' of which is much lamented in Guéranger's *Institutions liturgiques*), but rather in the creation of a bridge, built of liturgical chant, linking this modern abbey with its great liturgical past, for which no 'live' model was required.

If this sense of a connection to the past is, essentially, an imagined one, what is critical for our purposes is that it implicitly contained an equally important imagined connection to the future. The Solesmes project could never be described as essentially historical, for the primary aim of restoration was always renewal. There was no idea of the restoration of Gregorian chant as an exercise in authentic, 'historical' performance. The sole purpose

---

10   Prosper Guéranger, *Institutions liturgiques* 1 (Paris: Débécourt, 1840), xix; quoted in Bergeron, *Decadent Enchantments*, 9–10.
11   See Robert H. Winthrop, 'Leadership and Tradition in the Regulation of Catholic Monasticism', *Anthropological Quarterly* 58 (1985), 30–8.

of restoration rested in the belief that the modern re-kindling of liturgical life depended on its drawing energy and rigour from a re-connection with its earlier, more vigorous form, or, as Pothier put it: 'The music of the past better understood will be greeted as the true music of the future.'[12]

The application of scientific, comparative and philological methods to a study of the earliest medieval manuscripts of Western plainchant by the community at Solesmes was only one dimension of this grand project; the embodied performance of the repertoire was the other. The use of the camera provided a new technology for palaeographic work, and the monks employed 'the art of photography for their scholarly purposes on a scale so vast as probably to have been unprecedented',[13] while the invention of the phonograph facilitated recordings of the performance practices of the community.[14] The manuscripts were to provide the key to the past; the community was to embody its incarnation in the present by literally giving flesh and voice to the sonic evolution of the church at prayer.

One could argue that this radical approach, rooted in the past and projected into the future, set the agenda for the entire modern liturgical project, culminating in the liturgical documents of Vatican II. The reforming spirit of the late nineteenth and early to mid-twentieth centuries was comprehensively informed by this 'back to the future' logic – *nova ex veteribus* (or 'new things from the old'[15]). The renewal of the church's prayer was to be brought about by a re-understanding of her own past, informed

12   Joseph Pothier, *Les Mélodies grégoriennes d'après la tradition* (Tournai: Desclée, 1880), 6; quoted in Bergeron, *Decadent Enchantments*, 20.

13   F. Joseph Kelly, 'Plain Chant, the Handmaid of the Liturgy: A Challenge and a Prophecy', *Musical Quarterly* 7 (1921), 344–50 (at p.349).

14   For a summary of recordings produced by Solesmes, see Mary Berry, 'Gregorian Chant: The Restoration of the Chant and Seventy-Five Years of Recording', *Early Music* 7 (1979), 197–217. For a summary of performance styles which evolved in agreement or in conflict with Solesmes, see Lance Brunner, 'The Performance of Plainchant: Some Preliminary Observations of the New Era', *Early Music* 10 (1982), 316–28.

15   See Ernest B. Koenker, 'Objectives and Achievements of the Liturgical Movement in the Roman Catholic Church since World War II', *Church History* 20 (1951), 14–27 (at p.16).

by new scholarship and new sources, connecting the global, contemporary
church with her most ancient streams. Before the 'either/or' schism of
post-Vatican II practice, the modern liturgical movement followed a 'both/
and' schema of Derridian proportions.[16] The church was to reach back as
well as forward, to embrace the past by way of embracing the future. The
chasm created between the 'either/or' camps in the contemporary church,
particularly with reference to liturgical music, is at times so deep that it
requires an intrepid re-focusing of the historical lens on the early liturgical movement to realize that this was not always the case; that the sound
of Gregorian chant was never imagined as reactionary, but rather as the
contemporary and futuristic voice of the church.

The pastoral turn

Guéranger's words concerning a 'liturgical movement', inextricably linked
with the renewal of chant, were prophetic of aspirations for liturgy and
chant which would dominate the early twentieth century:

> Let us hope that the liturgical movement which is expanding and spreading will
> awaken also among the faithful the meaning of the Divine Office, that their attend-
> ance in church will become more intelligent, and that the time will come when, once
> more imbued with the spirit of the liturgy, they will feel the need to participate in
> the sacred chants.[17]

16   The 'both/and' paradigm permeates much of Derrida's published work, particularly
     in his deconstruction of dichotomies and dualities. One of the most explicit refer-
     ences can be found in his lecture entitled 'Interpretations at War: Kant, the Jew, the
     German', where he quotes a letter from Franz Rosenzweig: 'Let us then be Germans
     and Jews. Both at the same time, without worrying about the *and*, without talking
     about it a great deal, but really both' (Jacques Derrida (ed. Gil Anidjar), *Acts of
     Religion* (New York: Routledge, 2002), 142).
17   Guéranger, *Institutions liturgiques* 3 (Paris: Julien, Lanier et Cie, 1851), 170–71; cited
     in Robert L. Tuzik, *How Firm a Foundation: Leaders of the Liturgical Movement*

Solesmes set the agenda for the renewal of liturgy and chant, and a number of developments in the early twentieth century would result in the marrying of this influence with a turn towards wider, pastoral issues. Concerns about the fragmentation of community through urbanization in modern society, the isolation of the individual and the growth of secularization, as well as widespread unemployment, poverty and disempowerment in turn-of-the-century Europe, led to a renewed interest in recovering the *communio* character of the Eucharist, through which all Christians renew, in ritual, their essential unity with Christ and with each other.[18] This was an ecumenical impulse, with theologians from a variety of denominations contributing to an articulation of the growing sense that

> Everywhere there is awakening the realization that the church is something more than an external institution [...] the Church of Christ is, above all, a Unity [...] literally one body through union with Christ. This conception of the church as a creation and revelation of Christ, as an united organism living out of Christ, presses of its own accord toward the unifying and fraternizing of Christians who are separated by external barriers.[19]

One of the most influential contributions to this renewed understanding of Eucharist was promulgated by Benedictine theologian Odo Casel, who explained the liturgy as the 'fulfilment in ritual of what the Lord did for our salvation [...] we act out the mysteries as the body of Christ.'[20] In the church's performance of liturgy, the redemption achieved through the actions of Christ is re-actualized.

(Chicago: Liturgy Training Publications, 1990), 17, and Christopher Dorn, 'The Lord's Supper in Reformed Churches in an Age of Liturgical and Ecumenical Renewal: 1900–1968', *New Horizons in Faith and Order* 1 (2007), 46.

18   Dorn, 'The Lord's Supper in Reformed Churches', 56.

19   Friedrich Heiler, *Katholischer und evangelischer Gottesdienst* (München: Reinhardt, 1925), 9; cited in Bernard E. Meland, 'The Modern Liturgical Movement in Germany', *Journal of Religion* 11 (1931), 519.

20   Odo Casel (ed. Burkhard Neunheuser), *The Mystery of Christian Worship and Other Writings* (Westminster, MD: Newman Press, 1962), 9.

The official, papal endorsement of the connection between pastoral concerns for the 'Body of Christ' and the renewal of the liturgy came in the form of Pius X's *motu proprio* of November 1903, *Tra le sollecitudini*. Pius's understanding and appreciation of the integral nature of music and liturgy was formed as a young priest, when his passion for music led him to form church choirs and encourage congregational singing through experimentation with simple musical settings. He became increasingly convinced that Gregorian chant was musically, liturgically and pastorally the most appropriate music for both choir and congregation. *Tra le sollecitudini* became the point of departure for the pastoral, liturgical movement, stating that the most important and irreplaceable source of Christian identity as the Body of Christ resided in full and active participation in the sacred mysteries of the church. It was also the source of inspiration for a Belgian Benedictine, Lambert Beauduin, who recognized the implications of this document for the pastoral development of Christian communities through the liturgy. Eight years of work as a secular priest in Liège prior to his entering Mont-César convinced him of the necessity of including the entire Body of Christ in any liturgical movement which was to be authentic and truly involve itself in reform. In a seminal paper, delivered at the Congress of Malines in 1909, he proposed four measures towards the realization of this goal. These included the translation of the Roman Missal, the promotion of Compline and Vespers, the restoration of Gregorian chant, and annual liturgical retreats for parish choirs.

It is of interest that two of these four proposals for pastoral, liturgical renewal concern music, and one specifically concerns the role of Gregorian chant. Once again, the centrality of chant, not just as an aspect of monastic reform, but of a wider, pastoral reform, is reiterated. Reflecting on *Tra le sollecitudini*, Massey Shepherd wrote:

> It was one of the surer pastoral instincts of Pope Pius X to begin the modern phase of liturgical renewal in the Roman Church by a call to reform the Church's music, on the basis of the Solesmes' achievements in the sphere of Gregorian chant. No

proper liturgical spirit can develop among the faithful without an adequate vehicle of liturgical song.[21]

This 'vehicle' developed in a number of ways. Liturgical education and experimentation, including liturgical study weeks, pamphlets and popular publications by writers such as Beauduin, as well as the liturgical innovations at centres such as the Benedictine abbey of Maria Laach, led to the emergence of the 'Dialogue Mass', in which the congregation joined the altar servers in reciting the short responses and the Ordinary of the Mass in Latin. It was a short step to the promotion of the 'Sung Mass', at which the congregation was encouraged to sing these parts in Gregorian chant. Writing in 1951, Ernest Koenker declared that 'only a Mass in which the schola sings the proper and the congregation joins in singing the ordinary approximates the practice of the ancient Church.'[22]

Whether or not this is the case, it points to the appropriation of Gregorian chant as an important 'vehicle' through which active participation in the liturgy by the congregation was to be achieved. Anchored in the call of Pius X for 'special efforts [...] to be made to restore the use of the Gregorian chant by the people', the liturgical movement translated this into a call for pastoral inclusivity through the medium of chant.[23] In an ironic reversal of the contemporary tendency to identify congregational singing with the vernacular, and choral/schola singing with chant and polyphony, the so-called 'Gregorianists' of the modern liturgical movement were often accused of 'stealing' repertoire opportunities from choirs by giving over the Ordinary to congregational chant. In an interesting exchange in the *Musical Times* of 1931, a letter to the editor, signed 'J. McD', included the following response to a submission by Edward Maginty on the liturgical movement:

[...] if the Common of the Mass [Kyrie, Gloria, &c., called the 'Mass'] is henceforth to be given over wholly and entirely to the congregation, as Mr. Maginty seems to

21   Massey Hamilton Shepherd Jr. (ed.), *The Liturgical Renewal of the Church* (New York: Oxford University Press, 1960), 25.
22   Koenker, 'Objectives and Achievements of the Liturgical Movement', 18.
23   Reference to *motu proprio* text from Anthony Milner's 'Music in a Vernacular Catholic Liturgy', *Proceedings of the Royal Musical Association*, 91st session (1964/65), 27.

hint in his latest letter (and which really means an exclusive Gregorian rendering), perhaps he will kindly inform us in what way or under what conditions the other two styles of music, polyphony and the modern, can be propagated?[24]

Clearly, the 'High Art' camp of musical styles did not include congregational chant in its canons of taste. On the contrary, Gregorian chant was championed by those most invested in the 'pastoral' camp of renewal which, while not deprecating the role and importance of choral polyphony, clearly viewed the restoration of chant as an opportunity to restore also the singing role of the congregation.

This connection between liturgical renewal, pastoral inclusivity and social justice had one of its most explicit renderings in the development of the liturgical movement in the United States. A seminal figure in this story is the Benedictine Dom Virgil Michel. Inspired by Beauduin and the idea that liturgy creates and nourishes Christian community, he was to develop this notion into a sense of the inseparability of liturgical reform and social justice. In his review of a 1957 publication on Michel, Carl Fischer suggests that, for Michel, 'the liturgical movement is *the* social movement, *par excellence*'.[25] Similarly, in a more recent publication, Keith Pecklers links this sense of connectedness between liturgy and justice with the recovered theology of the church as the Mystical Body of Christ, manifest both in expressions of social justice and liturgical worship.[26]

The connection among social justice, the liturgy and Gregorian chant in the United States is perhaps most dramatically exampled through the figure of Dorothy Day, social activist and founder of the Catholic Worker Movement. Based in New York as part of the Catholic Worker Community, Day knew of the work of the Pius X School of Liturgical Music, founded by Justine Ward and Mother Georgia Stevens in Manhattanville,

24 'Letters to the Editor: The Movement in Roman Catholic Church Music', *Musical Times* 72 (1931), 632.
25 Carl M. Fischer, review of Paul B. Marx, *Virgil Michel and the Liturgical Movement* (Collegeville, MN: Liturgical Press, 1957), in the *American Catholic Sociological Review* 20 (1959), 181.
26 See Keith F. Pecklers, *The Unread Vision: The Liturgical Movement in the United States of America: 1926–1955* (Collegeville, MN: Liturgical Press, 1998).

New York. The Pius X school taught chant according to a variation of the Solesmes method, and Dom André Mocquereau, a choirmaster and leading proponent of chant investigation at Solesmes, was an occasional faculty member at the school. In 1935 Day sought the assistance of the school in the provision of a teacher to train a chant choir, which would help poor parishes in New York learn to sing Gregorian chant:

> That may seem a rather far cry from the work of the Catholic worker, at first glance, but I am sure I don't need to point out to you the fact that the entire Catholic social teaching is based, fundamentally, on liturgical doctrine. The group wishes to be able to open their evening meetings [...] with sung Compline. And they are especially anxious to learn a few of the simpler Gregorian Masses, in order to be able to offer their services free to poor parishes.[27]

The emergence of a strong pastoral dimension to the liturgical movement, with its first postulation in Belgium and perhaps its most widespread articulation in the United States, was intimately connected, both in official documentation (*Tra le sollecitudini*) and through grass-root practice (*semaines liturgiques*, the Pius X school, chant festivals and choirs) with the appropriation of Gregorian chant as a primary medium of 'active participation', the phrase which appeared for the first time in the 1903 *motu propio*, but which was destined to become the rallying call of the growing vernacular movement.

The Irish story

It is revealing, both of a historical reality and, no doubt, an Irish sense of humour, that two of the first publications on the liturgical movement in Ireland begin with a joke about the seeming incongruity of such a happening. In his 1961 article, Columba Breen writes:

---

27   Ibid., 276.

'Irish Liturgical Congress' [...] the phrase has a strange ring about it [...] Our mind is drawn to other, more familiar, perhaps inevitable associations – Irish whiskey, Irish Republican Army, Irish Catholic even. But Irish and the liturgy![28]

Similarly, in her 1998 article, Julie Kavanagh recalls an anecdote recorded by Bernard Botte, in which an Irishman declared that the story of the liturgical movement in Ireland was similar to the story of the snake in Ireland: there has never been any.[29]

There is no doubt that Ireland came late to an awareness or acceptance of the liturgical currents which were sweeping across Europe and the United States. Part of the resistance resided in Ireland's own complex liturgical history, where outward forms of Catholic liturgical practice were, by and large, forbidden or curtailed for a period of almost 300 years, stretching from the post-Reformation Penal period, to Catholic Emancipation in the nineteenth century.[30] The survival of 'the faith' during much of this time could not rely on the existence of a sustained, publicly proclaimed, communal site of prayer. Consequently, a domestic form of non-liturgical vernacular piety developed, with songs, prayers and blessings often married to traditional tunes associated with secular songs. This accounts, to some degree, for the highly devotional, individualistic nature of Irish Catholic liturgical practice that emerged post-Emancipation.[31]

28   Columba Breen, 'Glenstal Liturgical Congress', *Liturgical Arts* 29 (1961), 90.
29   Julie Kavanagh, 'The Glenstal Liturgical Congresses, 1954–1975', *Worship* 72 (1998), 421–44.
30   In his afterword to the second volume in the Irish Musical Studies series, Harry White writes of the implications for liturgical music of this historical curtailment: 'Put plainly, the impoverished condition of Roman Catholics in Ireland between 1500 and 1800 excluded the possibility of a high culture of sacred music.' See Harry White, 'Church Music and Musicology in Ireland: An Afterword', in Gerard Gillen and Harry White (eds), *Music and the Church* (Irish Musical Studies 2; Dublin: Irish Academic Press, 1993), 333.
31   For an account of traditional prayers and blessings associated with Sunday and the Mass that survived into the twentieth century, see Vincent Ryan, *The Shaping of Sunday: Sunday and Eucharist in the Irish Tradition* (Dublin: Veritas, 1997).

The first post-Reformation publications in Ireland of the plainchant revival date from the late eighteenth/early nineteenth century, and include an *Officium defunctum* published by Patrick Wogan in Dublin in 1793, and *A Plain and Concise Method of Learning the Gregorian Note* by Revd P. Hoey, also published by Wogan in 1800.[32] By the mid-nineteenth century, following Catholic Emancipation, Dublin was recognized as an important centre for Catholic publications:

> Not only had Dublin become an obvious centre for the Irish Catholic book trade, but astute Catholic publishers from London ensured that they either had independent offices in Dublin or were partnered with already established Dublin firms.[33]

The most significant revival of plainchant in nineteenth-century Ireland, however, was a result of Ireland's enthusiastic embrace of the Cecilian movement and its tenets. The Irish Society of St Cecilia was founded in 1878 by Revd Nicholas Donnelly, only ten years after the organization was birthed in Germany by Franz Witt, and its journal, *Lyra Ecclesiastica*, was the first Cecilian publication published exclusively in the English language. From its first issue, the journal was unambiguous in its support of Gregorian chant, sixteenth-century polyphony and some contemporary works written according to Cecilian principles, to the virtual exclusion of everything else.[34]

---

32 For a more detailed account of the revival of plainchant in Ireland in the eighteenth and early nineteenth centuries, see Bennett Zon, 'The Revival of Plainchant in the Roman Catholic Church in Ireland, 1777–1858: Some Sources and Their Commerce with England', in Patrick F. Devine and Harry White (eds), *The Maynooth International Musicological Conference 1995: Selected Proceedings, Part Two* (Irish Musical Studies 5; Dublin: Four Courts Press, 1996), 251–61.

33 Zon 'The Revival of Plainchant', 256.

34 For a more detailed account of Cecilianism in Ireland, see Kieran Anthony Daly, *Catholic Church Music in Ireland, 1878–1903: The Cecilian Reform Movement* (Dublin: Four Courts Press, 1995); Harry White and Nicholas Lawrence, 'Towards a History of the Cecilian Movement in Ireland: An Assessment of the Writings of Heinrich Bewerunge (1862–1923), with a Catalogue of his Publications and Manuscripts', in *Music and the Church* (as n.30), 78–107; and a review of Daly's publication by Helen Phelan in *Doctrine and Life* 46 (May/June, 1996), 311–13.

Cecilianism did not enjoy universal support in Ireland, as is suggested by the figure of Joseph Smith, organist, conductor and composer, who held a number of organ and teaching posts in Limerick and Dublin. Paul Collins notes that

> Smith took issue with those who held that Gregorian chant is '*par excellence* the music of the Church' and 'the one musical language alone capable of expressing the emotions of the mind acted upon by feelings of love and reverence for God.'[35]

This notwithstanding, the movement enjoyed great ecclesiastical support from the powerful Irish Catholic church that emerged in the wake of Catholic Emancipation and the Great Famine, personified in many ways by the towering figure of Paul Cullen. As rector of the Irish College in Rome, Cullen had been strongly influenced by the ultramontane ideology and, as the first Irishman to be elevated to the College of Cardinals, played an influential role in drafting the document on papal infallibility at the First Vatican Council. White suggests that Cecilianism introduced 'a code of musical aesthetics which could not but flourish in the actively conservative climate of Irish church politics in the late nineteenth century.'[36]

The shift in supremacy from German (Cecilian) to French (Solesmes) influences in chant reform at the turn of the century, particularly after the publication of the new *Vatican Kyriale* (1905), was not lost on Irish liturgical musicians, and Collins cites a report in the *Munster News* which notes that the ceremonies of Holy Week were celebrated at St John's Cathedral, Limerick, 'according to the approved Solesmes method.'[37]

---

35 Paul Collins, '*Soli Deo Gloria*: Catholic Church Music in Limerick, *c*1860–1950' (unpublished paper, presented at the Fourth Annual Conference of the Society for Musicology in Ireland, Mary Immaculate College, University of Limerick, 2006); see also Joseph Smith, 'The Reformation of Church Music', *Munster News*, 24 August, 1878, 4.

36 White and Lawrence, 'Towards a History of the Cecilian Movement in Ireland', 84.

37 Collins, '*Soli Deo Gloria*', citing 'Holy Week Ceremonies – St John's Cathedral', *Munster News*, 15 April 1905, 3.

One of the great Irish champions of the Solesmes reforms was Revd Dr John Burke of the National University, Ireland. In 1926 he inaugurated a chant summer school in Dublin, which, by 1929, included a full two-week programme of chant, liturgy, architecture and religious art. Burke was a passionate follower of Dom André Mocquereau, and only Mocquereau's age and declining health prevented him from accepting an invitation to teach at the Dublin programme.[38] The 1929 school included representatives of every diocese in Ireland, twelve overseas dioceses, ten male religious orders, seventeen female religious orders, as well as secular students and visiting bishops and abbots, bringing the number of participants to almost 200. It is interesting to note that, in the same year, Burke was invited to teach at the chant summer school in Oxford, where he presented on Irish music, postulating that the modal nature of Irish music and its lack of rhythmic constraint 'admirably prepares the Irish soul to understand and love Gregorian chant.'[39]

The Dublin summer school concluded with an optional examination, offered at four levels – primary, intermediate, advanced and diploma. In 1930 Dublin was recognized as the official Solesmes centre in Ireland, and the diploma was examined and recognized by Solesmes as a qualification for teaching chant in the Solesmes style. As the Society of St Gregory was only in its infancy in 1930 (having been founded in England in 1929), the Solesmes diploma for all of Great Britain was facilitated through the Dublin centre.

Burke was also responsible for reviving the practice of popular competitions for massed choirs singing plainchant, which had been part of the Cecilian legacy in Ireland. He introduced the 'Joseph Sarto Memorial' prize to the Feis Ceoil (a musical festival founded in 1895) in Dublin, and plainchant festivals and competitions soon began to appear throughout Ireland, often under the patronage of the bishops.[40] The liturgical festival

38 A full review of the summer school was published in *Revue Grégorienne* 14 (1929), 274–7.
39 *Revue Grégorienne* 15 (1930), 235 (trans. Charlotte Derenne).
40 Ibid.

in Limerick drew on the chant expertise of Doms Winoc Mertens, Maur
Ellis, and later, Paul McDonnell, from the Benedictine community at Glenstal Abbey, which would later play a seminal role in the modern liturgical
movement in Ireland. These festivals often featured massed choirs consisting of thousands of children:

> For example at the 31st International Eucharist Congress held in Dublin in June,
> 1932 a children's High Mass choir consisted of 2,700 boys and girls who sang not
> only the mass, *Ecce Sacerdos*, but also hymns in Irish.[41]

The inclusion of Irish language hymns alongside chant echoes Burke's passion for chant and Irish song, and the romantic urge to postulate ancient
connections between all things Celtic and Catholic. But it also played its
part in creating a voice for the newly emergent Irish State at the beginning
of the twentieth century, where Irish language song and Catholic church
music formed the core canon of musical education, so that 'the musical traditions that were excluded from the official canon in the previous century
found an honoured place in the schools of the young nation state.'[42]

The struggle for independence from England, which marked the early
part of the twentieth century in Ireland, was both a political and religious
affair. Nationalism and Catholicism became inextricably linked, to the
extent that, in her account of the Ireland which emerged as an independent
republic in 1949, Louise Fuller claims that '[A]ll of the evidence [...] points
to the fact that Catholic culture was *the* popular culture in most of the
Republic of Ireland in the 1950s'.[43] Most Irish schools and hospitals were
owned or managed by religious orders. The *Irish Independent*, the newspaper with the largest public circulation, advertized itself as a Catholic paper
until the mid-1950s. Raidió Éireann, the national radio broadcasting service,

---

41   Marie McCarthy, *Passing It On: The Transmission of Music in Irish Culture* (Cork:
     Cork University Press, 1999), 121.
42   Ibid., 184.
43   Louise Fuller, *Irish Catholicism since 1950: The Undoing of a Culture* (Dublin: Gill
     & Macmillan, 2002), 14.

instigated a practice in 1950 of broadcasting the ringing of the Angelus Bell each day, a practice which continues into the twenty-first century.

Mass attendance in the Ireland of the 1950s formed part of the fabric of social and cultural life, and non-attendance on Sundays or Holy Days was extremely rare, leading one writer to suggest that 'average Mass attendance in Ireland [...] is a record in the Catholic world today.'[44] In addition, most Catholics attended confraternities, sodalities, Benediction, novenas and devotions to Mary or the Sacred Heart on a weekly basis, as well as parish missions, pilgrimages and processions (particularly as part of Marian and Corpus Christi celebrations). At the heart of many of these devotions was the recitation of the rosary, the praying of which was also common during the celebration of the Mass. It was not unusual to spend two or three evenings a week involved in church activities, in addition to attendance at Sunday Mass; indeed, confraternities and similar gatherings provided a social outlet as well as a religious community. Processions engulfed the social fabric of towns and villages, as captured in this description by Irish writer John McGahern of a Corpus Christi procession:

> Coloured streamers and banners were strung across the roads from poles. Altars with flowers and a cross on white linen were erected at Gilligan's, the post office and at Mrs Mullaney's.
>
> The Host was taken from the tabernacle and carried by the priests beneath a gold canopy all the way round the village, pausing for ceremonies at each wayside altar. Benediction was always at the post office.
>
> The congregation followed behind, some bearing the banners of their sodalities, and girls in white veils and dresses scattered rose petals from white boxes on the path before the Host.[45]

The immersion of Irish social life in the culture of Catholicism, captured by McGahern, bears a strong resemblance to a description of another Corpus Christi procession, this time by Joseph Ratzinger, reflecting on his childhood in Bavaria:

---

44 Robert Culhane, 'Irish Catholics in Britain', *The Furrow* 1 (1950), 389.
45 John McGahern, 'Hell and damnation', *Irish Independent Weekender*, 31 July 1993, 1.

I can still smell those carpets of flowers and the freshness of the birch trees; I can see all the houses decorated, the banners, the singing; I can still hear the village band [...] I remember the *joie de vivre* of the local lads, firing their gun salutes![46]

In his article on Benedict XVI and the Eucharist, Eamon Duffy suggests that, for Ratzinger, this represented 'authentic catholic Christianity at its best', an experience which left him somewhat 'suspicious of those professional liturgists' of the liturgical movement, who implied that 'the Eucharist had been instituted to be eaten, not carried about on carpets of flowers or shot into the air over by lads with guns.'[47] Similarly, for many Irish Catholics in the later years of the liturgical movement, the liturgical reforms proposed did not seem to be filling the churches of the continent, and professional liturgists of Belgium, France and Germany were objects of 'suspicion and distain, because of their empty churches.'[48]

Nevertheless, a nascent Catholic, largely clerical, intelligentsia was beginning to wonder if all was indeed well with the particular brand of piety that filled Irish churches. Two new journals, *The Furrow* and *Doctrine & Life*, commenced in 1950 and 1951 respectively. As the liturgical movement gathered momentum, these became mouthpieces for some of the questions and innovations that were becoming increasingly difficult to ignore and which would culminate in the emergence of the Glenstal liturgical congresses in 1954.

The Glenstal congresses took their place in the tradition of liturgical study weeks and congresses, which were to mark the liturgical movement from the early twentieth century. The first liturgy week was organized in 1910 in Belgium, which quickly took the lead in organized and structured liturgical education and practice for the non-monastic community. The Centre de Pastorale Liturgique was founded in Paris in 1943, and provided the impetus for a number of congresses at Versailles and Maria Laach,

---

46   Joseph Ratzinger, *The Feast of Faith: Approaches to a Theology of the Liturgy* (San Francisco: Ignatius Press, 1986), 127.

47   Eamon Duffy, 'Benedict XVI and the Eucharist', *New Blackfriars* 88 (2007), 197.

48   John Cooney, 'John Charles McQuaid at Vatican II', *Doctrine and Life* 48 (1998), 215.

culminating in the international congresses of Lugano (1951) and Assisi (1956). Virgil Michel was central to the introduction of liturgical renewal to the United States through a series of 'liturgical weeks' that ran from 1940 to 1961.

If the story of liturgical renewal in Europe and the United States is also a Benedictine story, Cyprian Love reminds us that the Benedictine community in Ireland, and specifically the Benedictine community at Glenstal Abbey, stands 'in a relationship of proven inheritance, and also facilitated the introduction of the Movement in Ireland.'[49] The Benedictine monastery of Saints Joseph and Columba at Glenstal Abbey, Co. Limerick, can indeed boast of an interesting liturgical pedigree. The monastery was founded in 1927 from Maredsous Abbey in Belgium, which was itself founded by monks of Beuron, the founder house of so many Benedictine liturgical centres directly influenced by the tradition of Solesmes from the time of its founders, Maurus and Placidus Wolter. The story of the congresses at Glenstal began over a cup of coffee between the then Prior of Glenstal, Placid Murray, and the Dominican Thomas Garde, who had been leading a retreat for the community. Garde suggested to Murray that the Benedictines might be well positioned to initiate a liturgical congress in the tradition of the Benedictine love of liturgy.[50] The congresses commenced in 1954 and continued until 1975, when the torch for liturgical renewal in the post-Vatican II context was passed to the newly established National Institute for Liturgy.

A very interesting story emerges when one examines the position of Gregorian chant in this dual world of Irish liturgical realities: the world of

---

49   Cyprian Love, 'Glenstal Abbey, Music and The Liturgical Movement', *Studies in World Christianity* 12 (2006), 132.

50   Much of the information on the Glenstal liturgical congresses was facilitated through the kind assistance of Placid Murray and Vincent Ryan, members of the Glenstal community, who provided invaluable access to archival records of the congresses, as well as numerous formal and informal interviews during my research in this area (from 1995 to 2000) for my doctoral dissertation, 'Laus Perennis: The Emergence of a Theology of Music with reference to Post-Vatican II Irish Catholicism', PhD thesis, University of Limerick, 2000.

'traditional' and 'conservative' devotional practice on the one hand, and the smaller, but dynamic world of 'progressive' liturgical renewal, represented by the congresses, on the other. Once again, in contradiction to contemporary notions which ally 'traditional'/'conservative' faith positions with Gregorian chant, the story which emerged from the modern liturgical movement in Ireland was of the preservation and promotion of chant by the 'progressive'/'pastoral' movement and the wholesale embrace of the vernacular by the 'traditional' church.

This happened for a number of reasons. Firstly, the devotional nature of traditional Irish Catholicism was highly vernacular, even before Vatican II. Because so many people participated in paraliturgical events, there already existed a high level of vernacular singing associated with processions, pilgrimages and confraternity activities. One only need trace the emergence of popular hymnody in the post-Vatican II context to find its root in pre-Vatican II devotional practice. One of the striking examples of this was the extraordinary commercial success of the CD release *Faith of Our Fathers* in 1996, which featured a host of these hymns, made popular by devotional practice and transferred to the vernacular liturgies of the post-Vatican II context.[51] Hymns such as *Holy God, we praise thy name*; *Sweet Heart of Jesus*; *Hail Redeemer, King divine*; *Faith of our fathers*; *The Bells of the Angelus*; *To Jesus' Heart, all burning*; *Soul of my Saviour*; *Queen of the May*; *O Sacrament most holy*; *Lord of all hopefulness*; *Hail, Glorious Saint Patrick*; *I'll sing a hymn to Mary*; *Hail, Queen of Heaven*; *Jesus my Lord, my God, my all*; and *We stand for God* dominate the recording, with three short pieces of chant (*Tantum ergo*, *Ave verum*, *Regina coeli*) and one Irish language hymn (*Céad míle fáilte romhat, a Íosa*), illustrating the widespread popularity of vernacular hymnody among the pre-Vatican II Irish Catholic community. The popularity of chant festivals notwithstanding, the majority experience of Mass in the 1950s was of a 'Low' Mass with little or no sung chant, while, at the same time, the majority experience of religious song through paraliturgical events was clearly vernacular.

---

51   *Faith of Our Fathers: Classic Religious Anthems of Ireland* (RTÉ CD 198, 1996).

Conversely, while the liturgical movement in Ireland fully supported the increased use of the vernacular in the Mass, it is clear from a perusal of minutes and publications from the Glenstal congresses that the 'pride of place'[52] accorded to Gregorian chant in landmark liturgical documents such as *Mediator Dei* (1947), *Musicae sacrae disciplina* (1955) and culminating in *Sacrosanctum Concilium* (1963), was fully recognized and facilitated.

No minutes of the congress exist from 1954 to 1959. The lectures from these first six years, however, were published in 1961 by the Furrow Trust, Maynooth.[53] The devotional piety characteristic of Irish Catholicism prior to the Second Vatican Council is addressed in this volume by Daniel Duffy in a survey entitled 'Eucharistic Piety in Irish Practice'.[54] Duffy notes the large congregations attending Mass and receiving communion frequently, but also the largely silent participation, the 'telling of beads' throughout the celebration. Prayer manuals, when used, are frequently interspersed with aspirations. Corpus Christi processions, Forty Hours devotions and Exposition are popular and well attended. Duffy concludes that there is little real preparation for or understanding of the Eucharistic liturgy, reflected in the continued use of alternative prayers, unceremonious entrances and exits, and an extreme shyness of singing at liturgy: in all, a liturgical practice and attitude out of contact with liturgical modernity.

In his own contribution, 'Liturgical Piety According to the Encyclical "Mediator Dei"', Dom Placid also notes the lack of real understanding of the liturgical reform, beyond its exterior manifestations. Many priests would appear to feel that

> [t]heir duty [...] is to safeguard the elementary things among the general body of the faithful before they could attempt to go on to the refinements of the Liturgy. This

52   *Sacrosanctum Concilium*, art. 116, cited from Austin Flannery (ed.), *Vatican Council II: The Conciliar and Post Conciliar Documents* (Northport, New York: Costello Publishing Company, 1975), 32.

53   Placid Murray, OSB (ed.), *Studies in Pastoral Liturgy* (Maynooth: The Furrow Trust, 1961).

54   Daniel Duffy, 'Eucharistic Piety in Irish Practice', in *Studies in Pastoral Liturgy* (as n.53), 182–97.

attitude is based on a misconception of the nature of the Liturgy and belittles the Liturgy, considering it to be no more than rubrics or outward ceremonial.[55]

The volume notes that the afternoon session of the first day of the 1959 congress was dedicated to the 'Chants of Holy Week'. Conducted by Fr Kieran O'Gorman, Director of Sacred Music in the Diocese of Killaloe, it consisted of a practical introduction to chants for use in an average parish liturgy. O'Gorman's sense of the pastoral potential of chant is clear in his concluding aspiration, where he predicted that '[I]f we succeed in Holy Week, it is but a short step to active participation in every Mass, be it sung or read.'[56]

The three congresses from 1960 to 1962 were published in a second volume of *Studies in Pastoral Liturgy*, edited by Vincent Ryan, OSB.[57] In 'The Mass and the People in Irish Parishes', William Conway suggests that a regular *Missa Cantata* in every parochial church would be desirable. Sung responses such as the *Amen*; *Et cum spiritu tuo*; *Gloria Tibi, Domine*; and *Deo gratias* 'give visible expression to the nexus between the celebrant and the congregation.'[58] Sung participation in the Mass is taken up again by Kieran O'Gorman, rooting the modern liturgical awareness of the role of music in the writings of Pius X and his conviction that participation in worship was the most critical and indispensable source of Christian living.[59]

Minutes of the liturgical congresses were kept from 1960 onwards, firstly by Dom Placid and later, in a more sporadic fashion, by Dom Paul McDonnell, OSB. The intrinsic connection between music and liturgy is highlighted by a discussion on the possibility of establishing a music

55   Murray, 'Liturgical Piety According to the Encyclical "Mediator Dei"', in *Studies in Pastoral Liturgy* (as n.53), 132–9 (at p.132).
56   'Chants of Holy Week', in *Studies in Pastoral Liturgy* (as n.53), 287.
57   Vincent Ryan, OSB (ed.), *Studies in Pastoral Liturgy* 2 (Maynooth: The Furrow Trust, 1963).
58   William Conway, 'The Mass and the People in Irish Parishes', in *Studies in Pastoral Liturgy* 2 (as n.57), 107–119 (at p.115).
59   Kieran O'Gorman, 'Participating in the Mass by Song', in *Studies in Pastoral Liturgy* 2 (as n.57), 168–76.

sub-committee within the congress. In the minutes of the annual general meeting of the committee on 16 May 1961, it is noted:

> A suggestion in a letter of Fr. D. Linehan (Cork) to form a musical sub-committee on the Congress. The general feeling was that the musicians should get every encouragement, but that the formation of a committee might emphasise the difference between 'liturgy' and 'music'.[60]

The minutes note the organization of a study day for 19 October 1966, including representatives from the Dioceses of Achonry, Cloyne, Derry, Elphin, Ferns, Galway, Kerry, Kildare, Killala, Kilmore, Limerick, Ossory, Raphoe, and Waterford and Lismore. The guest speaker for the study day was Fr Pierre-Marie Gy, OP, director of the Institut Supérieur de Liturgie in Paris. The question of music was raised by a Mr Ó Cléirigh, one of three lay representatives present. The Prior referred to the relative paucity of sung Masses in Ireland. Fr Gy favoured an optimistic attitude, noting how much had been achieved in France, where, generally speaking, there were no Sunday Masses without chant, with the exception of Masses at seven or eight in the morning. He also emphasized the role of the schola as a support for the singing congregation.[61]

Even this short overview of some of the more pertinent records of the place of Gregorian chant in the liturgical congresses at Glenstal indicates an appreciation for the place of chant in the context of liturgical reform, a position which Cyprian Love suggests is still evident in the liturgical life of the Glenstal community: 'The traditional Benedictine option of Latin plainsong remains intact, though not slavishly so, in Glenstal's worship, alongside a growth of alternatives.'[62] It may seem ironic to some that one of the very few places where one can still experience Gregorian chant in a living liturgical context in Ireland is in the home of the most significant and sustained contribution to the modern liturgical movement in the country.

---

60   Minutes, Glenstal Liturgical Congresses, 1961.
61   Minutes, Glenstal Liturgical Congresses, 1966.
62   Love, 'Glenstal Abbey, Music and The Liturgical Movement', 137.

Conclusion

This brief overview of the modern liturgical movement, and particularly its manifestation in Ireland, suggests that contemporary discourse around 'traditional' and 'progressive' understandings of liturgy, as well as the identification of plainchant with the former and vernacular song with the latter, stands in sharp contrast to the practices and aspirations of the modern liturgical movement. The movement instigated by Solesmes was concerned with both restoration and revival, and the medium through which both of these aspirations were to be achieved involved the liturgical singing of Gregorian chant. The connection between liturgical reform and pastoral concerns, which marked the second phase of the movement, was one which was to be partially achieved through a popular revival of plainchant. In Ireland, the picture is far more complex than any simplistic bifurcation. The historical suppression of Catholic liturgical practice from post-Reformation to post-Emancipation in the early nineteenth century resulted in the development of a strongly pietistic, devotional religiosity, sonically expressed in Irish language songs and prayers. The revival of Catholic liturgical practice in the late nineteenth century was marked by an ideological adherence to Rome, characterized by strong clerical control and an embrace of Cecilian tenets. But the legacy of Cecilianism and the growth of a Solesmes-style revival in Ireland could also be characterized as a popular movement, not primarily through the liturgical use of chant, but through its mass popularity in competitions, festivals and paraliturgical events. Simultaneously, a vernacular culture of Catholic hymnody in English and Irish, nurtured through both domestic piety, national school education, and the widespread participation in extra-liturgical events, informed Irish Catholic culture in the emerging nation-state of the early twentieth century, an identity built on the preservation and celebration of 'traditional' Catholic values.

The embrace of the modern liturgical movement in the 1950s could not be described as a 'popular' movement, but was certainly a 'progressive' one. As the progressive voice of Irish Catholic liturgical reform, it also promulgated the centrality of liturgical chant, though never to the exclusion of the vernacular.

The inheritance of the modern liturgical movement is, therefore, a much more complex and inclusive one than contemporary practice might lead one to conclude. *Summorum Pontificum*, the Apostolic Letter of Benedict XVI, released on 7 July 2007, is an interesting response to the current liturgical divisions. Whatever the arguments in favour of or against this increased freedom to celebrate Mass according to the Missal promulgated by John XXIII in 1962, the public perception appears to equate 'Latin' and 'chant' with the older, 'traditional', 'Tridentine' Mass, and 'vernacular' and 'progressive' with the 'reformed' Roman Missal, promulgated by Paul VI in 1970.[63] If this simplistic perception becomes the ritual norm, one wonders if the resultant polarization will again lead to the abandonment of any attempt to engage in a reassessment of liturgical chant in the context of liturgical renewal. Against the backdrop of ever-increasing religious fundamentalism, might there be something to be gained from a re-examination of the inclusive (traditional, progressive, Latin, vernacular, congregational, choral) aspirations and practices of the modern liturgical movement?

63   A brief perusal of some media headlines concerning the *motu proprio* is of interest in terms of their reference to the 1962 publication as the 'Latin Mass' and the 1970 Missal as the 'Vernacular Mass'! See, for example, Alan Cooperman, 'Pope Poised to Revive Latin Mass, Official Says', *Washington Post*, 13 October 2006, A03; Laurie Goodstein and Ian Fisher, 'Wider Use of Latin Mass Likely, Vatican Officials Say', *New York Times*, 28 June 2007; and Paddy Agnew, 'Revival of Latin Mass criticised by some Jewish leaders', *Irish Times*, 9 July 2007, 10.

BENNETT ZON

Victorian Anti-Semitism and the Origin of Gregorian Chant

The history of Gregorian chant, arguably the most iconic music of the Catholic Church, has always excited controversy, especially in the reforming climate of post-Tridentine Europe. In post-Reformation England this once venerable musical tradition fluctuated dramatically alongside ideological sympathies. Gregorian chant became a plaything of church apologists, at times arguing partially unreconstructed Catholic positions, such as that of mid-sixteenth-century Chapel Royal musician and humanist John Marbecke,[1] and at other times eschewing Gregorian chant as musical anathema.[2] By the Victorian period, when genres of Catholicism blurred within established and disestablished churches, these arguments crystallized into a culture of extremes between ultra- and anti-Gregorians in both the Catholic and Anglican Churches. A correspondent in the Catholic magazine *The Tablet* suggests that 'One person would abolish all music but the Plain Chant of the Church; another dreads the very idea of barbarism.'[3] Indeed, there is a 'danger of becoming either ultra-Gregorians or anti-Gregorians.'[4]

---

1   See Hyun-Ah Kim, 'Renaissance Humanism and John Merbecke's *The Booke of Common Praier Noted* (1550)', PhD thesis, Durham University, 2005.

2   See Ruth M. Wilson, *Anglican Chant and Chanting in England, Scotland, and America, 1660–1820* (Oxford Studies in British Church Music; Oxford: Oxford University Press, 1996).

3   'Ecclesiastical Music. The Comparative Merits of Gregorian and Modern Music', *The Tablet* 8/350 (16 January 1847), 35.

4   Ibid.

The danger in this febrile atmosphere of deeply-rooted ideological conviction is everywhere abundant in the annals of Victorian church history,
with church hierarchies despairing to find their congregations so heavily
divided. A passionate observer of this ecclesiastical strife, the renowned
architect and Anglican convert to Catholicism, Augustus Welby Northmore
Pugin, was not alone in describing this disharmony 'as a stumbling block to
our separated service,'[5] i.e. a stumbling block to potential reunification of
the Anglican and Catholic Churches. At the same time, in the supposedly
disinterested field of historiography, historians viewed this divisive icon
of Catholic music, by and large, without denominational bias. Bound by
rules of 'objectivity', music historians shared this disinterest. Yet, as history
shows, lurking beneath their objectivity is a set of contemporary values just
as laden with cultural import as their counterparts in church. Although
denominationally disinterested, these music historians nonetheless speak
of strongly embedded historical attitudes towards quintessentially Catholic
music, and for that reason their writings are explored and interrogated here.
They provide a glimpse into the construction of an important component
in early Catholic history, and in the process shed light on a notorious aspect
of Victorian historical perspective.

Introduction

Today, despite advances in modern musicology, the origins of Gregorian
chant remain shrouded in mystery. Speaking of the commonly held belief
that chant is Hebraic in origin, Peter Jeffery says that

> Gregorian chant as we know it has little in common with the chant that is heard in
> synagogues today or that can be recovered historically by scholars. The two sister
> religions diverged in the first century of our era, and each has followed its own

5   Augustus Welby Pugin, *An Earnest Appeal for the Revival of the Ancient Plain Song*
     (London: Charles Dolman, 1850), 10.

historical trajectory since, despite frequent instances of both friendly and hostile contact between the two.[6]

The Victorians felt more confident, however. Undeterred by the lack of hard evidence, and buttressed by unerring confidence in a long, if controversial, history of plainchant in both Anglican and Catholic traditions[7] as well as a keen interest in the latest developments in Continental palaeography and publication,[8] Victorian musicologists plotted a history of Gregorian chant with a great sense of scholastic purpose.

Like all modern historians, they strove unflinchingly towards an 'objective historical truth'.[9] Yet the truth for Victorian musicologists was arguably compromised, for their intellectual mindset, and the attitudes they projected onto the history of Gregorian chant, was prefigured by inherited conceptions of their own national and human importance. These conceptions, moulded out of a flourishing imperial experience, assign ineluctable developmental superiority to Western, European – often English – man and his culture. Conveniently for Victorian cultural supremacists, the history of Gregorian chant embraces more than just Western cultural experience. It is also Semitic, and as such presents musicologists with a golden opportunity to reconcile the Western superiority of Gregorian chant with that of its Hebraic, and putatively less developed, predecessor. In this context, although seemingly neutral in empirical terms, Gregorian chant was never more historically politicized. Co-opted as a cipher for empire and its inexorable cultural conquest, the history of Gregorian chant, under the Victorians, expressed and confirmed the prejudices of their age.

6   Peter Jeffrey, 'Ratio Studiorum: The Shape of Modern Chant Studies', <http://www. music.princeton.edu/chant_html/what.html>, accessed Sept. 2007.
7   See Bennett Zon, *The English Plainchant Revival* (Oxford: Oxford University Press, 1999).
8   See Katherine Bergeron, *Decadent Enchantments: The Revival of Gregorian Chant at Solesmes* (Berkeley and Los Angeles: University of California Press, 1998).
9   Peter Novick, *That Noble Dream: The 'Objectivity Question' and the American Historical Profession* (Cambridge: Cambridge University Press, 1988), 2; cited in Keith Jenkins, *The Postmodern History Reader* (London and New York: Routledge, 1997), 11.

This essay explores these prejudices by locating histories of Gregorian chant within the intellectual culture of Victorian Britain. It does this by cross-examining a wide range of denominationally disinterested (and hence ostensibly more 'objective') musicology, including general histories of music, histories of national music and early writings in music psychology and ethnomusicology, within wider currents of Victorian anthropological literature. These sources are explored in four ways: first, by introducing Victorian theories of musical origins which undergird contemporary historiographies of Gregorian chant; second, by exploring notions of developmental simplicity in the music of the early church; third, by locating plainchant within Arnoldian theories of Hebraism, Hellenism and the origins of culture; and fourth, by looking at anti-Semitism and the Arnoldian paradigm in Victorian histories of chant. A conclusion projects into the early twentieth century to help explain how evolutionism supplanted developmentalism as an historiographical model in writings on the origins of Gregorian chant.

Victorian theories of musical origins

When, in 1859, Darwin revered the origin of species as 'that mystery of mysteries',[10] he solemnized a quintessential Victorian quest: the quest to know the origin of things. Musical origins formed an integral part of that quest. As Warren Dwight Allen says, 'it is a rare history of music that does not begin with "The Origins of Music."'[11] This is largely axiomatic for Victorian music histories. In these, attitudes towards musical origins not only establish conceptual delimitations, but campaign for ideological allegiances. William Stafford, for example, takes a sideswipe at wishful thinking when ascribing the origin of music to natural causes. Though

---

10   Charles Darwin, *On the Origin of Species* (London: John Murray, 1859), 1.
11   Warren Dwight Allen, *Philosophies of Music History: A Study of General Histories of Music, 1600–1960* (New York: American Book Co., 1939; repr. Dover, 1962), 183.

obscured by myth, 'Natural causes [...] may sufficiently account for its [music's] origin, without referring to a miracle for the event.'[12] In a peak of one-upmanship, Stafford's contemporary, George Hogarth, complains that although music is a complex and difficult art, it is nonetheless 'a gift of the Author of Nature.'[13]

These two important strands form just part of an expanding Victorian portfolio of musical origins. Later in the century, just two years before Darwin would revolutionize human thought, his contemporary Herbert Spencer elevated the argument from nature to a much higher level than the likes of Stafford had achieved. Articulating the first theory of musical origins framed in evolutionary language, he maintains that music evolved from intense, impassioned, speech:

> from the ancient epic poet chanting his verses, down to the modern musical composer, men of unusually strong feelings, prone to express them in extreme forms, have been naturally the agents of these successive intensifications [...] that on no other tenable hypothesis can either the expressiveness of music or the genesis of music be explained.[14]

Although hugely controversial, it was Spencer who became hegemonic in late Victorian musicology, rather than Darwin, not least for the adaptability of his theory to current developmental ideologies. Guided by the certainties of his convictions, he evolved a grand analogy in which development from speech to music mirrors development from savagery to civilization:

> That music is a product of civilization is manifest: for though some of the lowest savages have their dance-chants, these are of a kind scarcely to be signified by the title musical: at most they supply but the vaguest rudiment of music properly so called.[15]

12   William C. Stafford, *A History of Music* (Edinburgh: Constable and Co., 1830), 1.

13   George Hogarth, *Musical History, Biography, and Criticism: Being a General Survey of Music, from the Earliest Period to the Present Time* (London: John W. Parker, 1835), 1.

14   Herbert Spencer, 'The Origin and Function of Music', *Fraser's Magazine* (October 1857); see Herbert Spencer, *Literary Style and Music* (London: Watts, 1950), 69.

15   Spencer, 'The Origin and Function of Music', 68.

The durability and smug cultural satisfaction of Spencer's developmental analogy within an imperial environment left other theories of musical origins struggling to be heard. Nevertheless, other theories were developed, some eventually supplanting Spencer once, in the face of British imperial decline, anthropological rationalizations of empire became more generally redundant. Late-century theories often debate Spencer's presumption, postulating separate origins for music and speech. The psychologist and musicologist Edmund Gurney, author of the magisterial *The Power of Sound* (1880), takes a stab at Spencer, claiming that 'the speech of primitive man had a special relation to Music; [and] that his direct and normal expression of his intuitions and feelings contained the essential germs of Music, or was actually "a sort of music."'[16] For Gurney, moreover, 'we cannot judge music with the savage ear till we can remake ourselves into savages.'[17]

The critic Ernest Newman is even more vituperative:

> To us, there is a great psychological and aesthetic gulf fixed between excited speech and song – *not only between the speech and the song of to-day, but between the ruder speech and ruder song of primitive man* [...] Allowing for all the differences between our music and that of the savage who blows his reed and thumps his tam-tam, and for all the differences of general mental structure between him and us, we can still see that the same causes which incite us to music incited him.[18]

Newman echoes numerous critics of Spencer. Wallaschek, for example, not only distinguishes speech from music, but rhythm from melody, reasoning that 'to adduce speech and its modulations is not only unnecessary, but absolutely untenable. Men do not come to music by way of tones, but they come to tones and tunes by way of the rhythmical impulse.'[19]

---

16   Edmund Gurney, *The Power of Sound* (London: Smith, Elder, & Co., 1880), 490.
17   Ibid., 492.
18   Ernest Newman, 'Herbert Spencer and the Origin of Music', in Ernest Newman, *Musical Studies* (2nd edn, London: John Lane, 1910), 197–8. Original italics.
19   Richard Wallaschek, *Primitive Music: An Inquiry into the Origin and Development of Music, Songs, Instruments, Dances, and Pantomimes of Savage Races* (London and New York: Longmans, Green, and Co., 1893), 235.

Over time these and other criticisms of Spencer amassed, ursurping his theory of musical origins with a more pliant Darwinian model. Yet, ironically, it was not Darwin's equally speculative model of music origins (speech evolved from music) which ultimately bore musicological fruit, but his vastly influential theory of evolution. This would find pride of place in late-Victorian ethnomusicology, music psychology, criticism and analysis. However, in general music histories and histories of national music – where Victorian narrative conventions dictate a type of teleological emplotment missing from Darwin – Darwinian evolution, as a methodological template, remained conspicuous by its absence. There are some notable exceptions, such as Joseph Goddard's *The Rise of Music* (1908), but even this was followed by a more inexplicably conventional history of opera, *The Rise and Development of Opera* (1911).

Developmental simplicity and the music of the early church

While almost entirely speculative, theories of musical origins provided Victorian musicologists with a ready methodology, especially when writing histories for which documentary evidence was scarce. Under the influence of Spencer and the developmental analogy, to say nothing of earlier natural and religious models of musical origins, the very earliest musical forms – like savages – were deemed incomplete, as works in progress, *en route* to completion. Indeed, in the hands of some Victorians, the music of even the most renowned historical cultures – the Egyptians, Hebrews, Greeks, for example – often failed to evolve, or worse still, degenerated.

To greater or lesser extents, the strength of the developmental model is felt in every nineteenth- and early twentieth-century history of Gregorian chant, from 1819, when Thomas Busby wrote *A General History of Music, from the Earliest Times to the Present*, to 1936, when Alfred Einstein published *A Short History of Music*. Busby, like most of those who followed after him, locates the origins of Gregorian chant firmly in Hebrew music, with additional, probable, influences from Roman and Greek (pagan) temples.[20] Unusually for nineteenth-century musicologists, he is reservedly – perhaps frustratingly – unspeculative, simply regretting the absence of historical or musical evidence. Later writers provide increasingly more descriptive gloss, and it is in the gloss that the sheen of developmentalism becomes more visible.

Echoing what would later become a correlative to Spencer's developmental analogy (namely that just as humans progress from savagery to civilization they also progress from simplicity to complexity), Stafford describes early Christian music, tellingly, as 'simple', invoking one of the day's most common ciphers for developmentalism:

> The tunes, however, whether Hebrew, Greek, or Roman, used in the church at this early age, must have been extremely simple, and easy of execution, being sung in chorus, without any preparation, by people who, generally speaking, had not the least idea of music, and who professed, also, in every thing, to observe the greatest simplicity.[21]

Stafford's contemporary, Hogarth, repeats this claim, writing that the music 'probably resembled very much the rude, but frequently grand and imposing music still to be heard in various parts of the East, consisting of very simple strain or melody.'[22] For Hogarth, like Stafford and other developmentalists, simplicity is not, however, merely an indication of developmental position, but an expression of developmental evolution. Thus, for Hogarth, while the music of the Hebrews is simple, their 'history is that of a continual decline.'[23]

These same overlapping patterns of developmentalism continue unabated into the middle of the nineteenth century, insistently, and often subtly, representing Hebrew music as simple and unevolved. In a backhanded compliment, Henry Wylde, author of *Music in Its Art-Mysteries*

20   Thomas Busby, *A General History of Music, from the Earliest Times to the Present; Comprising the Lives of Eminent Composers and Musical Writers* 1 (London: G. and W.B. Whittaker, 1819), 249.
21   Stafford, *A History of Music*, 169–70.
22   Hogarth, *Musical History, Biography, and Criticism*, 6.
23   Ibid.

(1867), praises Jewish worship as 'pure and simple',[24] complaining that its influence marked early Christian music with a 'lack of artistic feeling and the stern asceticism [...] an antagonistic element to the progress of civilization.'[25] Wylde's somewhat later contemporary, John Stainer, spells out his developmentalism more succinctly, and more directly:

> That *monotone*, when used from century to century in the mouth of devout readers, will grow into a *cantillation*, or rude sort of chant, can be proved by the history of our early Church plain-song. Why should not the Hebrews have passed in their days through the same phase of musical development which other nations have done?[26]

This question underlies late Victorian musicology as well. Weber claims that early Christians 'could learn to sing the simple and natural Hebrew melodies, if they did not know them already from childhood',[27] and C. Hubert H. Parry, composer of *Jerusalem*, argues that 'Music was only cultivated by Churchmen and was of the simplest description – confined to melody only, and indefinite in pitch and rhythm.'[28]

Branding Hebrew music as simple, and possibly degenerate, did more than provide Hebrew music with a definition. It also helped to define Gregorian chant as the safeguard and developer of a previously undeveloped, unsystematized, often degraded, musical form. Where Hebrew music was simple and degenerate, later Christian music, was, arguably, more complex and evolved. The French musicologist Alexandre Choron suggests this when he claims that 'even in this state of degradation, it [early Christian music] still retained some constituent rules, and a certain variety in its changes and

24   Henry Wylde, *Music in Its Art-Mysteries* (London: L. Booth, 1867), 113.
25   Ibid., 113–14.
26   John Stainer, *The Music of the Bible, with an Account of the Development of Modern Musical Instruments from Ancient Types* (London: Novello, Ewer & Co., [1879]), 165. Original italics.
27   Friedrich Weber, *A Popular History of Music from the Earliest Times* (London: Simpkin, Marshall, Hamilton, Kent & Co., 1891), 178.
28   C. Hubert H. Parry, *Summary of the History and Development of Mediaeval and Modern European Music* (London: Novello and Co., 1893), 1.

character.'[29] Salvageable despite its origins, chant went native, gradually converting to Christianity and conveniently shedding, or reconstructing, its somewhat undesirable Jewish past. Frederic Ritter summarizes this when he declares that

> There is no doubt, however, that to the musical practice of the Greco-Romans, the Christian singers were far more indebted than to the Jewish musicians. For, whatever melodies might have been derived from these, such melodies were undoubtedly arranged according to the Greek musical theory.[30]

Ritter's contemporary, John Frederick Rowbotham, arrives at the same sentiment, but for different reasons. Rather than treating the history of Gregorian chant as a struggle from savagery to civilization, from simplicity to complexity, he views history as a constantly evolving and revolving epic struggle between man's two natures, the spiritual and intellectual on the one hand, and sensual and emotional on the other:

> And from the first we found two wings, the one inclined to spiritual passion, the other to the beauty of sensuous form, the one with their chants, that were but speech in music, the other with the gay dance, that brought rhythm and tune. And we have seen from the first how there were some men that leaned to one, and some to the other; the melancholy Semites, the happy Aryans, the fervent Hebrews, and the laughing Greeks. And we predicted that a day would come when these two forces should be brought face to face on the stage of the civilised world, and now behold it come! For the Christian and the Pagan are the Hebrew and the Greek; for the Christians, indeed, whose faith came from Judaea, and who for all their early centuries were led by Jewish teachers and apostles, did repeat, though they gave it new birth, the character and tradition of the Jews. And the chants of the Hebrew prophets were heard once more in the world. And now for the time they had conquered.[31]

---

29   Alexandre Choron, 'Summary of the History of Music', in John S. Sainsbury (ed.), *A Dictionary of Musicians from the Earliest Time* 1 (London: Sainsbury and Co., 1825), x.

30   Frederic Louis Ritter, *The History of Music, from the Christian Era to the Present Time* (3rd edn, London: William Reeves, 1892), 32–3.

31   John Frederick Rowbotham, *A History of Music* 3 (London: Trübner, 1887), 159–60.

Although Rowbotham lets the Hebrews win the race, they ultimately lose the battle, for his coda, 'now *for the time* they had conquered', implies, disappointingly, the expectation of degeneration, and with it the suggestion that the Hebrews are inadvertently bequeathing their musical descendants a potentially faulty inheritance, like original sin. Such musical sin is absolved only by conversion into the more structured, disciplined, Christian, Gregorian (or in its earlier incarnation, Ambrosian), chant. Though not overtly deprecating towards Hebrew music, William Rockstro suggests this, when he decries the seemingly irresponsible form of early transmission:

> the Melodies they sang were handed down, from generation to generation, by oral tradition only. Such a method of transmission, continued through long periods of time, must inevitably lead to extensive corruption of the original text, if not to its utter extinction. To remedy the first of these evils, and avert all danger of the second, S. Ambrose, Bishop of Milan, about the year 384, made a general collection of the Melodies then in use; reducing each to the purest attainable form; and laying down a code of technical laws which greatly diminished the risk of future deterioration.[32]

Locating plainchant within Arnoldian theories of Hebraism, Hellenism and the origins of culture

Although enlightened Victorians sought a more balanced understanding of the Jews, the period was rife with anti-Semitism. In addition to more overt, unsubtle expressions of anti-Semitism are rather insidious attempts to pit Jewish scholarship against itself, as in Baden Powell's twisted *Christianity without Judaism* (1857). As well as Oxford academics like Powell, evangeli-

---

32   William S. Rockstro, *A General History of Music, from the Infancy of the Greek Drama to the Present Period* (London: Sampson Low and Co., 1886), 15.

cals joined the bandwagon, especially in times of higher immigration,[33] and, following suit, British left-wingers supplied their own variety of invidious hatred.[34] In this atmosphere theologians were particularly keen to purge Christianity of its Hebraic roots. Ernest Renan's *The Life of Jesus* (1863) is one such example, drawing on a long history of developmental bifurcation delimiting Semitic and Indo-European races as an analogue to savagery and civilization. The Semitic race 'has the glory of having made the religion of humanity [Christianity].'[35] Within the anthropology of race this paradigm is no better articulated than in Matthew Arnold's *Culture and Anarchy* (1869), in his widely debated chapter 'Hebraism and Hellenism'. For Arnold the two qualify as cosmic rivals,

> not by necessity of their own nature, but as exhibited in man and his history, – and rivals dividing the empire of the world between them. And to give these forces names from the two races of men who have supplied the most signal and splendid manifestations of them, we may call them respectively the forces of Hebraism and Hellenism.[36]

Radicalizing contemporary racial terminology, Arnold proposes that 'The governing idea of Hellenism is *spontaneity of consciousness*; that of Hebraism, *strictness of conscience*.'[37] Cultural theorist Robert Young contemns these words as

> antithetical, centripetal and centrifugal [...] Hebraism involves a strict contraction of consciousness, while Hellenism produces its expansive free play, thus reproducing in subverting and containing, forward at work in society and history at large.[38]

33   William I. Brustein, *Roots of Hate: Anti-Semitism in Europe before the Holocaust* (Cambridge: Cambridge University Press, 2003), 88–9.

34   W.D. Rubinstein, *A History of the Jews in the English-Speaking World: Great Britain* (Studies in Modern History; Basingstoke: Macmillan, 1996), 112–13.

35   Ernest Renan (trans. Charles E. Wilbour), *The Life of Jesus* (London, 1863); see <http://www.infidels.org/library/historical/ernest_renan/life_of_jesus.html>, accessed 27 Sept. 2007.

36   Matthew Arnold, *Culture and Anarchy* (New York: Macmillan Co., 1936; originally published 1869), 128–9.

37   Ibid., 131. Original italics.

38   Robert Young, *Colonial Desire: Hybridity in Theory, Culture and Race* (2nd edn, London and New York: Routledge, 2003), 61.

Jonathan Freedman echoes this, when he characterizes Arnold's Hebraism as 'a single-minded Puritanism that must find correction by a Greek-inspired suppleness.'[39] Certainly Arnold promotes an extreme form of distinction:

> The uppermost idea with Hellenism is to see things as they really are; the uppermost idea with Hebraism is conduct and obedience. Nothing can do away with this ineffaceable difference. The Greek quarrel with the body and its desires is, that they hinder right thinking; the Hebrew quarrel with them is, that they hinder right […] Hebraism seizes upon certain plain, capital intimations of the universal order, and rivets itself, one may say, with unequalled grandeur of earnestness and intensity on the study and observance of them, the bent of Hellenism is to follow, with flexible activity, the whole play of the universal order, to be apprehensive of missing any part of it, of sacrificing one part to another, to slip away from resting in this or that intimation of it, however capital. An unclouded clearness of mind, and unimpeded play of thought, is what this bent drives at.[40]

Nonetheless, Arnold's bifurcation is remarkably unclear, and even Young is forced to admit that its seemingly dialectical stance weakens at the seams when probed for evidence of conceptual hybridity. Indeed, although Arnold projects a bluntly dialectical campaign of words, his historiographical concerns belie a more synthetic attitude. Arnold is quite specific on this account. When writing about human development, for instance, he indicates adamantly that the Hebrew/Hellene bifurcation is not an immutably teleological developmental model, but an admittedly loaded anthropological analogy:

> the evolution of these forces, separately and in themselves, is not the whole evolution of humanity, – their single history is not the whole history of man; whereas their admirers are always apt to make it stand for the whole history. Hebraism and Hellenism are, neither of them, the *law* of human development, – as their admirers are prone to make them; they are, each of them, *contributions* to human development.[41]

---

39 Jonathan Freedman, *The Temple of Culture: Assimilation and Anti-Semitism in Literary Anglo-America* (New York: Oxford University Press, 2000), 18.
40 Arnold, *Culture and Anarchy*, 130–31.
41 Ibid., 137. Original italics.

Thus, although the influence of Hebraism and Hellenism occurs within history, they are not diachronically fixed in a linear developmental sequence. Arnold intimates this when he describes their influence as malleable and cyclical, suggesting that history 'passes and repasses from Hellenism to Hebraism.'[42] The fact that, for Arnold, history passes and repasses does not exonerate him from the criticism of anti-Semitism, but it might absolve him of some of its greater evils. Although Lloyd Davies dismisses him simply as Jew-sneering,[43] Arnold is much more complex than that, because of the multi-dimensional nature of his construction. For David DeLaura, for example, Arnold aims at a new interpretation of life with a series of dualisms (feeling and thought; duty and desire, and so on) reinvigorating the individual and the culture in which he exists. Arnold's dualism is a mode of transcendence, not a mode of development,[44] his anti-Semitism vertical rather than horizontal.

Stephen Prickett takes issue with this idea, claiming that Arnold's distinction 'is less a picturesque balancing of terms than part of a long-term programme for hellenizing, or, better still, "indo-europeanizing" established Christianity.'[45] Indeed, for Prickett, and many others, Arnold seems as determined to reinvigorate Christianity as to overcome it. The more generalized reading of this agenda depicts the Jew as vestigial and atavistic, yet crucial to Hegel's christianizing historical programme.[46] More simplistically, what might lie behind Arnold's representations of the Hebrew and Hellene is, in some ways, a function of a much earlier controversy, the Christian 'usurpation myth', or the idea that Christians ousted the Jews from

42   Ibid., 135.
43   Lloyd Davies, 'Halakhic Romanticism: Wordsworth, the Rabbis, and Torah', in Sheila A. Spector (ed.), *British Romanticism and the Jews: History, Culture, Literature* (New York and Basingstoke: Palgrave Macmillan, 2002), 64.
44   David J. DeLaura, *Hebrew and Hellene in Victorian England: Newman, Arnold, and Pater* (Austin, TX and London: University of Texas Press, 1969), 167.
45   Stephen Prickett, 'Purging Christianity of its Semitic Origins: Kingsley, Arnold and the Bible', in Juliet John and Alice Jenkins (eds), *Rethinking Victorian Culture* (Basingstoke: Macmillan, 2000), 66.
46   Sander Gilman, *Difference and Pathology: Stereotypes of Sexuality, Race, and Madness* (Ithaca, NY: Cornell University Press, 1985), 150–62 and 191–216.

divine election.[47] The usurpation myth, perpetuated by conflict between the founding Jerusalem church and the Pauline church, was enshrined in gospel polemics and their later authoritative redactions. Believers embraced the myth as gospel truth, sowing the seeds for the likes of Matthew Arnold some 1,800 years later. Prickett intimates this when he and many others talk of Arnold 'purging Christianity of its Semitic origins', and certainly Arnold himself leaves no doubt in his reader's mind, as he says in *On the Study of Celtic Literature* (1867):

> The modern spirit tends more and more to establish a sense of native diversity between our European bent and the Semitic bent, and to eliminate, even in our religion, certain elements, as purely and excessively Semitic, and therefore, in right, not combinable with our European nature, not assimilable by it.[48]

Anti-Semitism and the Arnoldian paradigm in Victorian histories of chant

The psychology of eradication driving Arnold's and other Victorians' sentiments is as complex as the sentiments themselves. For Freedman,

> the figure of the Jew embodied a weirdly persistent paradox, in which the Jew was not only linked to something deeply problematic about culture, but also seen as integrally connected to its very operation. Although frequently installed as culture's debased other, the Jew is oddly, perhaps even scandalously, perceived as being its hidden truth.[49]

---

47 Hyam Maccoby, *A Pariah People: The Anthropology of Antisemitism* (London: Constable, 1996), 93.

48 Matthew Arnold, *On the Study of Celtic Literature* (1867), in Robert H. Super (ed.), *The Complete Prose Works of Matthew Arnold* 3: *Lectures and Essays in Criticism* (Ann Arbor: University of Michigan Press, 1962), 301.

49 Freedman, *The Temple of Culture*, 18.

In Victorian histories of Gregorian chant this hidden truth is at times a source of consternation, and at other times proof of a developmental project. When Henry Wylde praises Hebrew music, he also disparages its other arts, grudgingly accepting chant's Semitic history, but allowing for no other aesthetic influence:

> The pictorial and architectural characteristics of Jewish worship were wholly ignored by the founders of the primitive church of Christianity; but the immortal lyrics of 'the sweet singer of Israel' were in constant use amongst them.[50]

Renan's *The History of the People of Israel* (1887–93) perpetuates a similar attitude, as Prickett suggests, in which Jewish material culture is widely deprecated:[51] 'Outside their religion, the Jews had neither politics, art, philosophy or science; the very nature of their language made abstraction unknown and metaphysics impossible.'[52]

More importantly, when Rowbotham speaks of man's struggle to resolve his two natures, it reveals the strength of Arnold's Hebrew/Hellenic paradigm in the context of Victorian musicology. Rowbotham may as well be quoting Arnold *verbatim* when, as we have seen, he writes that

> from the first we found two wings, the one inclined to spiritual passion, the other to the beauty of sensuous form, the one with their chants, that were but speech in music, the other with the gay dance, that brought rhythm and tune. And we have seen from the first how there were some men that leaned to one, and some to the other; the melancholy Semites, the happy Aryans, the fervent Hebrews, and the laughing Greeks [...] For the Christian and the Pagan are the Hebrew and the Greek.[53]

Henry Tipper, author of *Music and Its Growth in Oriental, Christian & Renaissance Periods* (published before 1902), echoes this, saying that

50   Wylde, *Music in Its Art-Mysteries*, 113.
51   See Prickett, 'Purging Christianity of its Semitic Origins', 72.
52   Frederic E. Faverty, *Matthew Arnold the Ethnologist* (Evanston, Il: Northwestern University Press, 1951; repr. New York: AMS Press, 1968), 169.
53   Rowbotham, *A History of Music* 3, 159.

The History of the Hebrew, incomparably more than any other, has been counted worthy of the highest efforts of musical expression. His suffering and consolation, his triumph and despair, have been wrought into the minds of millions as an abiding spiritual force, both by the imperishable nature of his supreme moral power and intense genius, and by the nobly sustained interest of the great musicians, who have, with sublime song and epic, followed his efforts from the period of his sojourn in Egypt until the agonizing moment of the eclipse of his glory upon the cross at Cavalry.[54]

Nineteenth-century histories of Gregorian chant, which encapsulate this kind of self-conflict embedded within a developmental paradigm, generally occur only where Semitic music is transformed into Gregorian (earlier, Ambrosian) chant. Of these the majority deprecate their Semitic origins, using the racist language of developmentalism (e.g. Busby, Stafford, Wylde, Stainer, Weber) or its more subtly evolved dialectical form in Arnold (e.g. Rowbotham, Tipper). There are exceptions, however. For example, some histories locate Semitic origins in ways which do not lead ineluctably to completion in Gregorian chant. These seem to gather representation as the century progresses, gradually shedding racist developmental currents. First amongst these, though not originally in English, is Kiesewetter's influential *History of Modern Music of Western Europe, from the First Century of the Christian Era to the Present Day* (1848). Kiesewetter proposes, extraordinarily, that early Christian music developed spontaneously, because Christians would have eschewed Greek music as heathen and abandoned Hebrew influences as Jewish recidivism.[55]

Somewhat later, this idea would resurface in the work of the organologist and proto-ethnomusicologist Carl Engel, author of numerous books on ancient and national music. Favouring the origin of Gregorian chant in

---

54   H. Tipper, *Music and Its Growth in Oriental, Christian & Renaissance Periods; Together with Chapters on the Greater Tone Poets* (London: William Reeves [before 1902]), 19.

55   Raphael G. Kiesewetter (trans. Robert Müller), *History of Modern Music of Western Europe, from the First Century of the Christian Era to the Present Day, with Examples, and an Appendix, Explanatory of the Theory of the Ancient Greek Music* (London: T.C. Newby, 1848), 3–4.

Hebrew music, Engel reiterates the anti-Greek half of Kiesewetter's theory, writing in *The Music of the Most Ancient Nations* (1864):

> The apostles were Hebrews, accustomed from their childhood to the usages of their nation, and must have been practised in the music which they had been in the habit of using in worship before they became Christians. And it is not likely that the primitive Christians would have adopted in their worships the musical performances of idolators to which they were naturally averse.[56]

To support his claim, however, Engel invokes cultural analogies tellingly close to those found in Arnold's *The Study of Celtic Literature*.

Under the subheading 'Eastern Origin of Our Own Music', Engel compares – rather than contrasts – musical cultures across time:

> We have seen that the pentatonic scale actually exists at present in Europe in the music of some Celtic nations. We have found several names of our musical instruments to be of Asiatic origin. Further, in our Christian Church the intoning, chanting, and antiphonal singing are, in all probability, remains of the ancient Hebrew mode of performing in the Temple.[57]

Even Ritter implies this, when he proffers a relationship between Gregorian chant and folksong. Although modern European art music is 'ruled by entirely different laws from those of the Oriental nations',[58] Gregorian chant retains the implicitly pentatonic structure of folksong, thus being 'at once distinct from any previous effort of temple [Oriental] music.'[59]

The same attitude can be found late in the Victorian period, in Donovan's somewhat rambling *From Lyre to Muse* (1890), although Arnold's paradigm is translated into a northern/southern divide in the same way that Renan, in *The Life of Jesus*, places Jesus in a Judaism conceptually divided into Galilean (northern/Aryan) and Judean (southern/Semitic).

56   Carl Engel, *The Music of the Most Ancient Nations, Particularly of the Assyrians, Egyptians, and Hebrews; with Special Reference to Recent Discoveries in Western Asia and in Egypt* (London: John Murray, 1864), 358–9.
57   Ibid., 358.
58   Ritter, *The History of Music*, 63.
59   Ibid.

For Donovan, as arguably for Renan, what matters is the northern/Aryan connection; its southern/Semitic origins are of no concern:

> Of course, where the Gregorian chant originated, whether among the Egyptians, Hebrews, or Greeks, there is nothing to oppose, but everything to support the belief that it originated in the natural way. But what is pointed out here is, that when it reached the Northern people it was raised far above the spontaneous stage of evolution. It was drawn into relationship with very high and dignified language, whilst the mental status of the Northern people was yet only fitted for the spontaneous stage of religious song.[60]

Conclusion

As these examples show, most Victorian histories of Gregorian chant reveal traits of the Arnoldian paradigm, whether or not subscribing to anti-Semitic developmentalism. Indeed, such was the strength of this paradigm that even as late as the 1920s, Cecil Gray could write that

> Western European music has been able to develop peacefully and autonomously along its own lines, uninfluenced by the tyrannic [*sic*] prestige of ancient precedents and undisturbed by the seductive glamour of exotic cultural traditions [...] there is no denying the fact that however admirable the actual artistic achievement of the Greeks may have been, its influence upon modern art has frequently been pernicious in the extreme.[61]

Yet why is this? Why does Gray, and others like him throughout the Victorian period, characterize music in such grossly simplified, bifurcated, terms? What happened to change this view? And what difference did this change make?

60　J. Donovan, *From Lyre to Muse: A History of the Aboriginal Union of Music and Poetry* (London: Kegan Paul, Trench, Trübner, & Co., 1890), 160.

61　Cecil Gray, *The History of Music* (London: Kegan Paul, Trench, Trübner & Co. Ltd, 1928), 8.

As we have seen, the Victorians saw the world in largely developmental terms. These were enshrined in the Spencerian developmental analogy, and although eventually debunked by Darwinian evolutionism, they remained entrenched in general and national histories of music well after the rise of Darwinism. In studies of musical origins, the developmental model stuck, and along these lines bifurcated notions of musical origins were formed, thence influencing histories tracing the origins of Gregorian chant. Fed by currents of anti-Semitism, these notions mapped perfectly onto bifur-cated notions of a Hebrew/Hellenic divide, codified in the middle of the century in Matthew Arnold's *Culture and Anarchy*, and these, in turn, melded seamlessly into a fixed, although infinitely malleable, Victorian musicological ideology.

What happened to change this view? The answer may well lie in the phraseology Cecil Forsyth uses in *A History of Music* (1916); that is, in addi-tion to the fact that Hebrew music formed the basis of Gregorian chant,

> Hebrew melodies were continually altered and adapted to suit local require-ments. Hence we find them to-day in many forms with rather wide differences. Some such process of change and adaptation may have been sanctioned by the first Christians.[62]

The words of particular importance in this quotation are 'continually altered and adapted to suit local requirements' and 'process of change and adap-tation' – in other words the very clear language of Darwinian evolution-ism, *not* Spencerian developmentalism. Darwin had finally penetrated, in a serious way, the language of Victorian music historiography. There are other examples from around this time, as we have already intimated – Joseph Goddard, for example, in *The Rise of Music* (1908). Goddard looks at Hebrew music as 'an embryological music in which melody and regular accentuation are nascent'[63] and projects it as a starting point in evolution-ary movement – which he titles 'The Continuity of Art During the Early Centuries of the Christian Era'.

62   Charles Villiers Stanford and Cecil Forsyth, *A History of Music* (London: Macmillan, 1916), 22.
63   Joseph Goddard, *The Rise of Music* (London: William Reeves, 1908), 49.

What difference did evolution make? For Goddard, Stanford and other evolutionists, Hebrew music, like all music, had only the properties of a species evolving. It did not have fixed innate developmental properties, but the infinitely adjustable properties of evolutionary process: change, adaptation, descent with modification, and so on. Of course, this does not mean that evolutionism necessarily assuaged anti-Semitism – far from it. What it did do, however, was to provide an historiographical model which satisfactorily rejected predetermined ideological convictions of the likes of Arnold. In debunking anti-Semitism, it offered an alternative anti-ursurpation view of chant origins, a Hebrew music without the teleological *necessity* of Christian 'completion'. No longer was Jewish alterity a Christian prerequisite. Indeed, without this developmental prerequisite, anti-Semitism in histories of plainchant declined and a new ideologically unconstrained methodology emerged. The old certainties of Victorian conviction were gone, and with them the antiquated histories of musicological prejudice. Plainchant had a new lease of life, and it would not be long before its history would be written anew, questioning the very basis of its Hebraic origins.

THOMAS E. MUIR

Catholic Church Music in England: The 1950s

The conservative status quo

Superficially, the outstanding characteristic of Catholic church music in England during the 1950s was its conservatism. In many places the repertoire was virtually the same as in the 1930s; and this, in turn, had been defined by the consensus that had emerged by the 1900s. For example, 114 out of 127 pre-1962 publications surviving at Our Lady and St Michael's Church, Alston Lane, on the boundary between industrial and rural Lancashire near Preston, were printed before 1950.[1] At Our Lady of Mount Carmel, an inner-city parish in Liverpool, the figure is forty-four out of forty-six.[2] Not surprisingly, the bulk of their repertoire predates the Second World War. Except for sixty-three Gelineau psalm settings, only twelve out of 369 compositions at Alston Lane were written by composers active after 1950, while at Mount Carmel, the figure is four out of sixty-six. Even at Stonyhurst, the great Lancashire Jesuit boarding school, only twenty-two of the 1,071 pieces purchased between 1901 and 1962 fall into this category,

---

1   See Thomas Muir, 'Music at the church of Our Lady and St Michael, Alston Lane, near Preston, 1857–1962', *North West Catholic History* 33 (2006), 71–80 (at p.72). These figures apply to sheet music only. They do not extend to the contents of hymnals, Benediction manuals or liturgical books.
2   See Muir, 'Music at the church of Our Lady of Mount Carmel, Liverpool, *c*1860–1962', *North West Catholic History* 34 (2007); also Muir, *Roman Catholic Church Music in England, 1791–1914: A Handmaid of the Liturgy?* (Aldershot: Ashgate, 2008), 29.

despite the fact that forty-six out of 116 publications there were purchased between 1951 and 1962.[3]

The significance of such figures is highlighted by the behaviour of the major publishers. For example, 332 out of 1,343 pre-1962 publications in the library of the Church Music Association (CMA), a breakaway offshoot from the Society of St Gregory (SSG) established in the 1950s, are reprints of editions prepared before 1914. In every case the typeface is identical, the only differences being revamped dust-jackets, some alterations to music lists on the back, and a reference to the 1956 Copyright Act. Thus, not only did the repertoire remain static, so too did performance styles, since musicians would still have been following directions inserted by the original editors.

Such patterns were not just symptomatic of inertia, they were the consequence of archaizing trends that had gathered pace during the late nineteenth century, especially with the greater attention paid to plainchant and Renaissance polyphony. This was in sharp contrast with the interest in the latest trends displayed by English Catholics, not just in the early nineteenth century, but in the 1960s and 1970s after the Second Vatican Council.

Any appreciation of the 1950s scene therefore depends on a clear understanding of what had been inherited from the 1900s. Broadly speaking, this can be divided into four parts: plainchant, Renaissance polyphony, music developed from London embassy chapel traditions of the late eighteenth and early nineteenth centuries, and material composed for extra-liturgical devotions.

Plainchant

In the 1950s plainchant was sung in the style defined by the abbey of Solesmes. This stemmed from the papal decision in 1901 not to renew the monopoly over plainchant books held by Pustet, whose publications used

3   See Muir, 'Music at the church of Our Lady and St Michael', 73, and 'Music at the church of Our Lady of Mount Carmel'; also Muir, '"Full in the Panting Heart of Rome": Roman Catholic Church Music in England, 1850–1962', PhD thesis, University of Durham, 2004, 516, 528.

the 'measured' plainchant developed from the late Middle Ages onwards. Instead, under the *motu proprio, Col nostro,* of 1904, Pius X promoted the Solesmes method in the newly commissioned Vatican Typical editions of plainchant. Its chief characteristics are: (1) the principle of a single, undivided note-length; (2) rapid tempi, two-to-three times as fast as with measured chant; and (3) understated dynamics, again in sharp contrast with the heavy martellato style associated with measured chant.

Such plainchant was vigorously promoted across England during the 1930s, especially through schools. A principal agency was the SSG, founded in 1929 by Bernard McElligott. In 1931 and 1934, the SSG published *Plainsong for Schools*, in two parts, which were reprinted several times after 1945.[4] The SSG also held annual summer schools and in the 1930s even set plainchant examinations. Music teachers in Catholic schools across Liverpool archdiocese were expected to take such papers and their work was regularly inspected.[5]

The success of such campaigns was never more than partial. For a start, the essentially monastic character of Solesmes chant was not necessarily suited to a parish environment. Solesmes's plainchant notation, far more complex than the three basic note symbols used in measured chant, was alienating, and its arcane inaccessibility was compounded by arguments over performance styles among protagonists of the method.

Essentially there were two systems.[6] The first, found in the Vatican *Kyriale, Graduale,* and *Antiphonale,* was that advocated by Joseph Pothier. Taking his cue from the mantra 'sing the chant as you speak', he argued that plainchant should follow the rhythm of the text. Opposed to him was the practice advocated by André Mocquereau, and found in most of the

---

4   [Dominic Willson], *Plainsong for Schools: Masses and Occasional Chants* (Liverpool: Rushwoth and Dreaper; Paris, Tournai and Rome: Desclée, 1931, repr. 1948, 1961); *Plainsong for Schools* 2: *Masses and Occasional Chants* (Liverpool: Rushwoth and Dreaper; Paris, Tournai, Rome: Desclée, 1934, repr. 1958).

5   See Muir, 'Full in the Panting Heart of Rome', 205–7.

6   For a detailed account of the evolution of the two systems and the competition between them in the 1900s, see Katherine Bergeron, *Decadent Enchantments: The Revival of Gregorian Chant at Solesmes* (Berkeley and Los Angeles: University of California Press, 1998), 17–20, 101–28, 144–68.

Desclée-Solesmes editions circulating after 1905. This system was mainly worked out by Mocquereau while the Solesmes community was living on the Isle of Wight between 1901 and 1923. Consequently, it acquired an immediate foothold in England. His starting point was the concept of 'Arsis-Thesis'. Plainchant consisted of groups of two to three notes characterized by an initial 'impulse' followed by a 'relaxation' signalled by vertical and horizontal 'episema', or lines, placed above the notes. Such impulses were given through changes in pitch, dynamics, articulation, tempi and a slight lengthening or shortening of notes. Moreover, the Arsis-Thesis system applied not just to individual note groups, but to whole phrases, and indeed across the whole piece. Mocquereau therefore advocated a rhythmic equivalent to the Schenkerian concept of a 'foreground', 'middleground' and 'background' in plainchant analysis.[7] Its principal effect was to set up tensions between textual and musical rhythms. According to his supporters, this was a primary virtue in his method, but for the uninitiated, it probably made plainchant more difficult to sing.

Nevertheless, despite such problems, by the 1950s Mocquereau's method had become predominant. A key factor was Desclée's vast output of affordable volumes. For example, every seminary student at Ushaw College, near Durham, was given a copy of its 1950 edition of the *Liber Usualis*.[8] Its cachet was further endorsed by Decca LP recordings of the Solesmes monks under the direction of Dom Joseph Gajard, Mocquereau's pupil. Mocquereau's system was also used in *Plainsong for Schools*, and further support came from the English Benedictine Congregation (EBC). From the 1890s to the 1950s Stanbrook Abbey, led by Dame Laurentia McLachlan, was a major proponent of this style. Her *A Grammar of Plainsong*, first published in 1905 after close consultation with Mocquereau, was in its fourth edition by 1962.[9] Even before 1914, it had been instrumental in pushing the archdiocese of Birmingham into the Mocquereau camp. Support also

7   See Muir, *Roman Catholic Church Music in England*, 203–4.
8   I owe this information to Hugh Lindsey, the retired bishop of Hexham and Newcastle, who was a student at Ushaw during that time.
9   Benedictines of Stanbrook [Laurentia McLachlan], *A Grammar of Plainsong* (Worcester: Stanbrook Abbey; London: Burns and Oates; New York: Benziger, 1905, repr. 1926, 1934, 1962).

came from Downside Abbey, where Alphege Shebbeare, Anselm Dean (a Solesmes monk from Quarr), and Gregory Murray (who changed his mind in the 1950s) were active. Yet Mocquereau's dominance was never absolute. For example, despite the efforts of Justin Field, Dominicans and Cistercians used plainchant books without Mocquereau's 'rhythmic signs'.[10]

Renaissance polyphony

English interest in Renaissance polyphony was the result of its revival from the mid-nineteenth century onwards. As such it went through three major phases. The first began with the tentative interest shown by Vincent Novello and Samuel Wesley in the 1810s, notably with the former's publication, *Fitzwilliam Music*.[11] In the 1840s and 1850s this was picked up by ultra-montanes, notably Nicholas Wiseman, cardinal archbishop of Westminster, John Moore Capes, editor of *Selections from the works of Palestrina, 'Prince of Music'*, and James Burns, founder of the publishing company Burns and Oates. Burns's first partner was Sir John Lambert, editor of a wide range of plainchant publications. Ultramontane interest in Renaissance polyphony therefore developed in tandem with plainchant. This is hardly surprising. Renaissance composers often used plainchant motifs; notationally and stylistically, measured plainchant was much closer to Renaissance polyphony than Solesmes chant; and besides, Palestrina had played a major part in its Roman development. Renaissance polyphony, then, was directly associated with the glory days of Counter-Reformation Rome and, through its ties with plainchant, indirectly connected with its medieval heritage. As with plainchant, from an ultramontane perspective it was a useful device for promoting 'Roman' ways of doing things in England.[12]

10   See Muir, *Roman Catholic Church Music in England*, 219.

11   See Philip Olleson and Fiona Palmer, 'Publishing music from the Fitzwilliam Museum, Cambridge: The work of Vincent Novello and Samuel Wesley in the 1820s', *Journal of the Royal Musicological Association* 130 (2005), 38–73.

12   See Muir, '"Old Wine in New Bottles": Renaissance Polyphony in the English Catholic Church during the Nineteenth and Early Twentieth Centuries', *Nineteenth-Century Music Review* 4 (2007), 81–7.

The second phase of the revival began with the foundation of the German Society of St Cecilia by Franz Xaver Witt in 1867. Branches were quickly established across the Catholic world, notably in the USA and Ireland, and it was from there that they spread to England, especially through the seminaries. Of these the most important was Oscott, near Birmingham, where Wiseman had been rector.

Cecilians did three things. First, under the aegis of Franz Xaver Haberl, a complete range of plainchant volumes was produced by the firm of Friedrich Pustet from 1870 onwards. Second, they promoted the revival of Renaissance polyphonic works. Haberl, for example, was responsible for complete editions of all the known works of Palestrina, as well as all the sacred compositions by Lassus. As such, he built on work undertaken by Pietro Alfieri, Caspar Ett, and Carl Proske. Indeed, some of the latter's volumes in the *Musica Divina Sive Concentuum Selectissimum* series were still on sale in England during the 1900s.[13] Haberl's work also shows that, as with the English ultramontanes, plainchant and Renaissance polyphony were connected in the Cecilian mindset.

Third, Cecilians produced quantities of imitative Renaissance polyphonic compositions. Many of these circulated in Britain. For example, Edwin Bonney, choirmaster at Ushaw between 1899 and 1917, possessed several bound volumes containing works by at least forty Cecilian composers, including works by Johann Molitor and Witt from Germany, Lorenzo Perosi from Rome, John Singenberger from the US, and Joseph Smith and Joseph Seymour from Ireland. Equally striking, though, was the almost complete disappearance of such repertoire after the First World War – apart from some new editions of Perosi's Masses by Ricordi in the late 1940s. This may have been due to their allegedly poor quality, but equally important may have been the disintegration of the German music publishing industry, or at any rate its ability to penetrate the English market, as a result of the two world wars.[14]

---

13   This is recommended in Episcopal Commission on Ecclesiastical Music, *List of Church Music approved for use in the diocese* [of Salford] (Salford: Diocese of Salford, 1904), 20.

14   See Muir, 'Full in the Panting Heart of Rome', 485–7, 574–5.

Almost simultaneously, the close association between Renaissance polyphony and plainchant was weakened by the adoption of the Solesmes method with its radically different idiom, notation system and performance style.[15] Nevertheless, thanks to the work of Sir Richard Terry, such setbacks did not spell the end of the Renaissance polyphonic revival in England. From 1897 to 1901, and 1901 to 1923, Terry worked at Downside Abbey and Westminster Cathedral. The latter in particular became a showcase for a mass of rediscovered works, several of which Terry made more widely available to English Catholics through his editions in the *Downside Masses*, *Downside Motets*, *Polyphonic Motets*, and *Tudor Motets* series in the 1900s and 1930s. Most of these remained on sale throughout the 1950s.[16]

Terry did not just expand the range of Renaissance polyphonic compositions; he gave it a new twist. Hitherto, due to its association with ultramontane tendencies, the emphasis had been on Continental – and preferably Roman – composers. Terry paid equal attention to their English counterparts, especially Byrd, Tallis, and Phillips. Ideologically, this had a double implication. Terry denied the Anglican-inspired assumption that such composers represented the beginnings of a uniquely English tradition; instead he claimed they belonged to an international Catholic culture. In other words, one could be Catholic *and* English. In this way any tendency, encouraged by ultramontanism, to regard Catholics as purveyors of an alien foreign culture was finessed.

Like many Cecilians, Terry was also significant as a composer. Indeed his Masses and some of his motets, especially his settings for Holy Week, remained standard Catholic fare throughout the 1950s. As such he built on attempts by other composers, including some Cecilians, to marry Renaissance polyphonic styles with more modern techniques, a notable example being William Sewell's *Mass of St Philip Neri*, which was still being sung during the 1950s.[17] In turn this fitted in with Terry's promotion of a limited number of new works by professional composers, including some by

---

15   See Muir, 'Old Wine in New Bottles', 97–8.
16   See Muir (as n.15), 90–4.
17   Sewell's setting of *Alma Redemptoris Mater* was also sung at Westminster Cathedral on a number of occasions between 1949 and 1954; see Muir, 'Full in the Panting Heart of

non-Catholics, with a Tudor or plainchant inflexion. The most notable example of this was Vaughan Williams's *Mass in G Minor*. This pattern was picked up by George Malcolm and Colin Mawby at Westminster Cathedral after 1945 with the introduction of works such as Benjamin Britten's *Missa Brevis*, Edmund Rubbra's *Missa In Honorem Sancta Dominici*, and Lennox Berkeley's *Missa Brevis* and *Mass for Five Voices*.[18]

Terry's work was paralleled and continued, in the first instance, by William Sewell and Henry Collins at the Birmingham Oratory. Both produced dyeline editions of Renaissance polyphonic works, many of which found their way into the *Latin Church Music of the Polyphonic Schools* series published by J. and W. Chester. These were added to by Henry Washington, choirmaster at St Chad's Cathedral, Birmingham and the London Oratory after 1945. Further additions were made in the 1960s by Bruno Turner. At the same time, as the contents of the CMA collection illustrate, Catholics did not hesitate to use non-Catholic editions of Latin Renaissance works, especially OUP's *Tudor Church Music* and items edited by Edmund Fellowes in Stainer and Bell's *Church Choir Library* series. Here, as in so much else, they followed patterns that are clearly discernible in the 1930s, if not before.[19]

Finally, it should be remarked that during the 1950s Westminster Cathedral again became a showcase for Renaissance polyphonic performances, something that had never really been abandoned between the wars by Lancelot Long, who was Terry's successor. What was particularly interesting, however, was the highly distinctive sound, due to Malcolm's unusual approach to voice production – something he probably learned from Fr John Driscoll, choirmaster at the Sacred Heart Church, Wimbledon, in the 1930s. Malcolm focused on voices as they were, rather than attempting to reduce them to a standard uniformity; no attempt was made to eliminate 'chest' notes, and singers were encouraged to think in terms of whole phrases rather than individual clusters of notes. The total effect was one

---

Rome', filter on the database, table 'Westminster Cathedral' listing music advertised
for performance in monthly issues of the *Westminster Cathedral Chronicle*.

18   See Muir, 'Full in the Panting Heart of Rome', 245–56, 366–84.

19   See Muir, 'Full in the Panting Heart of Rome', 363–4; also Muir, 'Old Wine in New
Bottles', 95.

of chiselled power, discipline and wide-ranging dynamics – qualities still discernible in recordings of the same choir under the direction of James O'Donnell in the 1990s.[20]

Embassy chapel music and its successors

The great rival to Renaissance polyphony was music that had its origins in the repertoire performed in the London embassy chapels maintained by the Catholic powers in the late eighteenth and early nineteenth centuries. Apart from plainchant, this had two main strands: first, there was a native tradition of straightforward practical Masses and motets established by Samuel Webbe the elder and Vincent Novello. In later decades this was continued by composers such as John Richardson at Liverpool's Pro-Cathedral, Monsignor John Crookall at the seminary of St Edmunds, Ware, and Francis M. de Zulueta, SJ, at Corpus Christi Church, Bournemouth, in the 1890s and 1900s. Webbe's works, originally published in *A Collection of Motetts and Antiphons* and *A Collection of Sacred Music*, were reprinted by Thomas Boosey in several editions from the 1820s onwards into the twentieth century and in Cary's *Motets Ancient and Modern* series begun in the 1890s. As such, they remained available in the 1950s. Likewise, Vincent Novello's anthem arrangement of *Adeste Fideles* remained a standard staple with Catholic choirs at Christmas right up until Vatican II, as did Richardson's *Improperia* on Good Fridays.

The second strand began with a repertoire of grand Continental Masses associated with Haydn and Mozart and continued by composers such as Hummel, Weber, Gounod and Kalliwoda. English composers, notably Frederick George Nixon and Joseph Egbert Turner, OSB, added their quota too. Indeed Masses by the latter can be found in almost any old Catholic collection. While most of these works were intended for performance with an orchestra, organ realizations by Vincent Novello made them readily available to Catholic parishes. A further boost came after 1849, when Novello's son, Joseph Alfred Novello, produced the first of his

20   See Muir, 'Full in the Panting Heart of Rome', 361, 573–4, 578–9.

Cheap Musical Classics series. The key here was the replacement of engraving by a superior form of musical type. This, along with the development of lithography, enabled much longer print runs to be produced, thereby slashing the price and putting individual copies into the hands of every choir member. As a result, music in this style remained the dominant form throughout the nineteenth century.[21]

This pattern was reversed in the 1900s as a result of ultramontane and Cecilian pressure group activity culminating in Pius X's *motu proprio*, *Tra le sollecitudini*, of 1903. Among other things this attacked the allegedly secular operatic overtones associated with such 'modern' styles and stated that orchestral instruments could only be used in church with special permission from the bishop. In any case, the growth in the size of organs made it increasingly difficult to achieve a satisfactory balance with the limited number of orchestral instruments that were generally available at parish level. Nevertheless, much of this repertoire remained in use during the 1950s, especially the shorter plainer items which were less likely to fall foul of strictures against secular operatic vocal display.[22]

Music for extra-liturgical devotions

Music for extra-liturgical devotions grew rapidly during the nineteenth century, a natural consequence of the rising popularity of such services over that period. Except in monastic communities, this occurred at the expense of the Office. Consequently, at parish level there was a shift from psalm chants – many of them borrowed from the Anglicans – to vernacular hymnody and music for Benediction, the most widespread of all such devotions.[23]

21   See Philip Olleson, 'The London Roman Catholic Embassy Chapels and their music in the Eighteenth and Early Nineteenth Centuries', in David Wyn Jones (ed.), *Music in Eighteenth-Century Britain* (Aldershot: Ashgate, 2006), 101–18; see also Michael Hurd, *Vincent Novello and Company* (London: Granada, 1981), 50–2, 104–5; Muir, 'Full in the Panting Heart of Rome', 215–16, 479–84.

22   See Muir, 'Full in the Panting Heart of Rome', 526–9, 553–4, 571–3, 576–8, 597–8.

23   See Mary Heimann, *Catholic Devotion in Victorian England* (Oxford: Clarendon Press, 1995), 42, 178–82; also Muir, 'Full in the Panting Heart of Rome', 488–9, 517–19.

In England the principal musical texts for Benediction were the *O Salutaris*, the Litany and the *Tantum ergo*, an aspect first clearly identifiable in *A Collection of Music suitable for the rite of Benediction*, edited by Charles Newsham and revised by John Richardson in the early 1860s.[24] It was only a short step to group these into what was called a 'Benediction Service', early examples being the twenty settings provided in part three of the *Crown of Jesus Music*, edited by Henri Hemy. This first came out in 1864, and was the first Catholic hymnal to achieve a national circulation. As such it remained on sale into the 1890s, and copies were still used by some Catholic parishes in the 1950s.

Much Benediction music was written by British composers. Moreover, the regular metre of the *O Salutaris* and *Tantum ergo* texts encouraged borrowing from the hymn tune repertoire. The predominant form of such music therefore came to be block four-part harmony, with chants supplied for the central portion of the Litany.

During the 1930s the repertoire was consolidated, and it was in this guise that an essentially pre-1914 tradition was transmitted to Catholics in the 1950s. Two publications are outstanding: the *Complete Benediction Manual*, edited by Albert Edmonds Tozer and revised by Robert Hasberry in 1931,[25] and the *Benediction Choir Book*, edited in a cut-down edition by Richard Terry in 1937.[26] Hasberry's revisions were substantial. Only forty-one out of 213 items came from Tozer's 1898 publication; yet his approach was essentially backward-looking. Only twenty-three works had become available for inclusion after 1898, and since twelve of these were by Joseph Egbert Turner, who had died in 1897, this meant that there was virtually no twentieth-century input. Hasberry incorporated music, instead, from Newsham and embassy chapel sources that had been set aside by Tozer. Terry's volume, as the title implies, was aimed more at choirs than congregations, so it had a wider variety of vocal combinations alongside the

---

24   London: Burns and Lambert, n.d. [*c*1862]. See Thomas Muir, 'Charles Newsham, Henry Hemy, John Richardson and the Rise of Benediction Music in Nineteenth-century Catholic England, *Northern Catholic History* 47 (2006), 10–22.

25   London: Cary, 1898 (rev. 1931).

26   London: Burns and Oates, 1937.

standard four-part harmony format. Terry also provided more settings of texts outside the usual 'Benediction Service', as well as more plainchant, much of which was adapted from chant settings of Latin hymns and antiphons. A similar shift towards plainchant can be discerned in Vilma Little's collection, *Laudate Dominum: A Benediction Manual compiled chiefly from English* [Plainchant] *Mss*,[27] as well as in the substantial section devoted to Benediction chants in 1950s editions of the *Liber Usualis*.[28]

With vernacular hymnody, a key aspect was the exclusion of non-Latin texts from the Mass and Office imposed by the Vicars Apostolic in 1838. The change did not happen at once, partly because of divisions of opinion among the bishops. As a result, English hymns for use at Mass can be found in the *Crown of Jesus Music*. Nevertheless, the process was substantially complete by 1900. It meant that vernacular hymnody was primarily used in processions (copies of the *Westminster Hymnal* produced in 1912 and 1916 advertise band parts), in schools, in services associated with guilds and confraternities, and as a link between the variety of extra-liturgical devotions offered on Sunday afternoons and evenings.[29]

Its development occurred in stages. First, it had to be detached from the Latin plainchant hymns tied to particular Offices across the liturgical year. This was achieved partly by translation of the Office hymns, an important early monument being Edward Caswall's *Lyra Catholica* of 1849, and partly through the composition of new texts. Here, the contributions by Henry Newman and Frederick Faber were of enduring importance. All three, it should be noted, were Anglican converts and Oratorians. The next step concerns the shift from the remains of the melody-accompaniment

27 Liverpool: Rushworth and Dreaper, 1937 (repr. 1947).
28 See Muir, 'Full in the Panting Heart of Rome', 315, 336–42.
29 See Edward Yarnold, 'The Catholic Cultural Contribution: Architecture, Art, Liturgy and Music' in Vincent McClelland and Michael Hodgetts (eds), *From without the Flaminian Gate: 150 Years of Roman Catholicism in England and Wales, 1850–2000* (London: Darton, Longman and Todd, 1999), 335; also Muir, '"Hark an awful voice is sounding": Redefining the English Catholic Hymn Repertory: *The Westminster Hymnal* of 1912', in Peter Horton and Bennett Zon (eds), *Nineteenth-Century British Music Studies* 3 (Aldershot: Ashgate, 2001), 75–80.

format (often with echoes of a continuo bass approach) found in the *Crown of Jesus Music* to block four-part harmony, examples being the *St Dominic's Hymnal*, edited by Tozer in 1881[30] and *Arundel Hymns*, edited by Henry Howard (Duke of Norfolk) and Charles Gatty, of 1899–1901.[31] This coincided with the abandonment of melodies by Classical-Viennese composers that is so prominent a feature in the *Crown of Jesus Music*. It also reflects a shift from treating the hymn as a choral motet, sung only by the choir, to something that could be sung by either that body or the congregation, or both in combination. This aspect, of course, also applies to Benediction music at the same time.[32]

As with Benediction, such developments were consolidated in the early twentieth century. In 1912 the *Westminster Hymnal* appeared – 'the only collection in England and Wales authorized by the hierarchy.'[33] It therefore reflected the ultramontane obsession with uniform control. In essence, this was a musical version of the *Book of Hymns* issued by the bishops two years before.[34] As such, it drew directly on earlier hymnals, but eliminated non-Catholic texts. With melodies the situation was more complex. Terry, the principal musical editor, sought to eliminate non-Catholic tunes, and he stressed the value of uniform performance of the 'authentic' tune across the country. Unfortunately, problems with copyrights prevented him from using many earlier settings, so the gap was filled with compositions of his own and by extensive borrowing from early-modern German collections. Here he had to confess, however, that many such tunes were 'common property' among Catholics and Protestants alike.[35]

Nevertheless, despite such deficiencies, the *Westminster Hymnal* became the standard Catholic hymnal in England and Wales during the 1920s and 1930s. As a result, between 1936 and 1940 it was substantially revised by William Bainbridge and Murray, and it was in this guise that

30   London: R. and T. Washbourne.
31   London: R. and T. Washbourne/Boosey.
32   See Muir, 'Hark an awful voice', 69–71, 77–85.
33   London: R. and T. Washbourne.
34   London: R. and T. Washbourne.
35   See Muir, 'Hark an awful voice', 90–100.

its legacy was transmitted to Catholics in the 1950s. Yet by this time it was substantially different. Of its 276 items, only fifty-nine texts, thirty-five tunes and eight plainchant melodies belong to the 1912 edition; forty-six translations and five original texts were contributed by Ronald Knox; nine translations are by John Mason Neale, who was an Anglican; twenty-nine tunes are of Protestant origin; the number of plainchant settings was tripled; and twenty-two new hymn settings and 110 harmonizations are by Murray. Terry's input was therefore reduced to six tunes and twenty-four harmonizations.[36]

Such shifts were paralleled by developments elsewhere. *A Daily Hymn Book*, edited by Lancelot Long, has 384 items: 146 items use Latin texts, 155 are set to plainchant.[37] John Driscoll's series of *Cantionale* for different Jesuit establishments has similar tendencies. Of 480 texts in the *Stonyhurst Cantionale*, 293 are in Latin, and several melodies were drawn from non-Catholic sources.[38] This hymnal remained in use into the 1970s.

The explanation for such phenomena is twofold. First, it signals the reintroduction of congregational hymn singing at Mass. However, given the ban on English texts, Latin hymns had to be sung, hence the partial retreat to plainchant. Second, the ultramontane emphasis on a fixed, exclusively Catholic uniformity has been diluted. As a result, there was greater scope for originality. For example, the *Redemptorist Hymn Book with tunes* of 1947 has thirty-eight items, yet only sixteen texts and nine tunes come from either version of the *Westminster Hymnal*.[39] The fact that these are there, however, shows that conservative forces were still strong. Similarly, the preface to the *Leeds Catholic Hymnal*, edited by John Heenan, future cardinal archbishop of Westminster, claims that its object was to encourage Catholics to learn new hymns; but seventy-four out of ninety-four English texts appear in the *Westminster Hymnal*.[40] First published in 1954, this hymnal had run through twelve editions by 1963.

36   Ibid., 101–2; see also Muir, 'Full in the Panting Heart of Rome', 303–13.
37   London: Burns and Oates, 1931 (repr. 1948).
38   Roehampton: Manresa Press, 1936 (texts only), 1940 (full musical version in dyeline copy).
39   Anon. ed. No other publication details are supplied.
40   Farnworth: The Catholic Printing Press.

Papal legislation, questions of identity, and organizational factors

To sum up, much of the English Catholic repertoire of the 1950s was shaped by attitudes prevalent at the beginning of the century. In particular, it was supposed to conform to the template laid down in *Tra le sollecitudini* and elaborated in subsequent papal documents, notably *Divini cultus* (1928), *Mediator Dei* (1947), and the *Instruction on Sacred Music and Sacred Liturgy* (1958).⁴¹ *Tra le sollecitudini* asserted the primacy of plainchant and, next to it, Renaissance polyphony in the canon of church music. 'Modern' music, by contrast, was tolerated but viewed with suspicion, especially if it had a secular, operatic character. In other words: 'the more closely a composition for church approaches in its movement, inspiration, and savour the Gregorian form, the more sacred and liturgical it becomes; and the more out of harmony it is with that supreme model, the less worthy is it of the temple.'⁴²

There is little doubt that the 1903 *motu proprio*, while representing the personal thinking of Pius X, was the consequence of decades of pressure group activity by Cecilians and ultramontanes. Many of its ideas were anticipated in decrees by the provincial and diocesan synods convened by English ultramontane bishops, especially the first and fourth synods of Westminster (1852 and 1873). They also appear in pastoral letters by ultramontanes such as Henry Manning, Robert Cornthwaite, Cuthbert Hedley, and Louis Cassertelli. *Tra le sollecitudini* is also thoroughly ultramontane in its authoritarian measures for the enforcement of its decrees. Plainchant would be a compulsory subject in seminaries, and every diocese would have a music committee. Among other things, these could issue lists of approved

41 For translations, see Richard Terry, *Music of the Roman Rite: A Manual for Choirmasters in English Speaking Countries* (London: Burns, Oates and Washbourne, 1931), 253–69, 285–93; Clifford Howell (trans.), *An Instruction by the Sacred Congregation of Rites on Sacred Music and the Liturgy* (London: Herder, 1959); also Robert F. Hayburn, *Papal Legislation on Sacred Music, 95 A.D. to 1977 A.D.* (Collegeville, MN: Liturgical Press, 1979), 222–31, 327–32, 337–41, 356–77.
42 *Tra le sollecitudini*, clauses 3–6, in Terry, *Music of the Roman Rite*, 256–8.

music (thereby excluding all other repertoire). In England, such lists were
produced by Salford (1904), Liverpool (1906 and 1911), Westminster (1906
with subsequent revisions), and Lancaster (1929). Since these committees
were dominated by Cecilians, the emphasis was on Renaissance polyphony
and imitations thereof at the expense of more modern styles. Such pressure helps explain the tilt away from composers such as Mozart, Haydn
and Gounod after 1903.[43]

Pius X's *motu proprio* was also a liturgical document.[44] Liturgy was
the starting-point for all its thinking, whereas 'music is merely a part of
the liturgy and its humble handmaid.'[45] This raised, among other things,
questions of identity. The document insisted that 'the language proper to
the Roman Church is Latin.'[46] It was therefore hardly surprising that the
bulk of Catholic music in England used that language. Sixty out of sixty-six
compositions at Our Lady of Mount Carmel, Liverpool, for example, fall
into this category. This gave a European orientation to English Catholic
music, a factor reinforced by ultramontane influences. Yet, at the same
time, English Catholics were pulled in the opposite direction by nationalist
attitudes, not least because, although the Catholic Emancipation Act had
been passed in 1829, they still faced the accusation that their loyalties were
divided. As we have seen, the solution offered by Terry was to claim that
Catholic Renaissance polyphonic composers were English *and* Roman.
Some plainchant specialists, through assiduous research and publication
of English medieval chants, tried to do the same thing. The *Stanbrook
Hymnale* of 1963, building on work by Shebbeare and McLachlan, is a

43   See Muir, 'Full in the Panting Heart of Rome', 115–16, 128–33, 256–7; Muir, *Roman
      Catholic Church Music in England*, 187–94; Robert Guy (arranger, under the super-
      vision of Bishop Cuthbert Hedley), *The Synods in English being the text of the Four
      Synods in English translated into English* (Stratford on Avon: St Gregory's Press,
      1886); also Hayburn, *Papal Legislation*, 127–43, 195–219.
44   See clauses 1, 7–9, 22–3.
45   Clause 23.
46   Clause 7.

late manifestation of this.[47] Yet such an approach merely fudged the issue about whether there could be such a thing as 'English Catholic Music'. The balance between English and foreign composers in the 1950s repertoire is therefore of more than usual significance. Sometimes the former could be very high. English compositions account for 182 out of 369 items at Alston Lane, twenty-nine out of sixty-six items at Mount Carmel, 571 out of 1,071 items published between 1901 and 1962 at Stonyhurst, and 927 out of 1,689 pre-1962 items in the CMA collection. Elsewhere, though, the proportion could be significantly lower. English contributions account for 112 out of 611 compositions published between 1901 and 1962 at Ushaw, twenty-one out of 131 works performed at the Church of the Immaculate Conception, Farm St, London, in 1961, and 195 out of 895 works performed at Westminster Cathedral between 1948 and 1962.[48]

Such variations, though, demonstrate that English Catholicism was not as monolithically conformist as appears at first sight. Partly, this is simply the result of variety within its organization. First, there are the differences between the services, and therefore the music, performed in schools, seminaries, parishes, cathedrals and various monastic communities, many of which had distinct liturgical traditions of their own. Cutting across this are distinctions between rural, urban and suburban centres, between recently founded and older communities, and between communities in different parts of the country.[49]

On top of that, the semi-independent character of choirs must be recognized. Yet, just because they might not conform to ecclesiastical diktat, this did not mean they would break with their own past traditions. In most cases they consisted of unpaid volunteers; so, by definition,

47   Felicitas Corrigan, ed., *Stanbrook Hymnale* (Worcester: Stanbrook Abbey, 1963). See Muir, 'Full in the Panting Heart of Rome', 199–202, 307–8.

48   See Muir, 'Full in the Panting Heart of Rome', 529–33, 579–87; Muir, 'Music at the church of Our Lady and St Michael' (as n.1), 53; also Muir, 'Music at the church of Our Lady of Mount Carmel (as n.2).

49   Muir, 'Full in the Panting Heart of Rome', 534–7, discusses the amount of overlap between compositions found in different surviving music collections (see also pp. 555, 588–93).

they were difficult to coerce. Thus, by the 1950s, ultramontane attempts
to exclude women from choirs had been largely abandoned. The choir at
St Augustine's, Preston, for example, had nineteen sopranos and six altos,
only one of whom was a boy.[50] Yet, at the same time, even the most ama-
teurish body would have had an *esprit de corps* derived from the fact that
it was a specialist group of singers. Indeed, given the notorious reluctance
of English Catholic congregations to sing, they and the clergy were often
the *only* singers. They had separate rehearsals, could (in most cases) read
music, and were placed in a specified part of the building. Usually this
was a 'West Gallery'; so they were far away from clerical control, despite
all the official talk about their status as liturgical ministers. Sometimes, in
large establishments, however, this was mitigated by the appointment of
a clergyman as choirmaster, who worked alongside a specialist lay organist. This, indeed, was the pattern at Stonyhurst up to the mid 1950s. Yet
even this illustrated the difference in attitude between a cleric concerned
primarily with liturgy and many lay musicians. Symptomatic was a distinction between part-music intended for choirs and liturgical books with
plainchant intended for clergy and choirs. Similarly, there was the divide
between hymnals and Benediction manuals with four-part harmony and
the equivalent text-only volumes supplied to congregations.

Passive resistance by choirs, then, helps explain the survival of 'secular', 'modern' styles condemned by *Tra le sollecitudini* in repertoires of the
1950s. There is even a suspicion that, without Renaissance polyphony,
choirs might not have been persuaded to sing more monodic plainchant
at the expense of Viennese-Classical settings. This was because plainchant
could be sung by congregations; polyphony, by definition, could not. A
choir asked to abandon hard-learned Classical Masses therefore had to be
offered something else to justify its separate existence, if only to itself. In
this sense, then, choirs could be independent, but in a conservative way.

---

50   See Muir, 'Full in the Panting Heart of Rome', 539–43, for a discussion of the mem-
      bership of choirs. The data for St Augustine's, Preston, has been extrapolated from
      the biro signatures of choir members on copies of Johann Kalliwoda's *Messe*, opus
      137 (Mainz: Schott, n.d., but clearly a late nineteenth-century edition) handed in
      to the Talbot Library, Preston, and since then largely dispersed.

Factors for change

Organizationally, then, English Catholic music had the potential for new approaches, but these were smothered by the pressures for conservative conformity. Why then, did the situation change so radically after Vatican II? As far as the 1950s are concerned, the answer is four-fold: (1) the emergence of new musical forms and the reworking of old ones, (2) the impact of new music reproduction technology, (3) new liturgical ideas, and (4) the effects of fundamental social change within the Catholic community.

New and reworked musical forms

Some of the most significant new musical forms concerned psalmody. The impulse behind this was not new, as it stemmed from developments in linguistic scholarship beginning in the 1900s.[51] In particular, translators realized that the original Hebrew psalms were not necessarily organized in two-line verses, but that these could be sub-units of much larger stanzas of unequal length. They also appreciated that not only had account to be taken of the stress pattern in each line, but that English lent itself more readily to such treatment than ecclesiastical Latin. Taken together, such appreciations made nonsense of existing Solesmes-style renditions of psalmody, given that these assumed largely unmetrical two-line verses. It is remarkable, then, that musicians paid so little attention to this development before the 1950s.

During that decade, two new models were offered. One was Anthony Milner's *Vespers for Congregational Use: The Psalms newly rendered into*

---

51 See P.V. Higgins, 'The Psalms in the Vulgate', *Irish Ecclesiastical Review* 22 (1907), 372–79; L.C. Fillion, *The New Psalter of the Roman Breviary* (London/St Louis: B. Herder, 1915; original edn published from Paris in 1912); Francisco Zorrell, *Psalterium ex Hebraco Latinum* (Rome: Pontifici Instituti Biblici, 1928); Cuthbert Lattey, *The Psalter in the Westminster Version of the Sacred Scriptures* (London and Glasgow: Sands, 1944).

English from Hebrew by Fr Sebastian Bullough OP.[52] Each verse was sung
alternately by two groups, and to accommodate their varying lengths two
melodies were provided for each psalm. Milner believed that 'uniformity
is essential for Congregational music,' so he used a regular beat and chose
translations with a regular metre.[53] This, and the fact that he stuck to two-
line verses, suggests that he and Bullough only partially accepted the full
implications of the new Hebrew psalm scholarship.

This cannot be said of Gelineau psalmody, which eventually pushed
Milner's method into obscurity. It began in 1950 with *Le Livre de Psaumes*,
a straight French translation within the *Bible de Jerusalem* project. Its editors soon realized that, from a musical perspective, this was inadequate;
so T.P. Chiffot, OP and Joseph Gelineau were co-opted. The result was
not simply new translations. Gelineau and his friends produced a range
of volumes with new settings of every psalm.[54]

In England these methods were seized upon by Gregory Murray, and
preparations were made to adapt them for the English-speaking world.
Gelineau insisted on new translations, which were provided by a team of
editors headed by Murray and sponsored by The Grail. In addition, numerous psalm settings were produced in separate publications.[55] These were
accompanied by 160 through-composed antiphon settings, of which eighty-
nine were by Murray and twenty-seven by Gelineau.[56] Murray therefore
set his stamp on the form in England.

52   Hawkshead, 1955. See also Milner's *A form of Compline for Congregational use, Give
     thanks to the Lord (Psalm 136)* and *A form of Sunday Vespers* (London: Novello, 1958,
     1964 and 1965).
53   Anthony Milner, 'Music in a Vernacular Liturgy', in C. Cunliffe (ed.), *English in the
     Liturgy: A Symposium* (London: Burns & Oates, 1956), 122–33.
54   Joseph Gelineau, 'Introduction' in The Grail (ed.), *The Psalms: A new translation
     from the Hebrew arranged for singing to the psalmody of Joseph Gelineau* (London/
     Glasgow: The Grail/Collins, 1963).
55   Anthony Gregory Murray et al. (ed.), *Twenty-Four Psalms and a Canticle* (1955),
     Thirty Psalms and Two Canticles (1957), *Twenty Psalms and Three Canticles* (1957),
     and *Six Psalms and Three Canticles* (n.d.) (London: The Grail).
56   Other contributions were by Clifford Howell (twelve), Wilfrid Trotman (eight),
     Dorothy Howell (seven), Peter Peacock (five), Ingrid Brustle (four), Guy Weitz
     (three), Elway Bevin (three), and Joseph Samson (two).

The principal musical features were as follows.[57] For the verses Geli-neau provided forty-five tones grouped under six modes. Each tone con-sists of three, four or six sections of music, and in some cases these can be reduced to accommodate different numbers of lines in each verse. Gelineau noted that, although each line had a variable number of syllables, the number of accents was fixed. Each accent therefore marks the point where singers move on to the next bar. A regular pulse was maintained throughout, with preliminary 'up beat' notes provided where the text made this necessary. This means that, unlike in plainsong or Anglican chant, where the music is accommodated to the words, the text con-forms to the fixed tempo dictated by bars of equal length. In practice this results in a chordal, rather than melodic emphasis. Nevertheless, accents aside, Gelineau required normal speech patterns to be followed. Indeed, the accents were meant to coincide with the accentual pattern of English anyway.

Antiphons were composed in modern diatonic style. A deliberate contrast was thereby established between the antiphon and the verses. A particular feature was that, as long as the key or mode was compatible with that for the verse tone, settings by different composers could be associated with the same psalm text. On the other hand, not only was the thematic material of the antiphon and verse tone often related, but there was also a fixed relationship between the tempo in the antiphon and the pulse in the tone, usually at a ratio of 4:1 or 2:1.

The responsorial character of Gelineau psalmody, combined with its regular pulse and optional four-part harmonization, makes it well adapted for flexible combinations of a congregation, cantors and choir. Moreover, the verses can be sung without alternating antiphons, rendering it suitable for the Office. Yet, since it was designed for the vernacular, theoretically it should have been denied a place there and at Mass in pre-Vatican II days, when Latin was the established language. The same objections apply to Milner's settings. What, then, were they used for? The answer seems to

57   See J. Robert Carroll, *Guide to Gelineau Psalmody* (Chicago: GIA Publications, 1979).

have been retreats and informal religious gatherings. It may also have been heard privately at home on the radio and records.[58] Its full promise, then, lay in the future. Nevertheless, it is significant that Milner's titles refer to Vespers and Compline as possible venues. This suggests that either some erosion of the Latin monopoly on such occasions was already taking place, or that the early to mid-nineteenth-century tradition of English Catholic psalmody had not been entirely forgotten.

The next area to be considered concerns a direct challenge to the Solesmes method of singing plainchant. In 1958 Jan Vollaerts's book *Rhythmic Proportions in Early Medieval Chant* was published.[59] His ideas were quickly taken up by Murray, who had received an advance manuscript copy in 1956, and vigorously promoted in a series of articles culminating with Murray's book *Gregorian Chant according to the manuscripts*.[60] In the 1930s Murray had been a convinced supporter of Mocquereau; but now, citing evidence from medieval musical theorists from St Augustine onwards, and reinterpreting the staveless neumes in manuscripts hitherto cited by Solesmes, he and Vollaerts argued that plainchant notes were unequal in length and that the neumes indicated long and short notes on a fixed 2:1 ratio. In addition, Murray asserted the existence of triplet rhythms as well. This was a recrudescence of measured plainchant, and it is surely significant that Murray came to such conclusions at the same time as he was working on Gelineau psalmody with its accentuated patterns and rigid pulse.

Naturally, Solesmes was infuriated, but its eventual response, worked out in Eugène Cardine's *Gregorian Semiology*, itself involved a radical

---

58 See, for example, the remarks in the report of performances by The Grail at Westminster Cathedral in aid of World Refugee Year in 'From Our Notebook', *The Tablet*, 17 March 1962, 257.

59 Leiden: E.J. Brill, 1958 (2nd edn 1960).

60 London: L.J. Cary, 1963. See also Murray's 'Plainsong rhythm; The editorial methods of Solesmes'; 'Accentual cadencies in Gregorian Chant'; 'The authentic rhythm of Gregorian Chant'; and 'A reply to Fr Smits Van Waesbighe SJ' (Downside, 1956, n.d., 1959, and 1963 respectively).

change in direction.[61] Cardine argued that the staveless neumes in the earliest manuscripts did not just denote pitches; they indicated dynamics, articulations, nuances of tempo, and other aspects of performance technique.[62] Thus Gregorian rhythm was a 'symbiosis of text and melody'. There was no such thing as a theoretical *a priori* musical rhythm, as Mocquereau had stated. Consequently, the rhythmic tension between text and music was reduced.[63]

Next, there was the concept of 'coupure', an idea popularized in England by Laurence Bevenot.[64] Cardine argued that a neume or cluster of neumes was really a group of notes constituting what was, in effect, a broken chord. In Gothic buildings with a long echo, plainchant therefore produced a sliding kaleidoscopic pattern of heterophonic harmony, not a single melodic line. In this context it is interesting to note that composers such as Britten and Berkeley in their Masses used heterophonic accompaniments to melody in a similar manner. The idea was 'in the air'.

Nevertheless, as with Gelineau psalmody, the full import of such concepts lay in the future. After all, the *Graduale Triplex*, the first large-scale demonstration of such principles, was not published until 1979.[65]

This means that, in the 1950s, the most important technical challenge came with the composition of congregational Mass settings. Two composers led the way, and in both instances they responded to the difficulties encountered in trying to teach congregations plainchant. In 1948 Laurence Bevenot published his all-purpose *Four Settings of the Proper of the Mass*.[66] Each text was sung to a formula consisting of a recitative or monotone fol-

---

61   Eugène Cardine (trans. Herbert Fowells), *Gregorian Semiology* (Sablé-sur-Sarthe: Abbaye Saint-Pierre de Solesmes, 1982).

62   See Cardine (as n.61), 7–8, 18–22, and 112.

63   Ibid., 23.

64   See Laurence Bevenot, *Appraisal of Plainsong* (Panel of Monastic Musicians Pamphlet No. 4, 1978).

65   *Graduale Triplex: seu Graduale Romanum Pauli PP.VI cura recognitum et rhythmicis signis ad Solemnibus ornatum, nemis Laudunensibus (cod. 239) et Sangallensibus (Codicum Sangallensibus 369 et Einsidlensis 121) nunc autem* (Sablé-sur-Sarthe: Abbaye Saint-Pierre de Solesmes, 1979).

66   London: L.J. Cary.

lowed by a 'jubilus', or turn, usually on the final syllable of the line. This is very similar to plainchant psalmody. Although the reciting notes are equal in value, the syllables attached to them are, however, of different lengths 'according to the number of consonants following a vowel (all vowels are regarded as of equal length).' In this respect, Bevenot was moving away from the Solesmes concept of the equal indivisible note.

More radical were his four settings of the Mass in Re, Mi, Sol, and Fa.[67] True, plainchant-influenced melodies were used. What was new was the method of arrangement based, as Bevenot put it, on the I + II = III principle. These were in two parts, which could be sung independently or in combination by a divided choir or congregation, or by pitting a cantor against the latter, making it easy to learn.

Bevenot conceived his settings as stepping-stones towards plain-chant. Murray did no such thing. In 1950 he published *A People's Mass*.[68] In the preface, the challenge to Solesmes, Pius X, and all they stood for is unmistakable.

> In parish churches it would seem desirable for the congregation to take an active part in the singing of the Mass. Hitherto efforts to encourage the practice have largely failed because it has been assumed that the plainsong Masses of the Kyriale were within the capacity of unskilled singers. The simple fact is that these plainsong Masses were never intended for congregational use, they were composed for highly trained choirs and their worthy performance demands long hours of practice and a vocal technique far beyond the powers of an ordinary congregation. If our people are to sing the Mass, they must be provided with music which they can readily grasp, learn by heart and sing with ease: music which presents no greater difficulty than an ordinary hymn tune. *A People's Mass* is an attempt to supply that need.

This shows that Murray thought in terms of four-part block harmony, something he believed was well suited to the genius of the English people. This was no accident. Murray had been a pupil of Terry, and had collabo-rated with him in work on the *Benediction Choir Book* and revisions to the

---

67   Laurence Bevenot, *Mass in Ré* (1952), *Mass in Sol* (1957), *Mass in Fa* (1960), and
       Mass in Mi (1960) (London: L.J. Cary).
68   London: L.J. Cary.

Westminster Hymnal. As with a hymn, a Mass in block harmony could be sung by congregations and choirs separately or in combination with or without an organ. Moreover, to make it easier, the same thematic material was used across the whole setting.

A People's Mass was immensely popular. Over two million copies were sold in Latin and English versions before and after Vatican II. Moreover, it provided the template for other hymn-style Masses, especially after the introduction of a fully vernacular liturgy in the 1960s. Together with his work on Gelineau psalmody and measured plainchant, it establishes Murray's position as one of the most significant, independent-thinking musicians of Catholic England in the 1950s.

New Printing Technologies

It is a little known fact that businesses aim for a monopoly. By 1914, the English Catholic sheet music market was dominated by a few London-based companies, notably Novello and Co. and Cary and Co.; the vernacular hymn market was being cornered by R. and T. Washbourne (later amalgamated with Burns and Oates) through its production of the *Westminster Hymnal*, and plainchant publications were presided over by the Vatican Typical editions and Solesmes-Desclée collaborations. During subsequent decades the pattern changed little. German competition collapsed but with Renaissance polyphony the gap was filled by OUP, Stainer and Bell, the Catholic division of J. and W. Chester and J. Bank of Amsterdam. Overall, the effect was to reinforce the tone of conservative uniformity characteristic of the 1950s.

In the first instance all this was due to the mass production unleashed by the reintroduction of musical type and invention of lithographic printing noted earlier. Cheap, smart-looking vocal scores reduced the need to copy individual parts, thereby stifling tendencies to prepare arrangements – let alone original compositions – tailored to local conditions. In turn, mass production encouraged companies to enforce and extend copyright law, culminating with the passage of the 1911 Copyright Act. If the market could be supplied then it was worthwhile asserting a copyright monopoly.

The ultramontane passion for a permanent archaizing uniformity could also be turned to account. The *Westminster Hymnal*, for example, was officially endorsed by the hierarchy, and Pius X had commissioned a new series of standard plainchant books in 1904. Ultramontanes and publishers had a common interest, since uniformity of this sort created a captive Catholic market.

Such practices discouraged new music. Once a company had a full range of works by recognized composers, it had little incentive to look for new ones. Why go to the risky expense of preparing new typefaces if existing publications were selling well? If you chose to take the risk, it was safer to print old music such as plainchant or Renaissance polyphony. It was also cheaper, given that there were no royalties payable to living composers. Hence the 'stop-go' nature of English Catholic music publication. The 1890s and 1900s witnessed a surge in production as companies, especially Cary, filled up their catalogues; this was then followed by decades of relative stagnation.[69]

However, the introduction of Gestedner machines, wet photocopiers and Spirit Duplicators in the 1950s changed the rules of the game. For the first time it was possible to have cheap limited print runs produced locally and at almost instantaneous notice. Initially, such potential was often used to supplement existing stocks of sheet music. In this guise, the new technology reinforced the *status quo*. On the other hand, it opened the way for special arrangements and new compositions tailored for local needs. In the long run, and especially after Vatican II, this corroded the centralized uniformity promoted by ultramontanes and the established publishing industry.[70]

69   See Muir, 'Full in the Panting Heart of Rome', 479–81 and 500 for statistics compiled from a cross-section of music collections. The key point is that, while the number of *publications* rose, the number of *published compositions* fell from 3,714 between 1850 and 1900 to 2,652 between 1901 and 1950, despite the growth in the size of the English Catholic community in the same period.
70   See Muir, 'Full in the Panting Heart of Rome', 473–4, 479–81, 500 for statistical data.

New liturgical ideas

Despite appearances, Catholic liturgy in England was not static.[71] For instance, revisions to the Holy Week Triduum in 1951 and 1955, particularly the moving of Tenebrae from the night before to the morning of the relevant day, altered the whole atmosphere of what had hitherto been – from a musical perspective – a liturgical showpiece of the Catholic year.

More significant was the issue of congregational participation. This was not exactly new. Back in 1912 Terry had assumed that the *Westminster Hymnal* would promote congregational hymn singing, and the SSG in the 1930s had attempted the same thing with plainchant. The cause, nevertheless, received new impetus from a number of publicists in England, notably Joseph Connelly, James Crichton, and Clifford Howell. In the early 1940s they took control of the SSG, transforming it from a body primarily concerned with promoting plainchant to one that paid greater attention to liturgical change. Such writers appealed to the 1903 *motu proprio* and, with greater justification, to *Divini cultus*, *Mediator Dei*, and the *Instruction on Sacred Music and Sacred Liturgy*.[72] Yet, as so often with papal pronouncements, such documents proved capable of varied interpretation. *Divini cultus*, for example, discusses congregational participation in the context of singing plainchant.[73] *Mediator Dei* and the *Instruction* distinguish between 'interior' and 'exterior' participation; and even the latter could be confined to 'gesture', such as kneeling, standing, or making the Sign of the Cross.[74] As a result, the *Instruction* compromised between conflicting claims by demarcating the particular parts of the Mass that were the perquisite of the

---

71 For a general survey, see James Crichton, 'The Liturgical Movement from 1940 to Vatican II', in J.D. Crichton, H.E. Winstone and J.R. Ainslie (eds), *English Catholic Worship: Liturgical Renewal in England since 1900* (London: Geoffrey Chapman, 1979), 60–78.

72 See James Crichton, 'A Papal encyclical: past events casting their shadows before', *Music and Liturgy* 24 (1988), 4–7.

73 Clause 9; see Terry, *Music of the Roman Rite* (as n.41), 291.

74 *Mediator Dei*, clauses 80 and 105; *Instruction on Sacred Music and Sacred Liturgy*, clause 22.

officiating clergy, choir, and congregation respectively. The congregation, for example, was supposed to utter the Ordinary, the choir dealt with the Proper, and officiating clergy looked after the Canon. Yet, at the same time, the *Instruction* permitted vernacular hymns at Low Mass.[75]

Congregational participation therefore overlapped with attempts to promote a vernacular liturgy. Again, this was not new. Crichton's research shows how much experimentation took place in seventeenth-, eighteenth- and early nineteenth-century England, notably with work by John Goter, John Lingard, and F.C. Husenbeth.[76] Such tendencies were reversed by ultramontanes after 1850, but revived by Adrian Fortescue in the 1900s. Nevertheless, it should be noted that most of this activity concerned the provision of parallel translations or paraphrases of the Latin text that congregations might follow, but not necessarily utter. What was new in the 1950s was the widespread adoption of the Dialogue Mass. This had been discouraged by English bishops in the 1930s, but it received an important fillip during the Second World War through the medium of the *Simple Prayer Book*, which was issued in large numbers to the armed forces, as well as through Catholic servicemen's encounter with the form in Europe. Even here, though, it should be stressed that congregations were expected to respond in Latin, and at best only *read* the English translation. Nevertheless, even such limited change challenged the monopoly of sound hitherto held in so many places by the clergy, altar servers, and the choir.

Social change

It should be apparent that most of the changes observed so far were of potential rather than actual significance. On the surface, as noted at the start, the conservative *status quo* remained unruffled. What is more, although

75 *Instruction on Sacred Music and Sacred Liturgy*, clauses 22, 25, 29, and 33.
76 For a general survey, see James Crichton, *Worship in a Hidden Church* (Blackrock: Columba Press, 1988); see also Emma Riley, 'John Lingard and the Liturgy', in Peter Philips (ed.), *Lingard Remembered: Essays to mark the Sesquicentenary of John Lingard's death* (London: Catholic Record Society, 2004), 143–56.

Vatican II signalled massive changes, in one sense it did not cause them. As was demonstrated by Pope John Paul II, *Sacrosanctum Concilium*, the principal document concerned with music and liturgy, is more conservative than many have assumed.[77] For example, it still gave primacy of place to plainchant and encouraged the formation of diocesan music commissions. Moreover, the scope of vernacular liturgies and permission to use instruments other than the organ were left to the bishops.[78] In England, the key lay in the shifting of attitudes generated by deep-seated social change.

Obviously, the Second World War played a part. English Catholics did not just discover progressive European practices; the fact that they and their compatriots were fighting a common enemy weakened isolationist ultramontane tendencies and Protestant prejudices. This is illustrated by the ecumenical implications of the Sword of the Spirit movement. Musically, it meant that Catholics were more willing to use non-Catholic materials, as the revised edition of the *Westminster Hymnal* shows.

Then there was the growth of the English Catholic community, rising from 1.8 million in 1913 to 3.7 million in 1963.[79] Mere numbers do not tell the full story; after all, they simply kept pace with general population growth. What really mattered was the spread of Catholicism to the South and East (hitherto it had made little impact outside London), from inner cities to the suburbs, and from an Irish-inflected proletariat to the professional middle classes and businessmen.[80] This meant that a higher proportion of English Catholics were better educated and used to holding positions

77 See *Chirograph of the Supreme Pontiff John Paul II for the centenary of the Motu Proprio 'Tra le Sollecitudini' on Sacred Music* (2003), clauses 2, 8 and 10 (<http://www.vatican.va/holy_father/john_paul_ii/letters/2003/documents/hf_jp-ii_let_20031203_musica-sacra_en.html>, accessed Oct. 2009).

78 See Walter Abbott (ed.), *The Message and Meaning of the Ecumenical Council: The Documents of Vatican II with notes and comments by Catholic, Protestant and Orthodox authorities* (London and Dublin: Geoffrey Chapman, 1966), 137–8, clauses 116–117, 153, 120, and 101 respectively.

79 See *Catholic Directory* (London: Burns and Oates, 1913), 56, 100; also *Catholic Directory* for 1963, 763.

80 See Adrian Hastings, *A History of English Christianity, 1920–1985* (London: Collins, 1986), 134–6, 275–8, 473–6, and 561.

of responsibility. Hitherto, many of the Catholic intelligentsia, especially High Anglican converts such as Terry and Rubbra, had leant towards ultra-montanism. Yet, by definition, educated middle-class people are less likely to accept clerical authority unquestioningly. Simultaneously, changes in musical education and culture produced more instrumentalists, especially guitarists, woodwind and brass players, thereby altering the balance with choir singers and organists.

The introduction of vernacular liturgies in the 1960s gave such people their chance.[81] New hymns, Mass and responsorial psalm settings poured from local photocopiers, Gestedner machines and Spirit Duplicators. New companies, such as Mayhew-McCrimmon, peddled such music on a large scale. As a result, old-established businesses, notably Novello and L.J. Cary, were expelled from the market or driven to the wall. Simultaneously, Catholics raided other denominational repertoires, early examples being the *Parish Hymnal* and the hymnal *Praise the Lord*.[82] Folk groups and other mixed combinations of singers, keyboard players, and instrumentalists made their appearance. Yet significantly, all attempts to promote plainchant in English have largely fallen on stony ground. Finally, vernacular liturgy reoriented the international dimension of Catholic music in England. Hitherto, links with the US, while not negligible, had been restricted. For example, only seventy-two out of 1,343 pre-1962 publications in the CMA collection came from this source, accounting for seventy-seven works by Americans out of 1,689 compositions. All this has now changed. English Catholic musical culture is no longer primarily tied to a Latin Europe; it is associated with North America and other parts of an international English-speaking world.

81   For a limited survey, see John Ainslie, 'English Liturgical Music since the Council', in J.D. Crichton, H.E. Winstone and J.R. Ainslie (eds), *English Catholic Worship: Liturgical Renewal in England since 1900* (London: Geoffrey Chapman, 1979), 93–109.
82   John Rush (ed.), *The Parish Hymnal* (London: L.J. Cary, 1968); Wilfrid Trotman (ed.), *Praise the Lord* (London and Dublin: G. Chapman, 1966).

KEITH F. PECKLERS, S.J.

The Evolution of Liturgical Music in the United States of America, 1850–1962

Introduction

This chapter will consider the evolution of church music in the nineteenth and twentieth centuries as it grew within the North American context. Beginning with a consideration of European foundations in Europe, especially at Ratisbon and Solesmes, and Pius X's 1903 *motu proprio* on sacred music and its implementation on American soil, the subject will be examined in terms of tensions between the ideal presented by liturgical reformers and the reality of American parish life, the tension between Gregorian chant and vernacular hymnody, and the unique cultural and ecumenical dimensions present within the United States that had a profound effect on the way in which church music evolved there.

The nineteenth century proved to be a significant epoch for the reform of church music around the world. Sixteenth-century polyphony came to represent the 'golden age' of church music. Key in this reform was the Association of Saint Cecilia, founded in Germany by several church musicians: Caspar Ett (1788–1847) at Munich, and Carl Proske (1794–1861), John Mettenleiter (1812–58), Dominic Mettenleiter (1822–68), Joseph Schrembs (1815–72), Joseph Hanisch (1812–92), and Franz Witt (1834–88) at Ratisbon. Soon the leadership exhibited in Germany would serve as a catalyst for associate branches of the organization in Italy and in other parts of the world.

Fundamentally, the Association of Saint Cecilia endeavoured to diffuse principles and laws on church music among musicians who were not always so familiar with such documents. To that end, the association modelled appropriate liturgical music through conventions and assemblies that gathered musicians and clergy alike. These national and regional gatherings included more specific technical sessions on the craft of properly executing the singing of Gregorian chant, and also held regular competitions among choral groups as they worked at implementing that which was found in the documents.[1] In order to understand the development of liturgical music in North America, it will be necessary to consider first the musical situation in Italy and especially in Rome, where tensions arising from the more operatic and theatrical musical style that held sway in that period led to direct papal intervention.

Pope Pius VIII and the tension between secular and sacred music

On 24 August 1830 at the Basilica of Saint Mary Major in Rome, Pope Pius VIII approved the statutes for the Italian Society of Saint Cecilia with a solemn promulgation of *Bullarii Romani continuatio summorum pontificum*. This would gradually have influence on the society in other parts of the world and on the evolution of sacred music far beyond the confines of Italy. The document contained a Latin introduction, twenty-seven paragraphs in Italian, followed by six additional paragraphs in Latin. While later papal legislation annulled the statutes contained in this document, it nonetheless offers precious information on the establishment of that organization in Italy: how meetings were to be conducted; the paying of monthly dues and fines for those who violated the society's rules; distinctions made among professors of sacred music, chapel masters and organists, choir members and students; spiritual and temporal matters of its governance, etc. It was clearly defined as a lay confraternity specifically devoted

---

1   See Robert F. Hayburn, *Papal Legislation on Sacred Music, 95 A.D. to 1977 A.D.* (Collegeville, MN: Liturgical Press, 1979), 115.

to sacred music, and functioned not unlike other lay confraternities of the day. In fact, the term 'congregation' is used in the document to describe each chapter – the same term used for the nine lay confraternities at the Oratorio of San Francesco Saverio 'del Caravita' in Rome which were founded in the 1630s.

The validity of each congregation was determined by a minimum of forty members, with at least two 'guardians' who would supervise the group. There was a secrecy surrounding meetings of the group: 'members [...] shall never divulge or discuss either the subject-matter of their deliberations or the resolutions passed, except with those who were present at the meetings [...]'[2] The congregation also maintained an altar in the ancient Basilica of Saint Cecilia in Rome's Trastevere neighbourhood.

One of the most interesting sections of the document is found at Paragraph 28:

> But although these laws, which have been confirmed by Our Predecessors, must altogether remain in force, the Congregation of musicians, with great sadness of soul, already sees that abuses have been introduced here in the City of Rome. Many, appropriating to themselves fictitious privileges, dare to direct either prayers of sacrifice or psalms and hymns, which are arranged for many musicians and are tempered with a variety of sounds, oftentimes unworthy of the house of prayer, and they dare to entrust the playing of this music to lovers of this art. When this is done a great damage comes upon those who exercise the art of music, since such practices bring with them the end of true church music and in a way makes profane the holy temple of God.[3]

Thus, there was a need for a corrective document to challenge the growth of polyphony which was considered a more profane rendering of the pure and pristine Gregorian chant. With its juridical language focused largely on penalties to be imposed upon violators of what was stated in the document, it clearly demonstrates the papal desire for change in Italy's musical situation in the first half of the nineteenth century. Not surprisingly, the solemn tone of the document gave even greater impetus to the work of the

---

2   Chapter 11/Paragraph 14, as quoted in Hayburn (as n.1), 118.
3   Quoted in Hayburn, 120.

Saint Cecilia Association and it set that organization on a path of reform
that held significant sway in the latter part of the nineteenth century and,
indeed, well into the twentieth.[4]

It would, of course, take some time for the desires of Pope Pius VIII and
the Saint Cecilia Society to bear fruit. One of the key figures in the renewal
of nineteenth-century liturgical music in Italy was the composer Gaspare
Spontini (1774–1851). At the request of the archbishop of Jesi, Cardinal
Ostini, Spontini focused his work on surveying the state of sacred music
in that diocese located in the Marche Region, not far from the medieval
city of Urbino. After learning of Spontini's survey, the pope asked Spontini
to conduct a similar musical investigation in the churches of Rome and
appointed him as president of a commission on sacred music.

Spontini formulated the results of his investigation in a report entitled
'The Music in the Churches of Rome', which he presented to the pope. In
that undated text, Spontini expressed his dismay upon returning to Italy
after a period living outside of the country, at 'the scandalous abuses of
modern music in the Church.'[5] He continued that he felt supported in
his efforts at reforming sacred music since the pope himself had personally expressed to Spontini 'his extreme displeasure concerning existing
abuses.'[6] Describing the state of church music in Rome and throughout
Italy, Spontini wrote of the 'sad and numerous profanations of the holy
place by the introduction of unseemly music' – theatrical and operatic
music that was allowed to enter unquestioned into chapels and churches.[7]
He quoted from a resolution that had recently been adopted at a meeting of the Congregation of St Cecilia and was signed by Giuseppe Baini,
director of the papal chapel:

> [...] some singers managed to get possession of the works of the past, and arrogated to
> themselves the right of conducting the music in various churches. Not content with
> this they went a step further, and from being simple directors of music they aspired

4   See Hayburn (as n.1), 121.
5   Quoted in Hayburn, 122.
6   Ibid.
7   Ibid., 123.

to appear as composers. From this cause the House of God had been invaded by a horde of plagiarists, one brings into the Church the *Gerusalemme* of Zingarelli, an opera produced in the theatre, but here adapted to the words of the *Gloria*; another introduces the *Orazii* and the *Curiazii* of Cimarosa, another theatrical work disguised as a Mass; one the *Elisa* and *Claudio* of Mercadente, set to a Vesper; and, to pass over a multitude of similar horrors, quite recently, to our shame, we have heard the most popular airs, *finali* and duets of Rossini's *Gazza Ladra* and *Armida*, sung to the solemn and sacred words of the *Tantum Ergo*.

Such an eruption of profane music and of profaners of the Holy Temple cannot any longer be tolerated by the Ecclesiastical Superiors.[8]

Spontini then proceeded to compare the state of church music in Italy with that of other countries. He noted that with only several notable exceptions, the fundamental problem was that liturgical music had largely been left in the hands of inexperienced amateurs who had found their way into positions of musical leadership in churches and chapels which they did not deserve to hold. This was not the case in other countries, including Germany, France, England and Switzerland, and it was especially not the case in churches of the Reformation where a tradition of dignified liturgical music had been well-established since the sixteenth century.[9]

German foundations

In the early to mid-nineteenth century, Ratisbon had become an important centre for the study of Gregorian chant, and various attempts were registered to restore congregational singing. The reintroduction of polyphony would assist this task both in reforming modern church music but also in adding a more dramatic flair to Gregorian chant, which had been considered too monotonous and uninteresting by some. Thus, what emerged was a more emotional and dramatic rendering of Gregorian chant with quite

8   Quoted in Hayburn (as n.1), 122–3.
9   See Hayburn, 123–4.

elaborate melodies, metrical rhythms, and the accompaniment of the chant by various musical instruments. As the great Belgian liturgical pioneer Olivier Rousseau described it: 'The concert hall had invaded the sanctuary and had given its character to the sacred ceremonies.'[10] What happened in Germany is significant for what would happen in the United States later in the nineteenth century, since Benedictine monasteries which became centres of liturgical and musical renewal were largely founded as daughter houses of larger German and Swiss monasteries. Thus the Ratisbon tradition found its way across the Atlantic in a relatively short period of time.

At the Congress of Bamberg in 1868, like-minded church musicians and clergy from Germany, Austria and Switzerland formed themselves into the Allgemeiner Cäcilienverein. Two years later, on 16 December 1870, Pope Pius IX officially established the Association of Saint Cecilia with the brief *Multum ad commovendos animos.* While praising the work of German bishops in the musical reforms they had introduced, helped by promotional efforts of the St Cecilia Society, Pius IX continued the tradition initiated by his predecessor, Pius VIII, in lamenting the 'theatrical representations' adopted in the sacred music of many churches of the day.[11]

At the request of the pope, Friedrich Pustet published his version of the so-called 'Medicean' edition of the Tridentine Gradual of Paul V, which had been developed by Palestrina and other composers of the day, blending together medieval chant with musical innovations of the sixteenth century. Pustet's edition of the Gradual was declared authentic by the Sacred Congregation of Rites and praised by Pius IX in a brief of 1873. It would enjoy a thirty-year monopoly on publishing rights even though the text itself was corrupt, precisely because of the numerous embellishments which had only been made worse by Pustet.[12]

---

10   Dom Olivier Rosseau, OSB, *The Progress of the Liturgy* (Westminster, Maryland: Newman Press, 1951), 115.

11   See Hayburn (as n.1), 128.

12   See James F. White, *Roman Catholic Worship: Trent to Today* (New York: Paulist Press, 1995), 88.

The nineteenth-century reform of sacred music in North America

In Cincinnati, Ohio, the first American Society of Saint Cecilia was founded by the Revd Martin Henni on 22 November 1838. Six years later, in 1844, Henni was named the first bishop of Milwaukee and soon established that diocese's first seminary in the Milwaukee suburbs at Saint Francis. He imported its first rector from Germany, the Revd Joseph Salzmann, and together they founded a sort of 'teachers' college' for future teachers in the diocese's parish grade schools and also to serve as church musicians. In response to Salzmann's request that Ratisbon might send several competent church musicians across the Atlantic to serve as instructors, John Singenberger and Max Spiegler arrived at Saint Francis in April 1873. Together they began their work immediately, and the first item on the agenda was the establishment of an American branch of the St Cecilia Society, which held its first meeting on 7 May 1893.

Singenberger quickly emerged as the leader in the movement to reform sacred music in North America. Not only had he been schooled at Regensburg and therefore exposed to the important work being done there on the revival of Gregorian chant, but he also demonstrated significant entrepreneurial skills that would lead him to help others in implementing the Ratisbon vision. He soon began choral festivals throughout the United States to expose American Catholics to this new form of church music, and in 1874 he founded the magazine *The Caecilia*, which aimed to help familiarize members of the American branch of the St Cecilia Society with church laws on sacred music. He also wrote books and guides for organists and choir directors and composed Masses, motets, and organ music according to the musical style developed at Regensburg.[13]

In 1875 Milwaukee was created an archdiocese, thereby raising Henni to the rank of archbishop. He wasted no time in exerting the influence of his new ecclesiastical rank. One of his first official actions as archbishop of

13   See Hayburn (as n.1), 129–30.

Milwaukee was to petition Pope Pius IX for the special apostolic establishment and confirmation of the Saint Cecilia Society in the United States, just as had been granted for the church in Germany and Italy. That concession was granted on 6 February 1876, and the papally sponsored US branch of the Association of St Cecilia was officially constituted. Several months later, Henni petitioned the pope for a plenary indulgence that might be granted to the US Society on the feast of St Cecilia, which was duly granted by the pope provided that members 'contritely confess their sins and received Holy Communion in a church in which the Society is established', and 'pray devoutly according to the intentions of His Holiness.'[14]

Henni's and Singenberger's efforts at Saint Francis and within the American branch of the Saint Cecilia Society were further supported by German and Swiss-American monasteries that were flourishing throughout the United States, especially in the Midwest. The abbey of Saint Meinrad in southern Indiana, which had been founded from the Swiss monastery of Einsiedeln, soon became one such important centre for promoting Ratisbon chant that had already been widely diffused throughout Europe.

There were significant cultural differences regarding liturgical music among the various immigrant groups arriving in the United States at the time. In Germany, for example, congregational singing – including the regular usage of vernacular hymnody – was quite commonplace in areas like Bavaria even prior to the sixteenth-century Reformation. The situation in Ireland was different, largely complicated by English oppression and the need to celebrate Mass secretly so as not to be discovered. These Masses often took place behind barns in what came to be called 'rock Masses' and carried with them the tradition of a silent rendering of the Mass which included little if any congregational singing.

Be that as it may, while Ratisbon held sway throughout the nineteenth century with its promotion of a more innovative and dramatic form of Gregorian chant, the French Benedictine monks of Solesmes were quietly working away at careful study of hundreds of medieval chant manuscripts. Re-founded by Prosper Guéranger in 1833 after it had been suppressed during the French Revolution, Guéranger endeavoured to promote a strict observance of the Roman Rite in the monastic celebration of both Mass

---

14   Quoted in Hayburn (as n.1), 130.

and the Hours. Thus, the development of a laboratory in which monks would devote themselves to chant research would aid the ultimate goal of the Romanization of nineteenth-century French Catholic worship. The chant discoveries at Solesmes, however, would have global repercussions and would set the stage for the evolution of liturgical music in the twentieth century.

The Jesuit musicologist Angelo De Santi had been significantly influenced by the research done at Solesmes, the results of which stood in sharp contrast to the form of chant that had been promoted at Regensburg by individuals like Pustet and officially sanctioned by the Holy See. De Santi made his opinion known to the newly elected Pope Pius X and, not surprisingly, was asked to formulate a significant number of the principles found in the pope's 1903 *motu proprio*, *Tra le sollecitudini*, which was dedicated to the subject of sacred music and more particularly, sacred music reform. Prior to his nomination as Cardinal Patriarch of Venice and then his election as Pope Pius X, Giuseppe Sarto had been an organist and choirmaster, so the topic of his first *motu proprio* hardly came as a surprise.

In his *motu proprio*, the pope called for a return to the pure Gregorian chant as recovered by the monks of Solesmes, so that Catholic laity and clergy alike might better participate in the liturgy. Even though other popes had written their own documents on the subject of sacred music, Pius X wrote more than all the popes combined. Faithful to the spirit of Solesmes, it challenged the use of overly dramatic and theatrical music, calling for a return to music that was appropriate to the house of God and truly 'liturgical'.

Early twentieth-century developments in England

In England, John Ainslie noted that both 'tradition and ethos' militated against congregational singing and, indeed, despite great loyalty to the church in light of Modernism, the attention given to *Tra le sollecitudini* was minimal. Writing on the English situation, Ainslie affirmed:

Pius X's injunctions concerning the fostering of congregational music went largely
unheeded, as did his exhortations on the cultivation of better plainsong among
choirs. There were many parishes in England where neither of these forms of music
was practised and many where they were not known at all. There were few teachers
equipped to teach them – very few in the case of the chant – and few choirs, whether
of men or boys mixed, which could count on three or four good readers to make
feasible the performance of the simplest piece of polyphony. For all the nostalgia for
the beautiful singing of the past, there were far too many parishes where the music
of the liturgy, even if rubrically correct, was far from beautiful.[15]

A notable exception to the problem of congregational singing in England
was the Evening Service – rosary, novenas, and litanies – which always
included hymns. Thus, even if the Mass did not habitually offer a sung
Mass on Sunday mornings, it nonetheless would always offer eucharistic
Benediction in the evening, with the congregation singing *O Salutaris* or
Tantum ergo with gusto. Similarly, congregants were accustomed to singing hymns such as *Hail, Queen of Heav'n, the Ocean Star* or *Sweet Heart
of Jesus, Fount of Love and Mercy* as familiar hymns sung during Sunday
evening devotions. And of course, a constant was Faber's *Faith of our fathers*,
with its especially nationalistic tone: 'Mary's prayers shall win our country
back to thee'. Nonetheless, what remained was a clear distinction – indeed,
a certain distance between liturgical music and more devotional hymns,
where parishioners would easily sing the latter but not the former.[16]

Despite the significant number of English Catholics with Irish roots,
Ainslie noted the paucity of Irish music in the *Crown of Jesus Hymn Book* of
1861 and the first edition of the *Westminster Hymnal* (1912). Except for the
annual singing of *Hail, Glorious Saint Patrick* on 17 March, there was precious little by way of Irish contribution. The well-known tune *Slane*, often
sung to the text 'Be thou my vision', only arrived in English hymnals after
the Second Vatican Council, and only thanks to Anglican sources.[17]

---

15   John Ainslie, 'English Liturgical Music before Vatican II', in J.D. Crichton, H.E.
      Winstone and J.R. Ainslie (eds), *English Catholic Worship: Liturgical Renewal in
      England since 1900* (London: Geoffrey Chapman, 1979), 49–50.
16   See Ainslie (as n.15), 48.
17   Ibid., 49.

That said, however, it should be noted that there were various attempts to promote Gregorian chant in England, and a more liturgical conscious-ness within sacred music itself. Westminster Cathedral itself offered an important model of how chant could be employed, as well as places like Downside and Ampleforth Abbeys, and, of course, Brompton Oratory in Knightsbridge. The Society of Saint Gregory was founded on 12 March 1929 and made its own contribution, as it focused on four principal aims: (1) to maintain the dignity of the liturgy as the 'supreme instrument of congregational worship'; (2) to implement the wishes of Pius X in his *motu proprio* and also of Pius XI in his Apostolic Constitution of 28 Decem-ber 1928, *Divini cultus*, on the same subject; (3) to offer a yearly course in plainsong and polyphony for choir directors, teachers, and others who may be interested; and (4) to foster membership. The first meeting of the Saint Gregory Society led to a three-day meeting at the Dominican Col-lege of Blackfriars, Oxford, which took place in August of the same year. Proponents of a renewed liturgical life in the United Kingdom through a recovery of the church's musical tradition found mutual support and encouragement at Blackfriars.[18]

In July 1930, just one year after the founding of the Saint Gregory Soci-ety, Archbishop Downey of Liverpool wrote in *Plainsong for Schools*:

> Here in Liverpool, and, I am told, also in Birmingham, Cardiff and Nottingham, many people have been converted to the Plain Chant movement by the simple les-sons and practical demonstrations given by members of the Society of Saint Gregory [...] It has been gratifying to see the way in which the music of the Church has been appreciated by those who have taken the trouble to master its principles and method. Like the liturgy, it is in itself a prayer; an act of worship.[19]

18 Ibid., 50.
19 Quoted in Ainslie (as n.15), 53.

Twentieth-century developments in the United States

In the late nineteenth and early twentieth centuries, the American situation largely replicated what was happening in England. One of the most significant publications to appear in the United States during that period was Singenberger's *Guide to Catholic Church Music*. First printed in 1905 and reprinted in 1911 with a supplement, Singenberger's publication offered a 270-page text which listed what was considered to be acceptable church music. It contained both the names and publishers of more than one thousand Masses along with hundreds of settings of the Proper of the Mass, motets, supplementary Offertories, as well as organ selections. Singenberger's *Guide* became standard in many parishes and dioceses, and many diocesan bishops required their clergy and parish music directors to strictly adhere to what was found within that text.

In fact, this led to what came to the called 'white lists' for approved liturgical music and 'black lists' for that music which was no longer permitted. At the end of the day, however, whether the music was appropriate or inappropriate, a fundamental problem remained, and that was that in many parts of the English-speaking world, especially in North America, Catholics were not accustomed to singing in church. The exception were German immigrants, where they were to be found, as they brought with them a strong tradition of vernacular hymnody and musical participation. Given their own history, Irish immigrants saw singing as a 'Protestant custom' which was not to be embraced by Roman Catholics.

The situation was further complicated by the fact that chant continued to be viewed by many as cold and uninteresting, and even a *motu proprio* from the new pope was not about to change people's minds.[20] Where Catholic hymnody did exist, it tended to be fairly limited to the sentimental and devotional. Members of some congregations argued that even when singing sentimental Marian hymns like *Bring Flowers of the Fairest*, they were nonetheless singing 'liturgically'. But the liturgical pioneers of that period contested such talk. Virgil Michel, the German-American

---

20   See Keith F. Pecklers, *The Unread Vision: The Liturgical Movement in the United States of America, 1926–1955* (Collegeville: Liturgical Press, 1998), 256–8.

Benedictine and founder of the US liturgical movement, argued that the communal singing of hymns was 'liturgical' when it was in keeping with the 'liturgical spirit'.[21]

Despite the odds, liturgical pioneers and church musicians continued to promote Gregorian chant as the sung prayer of the mystical body of Christ.[22] The American branch of the Association of St Cecilia took the lead, greatly assisted by their monthly journal, *The Caecilia*, which set high musical standards for its composers. They were diligent in their attempts to abolish eighteenth- and nineteenth-century rococo music in churches, while advocating a return to Palestrina and the polyphony of the sixteenth century. While the Cecilian movement was originally centred in the Midwest – Milwaukee, Chicago, and Minneapolis-St Paul – as was the case with the wider US liturgical movement, the movement gradually expanded to the dioceses of Covington, Kentucky, San Francisco, and Portland, Oregon, while the country's east coast remained largely untouched by Cecilian efforts. Seen as an elitist and effete group, they had enemies on both sides of the Atlantic. The Liturgical Arts Society made its own contribution to the promotion of chant, forming a *schola cantorum* within the organization in 1934. Even though it was small in number, the *schola* set out to prove that chant was possible in American Catholic parishes. For a number of years, the 'Quilisima Club', as they were called, sang at principal Eucharists on Sundays and feasts in New York City churches.[23]

The greatest contribution to the promotion of chant in the United States and proper training in liturgical music was the Pius X School of Liturgical Music founded in 1916 by Mrs Justine B. Ward and Mother Georgia Stevens, RSCJ. Inspired by the *motu proprio*, Ward and Stevens opened a school for the teaching of Gregorian chant at the College of the Sacred Heart, Manhattanville, New York.[24] Ward was an accomplished

21   See 'Editor's Corner', *Orate Fratres* 3 (1929), 381.

22   See Clement J. McNaspy, SJ, 'Singing in the Church', *The Caecilia* 71 (1943–44), 207.

23   See John La Farge, SJ, *The Manner is Ordinary* (New York: Harcourt, Brace, and Company, 1954), 290.

24   See Catherine Carroll, *A History of the Pius X School of Liturgical Music: 1916–1969* (Washington: Catholic University of America Press, 1987).

musician and a newcomer to Catholicism. She was a frequent visitor to the Benedictine monastery of Solesmes, France, then in exile on the Isle of Wight. She essentially brought the Solesmes method of chant to North America since her own methodology was largely dependent upon chant studies taking place at that monastery.

Ward soon came to know John Young, SJ, a distinguished choirmaster at Saint Francis Xavier Parish in New York City who had earned a reputation for successfully teaching chant to choir members of that parish. Young was responsible for producing chant recordings using what came to be known as the Ward Method, and for incorporating the exercises and drills from the Chevé manuals for teaching music into the Ward Method. The Chevé *Méthode* was a popularized sight-reading manual used in Belgian, French, and Dutch schools in the late nineteenth century. Ward borrowed the use of numbers and intonation exercises from Chevé in developing her own method. By 1915, the first and second books of her method were published and used by a number of schools in the New York area. And by 1925, only ten years after the first publication of her manual, more than 13,000 teachers had studied Ward's method of chant. While teaching children the method during the academic year, Ward and Stevens focused their attention on adult education in the summers, often inviting chant specialists from Solesmes as summer faculty.

Gradually, other musical institutes grew around the United States, such as the St Cloud Music Institute in Minnesota, founded in 1928 by the Benedictine chant specialist Ermin Vitry. In 1935, the archbishop of Saint Paul, Minnesota, John Murray, launched a summer institute in liturgical music for choir directors, required for their certification by the archdiocesan Commission on Sacred Music. Six years later, in 1941, the Catholic Choirmasters' Correspondence Course was inaugurated in Pittsburgh, Pennsylvania, by the music director of Sacred Heart Parish, Pittsburgh, Clifford A. Bennett. The name was soon changed to the Gregorian Institute of Pittsburgh, and eventually to the Gregorian Institute of America when it re-located to Toledo, Ohio, in 1945. Summer institutes in liturgical music were also offered at the University of Notre Dame, De Paul University in Chicago, St Joseph's College in Collegeville, Minnesota, The

Catholic University of America, The Newton College of the Sacred Heart in Massachusetts, and The College of St Joseph in New Mexico.[25]

Even as liturgical pioneers and church musicians did their best to encourage Gregorian chant in dioceses around the United States, there was little encouragement in the 1930s and 1940s to explore a peculiarly American form of liturgical music. It was not until the time of the Second Vatican Council (1962–65) that American Catholics began to make greater use of hymnody and incorporate American hymn tunes and African-American spirituals into the liturgy. Thus, parishes and religious communities were noted for their liturgical singing when they learned to sing chant well: when they gathered to chant Sunday Vespers or sung a Gregorian setting of the Mass on Sunday morning in unison. Holy Cross Parish in St Louis became famous for such 'liturgical singing' thanks to its pastor, Monsignor Martin Hellriegel, who was one of the country's leading liturgical pioneers and who succeeded in convincing his parish of the value of chant. Parishes like Holy Cross, however, were more the exception than the norm. In light of the great economic depression of the 1930s, some Catholics argued that they had little to sing about at Mass or anywhere else for that matter. The archbishop of St Louis, John J. Glennon, responded by urging US Catholics to allow their liturgical singing to express their own lament as a corporate body:

> In these days of depression a large percentage of people is dependent on the govern-ment for its daily bread. Everybody is poor now, so there is a tendency for humanity to become disconsolate, thinking that all is lost when money is gone. In the Christian ages of the past the people did not have banks, they did not have usury, they did not have millionaires and factories; but their voices, hearts, and souls were attuned to the service of God, and it is the songs of the poor, the humble, and the lowly that God hears. He is their Father. He is your Father, too, and He listens to your song when you sing His praises as you do [...] In your song let there be charity and peace, thus you will be able to promote by means of the Gregorian chant, the gospel, the peace, and the charity of Christ.[26]

25   See 'Summer Schools in Catholic Church Music', *The Caecilia* 79 (1952), 157–60.
26   'Address by the Most Rev. John J. Glennon, D.D., Archbishop of St. Louis, Mo., at Organists Guild Meeting', *The Caecilia* 62 (1935), 194.

North American church music in its ethnic and ecumenical contexts

A unique phenomenon in the United States was the effect that ethnicity played upon the evolution of liturgical music in the nineteenth, but especially in the twentieth, century. This was particularly the case in German and Polish national parishes where those immigrant groups brought with them a tradition of congregational singing from their homeland. Despite the *motu proprio* of 1903 and the subsequent papal decrees of 1928 prohibiting vernacular hymns during Mass, congregational singing in German and Polish was normative in many of those parishes. Both ethnic groups sang the Mass back in the late 1930s and 1940s. Communities such as St Stanislaus Koska Parish in Chicago became famous for such vernacular singing. In 1947, one non-Pole who was a newcomer to Sts Peter and Paul Parish in Detroit complained that 'every high Mass [...] is sung in Polish. When the priest intones the *Gloria*, the choir responds with a Polish hymn.'[27] By 1948, Polish hymns were sung at the principal Mass of St Francis Parish in Detroit and the pastor reported that the church was 'packed to capacity'.[28] Poles were admired for the carols that they sang at the *Pasterka* (Shepherd's Mass) early on Christmas morning, as well as for the haunting tones of the *Gorzkie Zale* (Bitter Lamentations), sung by a number of Polish congregations during Holy Week.[29]

Just as the expression of lament through liturgical singing was discussed in light of the economic depression of the 1930s and also during the Second World War,[30] it became an important part of African-American self-discovery as that constituency tried to come to terms with their history

27   Leslie Woodcock Tentler, *Seasons of Grace: A History of the Catholic Archdiocese of Detroit* (Detroit: Wayne State University Press, 1990), 423.
28   Ibid., 350.
29   Ibid., 181.
30   See 'The Editor Writes', *The Caecilia* 69 (1941–42), 178–81.

of long suffering and oppression because of the slave trade.[31] In fact, it was precisely through the experience of slavery that African-American spirituals and gospel music grew in the Bible Belt of the deep South in the first place. Evolving within the nineteenth century, that music became a means of liberation from the oppressive experience of slavery, enabling African Americans to become subjects rather than objects of their own experience. In singing *Nobody Knows the Troubles I've Seen* or *Precious Lord*, they knew that it was their own story being told in the singing.

That musical genre would continue to develop, to arranged spirituals in the 1870s, to folk gospel in the 1890s. In the early twentieth century the idiom of African-American spirituals and folk gospel music grew into 'gospel music' with the expansion of gospel quartets and gospel groups in the 1940s and gospel choirs in the 1950s. While this musical idiom did eventually find its way into African-American Catholic parishes, it did not happen in any substantial way until the civil rights movement and the advent of Vatican II. There were, however, some early voices within the liturgical movement who encouraged greater liturgical and particularly musical participation by black Catholics, and several black parishes were already noted for their music and worship as early as 1933.[32]

In addition to the ethnic dimension to church life in North America, another significant aspect was and is its ecumenical diversity, and this is especially evident regarding the history of liturgical music, particularly in the twentieth century. A closer look at this important dimension makes it clear that the evolution of church music on American shores was much more than a mere passage of chant from Europe to North America. In an interesting chapter entitled 'Twentieth-Century American Hymnody and Church Music', Paul Westermeyer notes that prior to 1955, when Gilbert Chase first published his seminal work *America's Music*,[33] the standard opinion was that church music in the US had largely been imported from

31   See 'The Meaning of Spirituals', *Catholic Art Quarterly* 17 (1953), 69; also Theophilus Lewis, 'The Negro Spirituals As Hymns of a People', *America* 61 (1939), 43–4.

32   See editorial, *Orate Fratres* 7 (1933), 179.

33   Gilbert Chase, *America's Music: From the Pilgrims to the Present* (Urbana: University of Illinois Press, rev. 3rd edn 1987).

Western Europe.[34] Chase called that theory into question by demonstrat-
ing that church music in North America has its own distinct genius and
identity.

First World War concerns of a nation at war were evident in the Episcopal hymnal of 1916 and the 1917 supplement to the Presbyterian hymnal of
1895. Both hymnals included Rudyard Kipling's *God of Our Fathers, Known
of Old*, Francis Scott Key's *O Say Can You See*, and Julia Ward Howe's *Mine
Eyes Have Seen the Glory of the Coming of the Lord*. Westermeyer notes that
because of 'war time animosity against Germany', the editors of the 1916
Episcopal hymnal camouflaged classic German chorales with English titles.
So *Herzlich tut mich verlangen* became the 'Passion Chorale' – a practice
maintained by the editors of the 1940 Episcopal hymnal.[35]

Westermeyer identifies a particular shape to the unfolding of hymnody
in North America in the twentieth century which was three-fold in scope:
ecumenical and historical; gospel hymnody; and social concerns. While
the first two were linked together already by the end of the nineteenth
century, the 'Social Gospel' movement of the twentieth century had its
own influence on church music across denominational lines. Henry Sloane
Coffin's *Hymns of the Kingdom of God* and Mabel Mussey's *Social Hymns
of Brotherhood and Aspiration* exemplified the sort of social consciousness
that was evolving in American hymnody and the effect that such liturgical
music would have in promoting more socially-committed worship linked
to mission.[36]

George Pullen Jackson lamented the fact that American urban congregations tended to omit American folk hymns from their service books.
Having studied at the Royal Conservatory of Music in Dresden, as well as
Vanderbilt, Munich, Bonn and at the University of Chicago, he had a very
impressive portfolio. Taking an interest in the Sacred Harp Singers and

---

34   See Paul Westermeyer, 'Twentieth-Century American Hymnody and Church Music',
     in Jay P. Dolan and James P. Wind (eds), *New Dimensions in American Religious
     History: Essays in Honor of Martin E. Marty* (Grand Rapids: William B. Eerdmans,
     1993), 178.
35   See Westermeyer (as n.34), 188–9.
36   Ibid., 186.

other groups devoted to white spirituals of the South, Jackson is credited with introducing that music to the wider public, which contributed to the gradual inclusion of folk hymns into American hymnals.[37]

As the ecumenical liturgical collaboration grew significantly in the twentieth century, especially in the 1940s and 1950s, denominational hymnals came to represent an increasingly broad ecumenical breadth. Already in 1861, *Hymns Ancient and Modern* had brought together a wide range of hymns drawn from diverse traditions and became a sort of *editio typica* – a model to be emulated. This is well demonstrated in the Baptists' 1898 hymnal edited by E.H. Johnson with its curiously Roman title, *Sursum Corda*.[38] The greatest beneficiaries were Roman Catholics, of course, whose hymnals gradually came to include Anglican, Lutheran, and Methodist classics – a welcome change from Catholic hymns like *Mother Dear, O Pray for Me*. One need only think of how much Catholics have benefitted from the rich theology contained within the hymns of Charles and John Wesley to get the point.

Just as in the Catholic Church, other denominations founded and sponsored their own organizations and institutes aimed at furthering musical education in church life. In 1896, soon after becoming Dean of the School of Music at Northwestern University in Evanston, Illinois, Peter Christian Lutkin launched a department of church music whose influence extended far beyond the Methodist confines of that university. In that same year, 1896, the American Guild of Organists was founded to 'advance the cause of organ and choral music' and 'to improve the proficiency of organists and conductors'. The Hymn Society in the United States and Canada (formerly the Hymn Society of America) was founded in 1922 with the scope of promoting congregational singing. In 1926 the widely acclaimed Westminster Choir College was founded by John Finley Williamson, emerging from his work at Westminster Presbyterian Church in Dayton, Ohio, and it continues to thrive today at Princeton, New Jersey. Two years later, in 1928, one of the founders of the American Guild of Organists,

37   Ibid., 183.
38   Ibid.

Clarence Dickinson, started a School of Sacred Music at Union Theological Seminary in New York which exhibited a wide breadth of ecumenical
interest and served church musicians from throughout the United States.
The Methodist Church Music Society was founded in 1935, the American
Guild of English Handbell Ringers in 1954, and the Moravian Music Foundation in 1956. Among the largest church music programmes were those
developed by the Southern Baptists at their seminaries in New Orleans,
Louisville, and Fort Worth, Texas.[39]

Conclusion

In 1962, with the advent of the Second Vatican Council, the efforts at the
promotion of Gregorian chant soon gave way to the abandonment of the
church's musical heritage almost overnight, in favour of the newfound freedom of liturgical experimentation promoted by the vernacular concessions
granted by the same council. What did take hold and, indeed, has lasted to
this very day, was taking stock of the ethnic and ecumenical foundations
laid by nineteenth- and twentieth-century leaders in church music. That
cultural and ecumenical awareness within liturgical music and the sort
of musical borrowing across denominational lines has only grown more
constant in the past forty-five years and continues to enrich the worship
lives of all our churches.

39   See Westermeyer (as n.34), 195–6.

ANN L. SILVERBERG

Cecilian Reform in Baltimore, 1868–1903

This chapter traces the reform of liturgical music during one of its most controversial and least researched phases. Focusing on a single American city illustrates how a portion of the ethnically diverse, rapidly growing American Catholic church responded to the imported Cecilian liturgical music aesthetic, an aesthetic which was approved and eventually legislated for by the Vatican.

The Cecilian movement was, in some respects, an effort to return to the dictates of the sixteenth-century Council of Trent regarding liturgical music: it attempted to limit liturgical music to chant and *a cappella* choral polyphony in the strict sixteenth-century style. By resurrecting and reinstituting the church's ancient repertory of chant – a reinvigorated body of plainsong or Gregorian chant – and reintroducing the serenely controlled harmonies of the sixteenth century into Catholic liturgies, the Cecilians hoped to prune away distracting musical excess and return Catholic liturgical music to the pure wellspring of musical devotion.

The ideals of the Cecilian movement were quite simple: chant was held to be the most appropriate of all musical styles for liturgical use, and choral polyphony in the style of Palestrina and his contemporaries was to be the only acceptable polyphonic style. Music accompanied by instruments, instrumental selections, and any music with a secular taint – either by virtue of its musical style or by virtue of its prior text or context – was to be banished from liturgical use. Therefore, advocates of the Cecilian movement wished to expunge the orchestral Masses of composers such as Haydn, Mozart, and Beethoven, and any music they judged to be 'theatrical', from liturgies. Reformed church choir repertories, writings, music editions, and music catalogues were among the means of promoting these ends. Cecilian advocates upheld Gregorian chant and Renaissance-style polyphony as spiritually and aesthetically uplifting models for universal liturgical use, even as editions of this music were being created. But aside from the obvious inclusion of instrumental accompaniments, what was 'wrong' with the orchestrated Mass settings of famous composers such as Haydn, Mozart, Beethoven, and Weber? And what was chant anyway? How was it to be sung, and could or should it be accompanied in any way? If not, how were singers to be trained to remain on pitch? Which editions of chant were best? And how were musicians to get hold of Renaissance-style polyphony? Could and would living composers contribute works in an appropriate style? All of these questions had to be answered for the Cecilian movement to progress. More importantly, parishioners, singers, choir directors, priests, and prelates had to be convinced of the benefits of adopting the Cecilian repertory for the movement to succeed.

The Cecilian movement was the dominant reforming force in Catholic church music during the second half of the nineteenth century. It left an indelible mark on the development of liturgical music, and indirectly inspired Pope Pius X's *motu proprio* of 1903, *Tra le sollecitudini*.[1] This document essentially enshrined the ideals of the Cecilian movement and attempted to establish these ideals as universal, permanent models for Catholic liturgical music. Both the Cecilian movement and *Tra le sollecitudini* were efforts to greatly restrict and tightly control the style of music acceptable for use in Catholic liturgies. From the 1840s to 1903, a strand of reforming, purifying effort can be found in Catholic liturgical music history. Yet this strand never managed to thoroughly control Catholic liturgical music. In some places, 'serious' or 'solemn' Catholic music, Gregorian chant, boys' choirs, and *a cappella* Renaissance-style choral polyphony prevailed, sometimes for a considerable time, but this musical situation was far from universal. The Cecilians' earnest effort to narrow the scope of acceptable liturgical music was ultimately extinguished, only to be replaced by a document with similar goals issued by the pope himself

---

1   Robert F. Hayburn includes a translation and analysis of this document along with a discussion of its evolution in his monograph *Papal Legislation on Sacred Music, 95 A.D. to 1977 A.D.* (Collegeville, MN: Liturgical Press, 1979).

and unquestionably enjoined on the church universal. The evolution of a repertory of sacred works that were deemed unacceptable for liturgical use but still beautiful and worthy of listeners' attention was to some extent a by-product of the Cecilian movement. For example, many orchestrated Mass settings became essentially 'oratorios' – sacred music to be heard in concert rather than liturgical music *per se* – and a good deal of this music retains this connotation and context today.

Although the aesthetic model invoked by the Cecilian movement can readily be traced to the Council of Trent, the movement gained momentum in the first half of the nineteenth century with the formation of Cecilian Leagues in Bavaria and Austria, and by the middle of the nineteenth century, Regensburg had become an important centre for Cecilian music training.[2] The Revd Carl Proske had assembled an extensive library of polyphonic choral music in Regensburg, and this collection became an important starting point for the Cecilian movement's evangelical approach to polyphonic music.[3] Regensburg Cathedral, its boys' choir, and its choir school became models of the Cecilian ideal, and by the mid-nineteenth century, these institutions had become the training ground for musicians seeking to present the Cecilian repertory. The music library became a source for new anthologies of appropriate polyphonic liturgical music.

Among the faithful drawn to Regensburg for training in liturgical music were John Singenberger (1848–1924) a German-speaking Swiss, and Joseph Graf, a German priest. Singenberger became the Cecilian movement's chief lay evangelist in the United States: he was the musician sent to America in response to a request from Bishop John Martin Henni of

---

2　　Many sources may be consulted for further information about the Cecilian movement in Europe. Among them are Siegfried Gmeinwieser, 'Cecilian movement', in Stanley Sadie (ed.), *The New Grove Dictionary of Music and Musicians* 5 (2nd edn, London: Macmillan, 2001), 333–4; and Hubert Unverricht (ed.), *Der Caecilianismus: Anfänge–Grundlagen–Wirkungen: Internationales Symposium zur Kirchenmusik des 19. Jahrhunderts* (Eichstätter Abhandlungen zur Musikwissenschaft 5; Tutzing: Schneider, 1988).

3　　For more on Proske, see the article by August Scharnagl and Raymond Dittrich in the *New Grove* (as n.2) 20, 432–3, which also provides a bibliography.

Milwaukee, Wisconsin, for a suitably trained individual to open a school that would in turn send appropriately trained musicians to the parishes of his diocese. Arriving in Wisconsin in 1871, Singenberger soon set up a music school, founded the American St Cecilia Society, and created a publication for it (*The Caecilia*). Joseph Graf's peripatetic career took him to France, Ireland, and finally America, where he eventually led the choir of Baltimore Cathedral. He later served as choirmaster at the newly founded Catholic University of America in Washington, DC.

Transferring the Cecilian movement from its roots in Bavaria and Austria to the international church was not an easy task.[4] Many composers of the era, perhaps most notably Rossini and Verdi, were clear (but apparently not vocal) opponents. Rossini crowned his *Petite Messe Solonnelle* with a tongue-in-cheek dedication to 'Good God', excusing himself as an opera composer and openly raising the question of whether the work was 'sacred' or not when he completed it in 1863. Verdi, moreover, completed his imposing, highly operatic *Requiem* approximately ten years later, its first performance taking place on 22 May 1874 at a 'dry' Mass featuring no consecration of bread and wine in a church not far from La Scala. (The renowned opera house was the site of the wildly successful second performance days later.) Leading composers had not lost their taste for setting liturgical texts in a manner that can only be described as thoroughly theatrical. Re-textings of secular music for use in liturgies was common, if not rampant. Franz Liszt was a dominant figure in European avant-garde music and music-making throughout his many-faceted career, which stretched from the 1820s through the 1880s. When he took minor orders in 1865 he added to his mystique and also gained friends in high positions in the Catholic Church. As a church music composer, Liszt was truly an enigma and a dilemma: an enigma because he continued to write church music without much regard for obedience to any sort of standard, despite the controversy that surrounded polyphonic church music, and a dilemma because it was difficult, if not impossible, to ignore the work of

---

4   While there were parallel developments in Italy, these seem to have been less vital internationally.

such a famous composer – particularly one who had actually taken holy orders. Liszt himself did not help much, noting that he felt that church music should be dramatic but not theatrical. Works such as the *Missa Choralis* (Gregorian Chant Mass) obviously included melodies drawn from medieval chants, but their harmonies, voice leading, and overall structure could hardly be considered to resemble the style of Palestrina.

The effort to transplant the Cecilian movement to the far shores of the American church was arduous and only moderately successful, even at the height of its success. In order to succeed in the United States, the movement's advocates had to convince the American church hierarchy (most of whom were Irish or of Irish descent) to support their goals. By contrast, the Cecilian movement was closely tied to its Bavarian and German roots, and consequently to the culture of German-speaking immigrants. This barrier was difficult to overcome. Cecilian advocates, furthermore, were never truly able to discount the 'theatrical' liturgical music they attempted to supplant to the point that it was disowned. Ultimately, asking congregations, choir directors, and clergy to forego the Mass settings of Mozart, Haydn, Beethoven, and Weber – widely held to be beautiful – was too large a step. As the Cecilian movement attempted to become international, its leaders brought the controversy to Baltimore, where the debate on the correct style or styles of liturgical music was played out in the city's Catholic churches and in its two prominent Catholic newspapers, the *Catholic Mirror* and the *Katholische Volkszeitung*.

By the end of the nineteenth century, France had become the new focal point for Catholic liturgical music reform, due in part to the extensive work of Benedictine monks of Solesmes on medieval liturgical chant. Ultimately, in the early twentieth century, the Solesmes chant editions, analytical methods, and pedagogical tools were adopted nearly universally (they were in fact sanctioned by the Vatican) and the older chant editions put forth by the Cecilians were by and large abandoned. The previous Germanic hegemony of the Cecilian movement had been replaced by French, Belgian, and Italian influence. Twentieth-century reform efforts were somewhat more successful than the Cecilian movement had been, with a widespread effort to reintroduce Solesmes-style Gregorian chant pedagogy leading the way.

Exactly how did the Cecilian movement affect Catholic music in the United States? Why did it fade and fail near the end of the century? By looking at the context and content of the music used in Catholic churches of Baltimore, Maryland, in the second half of the nineteenth century, it is possible to infer some answers to these questions.[5]

Background to the Cecilian movement in Baltimore

The Cecilian movement arrived in Baltimore in the 1860s, but the city's Catholic history extends much farther back into the past. The city dates from the beginnings of the colony of Maryland, which was the only British American colony founded by a Catholic family (the Calverts, in the 1630s). Maryland was the home of Charles Carroll, the only Catholic signatory of the American Declaration of Independence, and one of Charles Carroll's distant relatives, John Carroll, became the first Catholic bishop of the United States.

John Carroll (1735–1815) was a Maryland native educated in Catholic schools in the United States and in Europe. Ordained in Europe, he became the bishop of Baltimore and thus first bishop to rule the entire US Catholic diocese – a gigantic territory – in 1789. Carroll was eager to show that Catholicism was compatible with the ideals and culture of the early republic, and he was equally eager to see that his Faith had the best possible chance to succeed among the diverse peoples of his enormous diocese. One major sticking point for Carroll, at least in his early years, was the exclusive use of Latin in liturgies as mandated by the Vatican. Carroll, however, seems to have backed away from his stance that the use of Latin was 'an Obstacle' to the church's progress in the United States by 1795; quite

---

5   For a full discussion of the background and progress of the movement in Baltimore, see the author's doctoral dissertation, 'The Cecilian Movement in Baltimore, 1868–1903', PhD thesis, University of Illinois at Urbana-Champaign, 1992.

possibly he understood that America would grow as a polyglot nation. He turned to the French to establish the first Catholic seminary in the United States, and the Sulpicians (Société de Saint Sulpice) opened the doors of St Mary's Seminary in Baltimore in 1791.

Something of Carroll's pioneering spirit along with the necessity of adjusting to local conditions seems to be a continuing thread in the long history of Baltimore's Catholic music. Just as Carroll was aware of the difficulty of persuading his compatriots that worship in Latin was a necessity, he realized that non-Catholics were likely to regard some Catholic practices with skepticism at best and outrage at worst. He felt, for instance, that a Corpus Christi procession featuring the Blessed Sacrament (the Eucharist) displayed in a monstrance carried through the streets could effectively incite anti-Catholic sentiment just as it provided the faithful with a singularly Catholic celebration, and he recommended that such processions be conducted on church grounds.[6] It is probably not much of a leap to think that Carroll would likely have approved of liturgical music that sounded compatible or appropriate to the overwhelmingly non-Catholic American majority.

Bustling as a port on the Chesapeake Bay and as a site of manufacturing, Baltimore was home to a number of music shops and publishers in the early and mid nineteenth century. Some of these sold and published collections of Catholic church music, a few of which were dedicated to or approved by John Carroll. Some collections even mentioned Carroll in their prefaces. John Aitken's Philadelphia collection, *A Compilation of the Litanies and Vespers Hymns and Anthems as They are Sung in the Catholic Church Adapted to Voice or Organ* (1787), is regarded as the first collection of Catholic church music to be published in the United States. Benjamin Carr also compiled a Catholic church music collection, published in Baltimore, entitled *Masses, Vespers, Litanies, Hymns, Psalms, Anthems & Motetts* [*sic*], *Composed, Selected, and Arranged for the Use of the Catholic Churches*

---

6   See the letter from Carroll to Enoch Fenwick of 25 June 1811, published in Thomas O'Brien Hanley (ed.), *The John Carroll Papers* 3 (Notre Dame, Indiana: University of Notre Dame Press, 1976), 152–3.

in the United States of America and Respectfully Dedicated to the Rt. Revs. John Carrol [*sic*] *D.D., Bishop of Baltimore*, which appeared in 1806.

The Aitken and Carr collections suggest the singular position of Catholicism and Catholic music in America in this era: they not only show that these music publishers felt that such collections could be successfully marketed; their contents suggest (but do not prove) a certain degree of leniency regarding the church's regulation of liturgy and liturgical music. The Handel aria 'Let the Bright Seraphims [*sic*]' is printed in the middle of a polyphonic (Latin language) setting of the Mass Ordinary in the Aitken collection, suggesting that it might have been sung at the Offertory. In his *Masses, Vespers, Litanies, Hymns, Psalms, Anthems & Motetts*, Carr suggested that movements of Handel's *Messiah* were suitable for use in church at various times of the year. Other English-language works abound in these collections, but their connection to official Catholic liturgies is not specified.

After John Carroll died, Archbishops Leonard Neale (1815–17), Ambrose Marechal (1817–28), James Whitfield (1828–34), Samuel Eccleston (1834–51), Francis Patrick Kenrick (1851–63), and John Martin Spalding (1863–72) ruled the Baltimore archdiocese. It was only during the tenure of John Martin Spalding that the Cecilian movement began to affect the city's church music, and in the decades leading up to that time, elaborate Catholic liturgical music became more and more a hallmark of at least a handful of Baltimore's churches. By the middle of the nineteenth century, sophisticated church music – music by acknowledged master composers such as Mozart, Haydn, and Beethoven – performed by soloists, choir, and orchestra, was heard in some of Baltimore's Catholic churches. Not surprisingly, the cathedral choir (a mixed choir of men and women) seems to have led the way. The archdiocesan archives contain a manuscript notebook detailing the works performed for Sunday High Mass during the early 1840s, when Florine Chateaudun was cathedral organist.[7] Among the composers listed are Beethoven, Cimarosa, Haydn, Mozart, and Weber.

---

7   The volume is titled 'Proceedings of the Choir' and covers the period from September 1840 to March 1842.

As the city grew, Catholic immigrants from Bohemia, England, France, Germany, Haiti, Ireland, Italy, Lithuania, and Poland, as well as migrants from other parts of North America, settled in Baltimore. In the eighteenth and nineteenth centuries, Catholic churches were founded in the city whenever and wherever sufficient Catholics could be found. These groups usually had a common ethnic heritage, and this was reflected in their social and musical lives and in the church music they sang and heard. During the nineteenth century, neighbourhood parishes were founded to serve virtually all the components of the city's ethnically diverse Catholic population. By the late nineteenth century, the city's Catholic population was ethnically and racially quite diverse. Thus the city's parishes show the progress of Cecilian music reform among various ethnic groups.

Judging from articles in the *Catholic Mirror* and the *Katholische Volkszeitung*, the Cecilian movement got its start in Baltimore in the early 1860s. By the time the St Cecilia Society (that is, the institution eventually known as the Allgemeine Caecilien Verein) won the approbation of Pope Pius IX in 1870,[8] the local movement had grown considerably. The pope's action officially blessed the movement's goals and indulgences were granted to members of the society. While this strengthened the Cecilians' position throughout the Catholic world, it by no means forced non-Cecilians to comply with its ideals. It merely meant that the pope acknowledged the work of the Cecilians to be valuable: a truly good (but nevertheless voluntary), spiritually salutary endeavour. Of course, this action also meant that church prelates were likely to think twice before disagreeing with the values of the Cecilian movement. In Baltimore, the Cecilian movement generated considerable controversy as it progressed during the 1870s and 1880s.

Two prominent events sparked by the contributions of three individuals marked the peak of the Cecilian movement in Baltimore. The two events were the 1876 national convention of the American St Cecilia Society, held in Baltimore during the summer of that year, and the Third Plenary Council of the Catholic Church in the United States, held in Baltimore in

---

8   The papal bull *Multum ad commovendis animos* was the document effecting this action.

1884. The music the gathered prelates heard at the latter council's official liturgies, as well as the council's rulings on music, showed distinctly Cecilian tendencies. The three individuals who were most important to the Cecilian movement's development in Baltimore were James Roosevelt Bayley, who served as archbishop of Baltimore from 1872 to 1877; John Singenberger, a Swiss immigrant and the national leader of the Cecilian movement;[9] and Joseph Graf, an immigrant priest and musician who led Baltimore's cathedral choir in singing Cecilian repertory. The remainder of this chapter concentrates on these events and individuals.

The progress of the Cecilian movement in Baltimore

During the 1860s, Baltimore's Catholic newspapers began to describe Cecilian reform. The *Katholische Volkszeitung*'s articles spoke in flattering terms of the reform in Germany and locally, and published more articles concerning it than the *Catholic Mirror*. Several of the city's German-speaking parishes, their choir leaders, and German priests (including Redemptorists) were central to the implementation of Cecilian reform in Baltimore. The German parishes most seriously involved were those of St Alphonsus, St James, and St Michael the Archangel. St Ann's, an English-speaking parish on the north side of the city, also embraced the reform for a time. Among the parishes not involved in the Cecilian movement, by contrast, were those of St Ignatius and St Martin (both English-speaking), the former staffed by Jesuits and the latter heavily Irish.

By 1875, the local movement had gained sufficient strength that plans were made to host the annual convention of the American St Cecilia Society

---

9   Singenberger was probably the most widely known advocate of the Cecilian movement in America. He came quite literally as a musical missionary for the Cecilian movement, arriving in 1871 at the request of Bishop John Martin Henni of Milwaukee, a German-speaking Swiss.

in the city. The plans were approved by Archbishop James Roosevelt Bayley, a vigorous advocate of liturgical music reform who had come into office in 1872.[10]

Bayley attempted to institute Cecilian music in the archdiocese during his five years as archbishop. He found the cathedral's long tradition of solo singing during the Offertory at High Mass particularly offensive and attempted to eliminate it. The archbishop's musical reforms, however, met with significant resistance. Even the changes in music he implemented at the cathedral received negative attention in the *Catholic Mirror*. During Bayley's tenure, Joseph Gegan resigned from his longtime position as cathedral choir director, and was replaced by Edmund G. Hurley, a layman from New York with experience leading choirs singing Gregorian chant. But love of chant was far from universal. In the summer of 1875, a writer identified only as 'Observer' characterized chant as 'coarse and unmeaning tunes (they cannot be called melodies) introduced ages ago' in a letter to the *Catholic Mirror*.[11] Needless to say, 'Observer' was not likely to convert to the Cecilian point of view on liturgical music.

At the end of 1875, plans were well underway for the upcoming convention of the American St Cecilia Society in Baltimore. In preparation, John Singenberger journeyed to the city. Regarding services at St Ignatius, he reported the following in an article which was published in the *Katholische Volkszeitung*:

> The Vespers, etc., were unchurchly, the chant shrieked, not sung [...] while the organist played the introduction in festive style to the point of being comical [...] Disgraceful music – particularly the world-weary, gushing, long solo before the exposed Host![12]

10   A priest in the Church of England prior to his 1842 conversion to Catholicism, Bayley was the nephew of Elizabeth Ann Seton, the founder of the Sisters of Charity, who was later canonized. For further details about Bayley's life and work, see, for example, *The Catholic Encyclopedia* 2 (New York: Appleton, 1907), s.v. 'Bayley, James Roosevelt'.
11   See *Catholic Mirror*, 22 July 1875.
12   *Katholische Volkszeitung*, 12 February 1876.

Finally, in the summer of 1876, at about the same time that Wagner's *Ring of the Nibelungs* had its first performance in Bayreuth, the American St Cecilia Society held its annual convention in the city of Baltimore, with the blessing of Archbishop Bayley.

The Baltimore Cecilian convention left a deep impression. In a general history of the city published in 1881, the historian Thomas A. Scharf summarized the events and effect of the convention as follows:

> A grand concert was given in St. Alphonsus' church, at which music selected in accordance with the severe view of the organization was elegantly rendered. It was an interesting occasion, but the societies have not yet succeeded to any extent in imparting their classical severity to the church music of Baltimore City. Some of the churches adopted the Gregorian chant, but, with rare exceptions, they have allowed it to fall into disuse, the tastes of the congregations plainly tending in the other directions.[13]

The convention was a flashpoint for the movement locally and it apparently polarized opinion. The *Catholic Mirror* of 12 August 1876, for example, carried a letter from 'Observer' – quite possibly the same author who had written the letter quoted above derogating chant. In it the letter writer made it clear that he/she regarded liturgical music as a marker of taste and class; it was a means of 'worshipping God like gentlemen.' The letter also praised the non-Cecilian repertory of orchestrated Mass settings, etc. as the most suitable type of liturgical music.

In October 1877, a little more than a year after the convention, Archbishop Bayley died and the local movement lost its most powerful supporter. Breaking with local tradition, but in line with the archbishop's views, his funeral music comprised Gregorian chant. Previously, archbishops' funerals had featured the Mozart *Requiem*.

The resentment some felt toward Cecilian music was intense. In 1883, a heated debate sprang up in the *Catholic Mirror* regarding a planned concert of church music given by the Catholic Choral Union and conducted by Edmund G. Hurley, who by this time was no longer choirmaster at the

---

13 John Thomas Scharf, *History of Baltimore City and County* (Philadelphia: Louis H. Everts, 1881; repr. ed. with new introduction by Edward G. Howard, Baltimore Regional Publishing Co., 1971), 673.

cathedral. The concert featured two works created for the Catholic liturgy but obviously not aligned with Cecilian standards: Mozart's *Requiem* and Rossini's *Stabat Mater*. The stated goal of the concert was 'to improve church music in this city', and this met with considerable objection on the part of Cecilian advocates. One of them (Joseph Graf) wrote: 'I utterly fail to see how, or in what sense, or in what degree, the production of Rossini's Stabat Mater [...] will "have a wholesome effect on the church music of this city" [...]' Hurley replied that, 'hearing these works with all their deformities, fiddling, and horn-blowings, the singers may be led to see the errors of their ways and may all the sooner become "genuine, liturgical, solid, pious, and edifying" singers of Cecilian music.'[14] It is worth noting that the Mozart *Requiem* escaped criticism, even from the staunchly Cecilian Graf.

Archbishop James Roosevelt Bayley was succeeded by James Gibbons, one of the city's native sons, as archbishop of Baltimore. During his long term in office (1877–1921), Gibbons became one of America's most beloved clerics. In 1886, he was the second American to become cardinal and was widely praised for his zeal, mild manner, and ability to successfully negotiate conflicts. It seems that Gibbons eventually allowed the reintroduction of the old orchestrated Mass settings and solos at the Offertory at Baltimore's cathedral. Still, it was apparently during Gibbons' tenure as archbishop that Joseph Graf became choirmaster of the cathedral.

Like John Singenberger, Fr Joseph Graf had been trained in Regensburg, at the heart of the Cecilian world. After working in Baltimore for some years, he became choirmaster at the Catholic University of America in Washington, DC, and later moved to New York City. Like Hurley before him, Graf strove to develop choirs that sang Gregorian chant and Renaissance-style polyphony. While in Baltimore, Graf developed a boys' choir and created an edition of one of Palestrina's Masses.

In 1884, the Third Plenary Council of the American Catholic Church was held in Baltimore, with Archbishop Gibbons presiding. The council's official liturgies featured an impressive array of Cecilian music, under the direction of Joseph Graf. The music heard at the council's ceremonies

14   *Catholic Mirror*, 1 December 1883.

brought the ideals of the Cecilian movement into the view of the entire American hierarchy. Fr Graf led a choir of boys and seminarians from St Mary's Seminary in singing the Mass Proper texts in Gregorian chant, while a mixed choir of men and women sang the Ordinary texts in settings by Palestrina and Cecilian composers of the nineteenth century. Only a few works by Palestrina were featured: the motet *O Beata Trinitas* and the *Missa Papae Marcelli*. Most of the Cecilian-era composers were not well known, but Graf and Singerberger were among them. Others included Franz Witt, the founding father of the Allegemine Caecilien Verein (he was also a priest) and several other Cecilian composers now obscure: Ett, Greith, Santner, Schuetky, and Stehle. Items included motets and other choral polyphony, all without accompaniment and in the best Cecilian taste.[15]

The council marked the final high point of the Cecilian movement in Baltimore, and Cecilian advocates surely hoped that it would have the long-sought effect of dispersing the Cecilian musical ideal throughout the United States as the gathered clerics made their way home. New regulations approved at the Third Plenary Council came close to adopting a Cecilian attitude, but fell far short of specifying precise limits on the repertory of liturgical music. The council's single ruling on sacred music (found under 'Title iii, Of Sacred Worship') reads: '(iv) Of sacred music. Profane melodies are forbidden. The music should accord with the sacredness of time and place. Psalms are not to be curtailed at Vespers. The Mass must not be interrupted by the length of the choir-singing.'[16] Precisely what constituted music in 'accord with the sacredness of time and place' and exactly how 'profane melodies' were to be identified was left open to conjecture.

Records show that some Baltimore parishes did indeed change their repertories in response to the Cecilian movement in the 1870s and 1880s. Not surprisingly, the most prominently 'Cecilian' parishes were heavily German: St Alphonsus, St James, and St Michael the Archangel were the most prominent churches to take up the Cecilian standard, and theirs were the choirs

---

15   A memorial booklet of the council's liturgies held in the Baltimore Diocesan Archives provides these details.
16   *The Catholic Encyclopedia* 2 (as n.10), s.v. 'Baltimore, Plenary Councils of'.

most involved in the 1876 Cecilian convention. St Ann's, on the northern edge of the city, was peripherally involved, largely because it was backed by a patron who was willing to fund a boys' choir at the attached school.

Individuals such as Joseph Graf edited Renaissance choral works with an eye toward reintroducing such works in liturgies. In Germany and Austria as well as in France, major efforts were made to unearth chant manuscripts and apply the knowledge gathered from them to new editions. The new musicological discoveries provided the fuel and the repertory for the Cecilians.

Justifying the rejection of musical works by Haydn, Mozart, and Beethoven was difficult, as this music was widely considered beautiful. Baltimore's Catholic weeklies, the *Katholische Volkszeitung* and the *Catholic Mirror*, documented the debate over Cecilian reform, detailing the cultural and spiritual values the opposing groups assigned to their ideal liturgical music repertories. Basically, the Cecilians found themselves arguing that while no one could plausibly deny the beauty of the orchestrated Mass settings of the masters (Mozart, Haydn, and Beethoven in particular), they were good as music, but not as liturgical music. Whatever pious legends might be ascribed to these composers, the Cecilians resolutely pointed out the secular spirit which they felt had clearly invaded these works. Accompaniment by an orchestra remained unacceptable to them, and thus, use of these Mass settings at liturgies was *verboten* as far as the Cecilians were concerned. Essentially, the work of the Cecilians helped move these works out of their original liturgical context and into a special category, akin to oratorio: suitable for concert use, perhaps, but not for liturgies.

Conclusion

Advocates of the Cecilian movement assigned themselves a tall order: convincing Catholics that churches should eschew the elegant, refined liturgical music penned by Haydn, Mozart, Beethoven and others, and instead invoke the solemn and serene sounds of Gregorian chant and *a cappella* Palestrinian vocal polyphony in liturgies. In Baltimore, Maryland, the battle was at least as much a discussion of the functions of musical aesthetics in relation to social class as it was a controversy over the spiritual value of music. In this American city, the movement never took permanent hold, even in the German parishes which for a time supported the Cecilian movement and sent their choirs to participate in the 1876 national Cecilian convention's events. Only one archbishop, James Roosevelt Bayley, was vocal and consistent in his advocacy of Cecilian ideals. His complaint about society ladies holding forth as vocal soloists at Mass in the cathedral made him unpopular with them, and the changes he insisted upon in the cathedral choir moved anti-Cecilians to produce concerts and write letters to the city's Catholic weeklies in protest. After Bayley's death, a much younger and far less polarizing archbishop, James Gibbons, was installed. Gibbons consistently tried to arrive at compromises designed to alienate the fewest possible constituents. Joseph Graf, an immigrant German priest, conducted the cathedral choir for several years during Gibbons' rule, providing strictly Cecilian music for the special liturgies held for the Third Plenary Council of the American Catholic Church, which met in Baltimore in 1884.

By 1900, the struggle was over; the Cecilian movement had lost impetus in Baltimore. Fewer and fewer press reports listed the performance of identifiably Cecilian works at liturgies, and more and more 'special events' (such as the fiftieth anniversary of a pastor's ordination) included notably non-Cecilian works, which were perhaps favoured by the honouree. The Cecilian chant editions issued by the Regensburg firm of Pustet eventually lost their status as the officially sanctioned Vatican edition. Based as they were on the printed Medicean edition first begun by Palestrina, these books could lay no claim to direct redaction from medieval manuscript sources, as the new Solesmes editions did. A truly international reform occurred only in the wake of Pope Pius X's *motu proprio* of 1903, which advocated reforms parallel to the Cecilian movement's ideals. This document's promulgation had a broad and deep effect on American Catholic church music.

Even H.L. Mencken, Baltimore's acerbic newspaper critic, had a positive reaction to the import of the *motu proprio*. In a column which appeared in the *Baltimore Herald* on 30 September 1905 he wrote:

> Pope Pius' effort to restore the early Gregorian music to the services of the Roman Catholic Church is evidently meeting with very gratifying success [...] Circles for the study of Gregorian chants have been formed in nearly every large city in the country, and in a few churches the restoration has been achieved without the slightest opposition. That his holiness' aim is a good one is agreed by everyone who is competent to judge; that it will succeed is sincerely to be hoped [...] thanks to Pope Pius, there will be an end to the incongruous mingling of the sacred and the profane. Unless the plans go for naught, church music will soon take its ancient, dignified place above and apart from all other music.[17]

Thus, even a notably secular American newspaperman had the sense that in the environs of the church, music should be distinctly different from that heard elsewhere.

The Cecilian movement left its mark on the music of the Roman Catholic Church, both in America and abroad. By returning to the centuries-old problem regarding the role of music in worship, the movement generated a heated debate on the nature and stylistic contents of the repertory. The final result of the Cecilian movement was a renewed focus on transcendental, transnational liturgical music, a focus which became the basis for the global reforms of the twentieth century.

---

17   Excerpted in Louis Cheslock, *H.L. Mencken on Music* (New York: Schirmer, 1975), 132–3.

ROBERT A. SKERIS

Musica sacra in the Archdiocese of Milwaukee, 1858–1958

After the council at Trent (1545–63) and the Thirty Years' War (1618–48), liturgical music in the Western church underwent a drastic change, which had serious consequences. Trent had issued a relatively brief decree (17 September 1562) prohibiting the use at Mass of any sort of music for voices or for the organ which was tainted with anything *lascivum aut impurum*.[1] On the positive side, the sacred synod emphasized the importance of the true and proper music of the Catholic liturgy, Gregorian chant, which meant, consequently, the traditional theocentric orientation of Catholic worship in contradistinction to the anthropocentric understanding of worship among the 'reformers'. This theocentric nature of Catholic liturgical rites found historical expression in the genesis and development of monodic Gregorian chant and its continuation in the early forms of polyphony.[2] Theobald Schrems has pointed out that the only 'reformer' to retain chant for a time in his new worship services was Martin Luther (1483–1546), who did so not out of liturgical considerations, but because

---

1   See Karl Gustav Fellerer, 'Church Music between Trent and Vatican II', in Fellerer (ed.), *Geschichte der katholischen Kirchenmusik* 2 (Kassel: Bärenreiter, 1976) 1–4. This expression had little to do with indecency, obscenity or depraved morals, as is often mistakenly assumed. The terms are meant rather in their root sense, and refer to the contamination or pollution of *musica sacra* by lack of seriousness or restraint. The root of Latin *impurus* is in Greek *akathartos*, which means 'not-clean', hence 'contaminated', as an 'impure' medicine would be poisonous. The Latin verb *lascivio* is the Greek *exubrizo*, which involves hubris, in the sense of contempt for just restraint in favour of boundless liberty.

2   See Michael Tunger, *Stiftskapellmeister Franz Nekes, 1844–1914: 'Der Aachener Meister heiliger Tonkunst' – Leben und Werk* (Aachen: Mainz Verlag, 2007), 15–35.

the faithful were accustomed to it. The liturgical iconoclasm of Huldreich Zwingli (1484–1531) or John Calvin (1509–64) eliminated the theocentric Catholic liturgy entirely, including its Latin chant, which they regarded as *barbarum murmur* (unintelligible muttering).[3]

It can safely be said that Gregorian chant formed the basis for the growth and development of the classical Roman Catholic vocal polyphony which perfectly combines contrapuntal art with rounded arches of melody and harmony. The singable melodic style, the harmony balancing consonance and dissonance, and the calmly flowing, chant-like rhythm are all stylistic marks of this liturgical music which, depending upon the length of the text, alternates polyphonic with homophonic passages and thus serves well the basic liturgical requirements through the very musical forms themselves. Many compositions of the so-called Roman school are regarded as models in this respect, and the chief representative of the style is Palestrina.

The aftermath of the Thirty Years' War witnessed another stylistic change in the period of the Enlightenment. New possibilities of expression and their subjective tendencies began to obscure the liturgical orientation inherent in *musica sacra* which called for objective expression. Increasingly, divine worship came to be regarded as an external backdrop against which musical forms and resources could develop. Instead of music *of* worship, or even music *for* worship, what developed was music *at* worship.[4]

---

3   See Theobald Schrems, *Die Geschichte des gregorianischen Gesanges in den protestantischen Gottesdiensten* (Freibourg: St Paulusdruckerei, 1930).

4   The terminology is that of K.G. Fellerer (see Fellerer (trans. Francis A. Brunner), *The History of Catholic Church Music* (Baltimore: Helicon, 1961), who rightly stresses that in all periods of its history, the central question in the development of church music is the relation of music to its liturgical function. Music *of* worship refers to the growth of musical expression with and out of the liturgical form (e.g. Gregorian chant). Music *for* worship recalls the gradual independence of a musical art which went its own way in the effort to enhance the inner liturgical expression with musical means, an effort which lasted approximately up to the Ars Antiqua. Music *at* worship indicates the leadership of secular music with its subjective art of expression and an emotional creativity, which perhaps reached its high point during the Baroque.

In the age of the 'Enlightenment', worship perforce lost its theocentric orientation and became primarily the service of man, as Kant had demanded.[5] The rationalistic, anthropocentric attitude of the age, exemplified in the Catholic Church by Josephinism, felt no need for artful church music which would only distract from the new goals of promoting virtue, moral edification, and human improvement. But a *musica sacra* which is art for art's sake can find no place in the Catholic liturgy, which is theocentric: its *musica sacra* is resonant dogma.[6]

This is not the place to describe, even summarily, all the baneful usages and customs which militated against the liturgical nature of *musica sacra* at that time. Suffice it to say that a restoration of sacred music was urgently needed in order to protect the divine liturgy (and hence ultimately the faith) against the inroads of secularization. This is why the nineteenth-century renewal of Catholic church music was not merely a product of romantic historicism.[7]

During the early decades of the nineteenth century, 'romantic' thoughts and attitudes manifested themselves in a great number of ways. Reaction to Enlightenment attitudes included a subjective searching for fulfillment of

5   See Immanuel Kant, 'Beantwortung der Frage: Was ist Aufklärung?', *Berlinische Monatsschrift* 4 (December 1784), 481–94. On church music and the spirit of the bourgeoisie, see Carl Dahlhaus, 'Kirchenmusik und bürgerlicher Geist', in Carl Dahlhaus (ed.), *Neues Handbuch der Musikwissenschaft* 6 (*Die Musik des 19. Jahrhunderts*) (Wiesbaden: Akademische Verlagsgesellschaft Athenaion, 1980), 152.

6   See Fellerer, *Geschichte* (as n.1), 217–18.

7   On the renewal of church music in central Europe during the nineteenth century, see the essays gathered in Johannes Overath (ed.), *Musicae Sacrae Ministerium* (Schriftenreihe des Allgemeinen Cäcilien-Verbandes 5; Köln: Luthe-Druck, 1962). Documentation of the history of the Cecilian movement has been published by Overath (ed.), *Der Allgemeine Cäcilien-Verband für die Länder der Deutschen Sprache: Gestalt und Aufgabe* (Schriftenreihe des Allgemeinen Cäcilien-Verbandes 3; Köln: Allgemeiner Cäcilien-Verband, Sekretariat, 1961). A good overview is provided by J. Schwermer ('Der Caecilianismus', in Fellerer, *Geschichte* (as n.1), 226–36) and Tunger (*Stiftskapellmeister* (as n.2)). For more on the history of the American branch of the Cecilian movement, see Ronald Damian, 'A Historical Study of the Caecilian Movement in the United States', DMA diss., Catholic University of America, 1984, especially chapters 1–3 (and particularly p.83 ff. on the 'Singenberger Era').

various yearnings, which, in spite of their polarization, strove for the Inconceivable, the Dynamic, the Vague and the Irrational. Mysticism and eternity were important aspects of this detachment from reality. The rationalistic individualism of the Enlightenment gave way to a subjective experience of personal feelings which gave a new meaning to the idea of religion.[8]

Such emphasis on the ego also affected religious poetry and its musical settings, and led to new forms of vernacular hymns through which emotionally tinged religious sensibility found expression in worship. On the one hand the nature of the liturgy is far removed from any subjective mysticism, while on the other hand liturgical worship attempts to transcend reality in temporal distance, seeking there that religious experience which the subjective individualism of time-bound actuality cannot supply. And so almost instinctively, many looked to the past, and this led to an idealized view of historical facts found in ecclesiastical architecture, for example, or in church music. Historical experience was reduced to the conception of an aesthetic ideal, and in the process the interpretation of history and its imitation established boundaries. The repristination and restoration of historical forms gradually became the ideal of music at worship. Gregorian chant and 'classical' polyphony were regarded as the ideal of 'medieval' church music, just as Romanesque and Gothic churches were considered the ideal worship spaces. In this process, genuine historicity was often lost in an idealized interpretation which led to an externalized presentation as the norm, thus encouraging more imitation. Both the *a cappella* ideal of the Palestrina style (e.g. Michael Haller (1840–1915), Regensburg and August Eduard Grell (1800–86), Berlin) and the promotion of large choirs which ensued are quite as far removed from historical reality as the 'reformed' versions of Gregorian chant, which had strayed far from its original character. Such tendencies are reflected in a (frequently extravagant) spirituality marked by the sort of unreal enthusiasm typified in Chateaubriand's *Le génie du*

---

8   On the Catholic European revivals of 1833 centred upon France (Guéranger at Solesmes), Germany (Möhler at Tübingen) and England (Pusey at Oxford), and their reaction against subjective tendencies of Christian and secular thought which regarded religion as individualistic, moralistic, and rationalistic, see R.W. Franklin, *Nineteenth-Century Churches: The History of a New Catholicism in Württemberg, England, and France* (New York: Garland, 1987).

Christianisme (1802) or his *Les martyrs, ou le triomphe de la religion* (1809). Viewed from such a perspective, *musica sacra* acquires greater importance in a liturgy which is moving away from Baroque splendour towards simplicity. But at the same time these influences led to greater interest in historical reality, and so efforts were made to grasp that reality under the conditions of the time and for contemporary audiences. Personalities like Dom Prosper Guéranger (1805–75) and Alexandre-Etienne Choron (1771–1834) in France, Giuseppe Baini (1775–1844) and Pietro Alfieri (1801–63) in Italy, and Johann Michael Sailer (1751–1832) and Anton Friedrich Justus Thibaut (1772–1840) in Germany – to name but a few examples – undertook and encouraged studies in Gregorian chant and ancient polyphony while urging the repristination and restoration of these forms of *musica sacra*. Such efforts were linked to a romantic sensitivity which continued to develop during the course of the nineteenth century, and also contributed to the blurring of a multifaceted attitude of piety.[9]

II

The year 1634 marked the first recorded visit of a European to what is now the state of Wisconsin, when a companion of the founder of Quebec, Sieur de Champlain, landed near the site of Green Bay. His name was Jean Nicolet. That same year the son of the first Lord Baltimore, Cecil Calvert, established an English colonial settlement in Maryland where Catholics were welcome.

---

9   Fellerer, *Geschichte* (as n.1), 217–18. The best available analysis of this complex phenomenon is now James Garratt, *Palestrina and the German Romantic Imagination: Interpreting Historicism in Nineteenth-Century Music* (Cambridge: Cambridge University Press, 2002), esp. 133–213. Thibaut's essay of 1824, as translated by W.H. Gladstone, 'On Purity in Musical Art', (London, 1877) was published in Singenberger's *The Caecilia* 7 (1879), with a commentary by Prof. Birkler; see also Damian (as n.7), 41–7. For Sailer, see Johannes Overath, 'Music at the Service of the Sacred', in R. Skeris (ed.), *Crux et Cithara* (Musicae Sacrae Meletemata 2; Altoetting: Coppenrath, 1983), 156–68.

As GianLorenzo Bernini was constructing the great colonnade of St
Peter's at Rome for Pope Alexander VII in 1661, Jesuit missionary Fr René
Ménard entered the present Taylor County in Wisconsin at the headwaters
of the Black River in aid of the starving Huron Indians.[10]

In 1682, during Henry Purcell's tenure as organist of Westminster
Abbey in London, the Fox Indian War disrupted missionary activity in
Wisconsin.[11] And in 1728, Fr John Baptist Chardon, SJ, was recalled to
Detroit (from DePere's St Francis Xavier chapel founded in 1670 by Fr
Claude Allouez, SJ), thus marking the end of organized missionary activ-
ity in Wisconsin until 1823. Less than a year after the last Jesuit departed
Wisconsin, the poet of *Nathan der Weise*, Gotthold Ephraim Lessing, was
born in the Oberlausitz, five years after Immanuel Kant first saw the light
of day at Koenigsberg in East Prussia.

Fifty years later, the number of immigrants arriving on the American
frontier was increasing apace. Among them was a Swiss seminarian named
John Martin Henni, who arrived in 1829, one of many Catholic settlers
from north central Europe, an area which may fairly be called the cradle
of what we know today as congregational singing in the vernacular. In fact,
at one important stage of its development, the very liturgy of the Western
church received important impulses from the Franco-Germanic cultural
area, and so it is perhaps not surprising that such newcomers to America
bequeathed to their descendants a distinctive legacy. Henni became the
first bishop of Milwaukee in 1843, and archbishop in 1875. Not unlike
other early American leaders, he actively recruited thousands of Catholic
settlers on the basis of the American system of competitive entry, government land sale, and homesteading.[12]

---

10   See H.L. Heming, *History of the Catholic Church in Wisconsin* (Milwaukee, 1896), 233.
      Geographic precisions suggesting the area between present-day Bayfield and Washburn,
      WI, were later offered by A.A. Schmirler ('Wisconsin's Lost Missionary. The Mystery
      of Father Menard', *Wisconsin Magazine of History* 45 (Winter 1961/62), 99).
11   See Peter Leo Johnson, *Crosier on the Frontier: A Life of John Martin Henni* (Madison:
      State Historical Society of Wisconsin, 1958), 60.
12   See Peter Leo Johnson, 'John Martin Henni', in *New Catholic Encyclopedia* 6 (New
      York: McGraw-Hill, 1967), 1018; also J.T. Ellis, 'United States of America, 2: Church

When as a result of emigration, art which has arisen in a definite social sphere is transplanted, so to speak, then it will either wither and die, or it will sink new roots, fructifying its new environment, or even becoming itself the foundation of a new, reshaped artistic position. (The helpful hymnologist regretfully remarks the great number of persons unwilling to admit that church music is an art, and that even an individual hymn is a complete unit, a *res facta* which can stand by itself.)[13] In the territory of Wisconsin during the nineteenth century, the country of origin was the source of development, which for the emigrants had been cut off at a definite point that in turn served as the beginning of further development which followed its own laws. K.G. Fellerer has pointed out that the decisive factors here are tradition, local influences, contemporary influences from the homeland, and independent stylistic development. Naturally, the effect of these factors is unequal, and sociological influences also make themselves felt.[14] For instance, many of the immigrants received pastoral

---

of the Early Immigrants 1815–1866', in *New Catholic Encyclopedia* 14 (New York: McGraw-Hill, 1967), 429–48. For patterns of immigration and settlement in Milwaukee from 1870 to 1920, see the modern gathering of sources for archdiocesan history, based upon the chronology presented in the various diocesan newspapers and supplemented by much recent archival research, in Steven M. Avella, *In the Richness of the Earth: A History of the Archdiocese of Milwaukee 1843–1958* (Urban Life Series 1; Milwaukee: Marquette University Press, 2002), 207–10. The situation of one particular ethnic group has been studied in detail by Robert R. Grimes, *How Shall We Sing in a Foreign Land?: Music of Irish Catholic Immigrants in the Antebellum United States* (Notre Dame: Notre Dame University Press, 1996), an excellent and thorough examination of issues raised by Thomas Day in his *Why Catholics Can't Sing* (New York: Crossroads, 1990). John Ogasapian's *Church Music in America, 1620–2000* (Macon: Mercer University Press, 2007), 144–52, gives an overview of the situation in the eastern United States during the late eighteenth and early nineteenth centuries based chiefly upon the researches of Grimes; at pp. 219–22 he treats the second half of the nineteenth century in brief, relying mainly upon Damian's thesis.

13   See H. Müller, 'Zum deutschen katholischen Kirchenlied', *Cäcilien-Vereins-Organ* 58 (1926), 33–8 (here 37–8).

14   See Fellerer, 'Fragen um das auslandsdeutsche Kirchenlied', in H. Konen and J.P. Steffes (eds), *Volkstum und Kulturpolitik: Eine Sammlung von Aufsätzen Gewidmet Georg Schreiber zum fünfzigsten Geburtstage* (Cologne, 1932), 1–16 (here 1–2).

care from religious priests (e.g. the Company of Jesus for pastoral work among the German-speaking in the eighteenth century), and this was not without influence upon the church music situation.[15]

III

In the years following his consecration as bishop on the frontier in Wisconsin, J.M. Henni travelled regularly to Europe in search of both financial and physical help for the growing numbers of souls entrusted to his pastoral care. He was a frequent visitor in local offices of what are called today the 'Pontifical Missionary Works' (at that time, for example, the Ludwigs-Missionsverein at Munich), and he preached in German, Austrian and Swiss dioceses seeking suitable volunteers for priestly work among German-speaking immigrants in the great American Midwest. Such a visit to the Lower Austrian town of Linz bore rich fruit when a young priest ordained for that diocese in 1842 arrived in Milwaukee on 7 October 1847, aged twenty-eight, after accepting Henni's invitation. The zealous priest was Joseph Salzmann (1819–74), who for more than a quarter of a century proved his worth as one of Henni's most successful and indefatigable collaborators. Salzmann organized what became St Francis Seminary (1856), collecting through speaking tours more than $100,000, an enormous sum for that time. A man of great vision who possessed the energy to carry out the plans which he and Henni had conceived, Dr Salzmann also raised the funds required for the establishment of a Catholic teacher training college on the grounds of the seminary property in Nojoshing, south of Milwaukee. In one of his presentations (to the Central-Verein at Louisville, Kentucky, in 1870) Salzmann explained his purpose in greater detail:

15   See Robert Skeris, *Divini Cultus Studium* (Musicae Sacrae Meletemata 3; Altoetting: Coppenrath, 1990), 95–9.

The Normal School (Teachers' Seminary) is by no means the crowning glory. My heart aims for a greater work; it desires to establish Fulda in America. In Fulda, at the tomb of St Boniface, the German Bishops decided to found a Catholic University. We also need a university; but first come the common schools and then the university. If your sons wish to enter one of the professions he need not then go to Europe or to one of the universities in this country, Hotbeds of indifferentism, whence he returns to you filled with the spirit of Irreligion. He need not become a priest. As an educated lay-man he can bring Honour upon his church and labour in her interests.[16]

The cornerstone was laid on 12 June 1870, the Normal School dedicated by Bishop Henni on 2 January 1871, and classes convened on 14 September of that year. In order to increase tuition revenue, Pio Nono College was established within the same structure of the Normal School, to offer business courses in preparation for professional work.[17] A year later, a 'music major' was added to the Normal School curriculum, with a three-year sequence of courses, which eventually graduated more than 500 organists and music teachers. In need of a qualified teacher who was both self-sacrificing and flexible enough to adapt to new and challenging conditions, Salzmann sought advice from the church music reformer Franz Xaver Witt (1834–88) at the church music school in Regensburg.[18]

16 See Avella, *In the Richness of the Earth*, 275, citing M.M. Gerend, 'Memories of By-Gone Days', *Salesianum* 7 (July 1912) 7–8. Details of Salzmann's career may be found in Joseph Rainer (trans. Joseph William Berg), *A Noble Priest: Joseph Salzmann, D.D., founder of the Salesianum* (Milwaukee: Hollinger & Schwartz, 1903), which is the second edition, in English, of Rainer's *Dr. Joseph Salzmann: Leben und Wirken* (St Louis, 1876). Rainer is quite correct in asserting that the American branch of the St Cecilia Society for the promotion of genuine church music 'owes its existence to him'.

17 Because the sovereign pontiff was celebrating his silver jubilee at the time, Salzmann chose the pope's name for the college.

18 The most complete record of Witt's life and work remains Anton Walter, *Dr. Franz Witt, ein Lebensbild* (Regensburg: Pustet, 1890). Witt founded the German Society of St Cecilia at Bamberg in 1868, and served as its president until his death twenty years later. For complete documentation, see n.7 above. Over the course of several years, Singenberger published English translations of Witt's principal essays in *The Caecilia*.

Witt's choice was a happy one. He recommended one of his own pupils, a twenty-five-year-old Swiss musician from Kanton St Gallen named John Baptist Singenberger (1848–1924). The young man arrived at St Francis, Wisconsin, on Good Friday, 11 April 1873, and he remained there for fifty-one years, helping to form and train hundreds of church organists, composers and music teachers during a long career marked by intense activity.[19] Industrious by nature, Singenberger was a devout Catholic who proved to be ideally suited to the successful accomplishment of Salzmann's plan. A year before his untimely death, Salzmann founded the American branch of the Society of St Cecilia, in the spirit of the reform initiated by Witt and his associates. John B. Singenberger was chosen first president of the society barely a month after his arrival in Milwaukee, at a meeting convened by Salzmann for the purpose of establishing a group similar to the one which young Singenberger had founded shortly before at the diocesan seminary of Chur in Graubuenden.[20] Six months later, on St Cecilia's Day in 1873, Singenberger conducted the first choral festival of the fledgling society, in the chapel of the Normal School, and three months later he published the first issue of the society's journal, *The Caecilia*, which through its successor publication is today the oldest continuously published music periodical in America.[21] The first annual meeting or convention of the American Cecilian Society was held at Milwaukee on 17 June 1874, shortly after Salzmann's passing. Papal approbation was granted in 1876 upon request of the new archbishop of Milwaukee, following the example of the parent organization in Germany.

19   See Robert J. Schmitt, 'A History of Catholic Church Music and Musicians in Milwaukee', MA thesis, Marquette University, 1968, 28–54, in addition to Damian, 'A Historical Study' (as n.7), 83ff. J. Vincent Higginson has authored two articles of note on 'Singenberger and the Caecilian Movement', *Catholic Choirmaster* 27 (September 1941), 101–4, and 'Singenberger the Musician', *Catholic Choirmaster* 28 (September 1942), 6–8, 54. John Singenberger's eldest son compiled a partial list of his father's compositions, showing some twenty Mass Ordinaries along with hundreds of motets, litanies, Mass Propers and vernacular hymns (see O. Singenberger, 'Compositions and Works of Prof. John Singenberger', *The Caecilia* 51 [July/August 1924], 35–40).

20   Details in J.V. Higginson, 'The American Caecilian Society', *Catholic Choirmaster* 28 (September 1942), 107–9, 114 (here 107–8).

21   The current name of the journal is *Sacred Music* (see www.musicasacra.com).

The decades of Singenberger's Milwaukee-based apostolate were fruit-
ful in many respects. Some of these deserve mention in the present context,
for instance his influence through the students he trained, and through
his publications.

Singenberger's tenure was co-extensive with the entire period (1872–
1922) during which music instruction was a major part of the curriculum
at the Catholic Normal School in St Francis, and hundreds of graduates
were trained there during the fifty-one years of its existence.[22] Indeed, if
one takes into account the regular continuing education courses Singenberger conducted so frequently during the summer vacation months, it
is likely that some 800 organists profited from his 'scholarly tutelage and
influence'.[23]

Typical of so many of Singenberger's first two generations of pupils
were Michael Ludwig Nemmers (1855–1929) and Caspar Petrus Koch
(1872–1970). Nemmers, born in an Iowa log cabin to Luxemburg-German
immigrant parents, was but sixteen years old when he entered the Holy
Family Normal School with its first group of students, and four years later
he graduated first in his class. During his long career as organist, teacher
and composer, Nemmers founded his own company to publish church
compositions, much as his teacher had done. 'Popular and Easy Liturgical Music' for small amateur choirs was, he felt, the need of the hour, and
in his fifty-five-year career (forty of them spent in the city of Milwaukee)
he published a great many Masses, motets, litanies and organ pieces of his
own as well as by other 'Caecilian' composers, chiefly Americans.[24]

Caspar Koch enrolled in Singenberger's course at St Francis in 1890,
and upon graduation he married his teacher's daughter before returning
to West Pennsylvania to seek his fortune as a church musician. A talented
organist and a gifted teacher, Koch was named city organist of Pittsburgh
by 1904, and professor of music at the Carnegie Institute of Technology
(known today as Carnegie-Mellon University), in addition to serving for

22   See P.L. Johnson, 'Joseph Salzmann', in *New Catholic Encyclopedia* 12 (New York:
     McGraw-Hill, 1967), 1007.
23   The estimate is that of F.J. Boerger, 'An Appreciation of John Singenberger', *The
     Caecilia* 60 (June 1933), 145–6.
24   See the article by his son Erwin Esser Nemmers, 'Michael L. Nemmers', *Catholic
     Choirmaster* 28 (September 1942), 112, 139.

decades as organist and choirmaster at Holy Trinity Church in Allison Park. In 1924 Caspar Koch designed the large Ernest Skinner organ for the Northside Carnegie's Music Hall, on which he played literally thousands of recitals until his retirement in 1954.[25] In addition to very successful pedagogical publications such as *The Organ Student's Gradus ad Parnassum* and a popular edition of the eight 'little' preludes and fugues long attributed to J.S. Bach, Caspar Koch published many organ transcriptions of orchestral pieces which regularly found a place in his recital programmes.

The skills taught by John Singenberger were diligently put into practice by men such as August Zohlen and his son Cletus at Holy Name Church in Sheboygan, by Fred Gramann in Waukesha, in Milwaukee by Thomas Stemper and his organist brother John followed by Max Fichtner at St Boniface, and by J.J. Meier at St Francis Church, to name but a few examples. Quite as many instances could be cited from the ranks of the other large groups whose musical preparation and liturgical formation were chiefly due to Singenberger's training of the women religious who directed the convent music departments in Milwaukee mother houses. From the pioneer days of the diocese in 1848 until the Civil War and later, religious sisterhoods served in the Catholic (and sometimes in the public) schools and gradually, at first in smaller parishes, nuns replaced the lay employees who had frequently acted as sacristan-schoolmaster-organist in one person, *per modum unius*. Singenberger's pedagogical efforts kept pace with the needs of the times, and while he had perforce concentrated at first upon the multi-talented lay teachers, as the years went by he did not fail to devote much energy and attention to the formation of convent musicians, with corresponding effects upon parish life and worship.[26]

25   Andrew Carnegie donated the first organ to the Hall in 1890 along with a City Organist, and the first series of free weekly organ recitals in the United States. Caspar Koch played the 1,000th free concert in 1914, the 2,000th in 1939, and his son Paul the 3,000th in 1967. The series came to an end on 1 January 1979, when the instrument was removed as the Music Hall was remodelled. At approximately 3,280 free recitals it was the longest running series of its kind in the country, according to William F. Rickenbacker, writing in the *National Review* on 18 March 1988.

26   On this process and its background, see Avella, *In the Richness of the Earth*, 72–83.

There were four religious orders of women that played notable parts in the development of Catholic culture and *musica sacra* in the Milwaukee diocese. Each of them was rooted in nineteenth-century German Catholicism, but only one of them was actually founded in the young diocese. This was the Congregation of Sisters of St Agnes, founded by Salzmann's companion, Fr Caspar Rehrl, in 1858 at Barton, north of West Bend, and which moved in 1870 to its present headquarters at Fond du Lac. The CSA sisters expanded greatly, combining the active and the contemplative life with success in the fields of education and health care.[27] The positive influence of John Singenberger and his pupils was felt in the schools and parishes to the north and west of Milwaukee through the apostolate of these devoted nuns.

The first of the three German groups to plant roots in the Milwaukee diocese were the 'Lake Drive Franciscans', as they were later known (Franciscan Sisters of Penance and Charity), whose ancestry goes back to a lay Franciscan group founded in 1848 at Ettenbeuren in the valley of the Kammlach, west of Augsburg, on the border between Swabia and Bavaria. After buying the property at Nojoshing, south of Milwaukee, in 1849, this order cared for orphans and managed the domestic services of the seminary built on the adjacent property a few years later. Since 1885 the sisters taught and mentored the hard-of-hearing at St John School for the Deaf, which formed part of the St Francis complex centred on the Normal School where John Singenberger held forth.[28]

In 1850 the School Sisters of Notre Dame arrived from Bavaria after an earlier visit by three nuns to explore the possibilities for a foundation,

27   Full details in M. Vera Naber, *With All Devotedness: Chronicle of the Sisters of St Agnes, Fond du Lac, Wisconsin* (New York: Kennedy & Sons, 1959). On the role of Austrian recruits to the American mission dioceses, and the contributions of the Leopold Foundation (Leopoldinen-Stiftung), see the work of a long-time chaplain to the CSA motherhouse, Benjamin J. Blied, *Austrian Aid to American Catholics, 1830–1860* (Milwaukee: Bruce Publ. Co., 1944). See also Imogene Palen, *Fieldstones '76: The Story of the Founders of the Sisters of St Agnes* (Fond du Lac: Oshkosh Printers, 1976).

28   On the early history of the order, see Mary Eunice Hanousek, *A New Assisi: The First Hundred Years of the Sisters of St Francis of Assisi* (Milwaukee: Bruce Publ. Co., 1949).

which was then realized with the support of the Ludwigs-Missionsverein and the energetic Bishop Henni. Mother Caroline Friess (1824–92) guided the growth of the order for some forty years.[29]

One of the most prominent Notre Dame musicians and Singenberger pupils was Sr Gisela Hornbach, SSND, whose *Mount Mary Hymnal* (1937) was widely used.[30] The archdiocese of Freiburg in Baden was the cradle of another congregation of women, the School Sisters of St Francis, who came to Milwaukee in 1873 to escape the effects of the *Kulturkampf* then escalating in Germany.[31] After many vicissitudes the order grew and expanded rapidly, numbering over 500 after some twenty years. Beginning in 1879, the convent musicians were trained in Singenberger's school, and one of his prize pupils, Sr Cherubim Schaefer, OSF, laid the foundations (at St Joseph's Convent) for what became the school of music of Alverno College, whose most distinguished leader was the late organist and composer Sr Theophane Hytrek, OSF. After John Singenberger's passing, the seeds he planted continued to germinate. His eldest son, Otto, adapted *The Caecilia* to the needs of Catholic church musicians of the time by concentrating upon music education in Catholic schools. Such education had received renewed attention after Justine B. Ward founded the Pius X Institute of Liturgical Music in 1916 and organized the New York Gregorian Congress of 1920, where some of the results of her pedagogical method were displayed.[32] Beginning in 1925 Sr Cherubim wrote, and Otto Singenberger published, articles outlining classroom music appreciation plans which were widely used in the Midwest.[33] John Singenberger himself continued

29 On the origins and development of the order in America, see Barbara Brumleve (ed.), *The Letters of Mother Caroline Friess, School Sisters of Notre Dame* (Winona: School Sisters of Notre Dame, 1991). Further documentation in M. Dympna Flynn, *Mother Caroline and the School Sisters of Notre Dame*, 2 vols. (St Louis: Woodward & Tiernan, 1928).

30 Sr Mary Gisela, *The Mount Mary Hymnal* (Boston: McLaughlin & Reilly, 1937).

31 See Sr Jo Ann Euper, *First Century of Service: The School Sisters of St Francis* (Milwaukee: School Sisters of St Francis, 1976), 2 ff.

32 See Dom Pierre Combe (trans. Philipe and Guillemine de Lacoste), *Justine Ward and Solesmes* (Washington: Catholic University Press, 1987), 2–6.

33 On this, see Damian (as n.7), 118–19.

his personal attention to the music instruction of these religious until the last years of his life.[34]

Under the leadership of Mother Benedicta Bauer, OP, Dominican Sisters from Bavaria finally began their apostolate in the Milwaukee diocese in 1863 at the urging of Bishop Henni. From the Lake Michigan port town of Racine the community branched out to the north and west, staffing parish schools whose music teachers had been formed by the spirit and example of John Baptist Singenberger.[35] That spirit remained a powerful influence after 'Chevalier' Singenberger passed to his reward, not least through the accomplishments of priest-musicians whom he had trained, and who in turn formed their own pupils.[36] By 1920 the Cecilian Society counted more than 5,000 paying members, surely the largest organization of its kind in the country at that time. One wonders, therefore, why anyone would claim that the organization 'had abandoned its original purpose out of deference for the 1903 *motu proprio* on church music.'[37]

34   A student nun's harmony assignments personally corrected by Singenberger are documented in Appendix C (pp. 263–73) of Damian (as n.7), along with pieces that Singenberger composed for the convent choir and dedicated to the Mother General at that time, M. Alfons, OSF.

35   The history of the Racine Dominican community is well told by Mary Hortense Kohler, *Rooted in Hope: The Story of the Dominican Sisters of Racine, Wisconsin* (Milwaukee: Bruce Publishing Co., 1962). See also the same author's *Life and Work of Mother Benedicta Bauer* (Milwaukee: Bruce Publishing Co., 1937).

36   Some of these Singenberger pupils are mentioned by Avella, *In the Richness of the Earth*, 277. The next generation included talented and zealous priestly personalities like Fridolin T. Walter, Joseph J. Pierron (who edited the *Ave Maria Hymnal* (Milwaukee: Bruce Publishing Co., 1928)), Raymond C. Zeyen, Elmer F. Pfeil, and Robert F. Mueller, among others.

37   Johnson, 'Salzmann' (as n.22), 1007 appears to assume that once the *motu proprio* was promulgated, all problems were resolved. But a century later, some of them remain. The basic principles of the American Society of St Cecilia were those of the German parent organization, whose influence upon the genesis of the 1903 papal document seems beyond question, through the influence of, for example, Lorenzo Perosi upon Giuseppe Sarto before he ascended the throne of Peter. For details (in spite of some factual inaccuracies and fanciful interpretations) see, for example, Robert F. Hayburn, *Papal Legislation on Sacred Music, 95 A.D. to 1977 A.D.* (Collegeville,

Singenberger's activity as publicist was quite considerable. In addition
to his own compositions and those of Cecilian colleagues, he published
instruction books for organists, choirmasters and church singers, as well
as hymnals in German and English by Joseph Mohr, for example, or by
himself. Singenberger's *Cantate* went through many editions, and was
still in print in 1932. That edition, for churches in which two-part singing
was customary, still carried the original letter of commendation by the
composer's fellow Swiss friend and supporter, Archbishop Messmer, who
in 1911 asked a question which is still apposite today:

> We are very anxious that the book be introduced in all the parishes of our Archdio-
> cese, and we earnestly hope that it will prove an efficient help towards introducing
> in our churches the old and beautiful traditional custom of congregational singing.
> When Protestant churches are filled with Christian worshippers it is in very many
> cases due to the beautiful church hymns sung by the whole congregation. It was the
> spirit of modern, unchristian innovation which deprived Catholics of our days of
> the beauty of the primitive and mediaeval mode of church music. Why should we
> not return to it ?

John B. Singenberger was not only the first president of the American Cecilian Society. From 1 February 1874 he was also the editor of the society's
journal *The Caecilia*, a position he retained until his death in 1924. This
was no mean feat, and its significance is matched only by Singenberger's
publication of the famous *Guide in Catholic Church Music* (Milwaukee,
1891). This book was inspired by the Vereinskatalog issued by the German
Cecilians, and was the forerunner of the 'White List' of the Society of St
Gregory under Nicola Montani. The *Guide* contained a 204-page catalogue
listing hundreds of compositions, chiefly by 'Cecilian' composers of the
late nineteenth century, arranged by choral voicing and, in the case of the

---

MN: Liturgical Press, 1979), 406–8 and in particular, 129–32 on Singenberger and
the American situation, including a valuable summary of the historical origins by
Dakota Bishop Martin Marty, OSB, which was first published by Singenberger in
the flagship issue of his English version of *The Caecilia*, called *Echo*. Since the market
for paid subscriptions was much smaller than anticipated, *Echo* ceased to resound
after only three years (1882–85). See also Damian (as n.7), 48–73.

Mass Propers, according to the liturgical year. The catalogue was preceded by twenty-one pages of prefatory documentation and indices.[38]

Singenberger's *Guide* had a powerful impact because of its official status: it was 'published by order of the First Provincial Council of Milwaukee and Saint Paul', which exercised legislative authority over the states of Wisconsin, Minnesota, and North and South Dakota. The Decree of the Provincial Council of Milwaukee (held 23–30 May 1886) provided for a catalogue of sacred music, to be approved by all the bishops of the province,[39] and urged that the St Cecilia Society 'be more and more propagated and earnestly recommended under the protection of the Bishops.' The then vicar apostolic of the Dakotas and former abbot of St Meinrad, Bishop Martin Marty, OSB, wrote in his preface that the *Guide* was 'presented to all who wish to be in harmony with the precepts and the spirit of the Church.' He added that

> In this communion of truth and grace God is everything and man is drawn and enabled by Him to perform those inward acts of adoration, praise and thanksgiving by which God is glorified and man sanctified. The outward form of these acts is truly sacramental, indicating as well as producing communion with God.[40]

After the promulgation of the *motu proprio*, *Tra le sollecitudini*, of Pius X, Singenberger published a second edition of the *Guide to Catholic Church Music* (St Francis, 1905) with an introduction by the metropolitan archbishop of Milwaukee in which the prelate offered explanatory comments on the pontifical document, concluding with the query, 'Who shall guide us in choosing the good and leaving the bad? Evidently not everyone is capable of forming a correct judgment in this matter [...]' The reply, of course, was unhesitating: '[...] our lifelong friend, Professor Singenberger, answers the description.' The professor's response to the challenge was to

---

38　Masses for four-part mixed choir totalled 308, with three each by Victoria, Lassus, Hassler and Viadana, one by Rheinberger, eight by Palestrina, and fourteen by F. X. Witt.

39　Caput XIII, 'De Cantu Sacro'; see *Guide in Catholic Church Music* (Milwaukee: H. Zahn & Co., 1891), v.

40　*Guide in Catholic Church Music*, vi.

place in the hands of pastors and church musicians 276 pages of catalogued compositions approved for use in divine worship, prefaced by the complete English text of the *motu proprio* in Fr Charles Becker's translation, along with a bibliography of nineteen articles containing informed commentary upon the 1903 document which had appeared in various ecclesiastical journals of pastoral or canonical tenor.[41] In addition to the usual catalogue categories of Mass Ordinaries, Litanies, Motets, Benediction Services, etc., there appeared a note explaining that since the Vatican edition of the chant books was not yet completed, and the decree of 8 January 1904 issued by the Congregation of Rites allowed it, the Medicaean chant books of Pustet in Regensburg could lawfully remain in use until the *Editio Vaticana* had been completed and published.

Loyal as always to the directives of the ecclesiastical authorities, Singenberger kept his promise in the *Supplement to the Guide* published in 1911. The sixty-eight pages of catalogued compositions commenced with the Gregorian chant books in the official (and since 1908 for the Mass and other parish services, complete) Vatican Edition as published with organ accompaniment by either Pustet or Schwann. The *Kyriale* in either modern or Gregorian notation was also listed in editions by Styria, J. Fischer or Desclée (for the Solesmes editions). In addition to the usual letters of recommendation from various diocesan bishops, the *Supplement* also reprints the 'Rules regarding Church Music to be observed in all the Churches within the province of Milwaukee, adopted by the Bishops of the Province January 29, 1906.' Singenberger's *Guide* is named 'the official catalogue of church music, vocal and instrumental, organ and orchestra. Pastors will see to it that every church choir gave the "Guide" in its repertoire and that it be purchased at the expence of the congregation.'[42]

The *motu proprio* of 1903 (VIII, 24) had called for the establishment of diocesan commissions for sacred music, and the 1906 Provincial Council decree specified the commission for the province of Milwaukee: two priest-

---

41   These included the *American Ecclesiastical Review*, *The Month*, *Dolphin*, and *Catholic World*.

42   J. Singenberger, *Supplement to the Guide to Catholic Church Music* (St Francis: 1911), v–vi.

professors at St Francis Seminary (Frs Charles Becker and Barn. Dieringer) and one layman, John B. Singenberger, who was also the recipient of a cordial letter from Archbishop Messmer dated 25 July, 1911. This letter pointed to the tasks and challenges facing Singenberger and the Society of St Cecilia even in the post-*motu proprio* era:

> [...] I cannot understand how in the face of the clear papal precepts, the many Conciliar laws, the repeated Episcopal ordinances and the instructive as well as interesting expositions in Catholic ecclesiastical periodicals there are still so many priests who do not seem to care what kind of music is sung or played in their churches as long as it suits the ladies of the organ loft or the set of pretended connoisseurs in the pew below. The fact that there is still so much worldly music sung in so many Catholic churches, even prominent Cathedrals, argues on the part of the responsible parties, which are always and at all times the clergy, either a sinful disrespect of the Church laws, or a humiliating fear of human opinion, or a shameful lack of proper information, from whatever source, of genuine and appropriate church music [...][43]

IV

A hundred years later, Messmer's letter to Singenberger bears a curious resemblance to descriptions of early twenty-first-century conditions in many areas of the church in the Western world. To the extent this is true, there may be lessons to be learned when one reflects upon the story of *musica sacra* in the archdiocese of Milwaukee from the mid nineteenth to the mid twentieth century. A few of these may be mentioned by way of conclusion.

One cannot fail to note the attitude of *sentire cum Ecclesia* which pervades the activity of the Cecilians in general as well as the entire life and work of John B. Singenberger in particular. His encyclopedic knowledge of the rubrics and the liturgical prescriptions of his time was legendary among

43   Ibid., iv.

his students.[44] When the earlier privileges of the Medicaean chant edition had been revoked and the *Editio Vaticana* was introduced, Singenberger discontinued instruction based on the older edition, for which in fact he had written textbooks. Henceforth the officially approved edition took pride of place, in classroom, sanctuary, and in the catalogue of the *Guide to Catholic Church Music*. With F.X. Witt and his teachers at Regensburg, Singenberger was firmly convinced that in terms of its activity or behaviour (*quoad actionem*), *musica sacra* is *ancilla liturgiae*, a handmaiden with a ministerial role to play. But in terms of its essence (*quoad naturam*), *musica sacra* is and remains an art 'which exhibits the Divine in material forms' which are 'truly sacramental', according to the 1891 edition of Singenberger's *Guide*.[45] This basic lesson remains critically important in our own day. In the words of the last ecumenical council, as *cantus sacer qui verbis inhaeret*, sacred music is in fact *pars necessaria vel integralis liturgiae sollemnis*.[46]

An attentive perusal of Singenberger's *Guide* or the many issues of *The Caecilia* that he edited reveals a noteworthy continuity of pastoral approach by the church and her musicians – in the twenty-first century, the twentieth century, the nineteenth century. The chief categories of *musicalia* recommended for pastoral praxis remain the same: Gregorian chant, choral music (including both 'classic' polyphony and 'modern' choral music), congregational singing, vernacular hymns, and organ music – each with its place in the symphonic unity of the divine liturgy. In the last analysis, the nineteenth-century initiative for the renewal of *musica sacra* embodied in the Cecilian movement begun in America at Milwaukee by Salzmann and Singenberger actually achieved the goal it had set for itself: church music as art music, to a very great extent cleansed of all profane and trivial elements, was once again officially acknowledged as a necessary and integral part of a theocentrically oriented liturgy. *Musica sacra* was recognized as

---

44   See Avella, *In the Richness of the Earth*, 279.
45   The Latin distinction is that of a father of the Second Vatican Council, cited by J. Overath, 'The Meaning of Musica Sacra and its Nobility', in R. Skeris (ed.), *Crux et Cithara* (Musicae Sacrae Meletemata 2; Altoetting: Coppenrath, 1983), 73–84 (here p.75). The words of Bishop Marty at p. vi of the *Guide*.
46   See the Constitution on the Sacred Liturgy (*Sacrosanctum Concilium*), art. 112.

being itself worship, and not simply ritual music during worship. And this was achieved only by stressing the perennially valid bonds linking today's *musica sacra* to theocentrically conceived church music – to Gregorian chant and classical vocal polyphony. These ideals of the 1903 *motu proprio* were those of J.B. Singenberger, who took to heart the motto which Witt had given to his nascent Society of St Cecilia: 'Our only desire is to carry out in practice the wishes of Holy Mother Church regarding music.' That remains the programme of the contemporary successor of the Cecilian Society.

Though its realization in practice has been achieved in varying degrees at different times during the history of the church, yet the basic unity of musical life as a whole remains a relevant principle, even for church music. There, the ultimate motivation for such unity is spiritual. The divine liturgy is both its starting point and its standard of measure. The church musician can ill afford to neglect musicology, not in order to have scholarship dictate to the choir loft, but in order to base pastoral decisions upon authentic information. 'Pastoral' aspects, in other words, cannot be urged at the price of artistic diminution. It is precisely musicology which can demonstrate that they are not in fact opposites. And at the same time *musica sacra* is a kind of pedagogy, not by 'adapting' the liturgy to the (perhaps half-formed) culture of peoples, but by 'converting' and 'elevating' the people into the liturgy.[47] *Quod Deus bene vertat!*

---

47   On this see Skeris (ed.), *Crux et Cithara*, 18–19; also Laszlo Dobszay, *The Bugnini-Liturgy and the Reform of the Reform* (Musicae Sacrae Meletemata 5; Front Royal, VA: Catholic Church Music Associates, 2003), 194–215 (especially pp. 200–1).

SUSAN TREACY

A Chronicle of Attitudes towards Gregorian Chant in *Orate Fratres/Worship*, 1926–1962

The pre-eminent voice of the liturgical movement in the United States was surely the journal *Orate Fratres*, which would later be renamed *Worship*. This essay will survey attitudes of those in the liturgical movement towards Gregorian chant over a span of thirty-six years, as revealed in the pages of *Orate Fratres/Worship*. During the time period under survey in this essay, there were only two editors of *Orate Fratres*, both Benedictine monks of Saint John's Abbey, Collegeville, Minnesota. The founding editor, Dom Virgil Michel, OSB, started the journal in 1926. After Dom Virgil's untimely death in 1938, the Revd Godfrey L. Diekmann, OSB, served as editor until 1965.

On 4 August 1903, Giuseppe Sarto, Patriarch of Venice, was elected pope. Taking the name Pius X, he issued only two months later his first encyclical, *E Supremi*, a document that would lay out the course of his pontificate and the motto that would encapsulate everything that he did.

> [...] We take courage in Him who strengthens Us; and setting Ourselves to work, relying on the power of God, We proclaim that We have no other program in the Supreme Pontificate but that 'of restoring all things in Christ' (Ephes. i., 10), so that 'Christ may be all and in all' (Coloss. iii., 2) [...] The interests of God shall be Our interest, and for these We are resolved to spend all Our strength and Our very life. Hence, should anyone ask Us for a symbol as the expression of Our will, We will give this and no other: 'To renew all things in Christ.'[1]

---

1   This motto – *Instaurare omnia in Christo* – has been variously translated as 'to renew all things in Christ,' 'to restore all things in Christ,' and 'that Christ may be formed in all.'

The first step of this mandate, 'to restore all things in Christ', was set in motion by *Inter sollecitudines*, the pope's *motu proprio* of 22 November 1903, on the restoration of church music. The following paragraph from this *motu proprio* was adopted by the liturgical movement as its own charter:

> Filled as We are with a most ardent desire to see the true Christian spirit flourish in every respect and be preserved by all the faithful, We deem it necessary to provide before anything else for the sanctity and dignity of the temple, in which the faithful assemble for no other object than that of acquiring this spirit from its foremost and indispensable fount, which is the active participation in the most holy mysteries and in the public and solemn prayer of the Church.[2]

Key to this restoration would be sacred music, and above all, Gregorian chant:

> The ancient traditional Gregorian Chant must, therefore, in a large measure be restored to the functions of public worship, and the fact must be accepted by all that an ecclesiastical function loses none of its solemnity when accompanied by this music alone.
>
> Special efforts are to be made to restore the use of the Gregorian Chant by the people, so that the faithful may again take a more active part in the ecclesiastical offices, as was the case in ancient times.[3]

Steps to restore Gregorian chant to the faithful began to be taken by those who were sympathetic and obedient to the pope's commands. There were not a few, however, who scorned or ignored the principles laid out by the Holy Father. In his *motu proprio* the pope also recognized the research of the monks of Solesmes and their efforts to restore the purity of the ancient chant. Pius X could be considered a bridge between the liturgical movement set in motion by Dom Prosper Guéranger of Solesmes and the modern liturgical movement, as inaugurated by Dom Lambert Beauduin in 1909 at the Catholic Conference at Malines. As a result of Dom Beauduin's speech, 'La vraie prière de l'Église', four resolutions were adopted by

2   Pius X, *Inter sollecitudines*, Introduction. This *motu proprio* is also known by its Italian name, *Tra le sollecitudini*.
3   Ibid., art. 3.

the conference, among them the resolution 'to work for a wider and more perfect use of Gregorian chant as desired by Pius X.'[4] These resolutions recognized that the pope's document on sacred music had ramifications for the liturgy in general.

In the United States the interest of the hierarchy in Gregorian chant for the people had preceded the official pronouncements of Sarto.[5] In 1866 the Second Plenary Council of Baltimore mandated that the 'elements of Gregorian chant be taught and exercised in the parochial schools.'[6] Eighteen years later the Third Plenary Council reiterated this, adding that

> with the number of those who are well able to chant the psalms increasing more and more, the major part at least of the faithful will learn to chant with clergy and choir the Vesper service and such like, as was the custom of the primitive Church and still is the custom in various localities. In this way the spiritual growth of all will be advanced, according to the words of St. Paul: 'Speaking to one another in psalms and hymns and spiritual songs' (Eph. 5:19).[7]

In 1874 John Singenberger emigrated from Switzerland to the United States and brought the Cecilian movement with him. In Milwaukee he founded the Amerikanischen Cäcilien-Verein and its monthly magazine, *The Caecilia*. A more cosmopolitan organization appeared in 1913, with the establishment of the Society of Saint Gregory of America, dedicated to

---

4   Olivier Rousseau, OSB (trans. Benedictines of Westminster Priory), *The Progress of the Liturgy: An Historical Sketch from the Beginning of the Nineteenth Century to the Pontificate of Pius X* (Westminster, MD: Newman Press, 1951), 165; quoted in Alcuin Reid, *The Organic Development of the Liturgy* (San Francisco: Ignatius, 2005), 79.

5   Giuseppe Sarto, as Patriarch of Venice, had issued a pastoral letter on sacred music in 1895. Earlier, as bishop of Mantua, he dealt with sacred music in the decrees of the 1888 diocesan synod. Both of these earlier documents concern the same issues as the *motu proprio*.

6   Paul Marx, OSB, *Virgil Michel and the Liturgical Movement* (Collegeville, MN: Liturgical Press, 1957), 77.

7   *Acta et Decreta Concilii Plenarii Baltimorensis* (Baltimore: John Murphy Co., 1886), n.119, quoted in William Busch, 'The Voice of a Plenary Council', *Orate Fratres* 21 (1947), 456.

seeing that the *motu proprio* of Pius X would be implemented. Its journal, the *Catholic Choirmaster*, began publication in 1915.[8]

Four other Americans who promoted Gregorian chant in the wake of the *motu proprio* were the Revd John Young, SJ, Justine Bayard Ward, the Revd Dr Thomas E. Shields, and Mother Georgia Stevens, RSCJ. Instrumental in the conversion of Justine Ward to the Catholic faith was Fr Young, who was choirmaster at St Francis Xavier Church, New York City. He had already been teaching Gregorian chant to the boys and men of his choir before the issuance of the *motu proprio*, and it was from him that Mrs Ward first learned Gregorian chant. For teaching Gregorian chant to the boys he used the Galin-Paris-Chevé method of number notation.[9] In 1910, when Dr Shields – then chairman of the Department of Education at the Catholic University of America – invited Justine Ward to provide the music portions of his series of grade school textbooks, she combined Fr Young's number system with Shields's enlightened pedagogical method. The result was the earliest version of the Ward Method of music pedagogy, which was 'directed toward Gregorian chant.'[10]

Justine Ward collaborated with Mother Georgia Stevens, RSCJ, to establish a school where teachers could be trained in Gregorian chant and the liturgy, so that the directives of Pius X could be promulgated throughout the United States and beyond. The Pius X Institute of Liturgical Music opened its doors in 1916 at the Manhattanville Academy (later College) of the Sacred Heart. By 1920 the Pius X Institute was so well established that Mrs Ward, along with Mother Stevens, Harold Becket Gibbs, and Joseph Bonnet, arranged an International Congress of Gregorian Chant. Among the invited guests was Dom André Mocquereau, choirmaster of the Solesmes monks and developer of the classic Solesmes method of Gre-

---

8   In 1964 both organizations merged, to become the Church Music Association of America. *The Caecilia* and the *Catholic Choirmaster* also merged, becoming *Sacred Music*.

9   See Francis Brancaleone, 'Justine Ward and the Fostering of an American Solesmes Chant Tradition', *Sacred Music* 136 (Fall 2009), 9.

10 Dom Pierre Combe, OSB (trans. Philipe and Guillemine de Lacoste), *Justine Ward and Solesmes* (Washington: Catholic University of America Press, 1987), 2.

gorian chant interpretation. For Justine Ward, her meeting with Dom Mocquereau was a defining moment; she determined to study the chant personally under Dom Mocquereau's tutelage. In 1921 she traveled to Quarr Abbey, on the Isle of Wight, where the Solesmes monks had been in exile since 1901. Dom Mocquereau's interpretation of liturgical chant, whose very objective was to elevate souls and lead them to God, was exactly what Justine Ward was looking for in her training of children. As she said of Dom Mocquereau: for him, 'art is not the main issue. The main issue is *prayer*, the prayer of the Church, to be precise, its solemn liturgical, official prayer, made in its name.'[11]

In 1922 the monks returned to their home, L'Abbaye de Saint Pierre, at Solesmes, and in 1923 Justine Ward moved into a house in nearby Sablé-sur-Sarthe. During the next few years she stayed numerous times at Sablé and visited the abbey for worship and for study with Dom Mocquereau. Early during her fifth visit – from 24 December 1924 to 12 June 1925 – Justine Ward met the young Benedictine Virgil Michel, of Saint John's Abbey, Collegeville, Minnesota. Sent by his abbot to Europe for philosophy studies, Dom Virgil discovered and became enamoured of the liturgical movement:[12] 'He was to spend a semester at St. Anselm's, travel and observe in various countries during the summer, go to Louvain for a year, and then occupy another summer in study trips in Europe, the Holy Land, and Egypt.'[13] In Rome he had met Dom Lambert Beauduin, who was teaching courses in liturgy at Collegio Sant' Anselmo.

All that Dom Virgil saw at the abbeys of Maredsous, Beuron, Maria Laach, Mont César, and Solesmes, as well as at other centers of liturgical renewal stimulated in him the desire to promote a popular liturgical movement in the United States. Writing to Abbot Alcuin from Solesmes on 18 January 1925, he commented: 'The liturgical project got a good boost at

11   *Monographie Grégorienne* 4 (1923), 31; quoted in Combe, *Justine Ward*, 10.
12   Virgil Michel left St Paul on 11 February 1924 and returned home on 28 August 1925. See Marx, *Virgil Michel* (as n.6), 43.
13   Marx, *Virgil Michel*, 25.

Solesmes and has otherwise developed without a loss of time.'[14] He urged
the abbot to take up the cause of the liturgy by arranging to translate various European writings on the liturgy and publish them in a 'Popular Liturgy Library.'[15] It was during this visit to Solesmes that Dom Virgil met
Justine Ward: 'Here they agreed that what the chant in America needed
was a liturgical movement. She invited him to give lectures on the liturgy
at Pius X the following year.'[16] After he left Solesmes, Dom Virgil wrote
from Louvain (14 March 1925) to Abbot Alcuin that Mrs Ward had also
offered to help in making the 'Popular Liturgical Library' available for
children.[17] In a letter of 10 May 1925, written from Sablé-sur-Sarthe, Mrs
Ward exclaimed to Michel:

> All that you write of the awakening of interest in the Liturgy in America and of the
> approval of your Father Abbot of the beautiful plan for a 'Popular Liturgical Library'
> fills me with joy. I often think of what Rev. Dr. Shields said to me a few months
> before his death: 'We are all taking part in a movement that is much greater than
> any individual and is more far reaching than we imagine; it has all the characteristics
> of the great epoch-making movements in the Church.'[18]

In addition to a 'Popular Liturgical Library', Dom Virgil also suggested to
the abbot that the monks begin a 'review', to be called *Orate Fratres*, which
would promote the liturgical movement in the English-speaking world.
Justine Ward and Virgil Michel were kindred spirits in their promotion of
Gregorian chant, in that they both saw the chant not merely as music, but
as *pars integrans* of the liturgy. As early as 1906, Mrs Ward had written:
'The music must pray, the prayer must sing.'[19] In a 1929 article in *Orate
Fratres*, Virgil Michel described chant's pre-eminently liturgical character

---

14   Letter to Abbot Alcuin Deutsch, 18 January 1925, quoted in Marx, *Virgil
      Michel*, 37.
15   Marx, *Virgil Michel*, 37.
16   Ibid., 47.
17   Ibid., 38.
18   Ibid., 98.
19   Justine Bayard Ward, 'The Reform of Church Music', *Atlantic Monthly* 97 (1906),
      455. This was later reprinted, along with an article from *Orate Fratres* by Roger
      Schoenbechler, OSB and the 1928 Apostolic Constitution of Pius XI, *Divini cultus*,
      as *The Chant of the Church* (Popular Liturgical Library Series 4, no. 5; Collegeville:

thus: 'The chant is primarily the sung prayer of the Church, and not first of all music or art.'[20] Dom Virgil's lectures in liturgy at the Pius X Institute came about as a result of his discussions with Justine Ward on the integral part played by chant in the liturgy.[21] Justine Ward's name appeared as an associate editor on the title page of the first issue of *Orate Fratres* (28 November 1926), and she continued in this capacity for seven years.

In the foreword to the first issue of *Orate Fratres*, Virgil Michel defined and stated the aims of the 'liturgical movement' by saying that: 'Our general aim is to develop a better understanding of the spiritual import of the liturgy, an understanding that is truly sympathetic.'[22] In discussing his hopes, Fr Michel cited the dictum of Pius X that the liturgy is the 'primary and indispensable source of the true Christian spirit.' He further characterized the liturgy as 'a great mine of the widest cultural life.' In this mine were included the 'literary, musical, artistic, historical, even ethnological and archeological aspects.' But all these should be 'always in subordination to the more fundamental aspect, that of spiritual import, which is its true essential nature.'[23]

In keeping with Michel's liturgical ideals, the publication of *Orate Fratres* followed the liturgical year, spanning the first Sunday of Advent to the twenty-fourth Sunday after Pentecost. The first issue consisted of four departments. There were several articles and an editorial, while 'Liturgical Briefs' – a sub-section of 'The Apostolate' – contained news of diocesan initiatives, workshops and summer schools of liturgical chant, and other events of liturgical interest. 'The Apostolate' proper focused on documenting practical experiences in liturgical worship. Later, in volume three, 'Book Reviews' were added to 'The Apostolate'. Starting with volume four, two more new sub-sections would be added – 'Questions and Answers' and 'Communications'. This format would be followed as a general rule for many years.

    Liturgical Press, 1930). Ward's article is also available at <http://musicasacra.com/publications/sacredmusic/pdf/ward.pdf>, accessed 24 June 2008.

20   Virgil Michel, OSB, 'The Chant of the Church,' *Orate Fratres* 11 (1937), 363.

21   See Marx, *Virgil Michel*, 80.

22   Virgil Michel, OSB, 'Foreword', *Orate Fratres* 1 (1926), 1.

23   Michel, 'Foreword', 2.

During the first ten years, articles on chant and congregational singing covered many aspects – historical, philosophical, and practical – of Gregorian chant. In volume one Justine Ward laid out a philosophical basis for the primacy of Gregorian chant in the church in her essay, 'Winged Words.' She did not neglect the experiential element, and provided an example of the transformation of Serravalle, a poor Italian village, through the use of Gregorian chant. In volume four she wrote a tribute to her recently deceased mentor, Dom Mocquereau.[24] Next to Ward, the most active writers (at this time) of articles on Gregorian chant were two Benedictines, Dom Gregory Huegle of Conception Abbey (Missouri) and Dom Ermin Vitry, an émigré from the abbey of Maredsous. His first article for *Orate Fratres* consisted of an evaluation of the progress made in the twenty-five years since the *motu proprio* on sacred music.[25] While being thankful for the advances made, Dom Vitry posited that they were 'meagre', and that so much more remained to be done:

> How shall we accomplish this end? By adopting and putting into practice the means proposed in the *Motu proprio.* These means are teaching and organization. This double theme will be the subject of study in future articles.[26]

In the first of these articles Dom Vitry emphasized that sacred music must be true liturgical music, the humble handmaid of the liturgy.[27] In volume three, Dom Vitry described the roles of priest, choir, and people in liturgical chanting.[28] Volume ten contained no fewer than five articles by Dom Vitry, but these were not intended as a 'continued series.' In his introductory essay, Dom Vitry stated his mission of emphasizing 'the organic union which must exist between the liturgical apostolate and the movement for the reform of church music', and he revealed that each successive article would 'treat of independent questions chosen at random from the field

---

24   Ward, 'Dom André Mocquereau of Solesmes', *Orate Fratres* 4 (1929–30), 199–207.
25   Ermin Vitry, OSB, 'Reflections on the Twenty-Fifth Anniversary of the Motu Proprio on Church Music', *Orate Fratres* 2 (1927–28), 240–5.
26   Vitry, 'Reflections', 245.
27   Vitry, 'What Sacred Music Really Ought to Be', *Orate Fratres* 2, 362–8.
28   Vitry, 'The Traditional Plan of Church Music', *Orate Fratres* 3 (1928–29), 171–7.

of daily experience.'[29] Pursuing further his theme of organic unity, Dom Vitry espoused Gregorian chant as the ideal way to achieve this union of the liturgical spirit with music.[30] Much of Vitry's advice was directed at priests;[31] nor did he shy away from controversy, for certainly Pius X's favouring of Gregorian chant over sentimental and theatrical music was not joyfully received by all Catholics.[32] Finally, in his tribute to Dom Joseph Pothier,[33] Dom Vitry touched on 'technical problems which divide the so-called "gregorianists"', despite his earlier avowal of maintaining an irenic spirit.[34]

Dom Huegle, in one of his articles during the first decade of *Orate Fratres*,[35] likewise broached the subject of the dislike many Catholics had for chant in 'Why is Liturgical Music So Austere?' Both monks were experts in Gregorian chant and served at various times as editor of *The Caecilia*, the journal of the American Cecilian Society.

In this first decade one other article, out of the many on liturgical music and chant, is worthy of mention. Gerald Ellard, SJ, one of the original founders of the American liturgical movement, wrote from Holland enthusiastically describing 'An Ideal Parochial High Mass'.[36] The Mass in question was at St Anthony Abbot Church, Rotterdam, and here Fr

---

29 Vitry, 'Liturgical Apostolate and Musical Restoration', *Orate Fratres* 10 (1935–36), 54–8.

30 Vitry, 'Liturgical Inspiration or Musical Methods', *Orate Fratres* 10, 248–56.

31 Vitry, 'Priestly Leadership in Sacred Music', *Orate Fratres* 10, 343–9; 'An Answer to an Inquiry', *Orate Fratres* 10, 439–45.

32 Vitry, 'Why People Do Not Like Gregorian Chant', *Orate Fratres* 10, 151–5.

33 Vitry, 'Dom Pothier and the Gregorian Restoration', *Orate Fratres* 10, 575–84.

34 Vitry, 'Liturgical Apostolate', 58.

35 Gregory Huegle, OSB, 'Why is Liturgical Music So Austere?', *Orate Fratres* 6 (1931–32), 56–60; 'May We Look for a Simplified Edition of the Vatican Gradual?', *Orate Fratres* 6, 115–20; 'Melodic Recitation of the Propers', *Orate Fratres* 6, 269–72; 'The Most Simple Mass in Gregorian Chant', *Orate Fratres* 6, 564–6; 'Church Compositions without Liturgical Foundation' (a three-part series), *Orate Fratres* 7 (1932–33), 211–215, 402–7; *Orate Fratres* 8 (1933–34), 24–9; 'Liturgy and the "Big Tone"', *Orate Fratres* 9 (1934–35), 467–70.

36 Gerald Ellard, SJ, 'An Ideal Parochial High Mass', *Orate Fratres* 3 (1928–29), 181–5.

Ellard heard the congregation of a thousand sing the Ordinary chants.
He marvelled at the artistic rendering of the chants by the faithful, later
observing that

> [T]he difficult Gradual was handled by the schola alone. But even then one heard
> half-suppressed singing among the people. Listening to this throng so joyously sing-
> ing the great articles of the Creed the writer was thinking of the vast congregations
> in America, forced to sit mute, while a florid rendition of the Credo is sung by a few
> choristers in an elevated loft at the rear.[37]

Taking stock – at the beginning of volume ten – of ten years of organized
liturgical renewal in the United States, the editors reminisced and saw
that, among other things:

> The chant movement, too, has made great advances, and has contributed not a little
> to further congregational participation in the Mass. Liturgical music in general is
> on a much higher level today than it was even five or six years ago, due primarily
> to the activities of the Society of St. Gregory and to the various diocesan Music
> Commissions.[38]

They cited the 'summer schools devoted to the liturgy and especially to
chant.'[39]

A point of controversy at the beginning of the second decade of *Orate
Fratres* concerned an article by the Revd Ferdinand C. Falque, who was
critical of aspects of the liturgical movement, including Gregorian chant.[40]
In the March issue he accused chant enthusiasts of lacking the true liturgical spirit and of legalistically imposing chant without making sure that it
was rendered beautifully. He noted

> the fact that a few decades of chant reform has not to date achieved anything like
> a popular response should be an emphatic enough manifestation of popular senti-
> ment. The decline of attendance at high Masses has been in very nearly the same
> proportion as efforts have been made to enforce chant.[41]

37   Ellard, 'An Ideal Parochial High Mass', 184.
38   The Editors, 'Nine Years After', *Orate Fratres* 10 (1935–36), 3.
39   The Editors, 'Nine Years After', 4.
40   Ferdinand C. Falque, 'The Liturgical Spirit in Reform', *Orate Fratres* 11 (1936–37),
     209–13.
41   Falque, 'Liturgical Spirit', 210.

Fr Falque suggested using other music that 'possesses the power of expressing the spirit of the liturgy [...] until a love of chant can be achieved.' In the next issue 'An Old Friend' wrote to the editor in polite protest over Falque's article, and took *Orate Frates* to task for seeming to promote Falque's view. The writer suggested that Fr Falque was expressing his personal preference, and that he took an evolutionary view in referring to chant as music 'in arrested development.' The 'Friend' closed by hoping that 'pens more able than mine will reply to the Reverend author of that article.'[42] In June the editor replied to Falque. Fr Michel focused on the criticism of poor renditions of the chant, and countered with four arguments: (1) many still resist obeying the *motu proprio*; (2) many choirmasters are ignorant of the correct way to interpret the chant, in accord with the Solesmes method, which is in tune with the liturgical spirit; (3) seminarians are not receiving proper training in Gregorian chant, not to mention liturgy; and (4) many diocesan chant directors tend to focus on chant as music, at the expense of the liturgy. In sum, many simply lack the will to promote the chant and render it beautifully and worthily.[43]

Later that year, in the September issue, Dom Virgil wrote what may be considered another reply to Fr Falque and to the 'Old Friend.'[44] Dom Virgil defined 'Modernism' and then chastised 'an ardent youth' who thinks the church should drop Gregorian chant as being outmoded, by noting that the chant is

> prayerful music, the best liturgical music, and is specifically music adapted for congregational participation because of its unisonous character. And there is no other music thus adapted to the entire spirit of that which is eternal in the liturgical worship of the Church. The facile slogan of today, that the chant is impractical, that 'it can't be done,' shatters to meaningless bits in the face of the many actual demonstrations of its practicality. An instance among many furnished materials for a most interesting article in the June issue of *Orate Fratres*.[45]

42 An Old Friend, 'Communications: "The Liturgical Spirit in Reform"', *Orate Fratres* 11 (1936–37), 281.
43 Virgil Michel, 'Timely Tracts: The Chant of the Church', *Orate Fratres* 11, 363–5.
44 Virgil Michel, 'Timely Tracts: Modernism and the Chant', *Orate Fratres* 11, 463–5.
45 Michel, 'Modernism and the Chant', 464.

Fr J.A. Winnen, in the lead article of the June issue, considered the fact
that the *motu proprio*, as well as Pius XI's anniversary document, *Divini
cultus*, had not been followed, and he attempted to answer the question
of whether Gregorian chant could be successfully implemented in small
parishes. His answer, from his personal experience as a missionary and as
a pastor in rural Maine, was a resounding 'yes'. Fr Winnen recalled the
sincere chanting of his African congregation of thirty-five years ago, and
then described the process he followed to build a liturgical, singing parish
of 250 families.[46]

The September issue also carried a review by the twenty-nine-year-
old Godfrey Diekmann, of Alec Robertson's book, *The Interpretation of
Plainchant: A Preliminary Study*. In his lively writing style, Dom Godfrey
referred to the 'comparative lack of success of the so-called Gregorian
revival, in spite of repeated pronouncements by the Church authorities.'
Although he disagreed with some of the author's ideas on the interpretation of chant, he appreciated the book, and averred that 'as long as the book
will be of substantial assistance in stimulating choir directors to greater
endeavor in vitalizing the Church's official song-prayer, its purpose will
have been accomplished.'[47]

The Christmas issue of volume thirteen sadly announced the death
of Dom Virgil 'on the vigil of this new liturgical year', and the editorship
of *Orate Fratres* fell to Godfrey Diekmann, OSB. Volumes thirteen and
fourteen contained no full-length articles on Gregorian chant. Volume
fifteen, however, featured many articles related to chant. The first number
of volume fifteen featured 'Advent Introits', an extract from Dom Dominic
Johner's *The Chants of the Vatican Gradual*, which had recently been translated and was soon to be published by the Liturgical Press.[48] A Mexican
Benedictine, Dom Juan Carlos Fernández, wrote of the power of unison
chanting to unite the faithful in prayer, and of 'the catholic, or universal
and popular character of our religion, which is brought out unmistakably

---

46 J.A. Winnen, 'It Must Be Done – It Can Be Done', *Orate Fratres* 11 (1936–37),
    337–45.

47 Godfrey L. Diekmann, OSB, '*The Interpretation of Plainsong: A Preliminary Study*',
    Orate Fratres 11, 525–6.

48 Dominic Johner, OSB, 'Advent Introits', *Orate Fratres* 15 (1940–41), 18–19.

in Gregorian chant.'[49] Monsignor Martin Hellriegel, another of the original pioneers of the liturgical movement, began in this volume a series of articles, 'Merely Suggesting', in which he shared many of the pastoral initiatives that he was inaugurating at Holy Cross Church, Saint Louis, where he had recently been assigned. Among the many initiatives designed to effect liturgically-oriented spiritual renewal among his parishioners, Gregorian chant held an important place. In the July issue Monsignor Hellriegel offered suggestions for the reform of the High Mass, especially during the summer months, when the practice of the High Mass seemed to fall by the wayside. Among other things, he suggested a brief plan of action for achieving congregational participation in chanting the Mass. First things first: the faithful should be taught to chant all the responses. After that, they can learn the Kyrie, Sanctus, and Agnus Dei, followed – after mastery of these – by the Gloria, and finally the Credo. He even suggested specific chants (as other writers did in previous volumes).[50] In his September article, Monsignor Hellriegel went further and described the process he used for bringing the children of his parish to full and active participation. Beginning in September of 1940, at the onset of the school year, the children were taught carefully and naturally to say the responses and Ordinary parts of the *Missa Recitata*. Monsignor noted that: 'Once or twice a month we recite the *Gloria, Sanctus, Agnus Dei,* etc. in English, but the children decidedly prefer the Church's mother-tongue.' October marked the commencement of instruction in learning to chant three Gregorian Mass Ordinaries. During the first week of Lent the children began to learn the third of these Ordinaries, Mass I (*Lux et origo*). By Easter they were ready to sing it along with the adult choir, which had also been following a similar plan of chant instruction.[51] In 'The Apostolate' section of the June issue was a full-length article by Dom Gilbert Winkelmann, OSB, on 'Introducing Congregational Singing' in a small parish in Wayzata, Min-

---

49   Juan Carlos Fernández, OSB, 'From Other Lands: Gregorian Chant and the People', *Orate Fratres* 15, 368–70.

50   Martin Hellriegel, 'Merely Suggesting', *Orate Fratres* 15, 390–7.

51   Hellriegel, 'Merely Suggesting', *Orate Fratres* 15, 442–8.

nesota.[52] Implementation of congregational singing of Gregorian chant in San Francisco was discussed by the Revd Edgar Boyle, archdiocesan Director of Liturgical Music, in the August number.[53]

Chant highlights of volume eighteen were two of the 'Timely Tracts' by the Revd H.A. Reinhold, a popular writer and an influential figure in the liturgical movement. 'H.A.R.', as he was known, chastised the choir for using rehearsal time for polyphonic motets and chant Ordinaries. Instead, he urged them to focus on the Propers, those chants rightly belonging to them, and to let the congregation chant the Ordinary. As a parting shot, he stressed the importance of restoring the original function of the Introit and Communion as processional chants.[54] In 'About Music and Other Things', H.A.R. commented on random issues related to chanting the Mass. Again he stressed that 'the ordinary belongs to the people', and perhaps in answer to chant perfectionists, he wrote: 'I have always found that congregational singing sounds only half as bad when you yourself join in. Maybe it is a psychological trick and an appeal to your own vanity. Yet it works!'[55]

Gregorian chant was not neglected during wartime conditions, and several articles and communications document positively its use in the armed forces. Captain George J. McMorrow wrote a letter, published in the February issue of volume nineteen, in which he reported that at Midnight Mass the soldiers 'sang the entire proper and the ordinary *a cappella*.

> Father, we want it to be known that the chant was welcomed, and men who had seldom heard it before commented most favorably upon the 'fittingness' of the music. Of course, 'it' can be done, but it takes work and perseverance and the desire to serve our Lord and the Church as He desires to be served. In short, we are of the opinion that in Church music the supernatural view of music must be taken, and it is then that the real beauty of the chant emerges. This is not to imply that there is any lack

---

52   Gilbert Winkelmann, OSB, 'Introducing Congregational Singing', *Orate Fratres* 15, 375–8.

53   Edgar Boyle, 'Congregational Singing in an Archdiocese', *Orate Fratres* 15, 417–19.

54   H.A. Reinhold, 'Timely Tracts: Choir and/or People', *Orate Fratres* 18 (1943–44), 73–6.

55   H.A. Reinhold, 'Timely Tracts: About Music and Other Things', *Orate Frates* 18, 514–20.

of music in the chant, but it is definitely an instrument of the liturgy, a beautiful instrument which reveals its lovely ancillary qualities best at Mass.[56]

Earlier volumes of *Orate Fratres* had reported on the natural aptitude of African and African-American people for Gregorian chant, along with their love for it. Volume twenty featured two full-length articles on this subject, one on an American parish and the other on missionary work in Uganda.[57] In the same volume a country pastor related the story of how the sung High Mass became a regular and cherished tradition at his parish. After starting with the children, he reached an impasse with his adult parishioners until a national eucharistic congress held in his diocese provided the inspiration to get everyone involved in chanting the Mass. In addition, after ten years, his parishioners also sang a number of other services, for example, Stations of the Cross, Forty Hours, and Holy Hours.[58]

Volume twenty-one of *Orate Fratres* is interesting in that it contains some historical documents relating to the themes of active participation in the liturgy and Gregorian chant. The Revd William Busch translated and published excerpts from documents of the Third Plenary Council of Baltimore (1884), and noted some earlier writers on the subject.[59] One of these was Fr Alfred Young, CSP, whose 1891 article, 'On Congregational Singing', reprinted from the *North-Western Chronicle*, mentions Gregorian chant in this exalted language:[60]

> Is it any wonder that holy Church has a song of her own, a sublime, poetic, truly oratorical chant, to which almost every word of her divine service of praise is attuned: all the magnificent, unsurpassed 'divine office' already mentioned: saving a few secret

---

56 (Capt.) George J. McMorrow, 'A Layman's View of the Chant', *Orate Fratres* 19 (1944–45), 189.

57 N.N., 'Story of a Negro Parish', *Orate Fratres* 20 (1945–46), 370–5; Revd O.S., 'Anima Naturaliter Liturgica', *Orate Fratres* 20, 468–76.

58 A Plug Country Pastor, 'How It Was Done', *Orate Fratres* 20, 564–70.

59 William Busch, 'The Voice of a Plenary Council', *Orate Frates* 21 (1946–47), 452–8.

60 Alfred Young, CSP, 'From Other Times: An American Prelude to Pius X: On Congregational Singing', *Orate Fratres* 21, 356–62.

prayers, every word of the missal. Open the three large volumes for the special use of the bishop, called the pontifical – almost all song, from beginning to end.[61]

With volume twenty-one, *Orate Fratres* began its third decade. The question of liturgy in the vernacular had been raised periodically in the pages of *Orate Fratres* throughout the years. In volume twenty-one, Clement McNaspy, SJ, revealed a little-known aspect of history. The Caughnawaga Indians were singing the Mass in Gregorian chant, but set to their own language, principally by Jesuit missionaries at the end of the nineteenth century. Fr McNaspy used this history to enter a plea for the use of English in the liturgy.[62] In the same volume a rationale for the use of Latin was put forth by the Revd Carlo Rossini, well known for his work in the field of sacred music.[63]

Volume twenty-two reflects the great interest in the recently issued encyclical of Pius XII on the sacred liturgy, *Mediator Dei*. Gerald Ellard, SJ, in his commentary and summary, reiterated the mission of the faithful as members of the Mystical Body of Christ to offer Mass with the priest and to participate actively by (among other things) 'joining in the High Mass chants [...] All this will take place in a setting that is architecturally, artistically, musically, the best man's gifts can here and now provide.'[64] Also, among the various articles related to congregational chanting is one by a self-admitted musically uneducated pastor who gradually coached his parishioners to a chanted High Mass.[65] Of special interest in this volume is Helene Iswolsky's article on the abbey of Regina Laudis in Connecticut, only recently founded, where the nuns chant the Divine Office and Mass in Gregorian chant.[66] With this volume a new writer made his first appearance. The English Jesuit, Clifford Howell, would become a frequent contributor to the pages of *Orate Fratres*.

---

61   Young, 'An American Prelude', 361.
62   Clement J. McNaspy, SJ, 'Iroquois Challenge: Chant in Approved Vernacular', *Orate Fratres* 21, 322–7.
63   Carlo Rossini, 'The Case for Latin', *Orate Fratres* 21, 176–83.
64   Gerald Ellard, SJ, 'At Mass with My Encyclical', *Orate Fratres* 22 (1947–48), 241–5.
65   Leo J. Trese, 'What Can Be Done?: A Pastor Proposes', *Orate Fratres* 22, 418–24.
66   Helene Iswolsky, 'Regina Laudis, Connecticut', *Orate Fratres* 22, 438–42.

For volume twenty-three of *Orate Fratres*, Fr Howell contributed an article to 'The Apostolate' on the theme of 'Let Us Be Practical: Some Thoughts on Chant Problems', in which he advocated that choirs not spend time on Ordinary chants, but instead let the congregation sing only the simplest Ordinaries (e.g. Mass XVIII and Credo III). Further, he suggested that Proper chants be simplified so that any *schola* could sing them. As an example, he included the beginning of *Benedicta sit*, the Introit for Trinity Sunday, as it appears in the *Liber Usualis*, followed by his own syllabic simplification of the chant.[67] This idea resulted in lively discussions in later issues.[68] In the November issue, Fr Howell related his visit of 14 August, along with Fr Gerald Ellard, SJ, to Monsignor Hellriegel's parish, Holy Cross. The English Jesuit was amazed at the beauty of the liturgy, the wholehearted chanting of the faithful, and the chanting of the Propers by a choir of boys and girls. For Holy Cross, this was a normal Sunday *Missa Cantata*, but Howell noted that it had been preceded by a Solemn High Mass.[69]

In volume twenty-four, Monsignor Joseph Schmidt reported on success at a mission parish in central Pennsylvania.[70] Another success story with chant – 'Homely Hints On...' – came from a pastor from Tiffin, Ohio, who wrote on teaching congregational chant in a small mission parish (Republic, Ohio), which had 'no school, no resident pastor, no special facilities of any kind.'[71] Likewise, 'Sunday in St. Meinrad's Parish' is Mary Fabyan Windeatt's account of the parish church in the town of St Meinrad, Indiana, near the archabbey.[72]

Dom Ermin Vitry returned in volume twenty-five with a lively article reminding readers of the inextricable union between chant and liturgical

---

67   Clifford Howell, SJ, 'Let Us Be Practical! Some Thoughts on Chant Problems', *Orate Fratres* 23 (1948–49), 267–75.

68   Martin J. Burne, OSB, 'Communications: "Let Us Be Practical"', *Orate Fratres* 23, 376–7; J. Vincent Higginson, 'Let Us Be Practical', *Orate Fratres* 23, 468–70.

69   Clifford Howell, SJ, 'A High Mass in St. Louis', *Orate Fratres* 23, 552–5.

70   Joseph Schmidt, 'A Parish Sings', *Orate Fratres* 24 (1949–50), 26–8.

71   Maurice C. Herman, 'Homely Hints On...', *Orate Fratres* 24, 267–70.

72   Mary Fabyan Windeatt, 'Sunday in St. Meinrad's Parish', *Orate Fratres* 24, 121–4.

prayer, and he went so far as to term the chant a sacramental.[73] He finished with an exhortation to provide for the spiritual and musical formation of children.[74] Volume twenty-five was the last of *Orate Fratres*, for in the next year the journal adopted a new name, *Worship*, in keeping with the growing momentum towards more use of the vernacular in the liturgy.

Nevertheless, Gregorian chant continued to be present in the pages of *Worship*. By now, Fr Clifford Howell was listed as an associate editor, and early in volume twenty-six he reiterated his concern that the choir was not singing the Propers and that the congregation remained mute while the choir sings the chants of the faithful, i.e. the Ordinary chants.[75] In response to Fr Howell's simplified chant from the previous volume, 'A Choir Director' offered suggestions as to various publications containing simplified versions of the Proper chants.[76] Another parish where congregational chanting was successfully nurtured was Sacred Heart, in Hubbard Woods, Illinois. Here the pastor was Monsignor Reynold Hillenbrand, another leader in the liturgical movement.[77]

The 1953 National Liturgical Week was held in Grand Rapids, Michigan, and was covered in volume twenty-seven of *Worship* by Fr Clifford Howell. The climax of the convention was the pontifical High Mass. Fr Howell greatly appreciated the Propers chanted by a *schola* and 'an immense congregation all able and eager to sing their responses and the common of the Mass.'[78] The year 1953 was the fiftieth anniversary of the *motu proprio* of Pius X, and celebrations were planned at different locations around the nation. From Davenport, Iowa, Fr Cletus Madsen wrote a somewhat depressing analysis of the fifty years since *Inter sollecitudines*. He concluded that despite the sublime ideals enumerated by Pius X, the majority of

---

73   As did Dom Jacques Hourlier, OSB, in *Reflections on the Spirituality of Gregorian Chant* (Orleans, MA: Paraclete Press, 1995), 47.

74   Ermin Vitry, OSB, 'Music and Prayer', *Orate Fratres* 25 (1950–51), 549–58.

75   Clifford Howell, SJ, 'The Mass is a Liturgy: Active Participation', *Worship* 26 (1951–52), 64–73.

76   'A Choir Director', 'Settings of the Proper of the Mass', *Worship* 26, 141–2.

77   Bob Senser, 'How a Parish Came to Sing', *Worship* 26, 257–60.

78   Clifford Howell, SJ, 'Liturgical Week 1953', *Worship* 27 (1952–53), 513–14.

American parishes were still ignorant of and unresponsive to these ide-als.[79] A few pages later the editor begged to disagree, saying that based on the letters he had received in the last year, there were reasons aplenty to be optimistic.[80]

Starting with volume twenty-eight, writings of men who would be major influences at the Second Vatican Council begin to appear. Giacomo Cardinal Lercaro was featured with an article on active participation, in the course of which he said that Pius X's privileging of Gregorian chant, among other musical aspects, 'became in effect a factor of incalculable efficacy for the restoration of divine worship and for drawing souls nearer to it.'[81] Cardinal Lercaro's article was a paper he presented at the Lugano conference (Third International Congress of Liturgical Studies); *Worship* followed the proceedings with great interest, and would continue to do so, as other international liturgical conferences were held in the ensuing years. Fr A.M. Roguet, OP, was another speaker at the conference, and considered chant to be 'the chief manner of participation'. However, he recognized that it is not easy to get the congregation to sing at Mass.[82] An article by the Revd Eugene A. Walsh, SS, chant director at St Mary's Semi-nary, Baltimore, approached the lamentable situation that many priests and seminarians do not know how to teach chant to their parishioners, despite their own extensive training in chant. Fr Walsh offered suggestions for the seminary curriculum, aimed at helping future priests develop singing congregations.[83] In 'How It Was Done', Monsignor Joseph Schmidt, who had written in volume twenty-four on getting the people of St Patrick's, his country parish, to sing, retells the story, this time in the context of the parish's pilgrimage to another church. The St Patrick's parishioners were well schooled in chanting the Mass by this time, because they had been

79   Cletus Madsen, 'Fifty Years After', *Worship* 27, 564–6.
80   'The Apostolate: Liturgical Briefs', *Worship* 27, 573.
81   James Cardinal Lercaro, 'Active Participation: The Basic Principle of the Pastoral-Liturgical Reforms of Pius X', *Worship* 28 (1953–54), 120–8.
82   A.M. Roguet, OP, 'The Theology of the Liturgical Assembly', *Worship* 28, 129–38.
83   Eugene A. Walsh, SS, 'For Seminary or Parish?', *Worship* 28, 38–43.

doing it since 1942.[84] The same volume features other reports of success with congregational chant, including one from a cathedral parish and one from a Mexican-American parish in Arizona.[85]

In volume twenty-nine Monsignor Hellriegel, in 'On Singers and Servers', began his article with a story about a little boy named Beppo, who was eager to become an altar server. This boy was the young Giuseppe Sarto, who would later become Pope Saint Pius X. Monsignor recounted the efforts that had been made towards full and active participation in the sacred liturgy, and he urged that children, especially high school students, should receive

> a solid training in classical music and folk-songs, but, above all, a thorough discipline in Church music, chant and polyphony. They should be able to learn at least six chant Masses (sufficient for the average parish) and some fifty well-chosen hymns for the various seasons of the Church year, evening services, Benedictions, etc.[86]

The Revd James King, SJ, shared his experience of teaching prep school boys to chant Gregorian Mass IX and psalm-tone Propers; he was convinced that young people would love Gregorian chant 'because it is beautiful music, perfect in its function.'[87] In the August issue, Fr Charles Dreisoerner, SM, offered a wealth of assistance to priests who might not know where to start in developing a singing congregation, including tips on how to introduce Gregorian chant in the parish.[88] In this volume, editor Godfrey Diekmann announced that Josef Jungmann, SJ, would be joining the roster of associate editors of *Worship*. Fr Jungmann, best known for his monumental *Missarum solemnia* (*The Mass of the Roman Rite*), was one of the most influential liturgical scholars in the years leading up to Vatican Council II.

The first issue of volume thirty celebrated the thirtieth anniversary issue of *Worship* (*Orate Fratres*), and the volume would feature another series of articles by Monsignor Martin Hellriegel, 'Towards a Living Parish.' All the articles in this series mentioned congregational chant. In this volume the

84   Joseph Schmidt, 'How It Was Done', *Worship* 28, 443–5.
85   'It Can Be Done', *Worship* 28, 201–3; 'It Can Be Done', *Worship* 28, 309–11.
86   Martin B. Hellriegel, 'Singers and Servers', *Worship* 29 (1954–55), 83–9.
87   James King, SJ, 'Prep School Experiment', *Worship* 29, 217–18.
88   Charles Dreisoerner, SM, 'The Priest's Part in Parish Music', *Worship* 29, 411–14.

simple psalm settings of Joseph Gelineau, SJ, were mentioned for the first time, by Fr Clifford Howell, as a remedy for the problem of congregational singing.[89] Near the end of the volume is a short article, a review separate from the 'Book Reviews' department, in which Fr Godfrey Diekmann introduces and promotes a new 'program for participation in low Mass', published by the World Library of Sacred Music. Everything needed for active participation was contained on one card easy enough for the average parishioner to use. Fr Diekmann, in explaining the rationale behind the programme, admitted that

> Most of our people in the United States attend low Mass all the time; most of our people do not handle any great amount of Latin well; most of our people do not understand what it means to participate in Mass.

The programme combined the Latin dialogue of the priest and people with some of the Mass prayers in the vernacular (Gloria, Apostles' Creed, Sanctus-Benedictus, Agnus, Domine non sum dignus) and judiciously selected English hymns. Fr Diekmann added that 'After the people have been thus trained to a true sense of participation, they are ready and eager for other and higher forms of participating in the sacramental and prayer life of the Church.'[90] The 'higher forms', one presumes, would include Gregorian chant.

Success stories that included Gregorian chant continued to be featured in *Worship*. Volume thirty-one gives an account of St Richard's, a new parish in a suburb of Minneapolis. An unusual feature of this parish was that not only did the congregation sing the Ordinary, but also during the Communion procession everyone chanted *Ubi caritas*.[91] At a San Antonio workshop designed to help priests lead their people into active participation, the Masses featured congregational chanting.[92]

---

89   Clifford Howell, SJ, 'A New Approach to Psalm Singing', *Worship* 30 (1955–56), 25–31.

90   Godfrey L. Diekmann, OSB, 'A Good Mass Program', *Worship* 30, 656–7.

91   Juniper Cummings, OFM Conv., 'They Did It', *Worship* 31 (1956–57), 215–22.

92   John M. Hayes, 'Timely Tract: A Workshop for Priests', *Worship* 31, 125–30.

To celebrate the tenth anniversary of *Mediator Dei*, the encyclical of Pius XII on the liturgy, Monsignor Martin Hellriegel opened volume thirty-two with an inspiring essay on the significance of this encyclical.[93] A new feature, beginning with this volume, was the column 'Responses', in which Fr Frederick McManus, an expert in canon law and liturgy, answered readers' liturgical questions. In March, Fr Robert Hayburn contributed the obituary of Fr Edgar Boyle, who had been the archdiocesan music director for San Francisco from 1932 to 1946. Reports of his indefatigable work on behalf of Gregorian chant had appeared countless times in the pages of *Orate Fratres*, and his funeral Mass could be cited as a measure of his success in promoting the ideals of the 1903 *motu proprio*. Fr Hayburn reported that: 'The ordinary of the Mass was sung by the congregation, which consisted of about 200 priests, 200 sisters, and 400 lay people; the proper by a choir of priests and seminarians.'[94] Some other voices occasionally appear in this volume of *Worship*. Mr Ed Marciniak, director of the Catholic Council on Working Life (Chicago), wrote of the decline of knowledge of union songs and of folk songs in general. The most startling idea he offered was that 'unless there is a *general* revival of folk singing in America, congregational singing of the Mass will advance slowly.'[95]

A noteworthy narrative unfolded in the pages of 'The Apostolate' for the September issue. The editor referred to a statement Cardinal Costantini made to the 1957 International Congress of Sacred Music, in which the cardinal recommended that missionaries need to study the indigenous music of those peoples they are evangelizing and 'incorporate their melodies into liturgical music.' He believed that some of these peoples have 'modes and melodies that are very similar to Gregorian chant [...]' Cardinal Costantini believed that music of the 'Occident' should not be used in the 'Orient'.[96] The next part of the narrative tells of a priest who wrote in to *Worship* and denigrated Gregorian chant as being too foreign for most Americans.

---

93   Martin B. Hellriegel, '1947 *Mediator Dei* 1957', *Worship* 32 (1957–58), 2–7.
94   Robert F. Hayburn, 'Rev. Edgar Boyle, R.I.P.', *Worship* 32, 244–5.
95   Ed Marciniak, 'We're Gonna Roll', *Worship* 32, 403–9.
96   'The Apostolate: Liturgical Briefs', *Worship* 32, 507–8.

The editor (Godfrey Diekmann) posed the question: 'Is it possible that our civilization is even farther removed from 'the tradition of the Occident' in the field of music than are the peoples of mission countries who have native 'modes and melodies that are very similar to Gregorian chant?' Fr Diekmann then used *Musicae sacrae disciplina,* the 1955 encyclical of Pius XII on sacred music to suggest that 'good' hymns be promoted for use at low Mass.[97] The final number of volume thirty-two contains the entire text of *De musica sacra et sacra liturgia,* the new Instruction on Sacred Music and the Sacred Liturgy, issued by the Sacred Congregation of Rites on 3 September 1958.[98] The text of the Instruction was followed by the commentary of Fernando Antonelli, OFM, Relator of the Historical Section of the Sacred Congregation of Rites.[99] Because Pius XII had followed the lead of his predecessors, Gregorian chant received much attention in the Instruction, which laid out in detail what the pontiff had said in his 1955 encyclical, *Musicae sacrae disciplina,* as well as in his 1947 encyclical on the Sacred Liturgy, *Mediator Dei.* Of particular interest was Fr Antonelli's commentary on participation of the faithful in sung Masses. Here he elaborated on the different degrees of participation that the Instruction recommends for helping congregations gradually to chant a high Mass. He mentioned, too, the very simple chants proposed as a minimum for the faithful, and he recalled – as an antidote to the lamentable reality of the prevalence of low Masses – the 1952 international Eucharistic Congress of Barcelona, at which 'a throng of 100,000 sang, "one heart and one soul," a very simple Gregorian Mass.'[100]

Volume thirty-two also contained the usual parish success stories concerning congregational singing of Gregorian chant, but a topic that was covered at least three times was the Gelineau psalms. Fr Eugene Walsh, SS, referred to earlier as a seminary chant director, wrote a glowing review of the Gelineau psalms as translated into English by the Grail, a women's

---

97   'The Apostolate: Liturgical Briefs', *Worship* 32, 508–10.
98   'Instruction on Sacred Music and the Sacred Liturgy', *Worship* 32, 590–626.
99   Fernando Antonelli, OFM, 'Commentary', *Worship* 32, 626–37.
100 Antonelli, 'Commentary', *Worship* 32, 632.

movement.[101] An LP recording of the Gelineau psalms was reviewed in volume thirty-three by James King, SJ.[102] This volume also contained further commentaries on the new Instruction and reports of various diocesan responses to it.

In a letter to the editor appearing in volume thirty-four, Fr Eugene Walsh mentioned the controversy over the Gelineau psalms, as it was raging in a number of periodicals, though he tried to maintain a *via media* between the disputants.[103] Some particularly interesting chant success stories are contained in volume thirty-four. Alexander O. Sigur tells of the Newman centre at Southwestern Louisiana State University, where the congregation sings the Mass and the *Liber Usualis* was often used for hymns.[104] Meanwhile, in Cambridge, Massachusetts, across from Harvard Square, stands St Paul's Church, a centre for congregational participation under the musical leadership of Theodore Marier, a nationally known figure in Gregorian chant and sacred music.[105] The year 1960 saw the passing of Dom Ermin Vitry, OSB, and editor Godfrey Diekmann wrote an affectionate tribute to this disciple of Abbot (now Blessed) Columba Marmion. The obituary also included part of a beautiful eulogy by Monsignor Francis Schmitt, choirmaster at Boys Town, where Dom Vitry had been part of the summer workshop faculty.[106] Dom Vitry's activities had been truly wide-ranging, and most recently he had been a regular, teaching chant at the Notre Dame summer liturgical institute.

The momentum towards the vernacular seemed to grow with volume thirty-five. Fr Clement McNaspy, SJ, contributed a lengthy article offering many justifications for the adoption of English in the liturgy.[107] Editor Diek-

101 Eugene A. Walsh, SS, 'Book Reviews: Twenty Four Psalms and a Canticle', *Worship* 32, 315–17.
102 James King, SJ, 'Book Reviews: The Gelineau Twenty-Four Psalms and a Canticle', *Worship* 33 (1958–59), 274–5.
103 Eugene A. Walsh, SS, 'Communications: The Gelineau Psalms', *Worship* 34 (1959–60), 356–8.
104 Alexander O. Sigur, 'It Is Being Done', *Worship* 34, 149–56.
105 William Leonard, SJ, 'A Parish Profile', *Worship* 34, 209–14.
106 Godfrey Diekmann, OSB, 'Dom Ermin Vitry, R.I.P.', *Worship* 34, 470–1.
107 Clement J. McNaspy, SJ, 'The Vernacular Re-Viewed', *Worship* 35 (1960–61), 241–50.

mann followed up McNaspy's article with his own three-page argument in favour of more use of the vernacular, and he looked forward to the coming council.[108] In a later issue, Fr Diekmann published extracts from letters written in favour of Fr McNaspy's article.

In the contents to volume thirty-six (1961–62) of *Worship* there are no occurrences of the words 'chant', 'Gregorian', or 'music'. There are no articles on these subjects, though there are three reviews of books on musical subjects. And there are advertisements for summer workshops in liturgical music and chant – at Pius X Liturgical Institute, Boys Town, and Webster College. On the eve of the Second Vatican Council, it seemed as if Gregorian chant was quietly being ignored as something that would hinder the faithful in achieving a true and meaningful participation in the eucharistic mystery.

108   Godfrey Diekmann, OSB, 'The Apostolate: Liturgical Briefs', *Worship* 35, 253–5.

JOHN DE LUCA

Disputatur inter Doctores: A Disagreement between Two Australian Bishops on the Binding Nature of a Papal *Motu Proprio*

The initial research for this chapter was undertaken as part of a doctoral thesis presented to the University of New South Wales in 2001.[1] Significant material relevant to the chapter's theme published since then includes a major biography of the principal protagonist, Patrick Francis Cardinal Moran, commissioned by Moran's present-day successor as archbishop of Sydney, Cardinal George Pell.[2] A journal article on Moran's contemporary and sometime episcopal critic, the archbishop of Adelaide, John O'Reily, has been added to the small but important body of research relating to this interesting colonial prelate.[3] A study of the relations between the popes of the late nineteenth and early twentieth centuries and the Italian state casts light on some of the motivating forces shaping the attitudes of the leading papal musical reformer of the period, Pope Pius X,[4] as does the recent work of probably the leading Australian scholar researching in the field of Italian history.[5]

---

1   John Anthony de Luca, 'A Vision Found and Lost: The Promotion and Evolving Interpretation of the Movement for Liturgical Musical Reform within the Sydney Catholic Church during the Twentieth Century', PhD thesis, University of New South Wales, Sydney, 2001.

2   Philip Ayres, *Prince of the Church: Patrick Francis Moran, 1830–1911* (Melbourne: Miegunyah Press, 2007).

3   Robert Rice, 'Archbishop John O'Reily: First bishop of Port Augusta and second archbishop of Adelaide – Some aspects of his theology and practice', *Australasian Catholic Record* 84 (2007), 169–84.

4   David I. Kertzer, *Prisoner of the Vatican: The Popes' Secret Plot to Capture Rome from the New Italian State* (Boston: Houghton Mifflin, 2004).

5   R.J.B. Bosworth, *Mussolini's Italy: Life under the Dictatorship, 1915–1945* (London: Penguin, 2006).

Since the publication of a *motu proprio* in 2007 by Pope Benedict
XVI, partially restoring the ceremonial of the post-Tridentine period to
the Roman Rite,[6] considerable point has been added to this chapter's consideration of conflicting episcopal attitudes to liturgical musical reform.
Such reform was the aim of the celebrated *motu proprio*, issued within
three months of his accession to the papacy, by Pope Pius X in 1903.[7] Conventional wisdom says that, in the secular sphere, all politics is ultimately
local. In all likelihood, this applies also to ecclesiastical politics, since the
church, irrespective of its claims to divine origin and guidance, is composed
of human beings, and therefore is not immune to the prejudices of the
people who comprise it, be they prelates or parishioners. This chapter looks
at divergent attitudes within the Australian Catholic church to the 1903
motu proprio, which sought to promote congregational sung participation
in the liturgy by stressing music's structural role rather than its decorative
function. Pius X wished to stress the active participation of the laity in
the liturgy as an essential prerequisite for their full involvement in the life
of the church. By proscribing music that he considered ornamental (be it
soloistic, the mixed-voice repertoire of the Classical and Romantic periods,
or purely instrumental) and replacing it with a restoration of monodic
plainsong for the congregation and the male-voice polyphony of the High
Renaissance as represented especially by the Roman School of Palestrina
and Victoria, Pius X gave official approbation at the highest level to the
aspirations of the nineteenth-century Cecilian movement.[8] The reality that
many ordinary church members enjoyed the existing musical repertoire,
approved of female choristers and soloists, and considered the reforms of
Pius X as elitist, was not lost on the then archbishop of Sydney, who openly
resisted the *motu proprio*'s reforms. Equally, the archbishop of Adelaide,
who had anticipated the reform programme of Pius X almost to the letter,

6   Benedictus PP. XVI, Apostolic Letter in the form of a *Motu Proprio*, *Summorum
     Pontificium* (Rome [Vatican City]: Libreria Editrice Vaticana, 2007).
7   Pius PP. X, *Tra le sollecitudini* (Rome [Vatican City]: Acta Sanctae Sedis, 36.329,
     1903).
8   See Karl Gustav Fellerer, 'Cecilian movement', in Stanley Sadie (ed.), *The New Grove
     Dictionary of Music and Musicians* 4 (London: Macmillan, 1995), 47–8.

sought to impose the reform agenda by decree. This chapter's story tells of the victory of populism over idealism in one remote part of the Roman Church: a determined bishop resisting a papal command.

Pope Pius X (Giuseppe Sarto) held office from 1903 to 1914. He is generally remembered as a pastoral rather than as a political or intellectual pontiff. Prior to his elevation to the papacy, he had served first as bishop of Mantua, and then as patriarch of Venice. As pope, his major musical reform is contained in the *motu proprio*, known by its Italian title, which was issued on 22 November 1903 (feast of St Cecilia, patron of music and musicians), barely three months after his accession to office. The haste with which this document was produced, confirmed by the fact that it was not until 1904 that the official Latin version appeared, may fairly be judged to indicate that liturgical musical reform was an issue close to the pope's heart.

As a young priest, Giuseppe Sarto had been an amateur choirmaster and church musician.[9] As a diocesan bishop, he had sought to improve liturgical musical standards in the two dioceses for which he had oversight. In furtherance of this aim, Sarto commissioned the Jesuit priest Angelo de Santi to draw up a list of liturgical musical norms to be implemented in the diocese of Mantua. This document was later revised and reissued in Venice when Sarto was appointed patriarch there. The late American scholar of papal musical legislation, Robert Hayburn, has ably demonstrated the close correspondence between Sarto's two decrees promulgated in Mantua and Venice, showing how the earlier decrees were in large part identical with the *motu proprio* of 1903.[10] De Santi, then, may be considered the effective author of the *motu proprio*, although the document undoubtedly reflected the deeply held convictions of Pius X himself.

---

9   See Iginio Giordani (trans. Thomas J. Tobin), *Pius X: A Country Priest* (Milwaukee: Bruce, 1954); also Rafael Merry del Val, *Memories of Pope Pius X* (London: Burns, Oates & Washbourne, 1939), and A.G. Cicognani, A.G. Ehman et al., *A Symposium on the Life and Work of Pope Pius X* (Washington, DC: Confraternity of Christian Doctrine, 1946).

10 Robert Hayburn, *Papal Legislation on Sacred Music, 95 A.D. to 1977 A.D.* (Collegeville, MN: Liturgical Press, 1979), 220–2.

Although geographically remote from the European heartland of Catholicism, and from its vibrant expression in the new world of the Americas, Australian Catholics at the beginning of the twentieth century were well acquainted with currents of thought in those older societies. The campaign to reform liturgical musical practice in the archdiocese of Adelaide conducted by John O'Reily (archbishop of Adelaide, 1895–1915) was based on the ideals of the Cecilian movement, and in many respects anticipated the reforms of Pius X. Not content with restricting his attempt to reform contemporary liturgical musical practices to his own diocese of Adelaide, O'Reily campaigned nationally in support of the Cecilian reform agenda. In the inaugural year (1895) of the *Australasian Catholic Record*, a scholarly ecclesiastical journal, O'Reily penned a lengthy article on the state of church music in Australia in which he called for the banning of '[...] the masses of Mozart and Haydn et hoc genus omne [and all those of that kind].'[11] Moreover, he suggested the drawing up of an *index expurgatorius*, or list of music considered unsuitable for use in Catholic worship. It was somewhat daring of O'Reily to choose the *Australasian Catholic Record* as the locus for his attack on current musical tastes, since this journal had been founded by Patrick Francis Cardinal Moran, archbishop of Sydney, a senior prelate who could be considered to have been O'Reily's patron. The musical practice in Moran's own cathedral church (St Mary's Cathedral, Sydney) embraced many of the so-called abuses that O'Reily was seeking to correct. To attack those abuses could be construed as criticism of Moran himself. O'Reily's article in the *Australasian Catholic Record* soon elicited a spirited riposte, not from Moran, but from Moran's associate, the director of cathedral music, John Albert Delany.[12] Delany's musical abilities were highly regarded in Australia, and his liturgical musical preferences suited Moran and the Sydney Catholic community. Although he was not totally opposed to some of the ideals being espoused by O'Reily (ideals which were soon to be enshrined in Pius X's reforming legislation), Delany had many reservations about the direction that liturgical musical reform was taking.

11   John O'Reily, 'Church Music in Australia', *Australasian Catholic Record* 1 (1895), 202.

12   J.A. Delany, 'Church Music in Australia', *Australasian Catholic Record* 2 (1895), 465–73.

O'Reily continued his national campaign for liturgical musical reform in a paper given at the First Australasian Catholic Congress, held in Sydney in 1900.[13] This paper was principally devoted to a critical study of the state of plainsong in Australian Catholic churches. In restricting himself to a consideration of plainsong, O'Reily left room for another speaker, one who shared O'Reily's Cecilian ideals, the Sydney lawyer John Donovan. Quite possibly, the division of labour between these two musical reformers at the First Australasian Catholic Congress was a diplomatic move on the part of O'Reily. The congress was being held in the diocese administered by Moran, Australia's senior ecclesiastic, a person of some standing with Vatican authorities, and one, moreover, who had been a patron of O'Reily himself. Moran had been the principal consecrator of O'Reily as a bishop, and had shown consideration for O'Reily in addressing pressing financial problems in O'Reily's own diocese of Adelaide. O'Reily probably considered it prudent to leave trenchant criticism to Donovan, a wealthy Sydney lawyer, the leading practitioner in equity law at the Sydney bar, a bachelor and significant donor to the church in Sydney and beyond. John Donovan will be seen to have played a pivotal role in the matter being considered in this chapter.

At the 1900 congress, O'Reily laid the blame for the reluctance of the laity to accept the use of plainsong in worship on the poor example being given by the clergy. Though personally in favour of plainsong, O'Reily considered that 'the condition in which the art of Gregorian singing finds itself in Australia is certainly regrettable. That art is a lifeless, spiritless thing, a mere dead body, without animation or beauty.'[14] So, clearly, O'Reily had no illusions about how difficult was the task to attempt to change public acceptance of the Cecilian reform agenda.

John Donovan, who was considerably more outspoken than O'Reily in criticism of the prevailing liturgical musical practice at the 1900 congress, was a prominent Sydney layman, well known to Cardinal Moran. Moran had secured a papal knighthood for Donovan in 1893 in recognition of

---

13   John O'Reily, 'Gregorian Chant', *Proceedings of the First Australasian Catholic Congress* (Sydney: St Mary's Cathedral, 1900), 810–814.

14   Ibid., 813.

his generous donations to Catholic charities and, indeed, to the fabric of
Moran's cathedral church itself. Donovan had been appointed to a committee in 1878, by Moran's Benedictine episcopal predecessor, to reorganize
the choir of St Mary's Cathedral along Cecilian lines, with boys' and men's
voices. This attempt at reform was not continued by Moran or his director
of music, John Albert Delany, quite possibly to Donovan's annoyance. In
his 1900 paper 'On Church Music', Donovan condemned the contemporary musical repertoire as entirely unsuitable for worship.[15] He considered
it to be self-indulgent, repetitious, and more a vehicle for the display of
soloists' technique than a useful adjunct to worship. Donovan cited, as a
particularly unsuitable example of this defective repertoire, the soprano aria
'Inflammatus' from Rossini's *Stabat Mater*, about which more will be said
later. In condemning the Masses of Haydn (and to a lesser extent, Mozart),
Donovan used phrases that had previously been employed by O'Reily in the
decrees he had issued in an attempt to reform liturgical music in his own
diocese of Adelaide. This congruity suggests the possibility that O'Reily
and Donovan were acting in concert, and that their target, at least in part,
was the recalcitrant Moran himself.

It is a moot point as to whether Donovan could be considered O'Reily's
mouthpiece at the 1900 congress. As a leading practitioner at law, Donovan was his own person and in need of no prompting to pursue causes
that he considered proper. However, O'Reily was a natural ally, and as a
metropolitan bishop, the senior and most articulate pro-reform ecclesiastic in Australia at the time. Each probably drew strength from the other, a
joint resolve that was needed to confront the very powerfully placed and
influential Cardinal Moran. The fact that Donovan used the expressions
hoc genus omne and *index expurgatorious*, both used previously by O'Reily,
could be explained by both men having had access to *Lyra Ecclesiastica*,
the monthly bulletin of the Irish Society of St Cecilia, where these phrases

---

15   John Donovan, 'On Church Music', *Proceedings of the First Australasian Catholic
      Congress* (as n.13), 815–25.

were first used in October 1878.[16] But it would seem more likely that the line of influence should be traced from the Irish-educated O'Reily to the native Australian Donovan.

The issuing of the 1903 *motu proprio* by Pope Pius X received wide publicity within Catholic circles in Australia. The two weekly Catholic newspapers in Sydney, the *Catholic Press* and the *Freeman's Journal*, featured both the text of the *motu proprio* itself, and detailed commentary on it. Advocates of liturgical musical reform, such as O'Reily and Donovan, felt vindicated by the papal decree. The fact that five papers on the topic of liturgical music were presented at the first significant national Catholic gathering following the publication of the *motu proprio* (the Second Australasian Catholic Congress, held in Melbourne in 1904), is a clear indication of the higher profile being given to liturgical music within the Australian church as a direct result of the papal intervention. The five papers included a commentary on the *motu proprio* by a Vatican official, Monsignor Antonio Rella, who was subsequently to become director of the Sistine Chapel Choir.[17] John O'Reily again spoke, this time with a more triumphalist tone. His paper was entitled 'The Pope on Church Music'.[18] O'Reily obviously felt vindicated by the papal endorsement of the reform agenda that he (O'Reily) had been fostering, not without opposition, for some time. The flavour of O'Reily's sense of vindication may be gauged from the following quotation: 'The Supreme Pontiff has spoken. The High Priest has said his word. His it is to rule the sanctuary, his to shape and fashion the public homage offered to God.'[19] Because of his superior ecclesiastical status, the last word at the 1904 congress was given to Cardinal Moran. Moran, predictably, did not pass up the opportunity to put

16   See Kieran Anthony Daly, *Catholic Church Music in Ireland, 1878–1903* (Dublin: Four Courts Press, 1995), 38–9.

17   Antonio Rella, 'A Brief Commentary on the Motu Proprio of Pius X', *Proceedings of the Second Australasian Catholic Congress* (Melbourne: Advocate Press, 1905), 478–83.

18   John O'Reily, 'The Pope on Church Music', *Proceedings of the Second Australasian Catholic Congress* (as n.17), 471–7.

19   Ibid., 471.

on record his personal opinion that the *motu proprio* was not of binding
nature so far as the Australian church was concerned. Moran contended
that the pope's legislation was intended for the older, established churches,
and not intended for the church in younger, missionary countries such
as Australia. Moran praised the pope's 'perfect musicianship' and agreed
that people 'ought to endeavour, as far as possible, to carry out his wishes.'
But he also stated firmly that 'the Holy Father was addressing the home,
and not missionary countries.'[20] In no uncertain terms, Moran indicated
his opinion that the 1903 *motu proprio* should not be considered as binding legislation so far as the Australian church was concerned. So there the
matter rested: *Disputatur inter doctores.*

Moran's 1904 argument on the non-binding nature of the *motu proprio*
for missionary churches was immediately taken up by his cathedral director of music, John Albert Delany. Writing that same year in the *Australasian Catholic Record*, Delany asked: '[...] can, then, the Catholic Church
in Australia be considered as any other than a Missionary Church? [...]
the writer ventures to think not.'[21] To the legal mind of John Donovan,
the Moran-Delany argument was specious, and he eventually determined
to test the argument in the highest court of appeal for any Catholic, the
Vatican Curia itself. But before making an appeal to Rome, there was an
opportunity to test Moran's opinion at the Third Plenary Council of the
Australian Catholic Church, scheduled to be held in 1905. Unlike the
congresses of 1900 and 1903, which were just 'talk-fests', plenary councils
were legislative bodies, proposing binding legislation for the local church,
legislation which would be ratified by the Vatican. To have the missionary
church argument debated by the Australian bishops in council, John Donovan's brother, Thomas, also a barrister but more well known as a successful
businessman, wrote to O'Reily soliciting his support for music reform at
the 1905 plenary council.[22] At this time, there was no official papal representative (apostolic delegate or papal nuncio) in Australia. Such formal
representation did not commence until 1914. It was Moran himself who

20   *Proceedings of the Second Australasian Catholic Congress* (as n.17), 477.
21   J.A. Delany, 'Pius X and Sacred Music', *Australasian Catholic Record* (1904), 376.
22   See T. Donovan/J. O'Reily, O'Reily Papers, Box 6 (Church Music 1895–1909),
      Archdiocese of Adelaide Archives; also Helen Harrison, *Laudate Dominum: Music at
      Adelaide's Catholic Cathedral, 1845–1995* (Adelaide: Powerhouse Press, 1997), 32.

was commissioned by the Vatican to preside at the 1905 plenary council as the pope's cardinal delegate, a presidency that he had also exercised at the two previous plenary councils in 1885 and 1895. With Moran in the chair, it was highly unlikely that any attempt to use the plenary council as a vehicle for dissent was likely to succeed. And this proved to be the case. The one concrete proposal concerning church music reform agreed to by the bishops at the 1905 plenary council was a call for the drawing-up of a list of music suitable for use in worship.[23] This proposal reversed both O'Reily's and John Donovan's previous calls for a list of proscribed music. But even this watered-down proposal was not implemented in the Sydney church during Moran's time as archbishop. The failure of the bishops at the 1905 plenary council to embrace any meaningful liturgical musical reform was probably the catalyst for John Donovan's next move: to appeal directly to the Cardinal Secretary of State in the Vatican.

Pope Pius X's Secretary of State was Rafael Cardinal Merry del Val, of mainly Spanish ancestry, but, significantly in the Australian context, English educated and English speaking. Possibly because of this English connection, Merry del Val's name was probably more well-known to informed lay Australian Catholics than the names of other members of the Roman Curia. For whatever reason, it was to Cardinal Merry del Val that John Donovan wrote, on Sydney's Australian Club letterhead, on 1 June 1909, seeking official clarification of whether Moran was correct in invoking exemption from the 1903 *motu proprio*'s reforms on the grounds that Australia was a missionary country. Donovan asked:

> Is the instruction of the Holy Father, commonly called the '*Motu Proprio*' on Church Music [...] intended to apply to all the Catholic World? Or, on the other hand, are 'Missionary Countries' (such as Australia is said to be) exempted from its operation, and if so, in what respect? [...] Cardinal Moran contends, or at any rate suggests, that this being a 'Missionary Country' the '*Motu Proprio*' is not intended to apply here [...] but I am unaware that the Cardinal has ever submitted this question to Rome.[24]

---

23   *Acta et Decreta Concilii Plenarii Australiensis III, habiti apud Sydney, A.D. 1905, a Sancta Sede Recognita* (Sydney: William Brooks Printer, 1905), n.193.

24   J. Donovan/R. Merry del Val, *Segreteria di Stato di Sua Santita* (Vatican, 1909), n.38504.

Donovan asked for a speedy reply to his inquiry, since he wished to prepare a paper correcting Moran's rejection of the binding nature of the 1903 *motu proprio*, and intended to present this paper at the forthcoming Third Australasian Catholic Congress, which was scheduled to be held in Sydney in September 1909. As will be seen below, Moran gave Donovan no opportunity to present his paper at the 1909 congress, effectively forestalling any possible criticism from Donovan.

The present writer, unaware at the time (1994) of the existence of John Donovan's letter to Cardinal Merry del Val, but interested in ascertaining whether Moran's argument concerning the non-binding nature of the 1903 *motu proprio* had ever been ventilated with the Roman authorities, conducted archival research on the matter in three Roman archives in May 1994. The first archive consulted was that of the Congregation for the Evangelization of Peoples, the Catholic Church's principal missionary office, formerly known as Propaganda Fide. The aim of the search was to ascertain whether Cardinal Moran had formally raised the question of the application of the 1903 *motu proprio* within the Australian context in any communication with the missionary dicastery. The search was assisted by the publication of an inventory of the archive's holdings prepared by a former prefect of the archive, Fr Josef Metzler, OMI.[25] As expected, the search proved negative. There was no record of any communication from Moran on this topic in the records of the dicastery of first instance to which Moran was answerable.

The second search was conducted in the archives of the former Sacred Congregation of Rites, now known as the Congregation for Divine Worship and the Discipline of the Sacraments. Because of a division in the functions of this office that took place during the papacy of Pope John Paul II, this archive is now found in the building presently housing the Congregation for the Causes of Saints. This search unearthed for the first time the previously-mentioned letter of John Donovan to the Cardinal Secretary of State, dated 1 June 1909. There was, furthermore, considerable

---

25   Josef Metzler OMI, *Sacrae Congregationis de Propaganda Fide Memoria Rerum: 350 Years in the Service of the Missions* (Rome, Freiburg and Vienna: Herder, 1976).

documentation relating to the stir within the Vatican dicasteries following receipt of Donovan's letter.[26] No evidence, however, came to light of any communication from Moran. The discovery of Donovan's letter will be discussed in more detail below.

The final search was conducted in the Vatican Secret Archives, to which the present writer was given access by the then prefect, the same Fr Josef Metzler who had previously been responsible for the Propaganda Fide archives. The records consulted were those of the Secretariat of State during the time of Moran's incumbency in Sydney. Once again, there was no sign of any communication from Moran to Rome on the issue of the 1903 *motu proprio*. This was a predictable result, considering Moran's sense both of his personal status and of his seniority to most curial functionaries.

With regard to the Vatican reaction to John Donovan's letter of 1 June 1909, the first thing to be noted is the promptness with which action was taken. On 12 July 1909, the Secretariat of State sent Donovan's letter to the Congregation for Divine Worship, directing that dicastery to attend to the matter. This typically bureaucratic response (that of shifting responsibility to another department) could validly be construed as recognition of Moran's status, and of an unwillingness to offend him. The Congregation for Divine Worship, however, researched the question of the application of general church directives, such as those contained in the 1903 *motu proprio*, to local churches in missionary countries that were under the jurisdiction of Propaganda Fide. The particular official charged with drawing up a response to Donovan's letter cited three precedents which indicated that Moran was in error. Despite this judgment, the advice given to the cardinal prefect as to how he might respond to a petitioner who had caused a high-ranking ecclesiastic to have been shown to be in error was simply to ignore both the question and the questioner. The cardinal prefect was advised that since the question had been asked by a layperson

---

26   See inter-office memorandum from Secretariat of State to the prefect of the Sacred Congregation of Rites (12 July 1909); also position papers prepared for the prefect for a reply to John Donovan (17 July 1909), SCR correspondence folders (1909), nos 196, 635.

('postulante e un semplice laico') and not by a bishop who had a right to a
response, the cardinal prefect was under no obligation to respond. So there
the matter rested. No reply was sent to John Donovan. Moran was wrong,
but Donovan was not to be told this. This deprived John Donovan of the
official judgment he had sought to use at the Third Australasian Catholic
Congress, held in Sydney in September 1909.

As it happened, Donovan was not invited to speak at the Third Australasian Catholic Congress. Cardinal Moran controlled the agenda, and he
clearly had no intention of providing a platform for his critics. In contrast
to the 1904 congress held in Melbourne, where five papers on the topic
of musical reform were delivered, some of which were, at least indirectly,
critical of Moran's stance on this issue, the topic of liturgical musical reform
was altogether avoided at the 1909 congress. To circumvent controversy,
Moran invited only a trusted medical practitioner, Charles W. MacCarthy,
to speak on a musical topic in 1909. MacCarthy had called for the composition of an Australian national song at the 1900 congress, a topic agreeable
to the nationalist sentiments of Moran. Presumably MacCarthy could
be relied on not to offend Moran. In his reply to Moran's invitation to
speak, MacCarthy makes no mention of anything controversial.[27] In the
end, MacCarthy delivered a paper on the uncontroversial topic of Irish
Music.[28] Since there was no separate section for liturgical music at the
1909 Sydney congress, MacCarthy's paper was included in the section for
literature, science and art.

An even more cogent indication of Moran's control of the situation
may be seen in the music chosen for the solemn High Mass celebrated in
St Mary's Cathedral as the high point of the Third Australasian Catholic Congress. If anything, the repertoire for this very public occasion
was counter-Cecilian. A mixed choir of some 270 voices, with orchestral accompaniment, performed the Australian premiere of Sir Charles

---

27   See C.W. MacCarthy/P.F. Moran, 7 July 1909, Sydney Archdiocesan Archives,
      U2314/5.94.
28   C.W. MacCarthy, 'Irish Music', *Proceedings of the Third Australasian Catholic Congress*
      (Sydney: St Mary's Cathedral, 1909), 602–25.

Villiers Stanford's *Mass in G.* An instrumental interlude replaced the proper plainsong Gradual (the item was the Norwegian violinist Ole Bull's air 'Solitude'). Most pointedly, in view of John Donovan having cited, at the 1900 congress, Rossini's *Stabat Mater* (and particularly the soprano aria 'Inflammatus') as a prime example of the sort of music that had no place in Catholic worship, it was precisely this aria that was 'glowingly sung by Miss Amy Castles' at the 1909 congress High Mass.[29] A determined and recalcitrant Cardinal Moran was indeed rubbing salt into the wounds of the would-be but vanquished liturgical musical reformers, and in so doing, confirmed an anti-reform pattern that was to continue in Sydney's Catholic churches for many decades to come.

The present writer's doctoral thesis examined the reluctant history of liturgical musical reform within the Sydney Catholic church during the twentieth century, a story that quite clearly reflected Cardinal Moran's recognition of the power of popular musical taste at the beginning of the century. An interesting study could be made of the similarities between the reform agendas for liturgical music of both Pope Pius X and his present-day successor, Pope Benedict XVI. An even more interesting study could be made of episcopal resistance to liturgical musical reform, one example of which this chapter has sought to illustrate.

29 Errol Lea-Scarlett, 'Music, Choir and Organ', in Patrick O'Farrell (ed.), *St Mary's Cathedral, Sydney, 1821–1971* (Surry Hills: Devonshire Press, 1971), 157–81 (at p.179).

JOHN HENRY BYRNE

Archbishop Daniel Mannix and Church Music in Melbourne, 1913–1963

On the 23rd of March 1913 – Easter Sunday – the train bearing the future Catholic archbishop of Melbourne arrived at that city's Spencer Street Station. Met by a crowd of 500 people, the prelate had arrived in Australia at Adelaide on the liner *Orama* and then travelled overland. He was to administer his archdiocese for forty-six controversial years, and his influence upon the archdiocese, and indeed upon his new homeland, was as profound as it was exhilarating.

In examining the influence that Archbishop Mannix had on the practice of liturgical music in Melbourne, it is necessary to look at the history of Catholic culture in the city that he was called to administer so far from his native Ireland. In the seventy years that elapsed between the European foundations of the settlement and the expansive wealthy city that it had become by 1913, the vast changes that had been achieved had been made under the administration of only two archbishops.

The nineteenth-century foundations

The tradition of Catholic liturgical music in Melbourne has long been regarded as one of the glories of what was basically an isolated Irish community transported to an isolated farming settlement at the south-east corner of Australia. With the foundation of Melbourne in 1835, a Catholic community arose that was entirely Irish with the exception of a single Frenchman. In the earliest days, any expression of Catholic faith consisted of the recitation of the rosary and the reading of prayers, as there was no priest to celebrate the Mass.

Despite these poor beginnings, three influences may be identified as contributing to the especially favourable circumstances from which the Catholic musical traditions of colonial Melbourne emerged when compared to England, Ireland or the other Australian colonies. The first was religious freedom. From the earliest days of the settlement, Melbourne Catholics were free to practise their religion with the full support, moral and financial, of the government. Such financial assistance was unknown in Britain, where the Catholic Emancipation Bill had been passed only in 1829 and had met with widespread opposition. For the Catholics of early Melbourne, the open practice of their faith was thus a comparatively new experience and one in which they could take considerable pride.[1]

Second was the existence of an atmosphere in which these Irish immigrants were able to create levels of cultural excellence in which they took enormous pride. Whether it was liturgical or social music, art or architecture, religious freedom or growing wealth, the predominately Irish Catholic population was able to display its cultural traditions publicly. Mocked as an ignorant 'bog-Irish' peasant class, they found themselves able to aspire to distinction and show their links to a flourishing European heritage. This is in contrast to Sydney, where the Catholic community was essentially founded upon a convict underclass of grinding poverty and social isolation.[2]

The third and most important factor was financial in nature. Due to the discovery of vast deposits of gold within fifteen years of the establishment of the settlement, Melbourne grew very rapidly from the poverty-stricken outpost of the 1830s to one of the wealthiest cities in the world with an economy that encompassed notorious slums and poverty, yet which also permitted conspicuous displays of wealth and brash confidence. Churches, convents, hospitals and schools were quickly financed, the most prominent of which was St Patrick's Cathedral, which took thirty-nine years to build.

1   See Ursula de Jong, 'William Wilkinson Wardell, his life and work, 1823–1899', PhD thesis, Monash University, 1983, 43.
2   See Patrick O'Farrell, *The Catholic Church and Community: an Australian History* (3rd edn, Kensington, NSW: New South Wales University Press, 1992), 40.

When it was completed in 1897, the cost of £217,000 had been fully met. The historian Brian McKinley places special emphasis on the incalculable wealth that flowed into Melbourne from the prodigious amount of gold discovered just outside the city, remarking that 'Melbourne was the wealthiest city in the British Empire, probably the world.'[3] Money was lavishly spent on luxuries, but most importantly, money was readily available in Melbourne churches for the formation and support of musical establishments for much of the nineteenth century.

The musical establishments of Melbourne's Catholic community centre upon the two principal city churches: St Patrick's Cathedral (erected between 1858 and 1897) and St Francis' Church (the first Catholic church in the colony of Victoria, erected between 1841 and 1845). Both had musical activities which were quite well documented in the periodicals of the day. St Francis' was erected by the first Catholic priest in Melbourne, Revd Patrick Bonaventure Geoghegan, an Irish Franciscan, who arrived on 15 May 1839. The Catholic population at the time numbered 2,073.[4] The suburban parish churches, while they appear to have been able to enjoy successful musical performances, are less well documented.

It is interesting to note that the Vatican decrees with regard to sacred music at the time of the foundation of Melbourne are all based upon an encyclical issued by Pope Benedict XIV in 1749. This encyclical was essentially a house-keeping document issued in preparation for the Holy Year of 1750, and while directed at the churches of Rome, it was also applicable to the whole church. The document urged the churches of Rome to get their affairs in order and ensure that the liturgy and its music were both dignified and appropriate. Furthermore, it delegated all minor details of implementation to the local bishop, thus giving local churches enormous freedom. From that date until 1903, for over 150 years, the Vatican was silent on the subject of liturgical music.[5]

---

3   Brian McKinley, personnal communication, August 1994.
4   See Henri Lemieux, *St Francis' Church, 1841–1941: A Century of Spiritual Endeavour* (Melbourne: The Fathers [of the Blessed Sacrament], 1941), 17.
5   See John Byrne, 'Sacred or Profane: The Influences of Vatican Legislation on Music in the Catholic Archdiocese of Melbourne, 1843–1938', MMus diss., Australian Catholic University, 2005, 41.

The first mention of Catholic liturgical music being performed in Melbourne is on St Patrick's Day 1843, when a solemn High Mass was celebrated for the first time in the colony. Garryowen wrote:

> In 1843, the Rev. Daniel McEvey, a young clergyman of exceptional ability, arrived from Dublin, and on 17th March (St. Patrick's Day) High Mass was solemnized for the first time in Port Phillip [...] The singing was very effective, as several gentlemen, members of the Philharmonic Club, volunteered their services as an amateur choir, and acquitted themselves creditably.[6]

In those days, before the discovery of gold, the colony was chronically poor and ill-resourced, but, as reported in the *Port Phillip Herald*, a similar choir furnished the music for the following St Patrick's Day in 1844, when 'the appropriate singing of the choir, composed of Protestant gentlemen who volunteered their services, had a most imposing and pleasing effect.'[7] By the following October, however, the church had its own male-voice choir, directed by William Clarke, formerly an organist from Liverpool who owned a music shop. Despite a favourable report in the press, Garryowen states that the ten men were better at 'trolling a catch than singing High Mass', and he quotes Revd McEvey as stating that 'they made a precious mess of it.'[8] No details of the music performed have been preserved, although Garryowen reports the accompaniment to have been 'a cornopean, a clarionet, and a seraphine'. This choir collapsed after that single performance. A second attempt to found a choir was made in 1845 for the opening of the church, and due to the enthusiasm and addition of female choristers it was a success.

Upon the arrival of the first Catholic bishop, James Alipius Goold, on 4 October 1849, St Francis' Church was officially elevated to the status of a cathedral and remained thus until the see was transferred to St Patrick's in

6   'Garryowen' [Edmund Finn], *The Chronicles of Early Melbourne, 1835 to 1852* (Melbourne: Fergusson and Mitchell, 1888), 139.
7   Francis Mackle, *The Footprints of our Catholic Pioneers: the Beginnings of the Church in Victoria, 1839–1859* (Melbourne: Advocate Press, c1926), 39.
8   Garryowen, *Chronicles*, 967.

1868. The discovery of gold quickly changed the church's situation, and in 1853 it became the first Catholic church to possess an organ. Bishop Goold had visited the great Crystal Palace Exhibition in London and returned with a treasure trove of paintings, vestments, plate and a large organ by Henry Bevington of Soho Square. This was the beginning of a new era for the Catholic Church in Melbourne.

An important milestone in the history of local Catholic music was marked by the blessing and dedication of the Ladye [*sic*] Chapel at St Francis' on Monday, 31 May 1858. The solemnity of the celebrations engendered much press coverage.[9] The liturgy was celebrated by the metropolitan of Australia, Dr Polding from Sydney, the bishop of Melbourne, Dr Goold, twelve priests, processions of children, an expanded choir, and included a performance of Haydn's *Nelson Mass* with full orchestra. According to Mackle, this was the first orchestral liturgy presented in Melbourne.[10] The director, William Wilkinson, formerly of Dublin, was the organist for St Francis' Choir at that time. Accounts referring to the early history of the St Patrick's Cathedral Choir are conflicting and confusing, but it is known that the first music heard in the then St Patrick's Church was in February 1858. The history of the Sisters of Mercy reports:

> The march of progress continued in 1858, when history was made in St Patrick's Church on February 21. On that day, the first choir to sing in the building was composed of Sisters of Mercy who duly impressed the large congregation.[11]

Reports concerning the foundation of the cathedral choir in 1868 suggest that the first years may have been difficult. Between that year and 1880 there were constant reports in *The Advocate* either commenting on performances by the choir or reporting on attempts to establish a new cathedral choir. In 1880 an account of the inauguration of yet another

9   See 'Blessing of Cathedral Ladye Chapel', *The Argus*, 1 June 1858, 5 and *The Herald*, 1 June 1858, 5.
10   See Mackle, *Footprints*, 112.
11   Mary Ignatius O'Sullivan, *The Wheel of Time: A Brief Survey of the Ninety-Six Years' Work of the Sisters of Mercy in Victoria, 1857–1953* (Melbourne: Advocate Press for the Sisters of Mercy, 1954), 17.

cathedral choir, under choirmaster and conductor Mr Plumpton, was reported, the new choir numbering sixty singers.[12]

Meanwhile, St Francis' Choir was now promoted as one of the leading choirs in Australasia, with comments that it attracted 'a large and fashionable audience and fulfilled the highest expectations of educated musicians'. From the 1850s, with the influx of new-found wealth, the resources soon became available to celebrate every major event at St Francis' with choir, orchestra and soloists. While it is unlikely that an orchestra was ever the weekly custom at any but the two most prominent churches, it seems that the smaller parish churches usually contented themselves with an organ or harmonium and perhaps a few instrumentalists on major occasions.

The fame of St Patrick's Choir, St Francis' Choir and the other principal choirs appears to have been founded upon their presentation of orchestral eucharistic liturgies. Although an orchestra is frequently mentioned as being a feature at such occasions, the number of instrumentalists per part, or even the orchestration used is invariably not recorded, and it is likely that some re-orchestration or adaptation of forces was not uncommon. This is borne out by a comment made in *The Advocate* regarding St Francis' Choir that 'this is the only church in Melbourne where the compositions of the great masters are heard with proper effects.'[13]

As local affluence grew, the liturgies continued to grow in size and lavishness until they endeavoured to rival the perceived traditions of European cathedrals. As well as the presentation of orchestral Masses by Haydn, Schubert, Mozart, Beethoven, and Gounod, there was a great interest shown in the role of the soloists, and the link between the church and the opera house became very close. Singers were well paid and usually contracted to a church, although guest artists frequently appeared when they visited Melbourne or when an opera company was in town. There grew an undoubted rivalry between the choirs of St Patrick's Cathedral and St Francis' Church, leading to some scandal among the wider public. Each endeavoured to obtain the most famous soloists, such as Armes Beaumont,

12   'Melbourne Intelligencer', *The Advocate*, 8 May 1880, 6.
13   'Melbourne Intelligencer', *The Advocate*, 10 February 1877, 8.

the notorious Anna Bishop, Dame Nellie Melba, Sir Charles Santley, Amy Castles, Catherine Hayes, and (the theatrically Polish) Ilma Di Murska. The cross-fertilization between church and opera could lead occasionally to highly suspect results, such as the masonically influenced 'Within these sacred halls' from Mozart's *The Magic Flute* being performed at St Francis' as a communion motet.[14]

As the century progressed, the liturgical music repertoire in Melbourne included the *Mass in C* by Beethoven and the *Messe Solennelle de Ste Cécile* by Charles Gounod. Other popular Masses included the two Masses by Weber, Haydn's six late Masses and his *St Nicholas Mass*, as well as the Masses by Schubert. It is interesting to note that the repertoire of Mozart Masses was not as extensive as could have been expected. The musical structure of the liturgical year appears to have been comparatively unsophisticated, as the same Masses and motets were performed with scant regard to liturgical season. One could guarantee Novello's arrangement of *Adeste Fideles* at Christmas, however, and Handel's *Hallelujah* on every possible occasion. Of a more overwhelming liturgical nature was a performance by St Francis' Choir, on 26 June 1881, of Rossini's vast *Petite Messe Solennelle*.[15] The performance was so well received that it was repeated the following week. This repertoire was expanded by some local compositions, many of which have been lost, although the 1861 *Mass in D* by G.O. Rutter (in a style akin to Beethoven) has recently been revived with great success at St Francis' Church.

It is apparent that the people took great pride in their choirs and the musical achievements that they had attained in just fifty years. The laity supported the choirs with its new-found wealth, viewing them as a valid means of religious expression and a source of pride to the Catholic community. There was also an undeniable gratification in attracting acclaim from the leading members of other denominations for their artistic achievements.

In Europe, meanwhile, rumblings were beginning to appear about the suitability and the questionable dignity of the presentation of Masses such

---

14   See 'Melbourne Intelligencer', *The Advocate*, 20 November 1869, 5.
15   See 'Melbourne Intelligencer', *The Advocate*, 2 July 1881, 7.

as the Rossini *Petite Messe Solonnelle*, Beethoven's *Missa Solemnis* and decid-edly inferior works such as the Masses of Paolo Giorza (1832–1914). The cult of the soloist with the prominent adulation of famous guest sopranos led some to question the entire direction that liturgical music had taken. Were people coming to hear Mass for the wrong reasons? Was the essential liturgical action being swamped by music and becoming simply a sacred concert? Was all this 'dignified and appropriate', as Benedict XIV had stipulated in 1749? The rise of the Cecilian movement in Germany began to ask these questions.[16] In Melbourne, however, these rumblings were seen as simply the musings of European theologians, with 'no relevance to our well-behaved choirs'. Melbourne's Archbishops James Goold (bishop, 1848–86) and Thomas Carr (bishop, 1886–1917) appear to have been sat-isfied with the *status quo*. They showed no interest in reforming church music, and almost no local voices appeared to advocate any change.

Reform of liturgical music and the Melbourne response

As the first official act of his pontificate, the newly elected Pope Pius X took decisive action to bring matters to a head. On 22 November 1903 he issued his *motu proprio, Tra le sollecitudini*, a decree stipulating that all liturgical music was to be restricted to plainsong, sixteenth-century polyphony, or works in that style. Women were banned from choirs, as were soloists and orchestras. Given the attitude of the local archbishop, as well as the close link between the foundation of Catholic Melbourne and its tradition of lavish liturgical music, it is not unexpected that such a papal decree was ostentatiously ignored in that city for the next thirty years.

The initial means of dissemination of the new decree in Melbourne was by means of a variety of papers given at the Second Australasian Catholic Congress held in late 1904. The papers concerning liturgical music and

---

16   See John Byrne, *Echoes of Home: Music at St Francis, 1845–1995* (Melbourne: Spectrum, 1995), 93.

its reform were presented by prominent local and overseas experts, who explained the new regulations and the reason for their implementation. Some papers expressed a sense of regret, but stated that the task of the local church was obedience. One paper attempted to explain why plainsong was so unpopular with choirs and the public, but encouraged everyone to endeavour to obey the wishes of the pope.[17]

In the following two decades, much discussion was held in the pages of the local Catholic press, especially *The Advocate*, and although both sides of the discussion argued with passion and scholarship, there was no apparent victor. The two leading proponents in favour of the new regulations were Archbishop John O'Reily of Adelaide and Revd George Robinson, parish priest of the large new Church of Our Lady of Victories in the Melbourne suburb of Camberwell. With their deaths, however, in 1915 and 1918 respectively, much of the passion went out of the discussions.

The arrival of Archbishop Daniel Mannix

Born in 1864 in Charleville, Co. Cork, Ireland, Daniel Mannix was set to become Melbourne's longest serving archbishop as well as Australia's most controversial churchman. Typical of the great tradition of prelates who were exported from Ireland in the nineteenth century, he was a man gifted with immense intellectual brilliance. He was president of the Royal Seminary of Maynooth (1903–12) before being appointed coadjutor to the ailing Archbishop Carr in 1913. He succeeded him as third archbishop of Melbourne in May 1917, remaining in that position until his death in November 1963.[18] Dr Mannix assumed virtual leadership of Australian

---

17   Ignaz von Gottfried, 'On the Probable Causes Why Plain Song is Held in Disfavour', in *Proceedings of the Second Australasian Catholic Congress, 1905* (Melbourne: St Patrick's Cathedral, 1905), 507.

18   See Barry Jones, *Dictionary of World Biography* (Melbourne: Information Australia, 1998), 494.

Catholics for more than forty years. He was deeply involved in the question of Irish independence, the opposition to conscription in Australia
during the First World War, the battle for state aid to Catholic schools,
and opposition to the influence of communism. His interest in liturgical
music appears to have been minimal.

Discussions with Revd Dr William Jordan, Revd Paul Ryan and
Revd Ernest Rayson emphasized the methods Archbishop Mannix used
to administer the various areas of his jurisdiction. He would search for the
most appropriate person in a certain area of action and give that person
total control and support. This fondness for delegation also showed itself
in his distaste for the centralized Roman authority of the church, which
he managed to disregard to a remarkable degree. In his biography, Walter
Ebsworth writes:

> The few letters that remain in the Dublin archives reveal a thorough knowledge of
> Canon Law, but a glimmer of disdain comes peeping through. In Australia, he largely
> ignored it. There was no diocesan Curia, never a concursus for parishes [...] never a
> visitation of parishes, and for years Melbourne had no vicar-general, although he del-
> egated full powers to the Administrator of the Cathedral. The only time he appointed
> Monsignori was before the International Eucharistic Congress in Sydney [1928]
> when he was told he could not have a Congress function in Melbourne unless he was
> attended by Monsignori, and accordingly, he wrote to his six Diocesan Counselors
> conferring the title on them, a privileged action jealously guarded by Rome.[19]

This distinctive attitude is further borne out by Michael Gilchrist, who
wrote that 'he liked to govern the Archdiocese with what he called a light
rein.'[20]

Although the reform of liturgical music as promulgated in 1903
held little interest for Mannix, in this he was following in the tradition
of Archbishop Carr. For thirty years, neither Carr nor Mannix made any
attempt to disturb the *status quo*, which was seen by them to be working
quite adequately. Despite the requirements of the Holy See, there was no
public education programme and no attempt to institute a tradition of
male choirs to replace the mixed choirs then prevalent in the churches of

---

19   Walter Ebsworth, *Archbishop Mannix* (Melbourne: H.H. Stephenson, 1977), 64.
20   Michael Gilchrist, *Daniel Mannix, Priest and Patriot* (Melbourne: Dove Commu-
      nications, 1982), 180.

the archdiocese. The principal churches all still had their orchestras and their admired soloists, and neither Gregorian chant or polyphony was to be heard to any serious degree. Despite this lack of action from the local church authorities, however, the subject of liturgico-musical reforms was not totally ignored by those with an interest in the subject.

The progress of reform under Archbishop Mannix, 1917–1928

As already noted, Archbishop Mannix displayed no interest in liturgical music during the first decade of his administration. His people were happy with their current practices, and the demands of a *motu proprio* from the other side of the world were of little influence. Liturgists and musicologists may have had their discussions in the pages of *The Advocate*, but Mannix appears to have regarded the issue with a benign indifference.

Interest in liturgical music returned to wider public attention in 1922, when an Australian tour by the Sistine Chapel Choir under the direction of Monsignor Antonio Rella was announced. Consisting of sixty-five male voices, the choir gave its first performance in Melbourne Town Hall on Saturday, 15 April. This first concert consisted of plainchant, and motets by Palestrina, Victoria, Allegri, Viadana, and Lorenzo Perosi. Perosi was the usual director of the choir but was indisposed. Rather surprisingly, the choir also sang a selection of choruses, solos and duets from operas by Verdi, Puccini, Lalo, Gounod, Massenet, and Wagner. Both leading daily papers, *The Age* and *The Argus*, gave the choir glowing reviews.[21] In an article in the Catholic paper *The Tribune*, Monsignor Rella deplored the state of local church music and attacked the presence of women in Catholic choirs despite the explicit instructions of the pope nineteen years earlier. He grudgingly stated: 'If it cannot be helped, women may then be suffered to continue until a different arrangement can be made.'[22]

21 See 'The Sistine Chapel Choir', *The Age*, 17 April 1922, 7 and *The Argus*, 17 April 1922, 9.

22 'Monsignor Rella on Church Music' *The Advocate*, 6 July 1922, 3.

In 1917 Cardinal Cattaneo assumed the position of apostolic delegate, and according to information given to Archbishop Kelly of Sydney, he 'thought of the Irish as a secondary race – and he – the Delegate – believed that the bishops should more actively foster an Australian clergy.'[23] Accordingly, Archbishop Mannix purchased a large rural property outside Melbourne at Werribee, and in 1923 he established Corpus Christi Seminary, conducted by Jesuits recruited from Ireland, England, the United States, and Australia. As was his usual custom, he gave them a free hand and encouraged not only spiritual development, but also academic excellence and intellectual initiative.[24] The rector, Revd George O'Neil, was an accomplished pianist who presented recitals of nineteenth-century music on Saturday afternoons. He was followed by Revd Henry Johnston, and although both of these men encouraged plainsong and polyphony, they were presented simply within the context of the Western musical tradition. Revd Johnston also instituted a custom of bringing leading musicians from Melbourne to perform for the seminarians. Thus, appropriate 'church' music was not selected for special emphasis.[25]

In 1924 an 'Association of Catholic Choirmasters' was formed and twenty parishes were represented. An ambitious programme of discussions and demonstration liturgies was announced, and Achille Rebottaro was elected president. This was an interesting choice, as Rebottaro was Director of Music at St Francis' Church and a fierce opponent of the reforms of the Holy See. The association collapsed within two years. Tom Dennett, son of the vice-president, T.A. Dennett, told David Rankin that the association 'didn't last long because too many people were not interested in reform – it was too difficult to push.'[26]

In this first decade of Mannix's period in office, it should be noted that music at St Patrick's Cathedral did take minimal notice of the demands of the Vatican while remaining faithful to popular taste. This was achieved

23 O'Farrell, *The Catholic Church*, 363.
24 Ibid., 365.
25 Revd Paul Ryan, personnal communication, June 2001.
26 David Rankin, *The History of Music at St Francis' Church 1839/1979* (Melbourne: Society of Jesus in Australia, 1979), 65.

by celebrating the Sunday morning Mass with the popular older style of music with soloists and, on special occasions, an orchestra, while Vespers on Sunday evening were celebrated with a male choir performing the newer style of music, including plainchant. Occasionally the two choirs would combine for the morning Mass when plainsong was required. On special occasions the Propers would be sung by the choir from the nearby Christian Brothers' College.[27]

At St Francis' Church, Achille Rebottaro presided over the traditional repertoire of orchestral Masses with soloists and (when they were in Melbourne) reinforcements from a visiting opera company. In 1922 the *Australian Musical News* reported that

> the authorities at St Francis have always taken great pride in the music of the church, and perhaps this accounts for the long list of eminent names which have been attached to the Church as organists, choirmasters and soloists [...] Following the tradition of St Francis', the Masses of Haydn, Mozart and Beethoven are given regularly in their entirety, Gregorian music not being favoured.'[28]

The popularity of this repertoire was borne out by a statement from Kitty Pendergast, a former choir member, as reported by Rankin:

> Under Signor Rebottaro, the reputation of the choir progressed rapidly. The young men from the Opera companies would go there often and sing in the chorus and anyone who had a voice was placed by their teacher in a Catholic choir [...] whether they were Catholic or not. It was everyone's ambition to sing at St Francis' where the soloists were paid.[29]

Vespers at this time were usually chanted in plainsong. However, after 1927 this practice was replaced by the recitation of the rosary.

Other churches in the archdiocese appear to have either stayed with the popular nineteenth-century orchestral style or attempted to combine it with some chant. There is little available reporting, however, so a

---

27 See Thomas Boland, *St Patrick's Cathedral: a Life* (Melbourne: Polding Press, 1997), 127.
28 *Australian Musical News*, 1 September 1922, 71.
29 Rankin, *The History of Music*, 54.

definite assessment is not possible. An interesting comment is preserved in the papers of Archbishop Spence of Adelaide, who attended a meeting of Australian archbishops at Dr Mannix's residence, Raheen, in Kew during the 1920s. According to Helen Harrison, Archbishop Spence wrote regarding the reforms that

> it was agreed that it would be impossible to carry out, here in Australia, the instruction of the late Pontiff, Pope Pius X, in his letter of 22 November, 1903. There was really no moral danger in mixed choirs, but the custom of allowing non-Catholics to be conductors, or members of the choir should be discouraged.[30]

Thus it may be seen that while the authorities were well aware of the demand for reform, there was no interest in seriously pursuing these reforms.

The progress of reform, 1928–1938

Resistance to the 1903 legislation was not confined to the Melbourne archdiocese. Church authorities in many parts of Europe and America were faced with opposition on the part of members of the local hierarchy and the wider faithful. The theoretical model upon which it was based was frequently found to be inadequate in its narrow requirements and contrary to the wishes and tastes of the Catholic population.

Realizing that further action was required, Pope Pius XI issued the Apostolic Constitution *Divini cultus* on 20 December 1928 in an attempt to clarify and reinforce the reform of liturgical music. As an Apostolic Constitution it was of the greatest possible weight and even more important than the 1903 *motu proprio*. This 1928 document acknowledged the widespread resistance to *Tra le sollecitudini*. The new document supported the teachings of the earlier one and attempted to emphasize the benefits of correct musical style rather than simply condemning inappropriate traditions. Its

---

30   Helen Harrison, *Laudate Dominum: Music at Adelaide's Catholic Cathedral, 1945–1995* (Adelaide: Catholic Archdiocese of Adelaide, 1997), 34.

tone was more conciliatory and less dogmatic than the 1903 document, and it called for the education of seminarians and school children in the correct musical style and the widespread establishment of choir schools. Moreover, not all instruments were banned. Pipe organs were permitted so long as the usual injunctions with regard to dignity and appropriateness were followed.

Articles in *The Advocate* quickly followed and there appears to have been a change in editorial policy. Whereas in earlier years this issue was the focus of discussion and argument, as the 1930s advanced all the published articles were in support of the new regulations, with no articles giving the alternative point of view. The influence of Jesuit Fr Henry Johnston became very evident, and he fulfilled the role that had been taken by Archbishop O'Reily and Revd George Robinson in earlier decades. Fr Johnston wrote many articles and gave lectures on the benefits of plainchant.

In December 1934, Melbourne was host to the Second National Eucharistic Congress to study and promote the role of the Eucharist in society and to mark the centenary of the foundation of the city. Unlike the 1904 congress, there were no papers presented on the role of music in the liturgy, but there were many opportunities to show what was considered appropriate. A public display of unparalleled Catholic pomp and grandeur, the congress concluded with a huge procession culminating in a public celebration of Benediction that was attended by half a million people in the middle of the city.[31]

The director of music for the congress was Dr Gerhard von Keussler, who was brought to Melbourne from Germany especially for the occasion. The music did not display the state of liturgical music in Melbourne at the time, but rather showed what it should become. With a single exception, all the music at the congress was totally in accord with the papal documents of 1903 and 1928. Upon his appointment, von Keussler announced that the two principal liturgies would feature the *Missa Papae Marcelli* by Palestrina and Beethoven's *Missa Solemnis*. The latter work was not

---

31   See 'The Glorious Closing Procession', in J. Murphy and F. Moynihan (eds), *The National Eucharistic Congress: Melbourne, Australia, December 2–9, 1934* (Melbourne: Advocate Press, 1936), 75.

presented, however, and was replaced with the strange choice of the Mass, op. 147 (1852), by Schumann – a highly Romantic, mediocre work totally inconsistent with the rest of the music presented.[32]

While there was no official statement from Archbishop Mannix until 1937, there is no doubt that he was aware of the necessity for reform and was taking action behind the scenes from the early 1930s. In 1930, under the influence of Fr Henry Johnston, Mannix made a decision that was to affect Melbourne's liturgical music for decades to come. In that year he selected the brilliant young son of a musical family and sent him to be trained for the task of eventually assuming control of music in the archdiocese. Percy Jones completed his schooling at fourteen, and at sixteen was sent to Propaganda College in Rome to study for the priesthood. Following brief studies in Dublin and Solesmes, he returned to Rome and took his doctorate in sacred music at the Pontifical Music Institute in late 1939. Returning to Melbourne on Christmas Day 1939, he was to direct music in the archdiocese for over thirty years.[33]

In 1932 Archbishop Mannix presided over the formation of another Catholic choirmasters' association which, this time, was to be active for three years.[34] It was during these years that the use of orchestras was discontinued, although there was no official announcement to that effect. In 1936 Mannix formed a diocesan commission for sacred music and in 1937, in an article entitled 'Christian Education and the Liturgy', he announced that he had approved certain recommendations of the commission, including the banning of female choristers.[35] Six months later the administrator of St Patrick's Cathedral published a single sentence of notification in the press: 'The Right Reverend Monsignor Lonergan wishes to advise that, in accordance with a previous direction by His Grace, the singing of solos by women at any function in the church is forbidden.'[36]

---

32   See 'The Music for the Congress', in Murphy and Moynihan (as n.31), 166.
33   See Donald Cave, *Percy Jones: Priest, Musician, Teacher* (Melbourne: Melbourne University Press, 1988), 37.
34   See Boland, *St Patrick's*, 127.
35   See Daniel Mannix, 'Christian Education and the Liturgy', *The Advocate*, 3 September 1937, 3.
36   'Melbourne Intelligencer', *The Advocate*, 3 March 1938, 18.

This simple statement and the formation of the diocesan commission were the sole public actions by Mannix with regard to the reformation of sacred music in Melbourne. The commission was to be a long-lasting creation, and despite several name changes over the years, it is still in existence and exerting a strong influence over diocesan liturgical music.

The question of what influenced Mannix to finally take action, however, may well be asked. David Rankin in his book on music at St Francis' Church postulates that the archbishop was influenced by an article in a rabidly anti-Catholic journal, *The Rock*, entitled 'Women in Priests' Beds'. While it is true that the ladies of St Francis' Choir stayed at the Blessed Sacrament Fathers' holiday house, it should be noted that the clergy were not in residence at the time.[37] Given his personality, this type of publicity is unlikely to have influenced Mannix, and a more probable reason is simply that pressure from the Vatican was becoming too intense to ignore. Mannix simply bowed to an inevitable change and took appropriate action.

On the part of those actively involved in music in the churches of the archdiocese during this decade, there was the slow acceptance, however grudgingly, of the inescapable changes. At St Patrick's Cathedral, von Keussler was offered the directorship of the choir following the 1934 congress and announced his intention of putting the reforms into place as soon as possible. He listed the polyphonic Masses and motets held in the choir library as well as works by Handel and Beethoven's *Mass in C*, which he, incorrectly, stated was still permissible.[38] From this it may be presumed that even he did not fully understand the new regulations. For some years following his appointment, a male-voice choir appears to have been operating together with a mixed-voice choir conducted by Contessa Filippini.[39]

At St Francis' Church, however, matters were more difficult. In 1928, following the First National Eucharistic Congress in Sydney, Archbishop Mannix invited the Blessed Sacrament Fathers to Australia to assume control of the church as a shrine for eucharistic devotion. Following their

37 See Rankin, *The History of Music*, 73.
38 See memorandum from Dr von Keussler to the members of St Patrick's Cathedral Choir, 21 September 1934.
39 Marius Tonti-Filippini, personal communication, April 1997.

arrival in late 1929, they immediately restored the discontinued practice of chanted Vespers.[40] The director of music, Signor Rebottaro, advertised at this time for more singers before launching an ambitious programme of works by French composers (the Blessed Sacrament Fathers were founded in France). This was to no avail, however, and Rebottaro was dismissed within two years and replaced by Thomas Dennett, a strong upholder of the new style.[41] The last orchestral Mass at St Francis' was Haydn's *Nelson Mass* at Christmas 1930, whereas at the cathedral, Gounod's *St Cecilia Mass* was performed at Christmas 1931 and 1932. At St Francis' the repertoire soon included parts of the plainsong Proper and a new selection of Masses by post-Cecilian composers such as Dubois, Perosi, Guilmant, and Ravanello. Plainsong and polyphonic Masses were only performed after the ladies of the choir were dismissed on 17 October 1937 and replaced by a small choir of eight tenors and eight basses – an event which engendered much ill-feeling.[42]

The aftermath

Despite these reforms of liturgical music eventually being imposed, the timing could not have been more disastrous for their success in the archdiocese. Within two years the world was to become engulfed by the Second World War, and the subsequent shortage of men meant that the new regulations were difficult to implement. The most fortunate beneficiary of these times was the choir of St Patrick's Cathedral. In 1939 a concert tour of Australia by the Vienna Mozart Boys' Choir (an offshoot of the Vienna Boys' Choir) was drawing to a close as war approached. The children were literally boarding their ship in Perth to return home when war was declared and they were interned as enemy aliens. Archbishop Mannix immediately offered them home and shelter in Melbourne. The children returned to the

40   See Rankin, *The History of Music*, 121.
41   See Byrne, *Echoes of Home*, 120.
42   Revd Ernest Rayson, personal communication, October 1995.

east coast and formed the basis for the modern choir of St Patrick's Cathedral. Their conductor, Dr Georg Gruber, became Director of Music at the cathedral and remained there for some months until he was interned.[43] He was quickly replaced by Revd Dr Percy Jones, newly returned from Rome, who remained there for thirty-two years, establishing a rich tradition founded upon polyphony and plainchant.

Other churches were not so fortunate, and the lack of men, the absence of choir schools, the unpopularity of the Gregorian tradition, and the difficulties in performing classical polyphony ensured that for the next twenty years, until the revolutionary edicts of the Second Vatican Council, the parish churches of the archdiocese of Melbourne endured a slow, but inevitable withering of the triumphs of past decades. Even at St Francis' Church, with its great and glorious tradition of church music, between the years of 1956 and 1961, music was only to be heard a few times a year when seminarians were invited to perform.[44]

In conclusion, the reason for the failure of these reforms in Melbourne may be attributed to the fact that the musical tradition was part of the establishment of Catholicism in Melbourne. It symbolized the freedom, pride and wealth of the young Irish Catholic community. This was seen and accepted by an archbishop who readily supported the wishes of his flock. There was also the benefit of being 10,000 miles from the authority of the Holy See. Finally, it must be admitted that for those in authority it was all just too difficult and unnecessary.

Time proved Archbishop Mannix and his flock to be correct. When the International Eucharistic Congress was held in Melbourne in 1973, the reforms of 1903 and 1928 having been reversed, St Francis' Choir announced the presentation of a Eucharist with choir, soloists and orchestra performing Mozart's *Coronation Mass*. On an extremely hot day, two hours before the Eucharist began, every seat was taken, every standing place was occupied, and people were even sitting in every inch of space on the sanctuary.[45] It was a revelation. One could imagine Dr Mannix smiling to himself; he had been right after all.

43   Otto Nechwatal, personal communication, January 1995.
44   See Byrne, *Echoes of Home*.
45   Roger Heagney, personal communication, May 2007.

Notes on Contributors

JOHN HENRY BYRNE, born in Melbourne, was educated at Xavier College before completing studies in teaching and librarianship at Melbourne University. Subsequent studies have included Bachelors of Music (Australian Catholic University) and Psychology (Monash University), and in 2005 he received his Master of Music degree. He has been a member of St Francis' Choir, Melbourne's oldest established choir, for 37 years, and is its archivist. He has published the history of the choir, entitled *Echoes of Home*.

PAUL COLLINS lectures in music at Mary Immaculate College, University of Limerick, Ireland. His research interests embrace music theory during the Baroque, seventeenth- and eighteenth-century keyboard music, and nineteenth- and early twentieth-century Catholic church music. His first book, *The* Stylus Phantasticus *and Free Keyboard Music of the North German Baroque*, was published by Ashgate in 2005. He is an advisory editor for the *Encyclopedia of Music in Ireland* (in preparation).

KIERAN ANTHONY DALY is a music graduate of University College Dublin (1978), Queen's University, Belfast (1991), and the University of Reading (1992). He is the author of *Catholic Church Music in Ireland, 1878–1903: The Cecilian Reform Movement* (Dublin: Four Courts, 1995) and is presently completing a doctoral dissertation on the Roman Catholic liturgical music performed in Dublin during the early twentieth century.

THOMAS DAY is Professor of Music at Salve Regina University in Newport, Rhode Island, United States. His scholarly publications include an edition of *Duetti, Terzetti, e Madrigali* by Antonio Lotti. He has published several articles on recent trends in music for Catholic churches today and the book *Why Catholics Can't Sing: The Culture of Catholicism and the Triumph of Bad Taste* (1990). He is also the author of *Where Have You Gone, Michelangelo? The Loss of Soul in Catholic Culture* (1993).

JOHN DE LUCA was ordained a priest of the archdiocese of Sydney in 1966. Asked to undertake subsequent musical studies for the archdiocese, he graduated from the New South Wales State Conservatorium of Music in 1973, majoring in organ. He was Director of Music in the archdiocesan major seminary, St Patrick's College, Manly, for some years before being appointed Director of Music at St Mary's Cathedral, Sydney, in 1971 (a position he held until 1975). He has lectured at the Sydney Conservatorium, has tutored in organ at the University of New South Wales and with private students, and has acted as an organ consultant and choral director. He holds the degrees of MMus and PhD from the University of New South Wales, and his major publication is *The New Living Parish Hymn Book*.

ECKHARD JASCHINSKI was born in Leverkusen, near Cologne, in 1952. Since 1977 he has been a member of the Society of the Divine Word (Divine Word Missionaries). From 1976 to 1982 he studied theology at the SVD seminary in Sankt Augustin (near Bonn). He was ordained a priest in 1983 and from 1983 to 1990 studied for his doctorate at the theological faculty of Paderborn. The title of his dissertation was 'Musica sacra oder Musik im Gottesdienst? Die Entstehung der Aussagen über die Kirchenmusik in der Liturgiekonstitution "Sacrosanctum Concilium" (1963) und bis zur Instruktion "Musicam sacram" (1967)' (Regensburg: Pustet, 1990). From 1992 to 1994 he gained pastoral experience in an African-American parish in Louisiana and since 1994 has been Professor of Liturgy and Homiletics at the SVD seminary in Sankt Augustin. In 1999 he obtained his post-doctoral lecturing qualification (Habilitation) at the Theological Faculty (SAC) in Vallendar.

THOMAS E. MUIR read history at Oxford and taught history and politics at Stonyhurst College, for whom he wrote the definitive history *Stonyhurst College, 1593–1993*, now in its second revised edition. Between 1997 and 2005 he read music at the universities of York and Durham, and his doctoral thesis forms the basis of his book, *Roman Catholic Church Music in England 1778–1920: The Handmaid of the Liturgy?* (Ashgate, 2008).

KEITH F. PECKLERS, S.J., has lived and worked in Rome since 1992. He is Professor of Liturgy at the Pontifical Gregorian University and Professor of Liturgical History at the Pontifical Liturgical Institute. He held the Gasson Chair in Theology at Boston College during the academic year 2006–2007. Fr Pecklers has published five books and numerous articles and reviews. His most recent volume, *Worship*, (Continuum and Liturgical Press) won the Catholic Press Association's First Place Book Award in 'Liturgy.' Fr Pecklers lectures widely throughout Asia, Europe, and North and South America, and is the founding president of the International Jungmann Society and founder of the International English-speaking Liturgical Community at the Oratory of Saint Francis Xavier 'del Caravita' in Rome. In addition to his academic and pastoral responsibilities, he is a Vatican commentator and 'on-air expert' for ABC News in the United States.

HELEN PHELAN is Associate Director of the Irish World Academy at the University of Limerick and programme director of the Academy's PhD programme in Arts Practice. She was course director of the MA Ritual Chant and Song programme from 2000 to 2009. Her publications are primarily in the area of ritual song, with particular reference to post-Vatican II Irish music and the music of new ritual communities in Ireland. Publications include articles for the *Journal of Ritual Studies*, *Public Voices*, *Orientalia et Occidentalia*, and *Irish Musical Studies*. In 2009, she was invited to be guest editor for a special volume on ritual and community music in the *International Journal of Community Music*. She is currently working on two invited articles for *The Oxford Handbook on Music Education* and *The Oxford Handbook on Music Education Philosophy*. She was editor of *Anáil Dé/The Breath of God: Music, Ritual and Spirituality*, published by Veritas Publications and is festival director of a world sacred music festival of the same name. She has scripted and narrated several documentary programmes on world sacred music for Lyric FM, Ireland's premiere classical music station. She is director of the 'Sanctuary' initiative, which coordinates Higher Education Authority Funding for cultural work with the refugee and asylum-seeking population in Ireland. From 2003 to 2005 she was Assistant Dean (Humanities) at the University of Limerick.

ANN L. SILVERBERG is Professor of Music at Austin Peay State University, Clarksville, Tennessee. She teaches music history, music literature, ethnomusicology, and music appreciation classes and serves on the Board of Directors of the Clarksville Community Concert Association. Her research interests include liturgical music, American music, music in China, and Chinese music. Silverberg holds a PhD in musicology from the University of Illinois, Urbana-Champaign in addition to Master's degrees in Anthropology (Vanderbilt University, 1998), Library and Information Science (University of Illinois, 1993), and Musicology (Indiana University – Bloomington, 1984).

ROBERT A. SKERIS has been a priest of the archdiocese of Milwaukee since 1961. He received his doctorate in theology from the University of Bonn in 1976, and from 1986 to 1990 served as Professor at the Pontifical Institute of Sacred Music in Rome. He was President of the Church Music Association of America from 1996 to 2004 and has been Director of the Centre for Ward Method Studies in the Benjamin T. Rome School of Music, The Catholic University of America, since 2000. His publications include the series *Musicae Sacrae Meletemata* (5 vols, 1976–).

SUSAN TREACY is Professor of Music and Chairman of the Department of Sacred Music at Ave Maria University, Naples, Florida. She has also taught at Franciscan University of Steubenville, Luther College, Emory University, and the University of Oklahoma. She studied at the Oberlin College Conservatory of Music and the Manhattan School of Music; she holds a PhD in historical musicology from the University of North Texas. Her research interests include Catholic liturgical music and seventeenth-century English devotional song, and she has published in *Explorations in Renaissance Culture*, as well as being a contributor to *Absolutism and the Scientific Revolution, 1600–1720: A Biographical Dictionary* (ed. Christopher Baker, 2002). In addition to having published scholarly articles, Dr Treacy writes regular columns: 'Musica Donum Dei' for the *Saint Austin Review* (StAR) and 'Repertory' for *Sacred Music*. Her practical manual of Gregorian chant – *A Plain and Easy Introduction to Gregorian Chant* – is published by Cantica Nova Publications. Dr Treacy directs the Women's

Schola Gregoriana at Ave Maria University, and while at Franciscan University she directed the Schola Cantorum Franciscana. She was a member of the editorial committee for *The Adoremus Hymnal* and is currently on the Board of Directors of the Church Music Association of America.

BENNETT ZON is Reader in Music and Fellow of the Institute of Advanced Study, Durham University, UK. He researches in areas of nineteenth- and twentieth-century historiography and aesthetics, with particular interest in music in long nineteenth-century Britain. He has published articles and reviews in *Current Musicology, Early Music, The Journal of the Plainsong and Medieval Music Society, Music and Letters, Studia Musicologia, Nineteenth-Century Music Review*, and *Recusant History*, and his more recent publications include articles in *Representing India* (Michael Franklin, ed., Routledge, 2006), *Europe, Empire and Spectacle in 19th-Century Britain* (Rachel Cowgill and Julian Rushton, eds, Ashgate, 2006), *Nineteenth-Century Contexts* (2007) and *The Cambridge History of World Music* (Cambridge University Press, 2008). Zon has published *The English Plainchant Revival* (Oxford University Press, 1999) and *Music and Metaphor in Nineteenth-Century British Musicology* (Ashgate, 2000). His recent work, *Representing Non-Western Music in Nineteenth-Century Britain* (Eastman Studies in Music, University of Rochester Press, 2007), was funded by an Arts and Humanities Research Council Research Leave Grant. Zon is General Editor and founder of the Ashgate book series *Music in Nineteenth-Century Britain*, and in 1997 founded the biennial conference on that topic. He is editor and co-editor of a number of volumes of *Nineteenth-Century British Music Studies, Proceedings of the Tenth International Conference on Nineteenth-Century Music* (Ashgate, 2002), and *Music and Orientalism in the British Empire, 1780–1940: Portrayal of the East* (Ashgate, 2007). He has contributed to numerous articles in the second edition of the *New Grove Dictionary of Music and Musicians, The New Dictionary of National Biography*, and the *Grolier Encyclopedia of the Victorian Era*. Zon is founder and General Editor of the international peer-reviewed journal *Nineteenth-Century Music Review* and is founding Director of the Centre for Nineteenth-Century Music, Durham University. He is also founding owner of the Nineteenth-Century Music JISCmail.

Index

Aachen (Aix-la-Chapelle) 30
active participation 28, 61, 80–1, 83, 94,
    212, 223, 225, 229–31, 238
Adelaide, archbishop of 237, 238, 240,
    241, 242, 259, 264
African-American spirituals 165, 167
Ainslie, John 159, 160
Aitken, John 177, 178
Alfieri, Pietro 126, 193
Allen, Warren Dwight 102
American Guild of Organists 169
Ampleforth Abbey 161
Annus qui 18, 26
Arnold, Matthew 110–113, 114, 115, 116,
    118, 119
Association of St Cecilia 158, 163
Australasian Catholic Congress 241, 243,
    246, 248, 258
Australasian Catholic Record 240, 244
Australian Catholic Church, Third
    Plenary Council of the 244
Austria 13, 19, 156, 173, 174, 185, 196, 201
    n 27

Bach, J.S. 17, 200
Baini, Giuseppe 154, 193
Baltimore, plenary councils of 179,
    183–4, 186, 213, 225
Bamberg, Congress of 19, 156
Bavaria 89, 158, 173, 174, 175, 201, 203
Bayley, Archbishop James Roosevelt 180,
    181–2, 183, 186
Beauduin, Dom Lambert 80, 81, 82, 212,
    215
Beethoven, Ludwig van 5, 15, 171, 172, 175,
    178, 185, 256, 257, 258, 263, 265, 267

Belgium 23, 29, 30, 31, 40, 41, 43, 83, 90,
    91
Bellens, Jozef 40
Benedict XIV, Pope 18, 26, 253, 258
Benedict XVI, Pope 89, 90, 97, 238, 249
Benedictines 23, 24–5, 75, 91, 218
Benediction Choir Book 131, 144
Benediction music 130–3, 138, 206
Bennett, Clifford A. 164
Bergeron, Katherine 75
Berkeley, Lennox 128, 143
Berlioz, Hector 3
Beuron Abbey 23, 24, 25, 91, 215
Bevenot, Laurence 143–4
Bewerunge, Heinrich 43–5, 47, 49, 54,
    64
Boyle, Edgar 224, 232
Bradshaw, Paul 73
Breen, Dom Columba 83
Britten, Benjamin 128, 143
Bruckner, Anton 21
Burke, John 87, 88
Busby, Thomas 105–6, 115
Byrne, Archbishop Edward J. 55, 56, 58,
    63, 64, 65

Caecilia, The 157, 163, 174, 198, 202, 204,
    208, 213, 219
Calvin, John 190
Cardine, Dom Eugène 142–3
Carr, Benjamin 177–8
Carr, Archbishop Thomas 258, 259, 260
Carroll, Charles 176
Carroll, Bishop John 176–7, 178
Casel, Dom Odo 79
Caswall, Edward 132

Catholic Choirmaster 214
Catholic Mirror 175, 179, 180, 181, 182, 185
Catholic Emancipation 84, 85, 86, 136, 252
Catholic University of America 165, 174, 183, 214
Catholic Worker Movement 82
Cecilian movement 7–8, 14, 18–19, 85–6, 163, 171–87, 208, 213, 238, 240, 258
Centre de Pastorale Liturgique 90
Chase, Gilbert 167–8
Chateaubriand, François-René de 192
Chesterton, G.K. 62
choirs 7, 11, 20, 27, 34, 47 (nn. 73, 74), 48, 49, 66, 80, 81, 83, 87, 88, 129, 131, 137–8, 145, 160, 167, 172, 181, 183, 192, 199, 227, 256, 257, 258, 259, 260, 261, 264
Choron, Alexandre-Etienne 107–8, 193
Cimarosa, Domenico 155, 178
Clemens non Papa, Jacobus 68
Collins, Paul 86
Col nostro 123
Cologne 13–14, 19
Complete Benediction Manual 131
Conception Abbey 218
congregational participation 53, 61, 147–8, 220, 221, 223–4, 233, 234, 238
congregational singing 20, 80, 81, 155, 158, 159–60, 166, 169, 194, 204, 208, 218, 223–4, 225, 231, 232, 233
Counter-Reformation 5, 25, 125
Crichton, James 147, 148
Crown of Jesus Music 131, 132, 133
Cullen, Cardinal Paul 86

Daily Hymn Book, A 134
Darwin, Charles 102, 103, 105, 118
Day, Dorothy 82
Delany, John Albert 240, 242, 244

De Meulemeester, Arthur 31, 41–3, 44, 51
De Prins, Francis Prosper 35–6, 39
De Prins, Léopold 35, 36, 37–8
De Regge, Ernest 51
De Santi, Angelo 159, 239
Deutscher Katholikentag 14
developmentalism 102, 106, 107, 115, 117, 118
Dialogue Mass 81, 148
Dickinson, Clarence 170
Diekmann, Dom Godfrey L. 211, 222, 230, 231, 233, 234, 235
Divini cultus 135, 147, 161, 222, 264
Donizetti, Gaetano 10
Donnelly, Bishop Nicholas 54, 85
Donovan, J. 116–17
Donovan, John 241–49
Donovan, Thomas 244
Downey, Archbishop Richard 161
Downside Abbey 125, 127, 161
Driscoll, John 128, 134
Duffy, Eamon 90

Eccleston, Archbishop Samuel 178
Editio Medicaea 23, 156, 186, 206, 208
Editio Vaticana 186, 206, 208
Einstein, Alfred 105
Ellard, Gerald 219, 220, 226, 227
Ellis, Dom Maur 88
embassy chapel music (London) 122, 129–30
Engel, Carl 115–16
England 44, 87, 88, 155, 159–61, 162, 179, 252, 262
Enlightenment era 3–6, 14, 16, 18, 190–2
E Supremi 8, 9, 211
Ett, Caspar 126, 151, 184
evolutionism 102, 118, 119

Faber, Frederick 132, 160
Falque, Ferdinand C. 220–1
Fellerer, Karl Gustav 190 n 4, 195

Filke, Max 59, 64, 66, 67
First World War 28, 40, 41, 126, 168, 260
First Vatican Council 8, 19, 86
Fischer, Carl M. 82
Fleischmann (senior), Aloys 47–8
Flood, William Henry Grattan 32
Forsyth, Cecil 118
France 5, 13, 19, 21–6, 75–6, 90, 95, 155,
    164, 174, 175, 179, 185, 193, 268
Franciscan Sisters of Penance and
    Charity 201
Franck, César 7, 68
Freedman, Jonathan 111, 113
Friess, Mother Caroline 202

Galin-Paris-Chevé method 164, 214
Gelineau, Joseph 121, 140–1, 142, 143,
    145, 231, 233–4
Germany 13–21, 23, 24, 35, 38, 46, 85, 90,
    126, 151, 155–6, 157, 158, 168, 179,
    180, 185, 193, 198, 202, 258, 265
Gibbons, Archbishop James 183, 186
Glennon, Archbishop John J. 165
Glenstal Abbey 88, 90, 91, 93, 95
Goddard, Joseph 105, 118, 119
Goller, Vincenz 47
Goold, Archbishop James Alipius 254,
    255, 258
gospel music 167
Gounod, Charles-François 7, 31, 47, 129,
    136, 256, 257, 261, 268
Graduale Triplex 143
Graf, Joseph 173, 174, 180, 183–4, 185, 186
Graff, Alphonsus 40, 45
Grammar of Plainsong, A 124
Gray, Cecil 117
Gregorian chant 2–3, 7, 9, 10, 19, 20,
    22–3, 25, 27, 29, 37–8, 44, 47, 61,
    74, 75, 76, 77, 78, 80–3, 85, 86,
    87, 88, 91–2, 93, 94, 95, 96, 97,
    99–119, 122–5, 126, 127, 132, 134,
    135, 136, 138, 142–4, 145, 146, 147,

149, 150, 151, 152, 153, 155–6, 157,
    158, 159, 161, 163–4, 165, 170, 171,
    172, 175, 181, 182, 183, 185, 186, 187,
    189–90, 192, 193, 206, 208, 209,
    211–235, 261, 265, 269
Gregorian Institute of America 164
Grell, August Eduard 192
Guéranger, Dom Prosper 21–2, 23–4, 25,
    75–6, 78, 158, 193, 212
Gurney, Edmund 104
Gy, Pierre-Marie 95

Haan, Alphonse 48–9
Haan, Gustav 48, 49–50
Haberl, Franz Xaver 23, 35, 48, 126
Haller, Michael 38, 49, 50, 192
Handel, George Frideric 16, 178, 257, 267
Hanisch, Joseph 151
Hasberry, Robert 131
Hayburn, Robert 232, 239
Haydn, Joseph 5, 47, 129, 136, 171, 172,
    175, 178, 185, 240, 242, 255, 256,
    257, 263, 268
Hebraism 102, 109–13
Hellenism 102, 109–13
Hellriegel, Martin 165, 223, 227, 230, 232
Hemy, Henri 131
Henni, Bishop John Martin 157–8, 173,
    194, 196, 197, 202, 203
Hillenbrand, Reynold 228
Hoey, P. 85
Hogarth, George 103, 106
Hornbach, Gisela 202
Howell, Clifford 147, 226, 227, 228, 231
Huegle, Dom Gregory 218, 219
Hugo, Victor 75
Hummel, Johann Nepomuk 129
Hurley, Edmund G. 181, 182–3
hymnals 133, 138, 160, 168, 169, 204
hymnody 92, 96, 130, 132, 151, 158, 162,
    165, 167–8
Hytrek, Theophane 202

Institut Supérieur de Liturgie 95
instruments in church, use of 6, 16, 19,
    26, 27, 130, 149, 171, 265
Ireland 19, 126, 158, 174, 179, 251, 252,
    259, 262
Irish College (Rome) 86
Irish Independent 30, 58, 88
Irish Society of St Cecilia 29, 36, 39, 53,
    54 n 1, 85, 242
Italian Society of St Cecilia 152–5
Italy 8, 10, 17, 19, 26–8, 151, 152–5, 158,
    179, 193

Jackson, George Pullen 168–9
Jefferson, Thomas 5
Jeffery, Peter 74, 100
Jesuits 8, 180, 262
John XXIII, Pope 97
John Paul II, Pope 149, 246
Johner, Dom Dominic 222
Joseph II, Emperor 5
Josephinism 191
Joyce, James 54
Jubilus Review 73
Jungmann, Josef 230

Kalliwoda, Johann 129
Kant, Immanuel 4, 191, 194
Katholische Volkszeitung 175, 179, 180,
    181, 185
Katholischer Verein Deutschlands 14
Kavanagh, Julie 84
Kelly, Archbishop Michael 262
Kenrick, Archbishop Francis Patrick 178
Kiesewetter, Raphael G. 115–16
King, James 230, 234
Koch, Caspar Petrus 199–200
Koenker, Ernest 81
Krutschek, Paul 20

Lassus, Orlande de 126
Lauri, Cardinal Lorenzo 63, 67

Lavery, Seán 73, 74
Leeds Catholic Hymnal 134
Lemmens, Jaak Nikolaas 29, 39, 45
Lemmens Institute 29, 31, 40, 42, 43
Leo XIII, Pope 8, 27
Liber Usualis 64, 65, 124, 132, 227, 234
Liszt, Franz 21, 174–5
Little, Vilma 132
Liturgical Arts Society 163
liturgical movement 28, 73–97, 163, 167,
    211–35
Love, Cyprian 91, 95
Luther, Martin 189
Lutkin, Peter Christian 169
Lyra Catholica 132
Lyra Ecclesiastica 29, 36, 38, 39, 45, 46,
    48, 49, 85, 242

MacCarthy, Charles W. 248
Malines (Mechelen) 29, 30, 31, 38, 39, 45,
    80, 212
Manhattanville Academy of the Sacred
    Heart 163, 214
Mannix, Archbishop Daniel 251, 259–69
Mantua 27, 239
Marechal, Archbishop Ambrose 178
Maredsous Abbey 24, 91, 215, 218
Maria Laach Abbey 23, 24, 81, 90, 215
Marmion, Abbot Columba 234
Marty, Bishop Martin 205
McCormack, John 59, 68
McDonnell, Dom Paul 88, 94
McGahern, John 89
McNaspy, Clement J. 226, 234, 235
McQuaid, Archbishop John Charles 63
Mediator Dei 93, 135, 147, 226, 232, 233
Melbourne 243, 248, 251–69
Mencken, Henry Louis 186
Mercadante, Saverio 7, 155
Merry del Val, Cardinal Rafael 245, 246
Mertens, Dom Winoc 88
Merx, Hans 50

Messmer, Archbishop Sebastian Gebhard 204, 207
Methodist Church Music Society 170
Mettenleiter, Dominic 151
Mettenleiter, John 151
Metzler, Josef 246, 247
Michel, Dom Virgil 82, 91, 162, 211, 215–7, 221
Milwaukee 157, 158, 163, 174, 189–209, 213
Minnesota 164, 205, 211, 215
Missa de Angelis 57, 59, 67
Mitterer, Ignatius 49, 66
Mocquereau, Dom André 83, 87, 123–5, 142, 143, 214–5, 218
Modernism 159, 221
Mohr, Joseph 204
Mont-César Abbey 80
Moran, Cardinal Patrick Francis 237, 240–49
Moran, David Patrick 33
Moravian Music Foundation 170
motu proprio (1903) *see Tra le sollecitudini*
Mount Mary Hymnal 202
Mozart 5, 35, 47, 129, 136, 171, 172, 175, 178, 182, 183, 185, 240, 242, 256, 257, 263, 269
Munster News 36, 37, 86
Murray, Dom Gregory 125, 140, 142, 144, 145
Murray, Archbishop John 164
Murray, Dom Placid 91
Musicae sacrae disciplina 93, 233

Napoleon Bonaparte 2, 8
Neale, Archbishop Leonard 178
Nemmers, Michael Ludwig 199
Newman, Ernest 104
Nixon, Frederick George 129
Nono, Charles Louis 34–5
Notre Dame Cathedral 2
Novello, Joseph Alfred 129
Novello, Vincent 125, 129, 257

O'Brien, Louis 68, 70
O'Brien, Vincent 57, 58, 59, 64, 68
O'Gorman, Kieran 94
O'Reily, Archbishop John 237, 240–43, 244, 245, 259, 265
Ostini, Cardinal Pietro 154

palaeography 23, 101
Palestrina, Giovanni Pierluigi da 7, 16, 21, 25, 39, 44, 49, 58, 64, 65, 68, 125, 126, 156, 163, 171, 175, 183, 184, 186, 190, 192, 238, 261, 265
Parish Hymnal 150
Parry, C. Hubert H. 107
Paul VI, Pope 97
Pecklers, Keith 82
Pell, Cardinal George 237
People's Mass, A 144, 145
Pepin the Short 2
Perosi, Lorenzo 126, 203 n37, 261, 268
Pius VIII, Pope 152, 154, 156
Pius IX, Pope 19, 23, 156, 158, 179
Pius X, Pope 8–10, 13, 27–8, 41, 53, 61, 80, 81, 94, 123, 130, 135, 144, 146, 159, 160, 161, 211, 212, 213, 214, 217, 219, 228, 229, 230, 237, 238–9, 240, 243, 245, 249, 258, 264
Pius X School of Liturgical Music 82, 163, 202, 214
Pius XI, Pope 64, 161, 264
Pius XII, Pope 226, 232, 233
Plainchant *see* Gregorian chant
Plainsong for Schools 123, 124, 161
Poland 19, 179
Polding, Archbishop John Bede 255
Pothier, Dom Joseph 22, 77, 123, 219
Powell, Baden 109
Praise the Lord 150
Prickett, Stephen 112, 113, 114
Propaganda Fide 246, 247
Proske, Carl 17, 20, 126, 151, 173
Pugin, Augustus Welby Northmore 100
Pustet, Friedrich 122, 126, 156, 159, 186, 206

Quarr Abbey 125, 215

Rankin, David 262, 263, 267
Ratisbon *see* Regensburg
Ratzinger, Joseph *see* Benedict XVI, Pope
Redemptorist Hymn Book with tunes 134
Redemptorists 36, 39, 40, 41, 180
Regensburg 7, 17, 18, 19, 23, 30, 35, 46, 48,
        49, 151, 155–6, 157, 158, 159, 173,
        183, 186, 192, 197, 206, 208
Rehrl, Caspar 201
Reinhold, H.A. 224
Rella, Antonio 243, 261
Renaissance polyphony 7, 10, 15, 16, 19,
        122, 125–9, 135, 136, 138, 145, 146,
        171–2, 183, 238
Renan, Ernest 110, 114, 116, 117
Rheinberger, Joseph Gabriel 47
Ritter, Frederic 108, 116
Robertson, Alec 222
Rockstro, William 109
Rogers, Brendan 61, 63
Roman Rite 6, 158, 238
Romanticism 6, 14, 15, 18
Roman Missal 80, 97
Roman Rite 6, 158, 238
Rossini, Carlo 226
Rossini, Gioachino 7, 35, 155, 174, 183,
        242, 249, 257, 258
Rousseau, Olivier 156
Rowbotham, John Frederick 108, 109,
        114, 115
Rubbra, Edmund 128, 150
Ryan, Vincent 94

Sacred Congregation of Rites 156, 233,
        246
Sacrosanctum Concilium 93, 149
Sailer, Johann Michael 17, 18, 193
Salzmann, Joseph 157, 196–7, 198, 201,
        208
Santner, Carl 184

Sarto, Giuseppe *see* Pius X, Pope
Schaefer, Cherubim 202
Scharf, Thomas A. 182
Schmidt, Joseph 227, 229
School Sisters of Notre Dame 201
School Sisters of St Francis 202
Schott, Anselm 24–5
Schrembs, Joseph 151
Schrems, Theobald 189
Schuetky, Josef 184
Second Vatican Council 11, 13, 73, 74, 77,
        78, 91, 92, 93, 122, 129, 139, 145,
        146, 149, 160, 165, 167, 170, 229,
        235, 269
Second World War 121, 148, 149, 166,
        268
Sewell, William 127, 128
Shepherd, Massey 80
Shields, Thomas E. 214, 216
Singenberger, John Baptist 42, 49, 50,
        126, 157, 158, 162, 173, 174, 180, 181,
        183, 198–209, 213
Singenberger, Otto 202
Sireaux, Joseph 40, 41
Sisters of St Agnes 201
Sistine Chapel Choir 243, 261
Smith, Joseph 37–8, 86, 126
Society of St Gregory 87, 122, 204, 220
Solesmes Abbey 9, 10, 21, 54, 74, 75, 76,
        77, 79, 80, 83, 86, 87, 91, 96, 122,
        123, 124, 125, 127, 139, 142, 144,
        145, 151, 158, 159, 164, 175, 186,
        206, 212, 214, 215, 216, 221, 266
Spalding, Archbishop John Martin 178
Spence, Archbishop Robert 264
Spencer, Herbert 103–5, 106, 118
Spiegler, Max 157
Spontini, Gaspare 154–5
St Cloud Music Institute 164
St Dominic's Hymnal 133
St John's Abbey (Minnesota) 211, 215
St Meinrad (Indiana) 158, 205, 227

Stafford, William 102–3, 115
Stainer, John 107, 115
Stanbrook Hymnale 136
Stanford, Sir Charles Villiers 249
Stehle, Johann Gustav Eduard 184
Stevens, Mother Georgia 82, 163–4, 214
Stokeley, W.F.P. 54
Stuyck, Jan Juliaan 40–1
Sulpicians (Société de Saint Sulpice) 177
Summorum Pontificum 97, 238
Swertz, Hans Conrad 46–7
Switzerland 155, 156, 213
Sydney 237, 238, 240, 241, 243, 245, 246,
    247, 248, 249, 252, 255, 260, 262,
    267

Tablet, The 99
Terry, R.R. 41, 127–8, 131–2, 133, 134, 136,
    144, 147, 150
Thibaut, Anton Friedrich Justus 16, 17,
    193
Tipper, Henry 114, 115
Tozer, Albert E. 131, 133
Tracy, Michael 33, 64
Tra le sollecitudini 9, 10, 13, 28, 41, 47,
    53, 54, 61, 80–1, 83, 130, 135, 136,
    138, 147, 151, 159, 161, 163, 166, 172,
    186, 203, 205, 206, 207, 209, 212,
    214, 218, 221, 222, 228, 232, 238,
    239, 243, 244, 245, 246, 247, 258,
    261, 264
Trent, Council of 18, 171, 173, 189
Turner, Joseph Egbert 129, 131

ultramontanism 14, 127, 150

Vatican Secret Archives 247
Vatican II *see* Second Vatican Council
Vatican Kyriale 86, 123
Vaughan Williams, Ralph 128
Venice 239

Verdi, Giuseppe 10, 26, 174, 261
vernacular hymnody 92, 130, 132, 151,
    158, 162
Victoria, Tomás Luis de 238, 261
Vitry, Dom Ermin 164, 218–19, 227, 234
Volkmer, Alois 45–6
Vollaerts, Jan 142

Wagner, Richard 182, 261
Wallaschek, Richard 104
Walsh, Archbishop William J. 54, 55
Ward, Justine Bayard 82, 163–4, 202,
    214–7, 218
Weber, Carl Maria von 129, 172, 175, 178,
    257
Weber, Friedrich 107, 115
Wesley, Charles 169
Wesley, John 169
Wesley, Samuel 125
Westermeyer, Paul 167, 168
Westminster Choir College 169
Westminster Cathedral 127, 128, 137, 161
Westminster Hymnal, The 132, 133, 134,
    145, 146, 147, 149, 160
Whitfield, Archbishop James 178
Winnen, J. A. 222
Winthrop, Robert 76
Wiseman, Cardinal Nicholas 125, 126
Witt, Franz Xaver 19, 20, 35, 49, 85, 126,
    151, 184, 197 n 18, 198, 208, 209
Wogan, Patrick 85
Wolter, Maurus 23, 24, 91
Wolter, Placidus 23, 91
Wylde, Henry 106–7, 114, 115

Young, John 164, 214
Young, Robert 110, 111

Zingarelli, Niccolò Antonio 155
Zulueta, Francis M. de 129
Zwingli, Huldreich 190